The World's
Best
Storybook

The World's Best Storybook

TREASURE PRESS

The texts and illustrations in this book formerly appeared in: Grimms' Fairy Tales, Hans Andersen's Fairy Tales, Tales from the Arabian Nights, Favourite Stories from Around the World, published by Octopus Books Limited.

Grimms' Fairy Tales — The Brothers Grimm — translated by Vladimír Vařecha — illustrated by Luděk Maňásek (The Frog Prince, The Golden Goose, Allerleirauh, The Worn Out Dancing Shoes, Rapunzel, The Fisherman and His Wife, The Poor Miller's Boy, The Water of Life, Merry Andrew, The Six Swans, The Two Brothers, Clever Grethel)
Hans Andersen's Fairy Tales — retold by Vera Gissing — illustrated by Dagmar Berková (The Constant Tin Soldier, Ole Close-Your-Eyes, The Swineherd, The Nightingale, The Ugly Duckling, Five Peas in a Pod, The Little Match Girl, The Snow Queen, Little Ida's Flowers, The Snowman, The Tinder Box, The Emperor's New Clothes, The Darning Needle)
Tales from the Arabian Nights — retold by Vladimír Hulpach — translated by Vera Gissing — edited by Anne Scott — illustrated by Mária Želibská (Abu Kir and Abu Sir, Prince Ahmed and the Fairy Pari Banu, Ali Baba and the Forty Thieves, The Evil Brothers, Fate and Riches, Hasan the Goldsmith)
Favourite Stories from Around the World — retold by Jane Ives and Jean-Luc Billeadeux (The Magic Tree — illustrated by Karel Teissig, The Pied Piper of Hamelin — illustrated by Vladimír Tesař, The Little Prince of the Sun — illustrated by Karel Teissig, Daedalus and Icarus — illustrated by Luděk Maňásek, Ondin and the Salt — illustrated by Vladimír Tesař, Orion, The Voyages of Sinbad the Sailor and Aladdin — text by Jane Ives and Jean-Luc Billeadeux, illustrations by Mária Želibská)

This edition published in 1985 by
Treasure Press
59 Grosvenor Street
London W1

Graphic design by Václav Bláha
© Artia, Prague 1985
Favourite Stories from Around the World
Text © Octopus Books Ltd. 1982

ISBN 1 85051 037 7
Printed in Czechoslovakia by TSNP Martin
1/18/10/51-01

CONTENTS

The Frog Prince

In the old days when wishing could still cast a spell, there lived a King whose daughters were all beautiful, but the youngest was so lovely that the sun itself, which had looked on so many things, was amazed whenever it shone on her face. Near the King's castle was a large dark forest, and in that forest there was a well under an old lime-tree. When the day was very warm, the King's youngest child would go out into the forest and sit down on the edge of the cool fountain. And when she felt bored she took a golden ball, threw it up in the air and caught it again, and that was her favourite pastime.

Now it so happened one day that the golden ball did not drop back into her little hand stretched out to catch but bounded away on the earth and rolled straight into the well. The Princess followed the ball with her eyes but the ball disappeared, and the well was deep, so deep that the bottom could not be seen. Then she began to cry and cried louder and louder, and there was nothing to comfort her.

As she was thus lamenting, someone called out to her. 'What is the matter, Princess? The way you are lamenting would move a stone to pity.' She looked round to see whence the voice was coming and saw a frog poking his thick, ugly head out of the water. 'Oh, it's you, old water-splasher!' said she. 'I am crying for my golden ball which has dropped down the well.'

'Be quiet and stop crying,' answered the frog. 'I have a way of helping you, but what will you give me if I recover your plaything and bring it up again?'

'Anything you wish to have, dear frog,' she said, 'my clothes, my pearls and diamonds, even the gold crown which I am wearing.'

'I do not care for your clothes, your pearls and diamonds, or your gold crown, but if you will love me and let me be your companion and play-fellow and sit by you at your little table, eat out of your little golden plate, drink from your little cup, and sleep in your little bed; if you promise me all this, then I will go down and fetch your golden ball again.'

'Oh yes,' she said, 'I promise you all you wish, if you but bring back my ball.' However, she thought to herself, 'What is this silly frog babbling about? He sits and croaks in the water with his mates, and cannot be a human being's companion!'

As soon as the frog received the promise, he dived his head under the water, sank down, and after a short while came swimming up again with the ball in his mouth and threw it onto the grass.

The King's daughter was overjoyed when she saw her lovely plaything again, picked it up and ran away with it.

'Wait, wait,' called the frog. 'Take me with you, I can't run as fast as you!' But what use was it for him to cry 'Croak, croak!' after her as loudly as he could? She did not listen to him, hurried home, and soon forgot all about the poor frog who had to descend into his well again.

The next day, when seated at the dinner-table with the King and all the courtiers, she was eating from her little golden plate, something came creeping splish, splash, splish, up the marble staircase, and when it got to the top it knocked at the door and cried, 'King's daughter, the youngest, open the door for me.' She ran to see who was outside, but when she opened the door and saw the frog sitting there, she banged the door to as fast as she could and went and sat down again at the dinner-table, though she was quite frightened. The King saw plainly that her heart was beating fast and said, 'My child, what are you afraid of? Is there a giant outside the door wanting to carry you away?'

'Oh no,' she answered, 'it is no giant, but an ugly frog.'

'What does the frog want with you?'

'Oh, dear father, yesterday as I was sitting at the well playing with my golden ball, it fell into the water. And because I was crying so bitterly, the frog brought it up again for me and, as he begged and insisted on it, I promised him he should be my companion. But I never thought that he could come out of the water. But he is here now and wants to come in here to me.'

Meanwhile, the knocking and shouting started again.

> 'Youngest daughter of the King,
> Open the door to me.
> Don't you remember what yesterday
> You said at the cool well-water?
> Youngest daughter of the King,
> Open the door to me.'

Whereupon the King said, 'As you have made a promise you must keep it. Just go and open the door to the frog.'

She went and opened the door, and the frog hopped in following her footsteps as far as her chair. There he sat and cried, 'Lift me up.' She hesitated till at last the King ordered her to do so. The moment the frog was on the chair, he wanted to sit on the table, and when he was sitting there he said, 'Now move your little golden plate nearer that we may eat together.' She did this, but it was plain to see that she did not do it willingly. The frog made a hearty meal, but not so the Princess: nearly every morsel stuck in her throat. At last he said, 'I have eaten my fill, and I am tired. Carry me now into your little room and make your silken bed ready that we may lie down and sleep.'

The Princess began to cry, and was frightened of the cold, clammy frog which she did not dare to touch and which was now to sleep in her pretty clean little bed. But the King lost his temper with her and said, 'He who helped you when you were in need shall not later be despised.'

So she took the frog with two fingers, carried him upstairs, and put him in a corner. But when she was lying in bed, he crept towards her and said, 'I am tired and want to go to sleep as well as you. Lift me up, or I will tell your father.'

She flew into a rage, picked him up, and threw him with all her might and main against the wall, shouting, 'Now you shall be quiet, you hideous frog!' But when he fell down he was no frog but a king's son with beautiful, kind eyes.

Her father's wish was that he should become her beloved companion and husband. He told her that he had been changed by a wicked fairy into a frog, and no one could have delivered him from the well but she herself, adding that tomorrow they would go together to his kingdom.

Then they went to sleep, and next morning when the sun wakened them **9** a coach came driving up with eight white horses, with white ostrich feathers on their heads and harnessed with golden chains. And behind stood faithful Henry, the young King's body-servant. He had been so grieved when his lord and master was changed into a frog that he had three iron bands placed round his heart lest it should burst with grief and sadness.

The coach was there to carry the young King into his kingdom. Faithful Henry helped both to get in, and once again took his stand behind overjoyed about this deliverance.

When they had driven only a little way, the Prince heard something crack behind him as if something had broken. He turned round and cried:

'Henry, the carriage is breaking.'

'No, sir, it's not the carriage
But a band from my heart is in twain
That for long was great pain,
While you sat inside a well
A frog by a bad witch's spell!'

Once more and then again there was cracking on the way. The Prince thought it must be the carriage breaking, but it was only the bands which were springing from faithful Henry's heart because his lord and master had been delivered and was happy.

The Constant Tin Soldier

Once upon a time there were twenty-five tin soldiers. All of them were brothers, for they had all been made from the same old tin spoon. They held rifles in their hands and every one of them looked alike with their lovely uniforms of red and blue. The very first words they heard in this world, when the lid was taken off the box in which they lay were, 'Tin soldiers!' It was the cry of a small boy, as he clapped his hands; he had been given the tin soldiers because it was his birthday. Straightaway he stood every one of them on the table.

They were like peas out of the same pod, the very image of one another, all that is except one, who was slightly different; he had only one leg, for he was the very last to be made and there was not quite enough tin left. But he stood on his one leg just as firmly and steadfastly as the others did on two. And it was this very soldier who met the most unusual fate.

There were many other toys scattered on the table where the little soldiers had been put, but by far the most attractive one was a magnificent paper castle. Through its tiny windows one could see right into the rooms. In front of the castle stood some little trees round a small mirror, which was made to look like a lake. Some wax swans swam on the lake, and were reflected in it.

It was truly very pretty, but prettiest of all was a little doll who stood in the open doorway of the castle. She, too, had been cut out of paper, but she wore a dress of the softest muslin, with a narrow blue ribbon round her shoulders like a shawl. In the middle of the ribbon sparkled a glittering coin the size of her face. The little maiden was stretching out both her arms, for she was a dancer, and one of her little legs was raised so high that the little tin soldier could not see it at all, and thought that she, like himself, had only one leg.

'That would be the wife for me!' he thought. 'But then she is too high and mighty. She lives in a castle, whereas I live in a box and, to top it all, there's twenty-five of us in it—that would be no proper home for her! Still, I am going to try to get to know her.' Then he stretched right out to his full height behind a snuff-box which also stood on the table. From there he had a perfect view of the little maiden, who stood persistently on one leg without losing her balance.

Later that evening, all the other tin soldiers were put back in the box and the people of the house went to bed. That was when the toys really began to play—at visiting, at fighting wars, and at having parties. The tin soldiers rattled in the box, for they wanted to play too, but they couldn't push the lid off. The nut-cracker turned somersaults and the slate pencil raced about on the slate. They all made such a noise that the canary woke up and joined in, chatting away in verse! The only two who never moved were the little tin soldier and the little dancer. She stood so erect on tiptoe, both her arms stretched out and he, too, stood steadfast on his one leg, without taking his eyes off her for a moment.

The clock struck twelve, and with a bang, the lid of the snuff-box sprang open. But there was no snuff inside, oh no, just a little black goblin. A Jack-in-the-box full of tricks!

'Tin soldier!' the Jack-in-the-box called out. 'Kindly keep your eyes to yourself!'

But the tin soldier pretended not to hear.

'Very well then, just you wait till morning!' threatened the Jack-in-the-box.

In the morning when the children got up, they put the little tin soldier on the window-ledge. Who knows if it was the fault of that Jack-in-the-box, or the wind, but all of a sudden the window flew open and the little tin soldier fell head first from the third floor to the ground. It was a fearsome fall, for he hit the ground with his cap and lay with his one leg in the air, his bayonet stuck between the paving stones.

The maid and the little boy ran down straightaway to look for him. But though they very nearly trod on him, they did not see him. If only the little soldier had cried out, 'Here I am!', they would have found him, but he didn't think it dignified to call out loudly when he was in uniform.

Then it started to rain and the drops fell faster and faster, till there was a real downpour. When it was over, two small boys came along.

'Look at this!' cried one of them. 'It's a tin soldier! Let's give him a sail!'

They made a little boat out of newspaper and put the tin soldier in it. Away he sailed down the gutter by the pavement with both boys running alongside, clapping their hands with glee. My word, what enormous waves there were in that gutter and what a current—but then, what a downpour! The little paper boat rocked up and down and every now and then it twirled right round, making the little soldier quite giddy. But he remained steadfast, never moving a muscle, never flinching, eyes forward, his rifle clasped to his side.

All at once the boat was swept under a covered drain where the soldier found it was as dark as his own box.

'Where am I going?' he wondered. 'It's all that Jack-in-the-box's fault! Oh, if only my little maiden was sitting here beside me, I wouldn't care if it was twice as dark!'

Just then, a large water-rat that lived in the drain appeared.

'Have you a passport?' asked the rat. 'Show me your passport!'

But the little soldier said not a word and clutched his rifle tighter than ever. The boat sailed on, with the rat following. Ugh! How it gnashed its teeth and shouted to the sticks and the straws, 'Stop him! Stop him! He hasn't paid the toll! He hasn't shown his passport!'

But the current grew stronger and stronger. The little soldier could already see clear daylight ahead, where the drain ended but he also could hear such a roar, loud enough to frighten the bravest of men. Just imagine, that drain ended in a great canal! Falling into it was as dangerous for the tin soldier as sailing down a mighty waterfall would be for us.

He was already so very near, he could not stop. The little boat flew like the wind, and the poor little soldier held himself as erect as he knew how. No one could call him a coward! The boat spun round three or four times, and filled with water right to the brim; surely it must sink! The little soldier was now up to his neck in water and the little boat sank deeper and deeper still. The sodden paper was falling apart more and more. Now the water closed over the soldier's head and he thought of the pretty little dancer whom he would never see again. In his ears rang the old song:

'Onward, onward, warrior!
Forward to your death!'

The paper fell apart completely and the tin soldier fell down, down and then he was swallowed by a large fish. It was so dark inside! It was even worse than the drain and no room to move at all. But the tin soldier remained undaunted, stretched out to his full length, clasping his rifle.

The fish flung itself about in a frenzy, twisting and turning horribly. At last it stopped and was perfectly still. Then suddenly, it seemed as if a streak of lightning flashed through it. A light shone brightly, and someone called, 'Here is the tin soldier!' The fish had been caught, taken to market, sold and brought into the kitchen, where the maid had cut it open with a large knife. Picking the tin soldier up by his waist with two fingers, she carried him into the sitting-room, where everyone was most curious to see this very remarkable little man, who had travelled the world inside the fish's tummy. But the little tin soldier wasn't one to boast—it was a mere trifle to him.

They stood him upon a table and there... well, fate plays a strange hand in life sometimes... the little tin soldier found himself in the very same room in which he had lived before. He saw the same children and the same toys still

standing on the table, and the magnificent castle with the prettiest little dancer. She was still balanced on one leg, with the other high up in the air, for she too was very steadfast! The tin soldier was so touched, he almost burst into tin tears, but this wouldn't have been the proper thing to do. So he gazed at the dancer and she gazed back at him, but neither spoke.

All at once, one of the small boys picked up the tin soldier and threw him straight into the stove—for no reason at all. That Jack-in-the-box must have most definitely had a hand in that!

The tin soldier now stood in the fiery glow and felt the fearsome flame, but he couldn't really tell whether it was the flame of a real fire, or the flame of love. His colour was all gone, but who knows whether he lost it during his travels, or through grief. He looked at the little dancer and she looked back at him, and he felt himself melting but still he remained steadfast as he clutched his rifle. Suddenly the door opened and the draught caught the little dancer. She flew like a fairy straight into the stove to the tin soldier. Instantly she was ablaze, and was gone. The tin soldier melted into a shrivelled lump and, when the maid cleared the ashes the following day, she found his little tin heart. But all that was left of the dancer was the shiny coin, and that was as black as a cinder.

Abu Kir and Abu Sir

Near the city of Alexandria lies a place called Abukir, which is a constant reminder of a certain tale about two men — Abu Kir the dyer, and Abu Sir the barber.

In those bygone, distant days they had neighbouring shops in the local square, and though they both excelled in their trade and were friends, their characters were vastly different.

Abu Sir was a serious, hard working fellow who earned respect from others, and as he was an honest, able barber, he did not lack for customers.

Now Abu Kir, the dyer, was quite a different man. He was a liar, a swindler and it was said he would rob his own grandmother of her last dinar! It was his custom, whenever someone brought material to be dyed, to demand payment in advance and then proceed to sell the stuff, usually at a profit. He would then make weak excuses and vain promises to the customers he had robbed, till eventually he closed the whole matter by swearing that some thief had stolen the material from right under his nose!

It came to pass that he became so notorious for his wicked deeds that he no longer dared to show his face in his shop. He preferred to while away the hours sitting at the barber's, safe from angry clients and their demands and protests. And what was more, at Abu Sir's he found now and then another victim simple-minded enough to fall into his snare.

But before long Abu Kir's dishonesty brought him poverty. The dye shop had to close, and he was so well known for his bad habits that nobody would

let him have anything on account. As for customers, they were a thing of the past.

So he took to complaining to Abu Sir, moaning over his fate, trying at the same time to convince him how greatly to their advantage it would be if they both moved out of Alexandria, where nobody really respected their trades nor their skills. He went on and on in this vein while the barber nodded his head, but remained silent. Time went by and Abu Kir did not miss a single day in painting the rosy, prosperous future which would be theirs, if only his friend would tear himself away from his shabby existence. The barber in the end gave in to his persuasive talk and agreed to the suggestion.

They sealed their partnership by reciting verses from the Koran, vowing they would work to their mutual advantage and help each other always.

Such an agreement was greatly to Abu Kir's liking, and it did not take long for him to turn it to his own advantage.

It so happened that they boarded a ship in Alexandria which was bound for foreign lands. As they had no money for their fares or for their food, Abu Sir

took out his barber's instruments and worked each day shaving the crew and cutting their hair. They repaid him with hard cash and simple food. The captain, being the richest, was the most generous, and every evening he invited both the partners to his cabin to dine at his lavish table. But Abu Kir was not really interested in such invitations. Why should he have been? After all, if he stayed on deck, he could have his fill of almost anything he fancied. He ate the simple loaves the sailors gave him as well as the selected dishes sent by the captain.

He is like a never-satisfied cannibal, Abu Sir often thought, but he let the dyer be, when Abu Kir was for ever excusing himself by saying he felt sea-sick.

After a long journey the ship moored in the harbour of a city, and the two partners found themselves lodgings ashore. The very next morning Abu Sir took all his instruments and went about the streets, practising his trade till the sun went down. He did this day after day, but the only things that Abu Kir did were sleep and rest and eat and complain that he felt giddy!

But after a few weeks the barber fell ill and was unable to go to work. Thank goodness I have a friend at hand, he thought, he is sure to look after me now. What a foolish thought!

Abu Kir certainly did not keep his part of the agreement. When he saw the money earned by the barber disappearing from the purse, he took what was left, crept out of their lodgings and left Abu Sir without any help at all.

He walked about the city, till he came to a dye shop. There was still in him a flicker of interest in his trade. He would find out how advanced they were in this city so distant from Alexandria. Also he fully realized that his bad reputation could not have followed him so far.

He was most surprised to see that all the materials had been dyed blue. It almost seemed that here in this town they did not know about all the varieties of colours, such as yellow, red, white, black, green, not to mention the different shades which Abu Kir could create on demand.

To make quite sure, he asked about it, and found his first thought was correct. This city knew no other colour but blue.

'What a chance for me,' Abu Kir said to himself. 'I should say it would be easy to get any dyer here to take me on, when I show what I can do.' But he was wrong. He walked from one dye shop to the next till he had been to them all. As he was a foreigner, nobody wished to employ him.

Indignant and exhausted by all this exercise the dyer decided to complain to the sultan himself. And the sultan not only listened, but on hearing of Abu Kir's capabilities, he pronounced he would give the dyer a trial.

20   'I can see you are a master of your trade and your work will be a credit to

this city. I shall tell my architects to accompany you on a tour of the town. Select the place where you want your dye shop to stand and it will be built according to your wishes.'

Abu Kir was quite overwhelmed by the sultan's unexpected generosity, in fact he was quite speechless at first. But as soon as he got used to the idea, he put the sultan's plan into action. He found a convenient place, and soon a building was erected to his specifications and filled with dyes and equipment bought with the sultan's money.

Then he set to work. First he mixed many colours in different dishes, and the colours were such that their brightness and beauty almost took one's breath away. Next he took five hundred lengths of material belonging to the sultan, and dyed each one a different shade.

He worked hard and well and with pleasure. He spared no effort to complete his task. The loiterers in front of the shop were amazed at his performance, and the sultan rewarded him handsomely. From that day on orders poured into the shop, but by then he no longer worked alone. He taught the art to several slaves and he only supervised. His wealth and business grew so swiftly that soon no other dyer could compete with him. In fact many of his rivals now offered their services, but Abu Kir refused them all. He repaid their former unkindness with unkindness.

He did not give a single thought to his old friend the barber, and it did not enter his head that it was his duty, according to their agreement, to care for him during his illness.

Poor Abu Sir, in the meantime, remained weak and helpless in the little room where they had settled. When he found out that the remains of his money had disappeared with Abu Kir, he was near despair.

But what could he do? He would have surely perished if the caretaker of that lodging house had not noticed that no person had gone out or come into his room for some time. It was he who investigated and took pity on the barber, caring for him and saving him from the verge of death by giving him good food and drink.

The caretaker was the one who told Abu Sir how successful and rich his former room-mate had become, and that he was a great favourite with the sultan. And Abu Sir was overjoyed and pleased for his friend. There was no envy, no reproach in his heart and he excused the dyer's dishonesty by saying to himself that he was probably working so hard for the good of them both that he had no time to pay him a visit.

At last he recovered enough to leave his lodgings and visit the dye shop. It was easy to find — everyone seemed to have heard of it — and when he saw the building as imposing as a palace, his respect for his friend grew.

The interior matched the grand exterior. And there was Abu Kir, relaxed on cushions, clad in expensive robes, issuing orders to his workers. But the minute he saw the barber, he cried angrily, 'Seize him! That is the thief, who has been stealing my materials for some time! He would have me work at a loss! Deal with him, so that he doesn't dare show his face in here again!'

Poor Abu Sir called for justice, but it was no use. He begged his friend to listen, but Abu Kir turned a deaf ear. The slaves obeyed the dyer's command and beat the barber till he was black and blue, and was hardly able to drag himself away. And while he was groaning and moaning in pain in the street, wondering how to ease his bruises, he decided that only a bath would ease the agony. But though he inquired everywhere, there was not a person in the town who had even heard of such a thing as a bath house! The only thing they could recommend was dirty sea water!

Abu Sir could scarcely believe such ignorance, which did not allow the body to be cleansed and refreshed in the proper manner. He came at last to the conclusion that the only solution was to go to the sultan and discuss the whole matter.

The sultan, who did not know the delights of a warm bath, of relaxing massage of limbs, or scented ointments, was most impressed by Abu Sir's words. He was eager that the barber should build a grand bathing place, and for this he opened wide the doors to his treasury.

The barber wasted no time. The bath house he had built was a credit to any sultan. Inside was everything anyone could want or desire — changing rooms, pools of hot and cold water with fountains rising in their centres, steam baths and private cabins. He engaged male and female slaves, picking those whose faces were beautiful and whose eyes were kind. He taught them the art of massage, and when all was ready, he sent messengers into the town to spread the word and bring in customers. How amazed and delighted everyone was, particularly the sultan! And as Abu Sir was a just man, he demanded a fee appropriate to each individual visitor, thus making the bath house available even to the man of most meagre means. And his wealth quickly grew, and before long he was richer than Abu Kir.

The dyer soon heard of the success of his old friend. He was so consumed with envy that he pondered day and night how to harm him.

After some time he decided to visit the bath house, and after Abu Sir had welcomed him in the friendliest manner without referring to the bitter experiences of the past, the dyer said, 'I have been looking for you for a long time now, for I wanted to look after you and make sure of your happiness. But now I can see that you live in luxury and don't even spare a thought for your

old friend!'

It was then that Abu Sir reminded him of their last meeting, and how he had him beaten by his slaves. What a thing for a friend to do a friend! But the dyer would not own up to such a deed. How was he to recognize the haggard, skinny beggar who came to see him as his friend, the barber?

They drank coffee together and again became friends. The artful Abu Kir flattered Abu Sir with fine words, and finally said, 'You have a magnificent bath house here; my dye shop cannot bring me in as much money. Just to prove to you how glad I am to see you so prosperous, I will tell you how to make your baths even more renowned. Make a mixture of lime and arsenic for your customers. It is amazing how easily it removes unwanted hair...'

'Thank you for your advice. I wouldn't have thought of such a thing. It just shows that two heads are always better than one,' said Abu Sir sincerely. And so they bade each other goodbye.

The dyer, of course, was not thinking at all of helping his friend, but of harming him as much as he could. He now hastened to the sultan to warn him. 'Sultan of our time! From this moment on you must not enter the bath house if you do not wish to lose your life! The barber, to whom you have given your trust and whom you have raised to the ranks of the rich, is an enemy of our faith and has prepared for you total destruction!'

'How can that be?' asked the bewildered sultan.

'If you go to the bath house, he will offer you a mixture — supposedly to remove unwanted hair. But this mixture is poisonous and would surely kill you.'

The sultan did not know whether or not to believe the dyer's words, so he hurried to find out whether he had spoken the truth. And sure enough — the minute he entered the bath house, there was Abu Sir, saying, 'Forgive me, Sultan, it is only now that I have remembered a certain mixture which rids the body of ugly unwanted hair, and which is in popular use in my country...'

'Show me that preparation!' the sultan commanded. When the barber brought him a rather foul smelling mixture, he began to think that this truly must be a poison prepared specially to bring about his death.

'Seize him!' he cried to the guards. And the poor unfortunate, unsuspecting man soon found himself in irons. Then he was led off to the palace, where the ruler decided that he would punish the culprit himself.

'Look at this,' he said to Abu Sir, taking out of his pocket a glittering ring. 'The power of this ring is such that if I put it on my index finger, and point at you, your head will fall from your shoulders. Such a death I choose for your deception and villainy.'

Surprise and terror caused the blood to drain from the unhappy victim's **24** face. But as the sultan prepared to place the ring on his index finger, it suddenly fell from his hand and rolled over to the barber's feet. Abu Sir picked it up. Everyone present looked on in horror, for now he, the condemned, was the master of life and death of all those in the palace.

Turning to the silent onlookers, he addressed the sultan, 'Oh, King of the age, fate has destined me to survive your test, so I could in turn test your fairness. Therefore take back this ring.'

With those words he handed the ring back to the sultan. The ruler was amazed at the barber's faith in him. Such a man surely could not be an enemy, thought he, and began to discuss the barber's crime.

Abu Sir heard the shameful tale with a sad, crest-fallen face. He then told of all his previous experiences with Abu Kir.

'How easy it is for me to see now who is the true enemy of my faith,' said the indignant sultan, and added decisively, 'Death, which the dyer was preparing for you, will now be his fate, as he so rightly deserves.'

And that is exactly what happened. But when Abu Kir was shorter by his head, Abu Sir persuaded the sultan to allow him to take back the body of his one time friend to their homeland and have him buried there with full honour. That he did this is proved by the place near Alexandria called to this day Abukir.

The Golden Goose

There was once a man who had three sons. The youngest was called Dummling, which means Dunce or Simpleton. He was despised, made fun of and ignored at every opportunity.

It so happened that the eldest brother decided to go into the forest to cut wood and, before he left, his mother gave him a nice fine sponge cake and a bottle of wine so that he wouldn't suffer from hunger and thirst.

When he got into the forest he met a little wizened, grey-faced old dwarf who bade him good day and said, 'Please give me a piece of the cake you have in your pouch and a drop of your wine. I am so hungry and thirsty.'

But the clever son answered, 'If I give you my cake and my wine, I shall have nothing left for myself. Go on your way.' And he left the little man standing there and walked on.

Soon after, when chopping the tree he miscalculated, missed, and the axe cut into his arm so that he had to go home and have it bandaged. And this had been the little grey man's doing.

Thereupon the second son went into the forest and, like the eldest, his mother gave him a sponge cake and a bottle of wine. He, too, met the old grey dwarf who stopped him to ask for a piece of the cake and a drop of wine. But the second son also spoke quite brusquely and said, 'Whatever you get, I shall lose. Go on your way!' and he left the dwarf standing there.

It was not long before he was punished. After dealing the tree a few blows he cut his leg and had to be carried home.

Then Dummling said, 'Father, now let me go out and cut wood.'

The father replied, 'Your brothers have been injured doing it. Don't meddle with it. You know nothing about cutting trees.'

But Dummling begged and begged till the father gave in at last and said, 'Go there then, you'll be wiser from your mistakes.'

His mother gave Dummling a cake, one that had been cooked with water and in ashes, and a bottle of sour beer. He came into the forest and also met the old grey dwarf.

The dwarf greeted him and said, 'Give me a piece of your cake and a drink out of your bottle. I am so hungry and thirsty.'

'I have only a plain cake baked in the ashes and sour beer,' said Dummling. 'But if you find it to your taste, we will sit down and eat together.'

Then they sat down, and when Dummling unwrapped his plain cake, it had turned into a fine sponge cake and the beer into good wine. They ate and drank and the dwarf said, 'You have a kind heart and are willing to share what you have with others, so I will bring good fortune to you. See that old tree there, go and cut it down, and you'll find something in the roots.' Then the little man said good-bye.

Dummling went over to the tree, cut it down and, when it fell, a goose was sitting among its roots with feathers of pure gold. He lifted it out, took it with him and went to an inn to spend the night. Now the innkeeper had three daughters and when they saw the goose, they wondered what a miraculous bird it was, and positively yearned to possess one of its golden feathers.

The eldest thought to herself, 'I am sure I'll find an opportunity to pull out just one feather,' and when Dummling left the room for a while, she seized the goose by the wing but her fingers and hand stuck fast to it.

Soon after that the second daughter came with no other idea than to take a golden feather for herself. But as soon as she touched her sister she got stuck, too.

Finally, the third sister came with the same intention. Her two sisters shouted, 'Keep away for heaven's sake, keep away!' But she didn't understand why she should not come in, and thought to herself, 'Why shouldn't I be there, when they are there!' And she leapt forward, but scarcely had she touched her sister than she stuck to her. So they had to keep company with the goose all night.

The next morning, Dummling put the goose under his arm, and set out **27** without as much as a thought for the three girls who were hanging on to it. They just had to follow him at a trot, now right, now left, as the fancy took him.

Out in the fields they met the parson and, on seeing Dummling's procession, he said, 'Shame on you, you disgraceful girls! Why are you chasing this lad through the fields? It's indecent!'

With these words, he seized the youngest by the hand to pull her back. But the moment he touched her, he, too, got stuck, and had to run on behind.

Before long, the sexton came along and, seeing his master, the parson, following on the heels of three girls, was astounded and cried out, 'Hey parson! What's the big hurry? Don't forget we have a christening today!' And he ran up to him and caught him by the sleeve but he too stuck fast.

As they were thus trudging along one behind the other, two peasants with their mattocks came across the field. The parson calling out to them, begged them to cut him and the sexton free. However, the moment they touched the sexton, they stuck to him, and now there were seven of them running behind Dummling and his goose.

Next they came to a city where a King ruled who had a daughter, so sad that nobody could make her laugh. He had proclaimed that whosoever could make her laugh should marry her. When Dummling heard about this, he appeared before the Princess with his goose and its train of people. When she saw the seven people running one behind the other after him and his goose, she burst out into loud laughter, and laughed and laughed and couldn't stop.

Then Dummling asked for her to become his wife, but the King didn't like his would-be son-in-law, and made all kinds of excuses saying that he would first have to produce a man who could drink dry a cellar full of wine.

Dummling thought the grey dwarf might help him, so he went into the forest, and at the place where he had cut down the tree, he saw a man looking very miserable. Dummling asked him what was the matter.

The man answered, 'I am terribly thirsty and cannot quench my thirst at all. Cold water doesn't agree with me. I did empty a cask of wine, but what's a drop like that on a dry stone?'

'Well, I can help you,' said Dummling, 'just come along with me, and you shall have your fill.'

Then he took him into the King's cellar and the man fell upon the big casks and drank and drank until his hips ached, and before the day had passed had drunk the cellar dry.

Again, Dummling demanded his bride, but the King was annoyed to think that a low-born fellow, whom everyone called a simpleton, should walk off with his daughter. So he laid down new conditions. First he would have to produce a man who could eat up a mountain of bread. Without delay Dummling went straight into the forest. There, on the same spot as before, sat a man who was tightening his belt and looking the picture of misery.

He said to Dummling, 'I've eaten a whole ovenful of grated bread but what good is that when one is as hungry as I am? My stomach remains empty, and **29**

I am tightening my belt to help stop the pangs of hunger, but I fear I shall starve to death.'

Dummling was overjoyed to hear this and said, 'Get up and come with me. You shall eat your fill.'

He took him to the King's court. The King had all the flour in the whole kingdom brought to the palace, and a monstrous mountain of bread baked from it. Then the man from the forest stood before it and began to eat and, in a day, the whole mountain had disappeared.

For the third time Dummling asked for his bride, but the King again found an excuse and demanded a ship that could sail both on land and on water. 'The moment you come sailing along in it, you shall have my daughter for your wife.'

Dummling went straight into the forest and there he found the grey old dwarf. The dwarf said, 'I've drunk and I've eaten for you, and I'll also give you the ship you need. I am doing all this because you once took pity on me.' Then he gave Dummling the ship that could sail on both land and water, and when the King saw it, he could no longer refuse to give him his daughter.

The wedding was celebrated, and after the King's death Dummling inherited the kingdom and he and his wife lived happily ever after.

Ole Close-Your-Eyes

There is no one in the whole world who knows so many stories as Ole Close-Your-Eyes. How he can spin those tales!

In the evening, when children are still sitting quietly at the table or on their little stools, Ole Close-Your-Eyes usually comes along. He climbs up the stairs very softly, for he walks about in his socks. He opens the door so very gently and—swish! he squirts sweet milk into the children's eyes, not very much, but enough to make them shut their eyes, so they cannot see him. Then he creeps up close behind them and breathes lightly, so lightly, upon their necks. Straightaway their heads become very heavy, oh, so heavy! But it does not hurt the slightest bit, for Ole Close-Your-Eyes means it kindly and only wants them to be quiet, and quiet they are most of all when they are in bed. They have to be quiet, so that he can tell them his stories.

When at last the children are asleep, Ole Close-Your-Eyes sits down on their bed. He is smartly dressed, with a coat made of silk, but it is impossible to say what colour that coat is, for it shines now green, now red, now blue, according to the light and how he moves about. Under each arm he holds an umbrella. One, which has pictures painted on it, he opens over good children, who afterwards have the most delightful dreams all night long. And the other umbrella, which has nothing on it, he opens over naughty children, and then they sleep rather heavily and wake up in the morning without having dreamed at all.

And now let us hear how Ole Close-Your-Eyes visited a little boy called Hialmar every night for a whole week and what stories he told him.

MONDAY

'Just you wait,' said Ole Close-Your-Eyes in the evening, as soon as he had got Hialmar into bed. 'Now I will decorate this room!' And, all at once, all the flowers in their pots grew into large trees, with long branches that spread right up to the ceiling and along the walls, so that the room looked like a beautiful arbour. The branches were full of flowers and every flower was more beautiful than even a rose, and had a wonderful smell. Moreover, if you were to eat one, you'd find it sweeter than jam. Fruit glittered like gold and there were cakes full of currants. It was truly delightful! But all at once, something started to moan and to complain most awfully in the table-drawer, where Hialmar's school books were kept.

'What is the matter?' wondered Ole Close-Your-Eyes, as he went up to the table and opened the drawer. It was the slate who was rather distressed, for a wrong figure had got into the sum on it and the other figures were pressing and squeezing together, till the whole sum nearly fell to pieces. The pencil was hopping and skipping about like a little dog, he really wanted to help that sum, but he could not! And Hialmar's copybook was there too and it moaned and groaned in a most unpleasant manner! On each page at the beginning of every line was a capital letter with a little letter next to it; this was the example. And by its side were other letters intended to look like the example. Hialmar had written these, but they seemed to have fallen over the lines upon which they should have been standing.

'Now this is the way you should hold yourselves,' said the example. 'Slightly slanting, like this, and turning round sharply and smartly!'

'Oh, we would like to do that,' said Hialmar's letters, 'but we can't, we are just not up to it!'

'In that case you need the powder medicine!' said Ole Close-Your-Eyes.

'Oh no,' the letters cried, and stood up so straight they were a joy to behold.

'Well, I can't tell any more stories now,' said Ole Close-Your-Eyes, 'for I have to drill those letters! Left right! Left right!' So he drilled the letters and they looked so straight and healthy, as if they were the examples themselves. But when Ole Close-Your-Eyes went away and Hialmar looked at them the next morning, they were just as badly formed as before.

TUESDAY

As soon as Hialmar was in bed, Ole Close-Your-Eyes touched with his little magic wand every piece of furniture in the room, and they all started to chatter and they all chattered only about themselves, with the exception of the spittoon. He was standing there quietly, annoyed at their vanity talking only about themselves, thinking only about themselves, without even remembering him, who stood so modestly in the corner and had to put up with being spat upon.

A large picture in a gilt frame hung over the sofa. It was a landscape. In it you could see tall old trees, flowers in the grass and a big lake with a river that flowed round the wood, passing many palaces on its way to the stormy sea.

Ole Close-Your-Eyes touched the painting with his magic wand and immediately the birds started to sing, the boughs of the trees swayed to and fro and the clouds actually moved, you could see their shadows flitting over the landscape.

Ole Close-Your-Eyes lifted little Hialmar up to the frame, and Hialmar put his legs right into the picture; there he stood in the tall grass and the sun shone down upon him through the branches of the trees. He ran to the lake and sat down in a little boat which was anchored there. It was painted red and white, with sails glittering like silver. Six swans, all with golden garlands round their necks and shining blue stars upon their heads, pulled the little boat along, past the green woods, where the trees were telling stories about thieves and witches and the flowers were talking about the pretty little elves, and of what the butterflies had said to them.

The most beautiful fishes with scales like gold and silver swam behind the boat. Every now and then they leapt above the surface, splashing the water. And birds red and blue, big and small, flew after him in two long rows; the gnats danced and the cockchafers mumbled, 'boom, boom'. They all wanted to go with Hialmar and every one of them had a story to tell.

A voyage it was to be envied! Now the woods were dense and gloomy, now like the most beautiful gardens filled with sunshine and flowers and in those gardens there were big palaces built of glass and marble. Young Princesses stood on the balconies, and they were all little girls whom Hialmar well knew and with whom he had often played. They all stretched out their hands to him, each holding a pretty little sugar pig, like those sold in sweet shops. Hialmar seized the end of one of the sugar pigs as he sailed by and, as the Princess was holding on tight, each got half, the Princess the smaller, Hialmar the larger. At every palace little Princes were keeping guard, they had gold swords at their side and they were throwing raisins and tin-soldiers all around—they were true Princes!

Hialmar sailed sometimes through woods, sometimes through large halls or the middle of a town. He also passed through the town where his nurse lived—one who had looked after him when he was just a little boy, and who loved him dearly. Now she nodded and beckoned to him as he passed by, waving and singing the pretty song she had herself composed and sent to him:

'How many times I think of you,
My Hialmar, my boy!
How I'd kiss your cheeks, your lips,
You were my pride and joy!
Your very first words I heard you try
But then time came to say goodbye.

May the good Lord be your guide
And stay always at your side.'

And all the birds sang with her, the flowers danced on their stalks, and the old trees nodded their heads, as though Ole Close-Your-Eyes were telling the stories to them as well.

WEDNESDAY

Oh, how hard it rained, how it poured! Hialmar could hear it in his sleep. And when Ole Close-Your-Eyes opened the window, water came in over the ledge. There was quite a lake outside, with a magnificent ship right by the house.

'Do you want to sail with me, little Hialmar?' asked Ole Close-Your-Eyes. 'We can visit foreign lands tonight and be back here again first thing in the morning!'

And so Hialmar found himself standing on deck, dressed in his Sunday clothes. The weather had cleared. The ship sailed through the streets, cruised

round the church, and soon they were on the wide, wild sea. They were sailing for such a long time, that there was no land in sight, only a few storks, who had also left their home and were travelling to warmer lands. The storks flew one behind the other and had been flying thus for a long, long time. One of them was so weary, his wings could hardly keep him up. He was the last in the row and was soon far behind the others. He sank lower and lower, his wings outspread; he managed to move them a few more times, but it was no use. His feet touched the ship's rigging, he slid down the sail and, plonk! there he was, standing on deck.

The cabin-boy picked him up and put him in with the hens, ducks and turkeys. The unfortunate stork stood among them quite confounded.

'What a funny fellow!' babbled the hens.

And the turkeycock thrust out his chest as hard as he could and asked the stork who he was. The ducks waddled backwards, nudging each other and quacking: 'Move over, move over!'

The stork told them about warm Africa, about the pyramids and the ostrich, who races the desert like a wild horse. But the ducks did not

understand him and only nudged each other, remarking: 'Don't you think him stupid?'

'Yes, indeed, he is stupid!' said the turkeycock and began to gobble. With that the stork lapsed into silence and thought of his Africa.

'What beautiful, slender legs you have,' said the turkeycock. 'How much did they cost you per yard?'

'Quack, quack, quack!' laughed the ducks, but the stork pretended not to hear the question.

'You should have laughed with us!' said the turkeycock, 'for it was a very witty joke! Or was it, perhaps, slightly common for you? Oh, oh! You're not that grand yourself! Come on, let's keep ourselves to ourselves!' With that he turned and gobbled on, and the ducks quacked on: 'quack, quack, quack!' It was indeed the most horrible noise, but they probably thought it pleasant.

Hialmar went over to the hen-house, opened the door, called the stork, and the stork immediately hopped out on deck. He had rested enough and bowed his head to the boy, as if to thank him. Then he spread his wings and flew away to warmer regions. The hens cackled, the ducks quacked and the turkeycock turned purple.

'Tomorrow we'll make a soup out of you all!' Hialmar threatened but then he awoke, and found himself in his own little bed. It was indeed a strange journey that Ole Close-Your-Eyes had taken him on that night.

THURSDAY

'I'll tell you what,' said Ole Close-Your-Eyes. 'Don't be scared and you'll see a little mouse!' And he held out his hand with the tiny, pretty little animal in it. 'She has come to invite you to a wedding. This very night, two little mice here intend to enter into matrimony. They live under the floor of mother's pantry. Apparently it is the most beautiful apartment!'

'But how am I to get through a little mouse-hole?' asked Hialmar.

'Leave that to me!' said Ole Close-Your-Eyes. 'I'll make you small!' He touched Hialmar with his magic wand and Hialmar started to shrink and shrink, till he was no bigger than a finger. 'Now you can borrow the tin soldier's clothes. I think they will suit you, and a uniform looks so imposing when in company.'

'Agreed then,' said Hialmar and in a trice he was dressed like the smartest tin soldier.

'Would you please be so kind as to sit in your mother's thimble?' asked the little mouse. 'I would consider it a great honour to be allowed to pull you!'

'Heaven forbid that a young lady would go to such trouble!' Hialmar   **37** protested. But they were already on their way to the mouse wedding.

First they came to a long passage under the floor, which was only just high enough for the thimble to be pulled along. The whole passage was lit with lighted tinder.

'Isn't there a lovely smell in here?' said the mouse who was pulling the thimble. 'The whole passage has been rubbed with bacon-rind! There is nothing in this world to beat it!'

And now they were in the bridal apartment. On the right hand side stood all the lady mice, gossiping and whispering and cracking jokes. On the left hand side stood all the gentlemen mice, stroking their whiskers with their paws. In the middle of the floor were the bride and groom.

They stood in the scooped out rind of a cheese and were ardently kissing each other before everyone's eyes. They were, after all, betrothed, and were to be married straightaway.

More guests arrived every moment. The mice nearly trod each other to death and the bride and groom had placed themselves right by the door, so no one could go in, nor out. The whole apartment, like the passage, had been

rubbed in bacon rind. That was all the refreshment they had but, as a dessert, a pea was exhibited, in which a little mouse who belonged to the family had bitten out the names of the bride and groom, or rather their initials. It was something quite extraordinary.

All the mice agreed that it was a truly memorable wedding.

Hialmar then rode back home. He had certainly been in the most distinguished company. Though he felt slightly abashed at allowing himself to become so small and wearing the uniform of one of his own tin soldiers.

FRIDAY

'It is truly incredible how many old people want my company,' said Ole Close-Your-Eyes. 'Particularly those who have done something wicked. "Dear, good Ole," they say to me, "we can't sleep a wink all night. We lie awake and see all our bad deeds sitting like ugly goblins on the edge of the bed, sprinkling scalding water over us. If you would be so kind as to come and chase them away, so that we could have a good sleep!" And then they sigh deeply, "We'd be happy to pay you! Good night, Ole! You'll find the money behind the window!" But I don't do anything for money!' said Ole Close-Your-Eyes.

'What are we doing tonight?' asked Hialmar.

'Well, I am not sure if you would like to go to yet another wedding tonight. But it will be quite different from yesterday. Your sister's big boy doll, Herman, is going to marry the doll Bertha. Besides, it is Bertha's birthday as well, so there'll be a lot of presents.'

'I know this very well!' said Hialmar. 'Whenever the dolls need new clothes, my sister lets them celebrate either their birthday or their wedding. It must have happened at least a hundred times already!'

'Yes, but tonight they will be married for the hundred-and-first time. And this hundred-and-first marriage has to be the last. So this is sure to be a special wedding. Come on and look!'

Hialmar looked upon the table. A little doll's house stood there, with lighted windows and tin soldiers at the door presenting arms. The bridal pair were sitting on the floor, leaning against the leg of the table and looking somewhat worried. They probably had their reasons. But Ole Close-Your-Eyes, dressed in his grandmother's black gown, was marrying them! When the ceremony was over, all the furniture in the room started to sing this pretty song, written specially by the pencil:

'We sing fond farewell
To the bridal pair
With kid-leather skin
Yet straight and so fair.
For beau and belle hurrah, hurrah!
Let our song echo near and far!'

Now the presents were brought to them. Nothing edible, of course, would they accept. They had enough love to live on!

'Shall we live in the country, or go abroad?' asked the bridegroom. They consulted the swallow, who was well-travelled, and the old hen, who had hatched five broods of chickens. And the swallow spoke of beautiful warm regions, where bunches of grapes grow large and heavy, where the air is balmy and mountains are tinged with colours here unknown!

'But they haven't got our cabbage!' said the hen. 'Once in the summer I lived with all my chicks in the country, where there was a gravel-pit in which we could dig and scrape about, and from there we had access to a garden full of cabbages! Oh, how green they were! I can't even imagine anything more beautiful!'

'But surely, one head of cabbage looks exactly like another!' said the swallow; 'and then the weather here can be so awful!'

'Yes, but we are used to that!' the hen argued.

'But it is so cold here. It freezes!'

'That is good for the cabbages!' said the hen. 'And as for the heat, we have it too! Did we not, four years ago, have a summer which lasted five weeks? It was so hot, it was impossible to breathe! Besides, here you won't find all those poisonous animals which they have in foreign countries! And we don't have to fear robbers! Who doesn't consider our country the most beautiful of all, is an idiot! He doesn't deserve to live here with us!' And the hen burst into tears.

'I too have travelled. I've covered twelve miles in a coop! There is no pleasure at all in travelling!'

'Oh yes, the hen is a sensible woman!' the doll Bertha declared. 'I don't like travelling in the mountains, because one is always going up and down! No, we will go to the gravel-pit and stroll in the cabbage garden.'

And so it was settled.

SATURDAY

'Are you going to tell me another story?' asked little Hialmar, the moment Ole Close-Your-Eyes put him to bed.

'We've no time for that this evening!' said Ole, spreading his beautiful picture umbrella over him. 'Just look at those Chinese pictures!' The whole umbrella looked like a large Chinese plate with blue trees and pointed bridges, on which stood little Chinese men and women, nodding their heads. 'By tomorrow morning I must put the whole world in order,' said Ole. 'It is, after all, a festive day, a Sunday. I've got to examine the church tower, to see if the little goblins have polished the bells to make them ring nicely, I must look at the fields to see if the winds have swept the dust off the leaves and the grass. And the hardest job of all, I must take down all the stars from the sky and brighten them up. But first I have to number them; and the holes up there, into which the stars fit, have to be numbered too, to make sure the stars will return each to his proper place. Otherwise they wouldn't sit firmly and we would have falling stars tumbling down one after another!'

'Now listen to me, Mr. Ole Close-Your-Eyes,' said an old portrait, which hung on the wall near Hialmar's bed. 'I am Hialmar's great-grandfather. It is only fitting for me to give you my thanks for telling the boy stories, but you must not confuse him. Stars cannot be taken down and polished! Stars are heavenly bodies, same as our earth, and that is the good thing about them!'

'Thank you kindly, old great-grandfather,' said Ole Close-Your-Eyes,

'many thanks indeed! You are, after all, the head of the family, its very oldest head! But I am older than you! I am an old heathen; the Romans and the Greeks called me the God of Dreams! I have visited the most distinguished families, and I visit them still! I know how to deal with great and small! Now it is your turn to talk!' And with that Ole Close-Your-Eyes went away, taking the umbrella with him.

'So one is not allowed even to speak one's mind today!' muttered the old portrait sadly.

And then Hialmar awoke.

SUNDAY

'Good evening!' said Ole Close-Your-Eyes. Hialmar answered his greeting with a nod, jumping up at the same time to turn his great-grandfather's portrait to the wall, so he would not interrupt them as he had done the night before.

'Now tell me stories—about the five peas who all lived in one pod, about the proud cock courting the hen, and about the darning-needle, who was so conceited she fancied herself a sewing-needle!'

'That is too much at once!' protested Ole Close-Your-Eyes. 'I would actually rather show you something else! I will show you my brother, he too is called Ole Close-Your-Eyes, but he never visits anyone more than once. And whomsoever he calls on, he takes on his horse and tells him stories. He knows only two; one is wondrously beautiful, such as no one in the world can imagine; the other is so terrible and dreadful — indescribably so!' And Ole Close-Your-Eyes lifted little Hialmar up to the window, and said, 'Now you will see my brother, the other Ole Close-Your-Eyes! He is also called Death. You see, he is nowhere near as frightful as he looks in picture books, where he is all bones! See his clothes, they are embroidered with silver. He is wearing the most magnificent uniform! His cloak of black velvet flies above his horse. See how he gallops!'

And Hialmar saw the other Ole Close-Your-Eyes ride on, taking with him on his horse folk young and old. Some he placed in front of him, others behind, but always he asked first, 'What kind of a report have you?' 'Good!' said one and all. 'Very well, but let me see it!' he said, and so they had to show him

their reports. And all those who had 'very good' or 'excellent' written on theirs, were allowed to sit in front and to listen to the lovely story. But those who had 'fairly good' or 'bad' inscribed, had to sit behind and had to listen to the horrid tale. They trembled and cried, and tried to jump down from the horse but that they could not do, for they were as firmly fixed as if they had grown there.

'Why, Death is the most beautiful Ole Close-Your-Eyes!' Hialmar cried. 'I am not afraid of him!'

'And neither should you be,' said Ole Close-Your-Eyes. 'Just make sure you have a good report!'

'Most instructive indeed!' grunted the great-grandfather's portrait. 'It must help, after all, to give one's opinion!' He was now content.

So this is a story about Ole Close-Your-Eyes. This evening he may tell you more himself!

The Swineherd

Once upon a time there was a poor Prince. He had a very small kingdom, but it was still big enough for him to marry on, and to marry he wished.

Yet it was rather bold of him to dare to say to the Emperor's daughter, 'Would you like to marry me?' But the Prince did dare, for his name was quite renowned everywhere. Hundreds of Princesses would have been only too glad to say 'yes', but let us hear what the Emperor's daughter did.

On the grave of the Prince's father a rose bush grew. It was such a beautiful rose bush! It flowered only once every five years, and even then it had only one bloom. But that rose was so sweetly scented, that whoever smelt it forgot all his sorrows and worries.

The Prince also had a nightingale, which sang as if all the loveliest melodies were held in his throat. The rose and the nightingale were just right for the Princess. And so the Prince put them into silver caskets and sent them to her.

The Emperor had them carried before him into the great hall where the Princess was amusing herself with her maids of honour by playing 'visitors' — they never did any work. When she saw the silver caskets with the presents, she clapped her hands for joy.

'If only it was a little pussy-cat!' she said. But out came the rose.

'Isn't it prettily made!' said the Emperor. 'It is exquisitely made.' But when the Princess touched it, she could have cried.

'Ugh, daddy!' she shouted. 'It isn't an artificial one, it's real!'

'Ugh!' cried all the maids of honour. 'It's real!'

'Let's take a look at the second casket before we start getting cross!' suggested the Emperor.

Out came the nightingale. He sang so beautifully, that it was not possible to find any fault.

'*Superbe! Charmant!*' cried all the court ladies, for they all babbled in French — one worse than the other.

'How this nightingale reminds me of the greatly lamented late Empress's musical box!' said an old courtier. 'Yes, yes, — it has the very same tone, the very same eloquence!'

'Yes,' sighed the Emperor, bursting into tears like a child.

'I can hardly believe it's real!' retorted the Princess.

'Oh yes, it's a real bird!' said the men who had brought it.

'Let it fly off then!' said the Princess and flatly refused to let the Prince in.

But the Prince wouldn't be deterred. Smearing his face black and brown, he pulled his cap down over his eyes and knocked.

'Good morning, Emperor!' he said. 'Can you find a job for me, here at the palace?'

'People come thick and fast asking for work!' the Emperor replied. 'But let me see — I could do with somebody to see to the pigs. We've got a fair number of them.'

So the Prince was employed as the imperial swineherd. He was given a poor little room near the pigsty, and there he had to live. But he worked at something all day long, and by evening he made a pretty little cooking pot, with little bells all round it and whenever the pot started to boil, the bells tinkled prettily, ringing out an old melody:

'*Ah, my dearest Augustine,*
All is gone, gone, gone!'

But the strangest thing of all was, that if you held your finger in the steam which escaped from the pot, you would smell straightaway everything that was being cooked on every stove in town. Now this was something quite different altogether from a rose!

The Princess was walking past with all her maids of honour. Hearing the melody played by the pot, she stopped. She looked really pleased, for she too knew how to play 'Ah, my dearest Augustine' — it was the only tune she could play, and then only with one finger.

'I can play that tune!' she cried. 'That must be a well-bred swineherd! Listen, go and ask how much he wants for that instrument!'

One of the maids of honour had to run there and ask, but she put her clogs on first.

'How much do you want for that pot?' she asked.

'I want ten kisses from the Princess!' said the swineherd.

'Good gracious me!' said the horrified maid of honour.

'I shan't let it go for less!' insisted the swineherd.

'Well, what did he say?' asked the Princess.

'I can't even tell you!' answered the maid of honour. 'It's too dreadful!'

'Whisper it then!' And the maid of honour whispered it.

'What a saucy fellow!' said the Princess and walked away at once. But she had gone only a little way, when the bells rang out again so very prettily:

'Ah, my dearest Augustine,
All is gone, gone, gone!'

'Listen,' said the Princess, 'ask him if he'd like ten kisses from my maids of honour!'

'No thank you!' replied the swineherd. 'Ten kisses from the Princess, or the pot stays mine!'

'How annoying!' said the Princess. 'But you must all stand round me, so no one may see!'

And the maids of honour all stood round her, spreading their wide skirts and the swineherd got his ten kisses and the Princess got her pot.

What fun they had! That pot had to boil all evening and all day. There wasn't a single stove in the whole town but they knew what was being cooked on it, from the chamberlain to the cobbler. The maids of honour danced and clapped their hands in delight.

'We know who is to have soup and pancakes! We know who is to have cutlets and rice pudding. It is so interesting!'

'Frightfully interesting!' said the lady of the wardrobe.

'But not a word to anyone, for I'm the Emperor's daughter!'

'We wouldn't dream!' they all cried.

The swineherd — or rather, the Prince, but then they all thought him to be a real swineherd — the swineherd never let a day go by without making something. Now he made a rattle. When he swung it round, it played all the waltzes, jigs and polkas which have ever been heard since the creation of the world.

'Oh, it is *superbe!*' cried the Princess, as she passed by. 'I've never heard prettier compositions! Listen, go and ask him how much he wants for that instrument! But mind, there'll be no kissing!'

'He wants a hundred kisses from the Princess!' said the maid of honour who had been sent to the swineherd.

'The fellow must be quite mad!' said the Princess and she walked off. But after going a little way, she stopped. 'We have to encourage the arts!' she said. 'I am, after all, the Emperor's daughter! Tell him he'll get ten kisses, the same as yesterday and the rest he can collect from my maids of honour!'

'Oh, but we shouldn't like that at all!' objected the maids of honour.

'What nonsense!' said the Princess. 'If I can kiss him, so can you. Remember I feed you and pay you!'

And so the maid of honour had to return to the swineherd.

'A hundred kisses from the Princess,' announced the swineherd, 'or we both keep what we've got!'

'Stand round!' ordered the Princess, and the maids of honour stood round and the swineherd got on with the kissing.

'What's all that commotion by the pigsty?' wondered the Emperor, when he stepped out on to the balcony. He rubbed his eyes and put on his spectacles.

'Those maids of honour must be up to something! I'd better go and inspect!' He pulled up his slippers at the heel, for they were trodden down.

My word, how he rushed!

When he came into the courtyard, he went about on tiptoe. The maids of honour were engrossed in counting the kisses to see fair play, to make sure the swineherd wouldn't get too many, nor too few. So they didn't even notice the Emperor. He drew himself up on tiptoe.

'Well I never!' he cried, seeing the kissing pair, and he hit them over the head with his slipper, just as the swineherd was getting his eighty-sixth kiss. 'Out!' screamed the Emperor, for he was furious. And the Princess and the swineherd were turned out of his kingdom.

And there stood the Princess weeping, with the swineherd scolding, and the rain pouring down.

'Oh, poor me!' cried the Princess, 'if I had but taken that handsome Prince! Oh, how unfortunate I am!'

The swineherd went behind a tree, wiped the black and brown off his face, took off his filthy rags and stepped forth in all his princely splendour. He looked so handsome, the Princess couldn't help but curtsy before him.

'I've learnt to despise you!' said the Prince. 'You wouldn't have an honest Prince! You couldn't appreciate a rose nor a nightingale, but you kissed a swineherd for a simple toy! Serve you right!'

With that he went back to his own kingdom, slammed the door and bolted it. The Princess was left standing outside singing in earnest:

> *'Ah, my dearest Augustine,*
> *All is gone, gone, gone!'*

Allerleirauh

Once upon a time there was a King who had a wife with golden hair, and she was so beautiful that her equal was not to be found on earth.

Now it happened that she fell ill, and when she felt she was about to die she called the King and said, 'If you wish to marry again after I am dead, do not take anyone for wife who is not just as beautiful as I am and who has not such golden hair as I have. This you must promise me.' The King gave her his promise, and she closed her eyes and died.

For a long time the King was inconsolable and had no thought of marrying again. At length, however, his councillors said, 'There is no other way, the King must get married again that we may have a Queen.'

So messengers were sent out far and wide to seek a bride who would equal the late Queen in beauty. But there was none to be found in the whole world, and even if one had been found, there was none who had such golden hair. So the messengers returned home empty-handed.

The King had a daughter who was just as beautiful as her mother before she died, and she also had her mother's golden hair. When she had grown up, the King looked at her one day and saw that she was like his late wife in every way and suddenly he fell passionately in love with her. So he said to his councillors, 'I will marry my daughter, for she is the living image of my late wife and anyway, I can find no bride to equal her.'

The councillors were shocked when they heard this, and said, 'God has forbidden that a father should marry his daughter. No good can come from such a sin, and the kingdom itself shall go to rack and ruin.'

Even more shocked was the daughter when she learnt of her father's resolution, but she hoped to turn him away from his intention. So she said to him, 'Before I grant your wish, first I must have three dresses. One as golden as the sun, one as silvery as the moon and one as radiant as the stars. Also, I demand a mantle, made from a thousand different pieces of fur sewn together, and every animal in your kingdom must give a piece of its skin for this purpose.' What she really thought was, 'It is quite impossible to procure all that fur, and thus I shall turn my father from his evil design.'

The King, however, did not give up, and had the cleverest maidens in the kingdom weave the three dresses, one as golden as the sun, one as silvery as the moon and one as radiant as the stars. His huntsmen were ordered to catch every single animal in the whole of his kingdom and to take a piece of its skin. Thus a mantle was made of a thousand different kinds of fur.

At last, when everything was ready, the King had the mantle brought in, spread it out before her, and said, 'Tomorrow is the wedding day.'

The King's daughter now saw there was no longer any hope of turning her father's heart, so she made up her mind to run away. That night, when everyone was asleep, she got up and took three of her most precious things; a golden ring, a golden spinning-wheel and a golden reel. She pressed the three dresses — one like the sun, the other like the moon and the third like the stars — into a nutshell, put on the mantle made of all kinds of fur, and blackened her face and hands with soot. Then she commended herself to God and went away and walked the whole night until she came to a great forest. As she was tired, she sat down in a hollow tree, and fell asleep.

The sun rose and she slept on, and she was still asleep when it was broad daylight.

Then it so happened that the King whose forest it was came there hunting. When his dogs came to the tree, they sniffed and ran about barking. The King said to the huntsmen, 'Well, go and see what kind of wild animal is hiding there.'

The huntsmen obeyed his order and when they came back they reported,

'There is a strange animal lying in the hollow tree, such as we have never seen before. There are a thousand furs on its skin, and it is lying asleep.'

The King said, 'See if you can catch it alive, then fasten it to the carriage and take it back to the palace.'

When the huntsmen laid hold of the maiden, she woke up full of fright and cried out to them, 'I am a poor child forsaken by father and mother, please have pity on me and take me with you.'

Then they said, 'Allerleirauh—which means furs-of-all-kinds—you will be useful in the kitchen. Just come along, you can sweep up the ashes.'

So they put her in the carriage and drove home to the royal palace. There they showed her a small cupboard under the stairs where no light of day ever came, and said, 'Hairy animal, here you can live and sleep.' Then they sent her into the kitchen, where she carried wood and water, stirred the fire, plucked the poultry, picked the vegetables, swept up the ashes, and did all the hard work.

Thus for a long time Allerleirauh led a truly wretched life. Alas, fair princess, what is to become of you next!

However, it happened that a feast was to be held in the palace, and she said to the cook, 'May I run upstairs for a while and look on? I will only stand outside the door.'

The cook answered, 'Yes, go on up there, but mind you are back here again in half an hour and sweep the hearth.'

Then Allerleirauh took her little oil lamp, went into her cupboard, took off her dress of fur and washed the soot off her face and hands, so that her full beauty stood revealed again.

Then she opened the nut, and took out her dress which shone like the sun. Then, when she was ready, she went upstairs to the festival and everyone stepped aside for her to pass, for they did not know her and all of them thought she was no less than a king's daughter.

The King came to meet her, gave her his hand and danced with her and thought in his heart, 'Never have my eyes seen anyone so beautiful!'

When the dance came to an end she curtsied and, as the King turned his head, she vanished and no one knew whither. The guards standing in front of the palace were called in and questioned, but none had seen her.

Meanwhile, Allerleirauh had run back to her cupboard, quickly taken off her dress, blackened her face and hands and put on her fur-mantle. When she came back to the kitchen, she was about to start her work sweeping the hearth, when the cook said, 'Leave that alone till tomorrow, and make bread soup for the King. I, too, want to have a look upstairs; but don't let any hairs fall in, or you shall get nothing more to eat.'

Then the cook went away and Allerleirauh made bread soup for the King as best she could. When it was ready, she went to her closet to fetch her golden ring, and put it in the bowl in which the soup was to be served.

When the dance was over, the King had the soup brought to him and ate it. It tasted so good that it seemed to him he had never eaten better soup in his life. When he came to the bottom, he found the golden ring lying there, and could not understand how it had got there. Then he ordered the cook to appear before him.

The cook was terror-stricken and said to Allerleirauh, 'You must have let a hair fall into the soup. If that is so you shall get a beating.'

When he appeared before the King, the King asked who had made the soup.

'I made it,' answered the cook.

But the King said, 'That is not true, for the soup was made in another way, and much better than usual.'

So he answered, 'I must confess I did not make it, it was made by the wild, hairy animal.'

Said the King, 'Go and send it up to me.'

When Allerleirauh came the King asked, 'Who are you?'

'I am a poor child who has no father and no mother.'

Then the King asked, 'What do you do in my palace?'

She answered, 'I am only good enough to have boots thrown at my head.'

He asked again, 'How did you come by the ring which was in the soup?'

She answered, 'The ring? I know nothing about it.'

So the King learnt nothing, and had to send her away again.

Some time later, there was another festival and, as before, Allerleirauh begged the cook for permission to go and look on.

He answered, 'Yes, but come back again in half an hour and make the King the bread soup he is so fond of.'

So she ran into her cupboard and washed quickly. Out of the nut she took the dress that was as silvery as the moon, and put it on. Then she went upstairs looking like a king's daughter. The King came forward to meet her and was overjoyed to see her again and, as the dance was just beginning, they danced together. However, when the dance was over, she again disappeared so quickly that the King could not see where she had gone.

She hurried to her cupboard, made herself the hairy animal again and went into the kitchen to make the bread soup. When the cook had gone upstairs, she fetched the little golden spinning-wheel, put it in the bowl and the soup was poured over it.

Then the soup was taken to the King, who ate it and enjoyed it just as much as the time before. He sent for the cook and again he had to confess that it was Allerleirauh who had made it. Allerleirauh appeared before the King, but she answered that she was only good enough to have boots thrown at her head, and she knew nothing at all about the little golden spinning-wheel.

When the King held a feast for the third time, everything happened in just the same way as on the previous occasions.

But the cook said, 'You are a witch, Fur-Skin. You always put something into the soup that makes it so good that the King likes it better than mine.'

Yet, as Allerleirauh begged him so much, he let her off for half an hour as before.

This time she put on the dress which shone like the stars, and entered the hall. Again the King danced with the beautiful maiden and thought that she was more beautiful than ever before. And, while they were dancing, he slipped a golden ring on her finger without her noticing it. He had also given orders that the dance should go on for a very long time.

When it was over, the King would have held her fast by the hand but she tore herself loose, and sprang away so quickly among the guests that she vanished from his sight. She ran as fast as she could to her little cupboard under the stairs. But, as she had long overstayed her half hour, she had no time to take off her lovely dress and, instead, threw the fur-mantle over it. Nor did she, in her haste, make herself completely black, and one of her fingers remained white.

Then Allerleirauh ran into the kitchen, made the bread soup for the King and, as soon as the cook was away, dropped the golden reel into it.

When the King found the reel at the bottom, he sent for Allerleirauh whereupon he noticed the white finger and saw the ring he had slipped on it while they were dancing. He grasped her by the hand and held her fast and, as she was trying to break loose and run away, the mantle of fur parted a little, and the star-dress shone forth. The King caught hold of the mantle and tore it off. Then her golden hair fell around her shoulders and she stood there in full splendour no longer able to hide herself. When she had washed the soot and ashes from her face she was more beautiful than anyone had ever seen on earth.

The King said, 'You are my dear bride, and we will never part again!'

Whereupon their wedding was celebrated, and they lived happily ever afterwards.

The Worn Out Dancing Shoes

Once upon a time, there was a King who had twelve daughters, each one fairer than the other. They all slept together in one great chamber where their beds stood side by side, and at night when they were in bed, the King would come, lock the door and bolt it. But when he opened the door every morning, he would see that their shoes were worn out with dancing, and no one could tell how it happened.

Then the King issued a proclamation that, whosoever could find out where they had been dancing at night, might choose one of them for his wife and become King after his death. But anyone who came forward and did not find out the truth within three days and three nights would forfeit his life.

Not long afterwards a Prince came forward and volunteered to undertake the risk. He was well received and, in the evening, they led him into a room adjoining the bedchamber of the Princesses. The servants made up a bed for him there, and he prepared himself to watch where they went and danced. So that the Princesses might not do anything in secret, the door of their bedroom was left open.

However, the Prince's eyes began to feel like lead and he fell asleep. When he woke up in the morning, all twelve Princesses had been out dancing, for their shoes were standing there with holes in the soles.

Nor did things go any differently on the second and the third nights, so his head was cut off without mercy. And after him came many more brave men who volunteered for the risky venture, but all of them had to leave their heads behind.

Now it so happened that a poor soldier who had been wounded and could serve no longer, found himself on the road to the city where the King lived. While walking along he met an old woman who asked him where he was going. 'I really don't know myself,' he answered and added jokingly, 'I should like to find out where the King's daughters dance their shoes to shreds, and then become King.'

'That's not so very difficult,' said the old woman. 'You just mustn't drink the wine that is brought to you in the evening, and only pretend to be fast asleep.'

Then she gave him a little cloak and said, 'When you put this round you, you will become invisible, and can creep after the twelve maidens.'

With all this good advice, the soldier started to take the matter seriously. He took heart, went before the King and offered himself as a suitor. Like the others, he too was well received and dressed in royal clothing.

In the evening towards bedtime, he was conducted to the chamber near the Princesses' room and, when he was about to go to bed, the eldest Princess came and brought him a cup of wine. But he had tied a sponge under his chin, let the wine run into the sponge, and did not drink a single drop. Then he lay down, and after lying there for a few moments, began to snore like one in the deepest sleep.

The King's twelve daughters heard this and laughed. The eldest said, 'He, too, might have done better to save his life.' Then they got up, opened wardrobes, chests and boxes, and took out magnificent dresses. Then they dressed themselves before their mirrors, skipped about, and looked forward to the dancing.

Only the youngest said, 'You are all full of joy but I have a strange feeling that misfortune is about to befall us.'

'You are a silly little snow-goose,' said the eldest. 'You are always scared. Have you forgotten how many Princes have already been here without success? As for the soldier, I needn't even have given him the sleeping-wine. The fool wouldn't have woken up anyway.'

When they were all ready, they first cast a glance at the soldier, but he had his eyes closed, did not move or stir, and so they believed they were now quite safe. Then the eldest went to her bed and knocked on it. At once it sank into the earth, and they stepped down through the opening, one after the other.

The soldier, who had seen everything, did not hesitate, hung his little cloak about him, and stepped down after the youngest. In the middle of the staircase he suddenly trod on the edge of her dress. She was so frightened that she cried, 'What's happening? Who is treading on my dress?'

'Don't be so silly,' said the eldest, 'you only got caught on a hook.'

Then they went all the way down, and when they were down, they were standing in a magnificent avenue of trees, where all the leaves were of silver and shimmered and glittered. The soldier thought, 'I'd better take a token with me,' and broke off a branch. The tree made a tremendous crackling noise, and again the youngest cried, 'Something is wrong! Did you hear that noise?'

But the eldest said, 'Those are shouts of joy because we have freed our Princes so early.'

Thereupon they came into an avenue of trees where all the leaves were of gold, and finally into a third where there were leaves of diamonds. From both avenues of trees the soldier broke off a twig, and each time the tree made such a noise that the youngest started with fright. But the eldest insisted that it was festive shouting.

They went on and came to a big lake on which stood twelve little boats, and in each boat sat a handsome young Prince. They had been waiting for the twelve Princesses, and each took one into his boat, while the soldier seated himself in the boat with the youngest.

Then the Prince said, 'I don't know why, but the boat seems much heavier today. I must row with all my strength to push it forward at all.'

'Perhaps it is the warm weather?' said the youngest. 'I feel warm, too.'

On the other side of the lake there stood a fine castle from which came the jolly music of trumpets and kettle-drums. They rowed there, entered, and each Prince danced with his beloved.

The soldier, being invisible, danced along too, and when one of the Princesses held a cup of wine, he drank it up, so that it was empty before she lifted it to her lips. The youngest was alarmed at this, but the eldest always silenced her. They danced there till three the next morning when all their shoes were in shreds, and they had to stop.

The Princes ferried them back again across the water, and this time the soldier sat in front with the eldest. On the shore they took leave of their Princes, and promised to come again the following night.

When they got to the stairs, the soldier ran ahead, and lay down in his bed, and when the twelve came tripping up slowly and wearily, he was snoring so loudly that they could all hear it and said, 'We are safe with this one.'

Then they took off their fine robes, put them away, placed the worn out

dancing shoes under their beds, and lay down.

The next morning the soldier resolved not to say anything yet but to observe the strange goings-on still more. So he went again with them the second and the third night. Everything was just the same as the first time, and each time they danced till their shoes were worn out. The third time, however, he took with him a cup of wine as a token.

When the hour came for him to give his answer, the soldier took the three twigs and the cup of wine with him and went to the King. The twelve Princesses were standing behind the door, listening to what he had to say.

The King asked, 'Where did my twelve daughters dance their shoes to shreds in the night?'

The soldier answered, 'With twelve Princes in an underground castle,' and he described everything that had happened, and produced the tokens.

Then the King bade his daughters appear before him, and asked them if the soldier had told the truth. Seeing that they had been discovered, they confessed everything. Thereupon the King asked the soldier which one he would like to have in marriage.

He answered, 'I am no longer young, so please give me the eldest.'

The marriage was celebrated on the very same day, and he was promised the kingdom on the King's death.

Prince Ahmed and the Fairy Pari Banu

Three handsome sons had the Indian king; Husein the eldest, Ali the second, and Ahmed the youngest. The boys grew from babyhood in friendship and affection. Their greatest love and joy was their cousin Nur en Nahar, who spent all her days with them, for her father, the king's younger brother, died tragically soon after his daughter's birth.

The princess was not only sweet, kind and beautiful. Her uncle made sure she attended the very best school, so that when she was grown up, there was no one her equal in the whole wide world.

How could anyone be surprised then that her three cousins fell desperately in love with her, and each and every one desired her for his wife?

The king understood well what was going on in his sons' minds, so he called them to his side one day and said, 'My dear sons! Nur en Nahar deserves your love, but as only one of you can have her for a wife, I shall give her to the one who proves himself to be most worthy of her.'

'What should we do?' Husein asked impatiently.

'You will all go out into the world. Whoever brings the most valuable

and the rarest gift by the end of the year will win the princess, Nur en Nahar.'

All three at once agreed to their father's wise suggestion, and before very long they were speeding on horseback through the palace gates, accompanied by servants and advisers.

They travelled along the same path all day long, but as the sun began to set, they reached a crossroads: one path led to the right, the second to the left and the third went straight on.

'It is time to bid each other goodbye,' Husein said. 'It would be best for us all to meet here again in exactly one year's time.'

Then each one chose a direction to follow.

The eldest prince chose the path to the right, for he well remembered that it was supposed to lead to the far away Bishanghar Land on the banks of the Indian Ocean, and he knew it to be a region rich in the rarest merchandise.

He travelled many days and many weeks along caravan trails till at last he reached the capital of Bishanghar.

All he had heard proved to be true; what he saw in the bazaars and stalls in the streets was beyond all expectations. Such a variety of jewels, beautiful materials, exquisite flowers – all of which took his breath away. He walked tirelessly from stall to stall, yet he was unable to find a suitable gift for the princess.

His steps led him to a dark little back alley, where suddenly an old wrinkled man appeared before him. He held in his hands a vividly coloured carpet.

'I will sell, I will sell, it is the only one of its kind!' he cried, offering it to the prince.

'How much do you want for it?' Husein asked, more out of curiosity than an intention to buy.

'Three thousand gold pieces,' answered the seller, lowering his voice. 'But this is no ordinary carpet. If you sit on it, it will take you through the air wherever you wish...'

What a present that would make, thought the prince, and he said aloud, 'As it costs so much I must try it out first.'

And so he sat down upon the carpet with the old man behind him, and he ordered the carpet to take them round the town and back again. What an amazing journey it was too! Husein's head was still spinning long after they came back to earth!

Now he did not hesitate. He paid up to the very last gold coin, and then, as there were many months before the end of the year when he was to meet his brothers, he sat on the carpet again, deciding to visit distant lands...

64   Prince Ali chose the path to the left, and it led him into green hills which rolled down under high mountain peaks capped with snow. He journeyed for four months till he came to the city of Shiraz in distant Persia.

The moment he saw the sumptuous markets, the workshops and the palaces, which were richer far than those of Bishanghar, he knew he would find here what he was searching for.

He was not disappointed, though for the first two days he wandered in vain. But on the third day his attention was caught by shouts from the market place. 'A magic tube of ivory for sale, a magic tube!'

'How much do you want for that tube?' the prince asked the seller.

The man pulled him aside by the sleeve. 'Thirty five thousand pieces of gold,' he whispered. 'But it possesses a wondrous quality. When you look into it, you will see whatever you wish, though it may be a thousand miles away...'

'Lend it to me, so I can see for myself,' Ali asked, thinking of his father. And sure enough, the moment he put his eye near the glass lens set in the ivory, he saw the Indian king on the familiar gold throne.

'I shall be glad to buy it,' said the prince, taking the tube from his eye. And he paid the man there and then.

'Who could bring a more valuable gift than I?' he said to himself, as he wandered away from the market. There was ample time before he had to return home, so he spent another four months in the lovely land of Persia.

The youngest prince Ahmed was left to take the middle road. For six long months he travelled, through deserts and forests, plains and mountains, till he stopped at last in the city of Samarkand — the furthest point from where he bade his brothers goodbye.

Like Husein and Ali, Ahmed too was fortunate. The city was so magnificent that he gasped with admiration, and a gift for his cousin was there, as if waiting for him. Before he even got off his horse, a young boy ran to him, a lovely apple in his hand.

'Buy this apple, sir, for it is no ordinary fruit...'

'How much do you want for it?' asked the prince, whose throat was dry after the long journey, and he was tempted by the fruit.

'This is not just a common apple,' the boy continued, his face serious. 'It contains medicine for all illnesses, and it will even cure a dying man, if he only smells it. Give me forty thousand gold pieces, and it is yours.'

'Not so fast, young lad,' Ahmed laughed, but his heart missed a beat with excitement. What a present this would make for his cousin! 'I must convince myself first!' And he went in search of a man who was desperately ill.

He enquired in the streets, and eventually came to a house where a very old man, thin and withered, was preparing for death to take him. The prince hastened to his bedside and asked him to sniff the apple. Wonder of wonders! Before his eyes the yellow face of the dying man turned a healthy pink, his eyes cleared and he sat up in bed without any difficulty and shouted to his servant to bring food at once, for he was remarkably hungry.

That was enough for Ahmed. He counted out the forty thousand pieces of gold, handed them over to the boy and hid the precious fruit in his saddle bag.

Turning his horse round, he set off on his return journey without wasting any time. He had a very long way to travel. But, when after six months he reached the crossroads, his brothers were already waiting.

He embraced them affectionately and asked impatiently what gifts they were bringing to the princess. Meantime he himself was taking out the apple

from the saddle bag with the greatest care.

'I have brought a flying carpet,' Husein said, and Ali told him excitedly, 'I am bringing a magic tube, which shows you whatever you want to see...'

'Let us use it now!' Ahmed cried enthusiastically. 'Let us see what our cousin is doing at this very minute right now.'

The second brother placed his eye against the tube and immediately his face paled.

'Nur en Nahar is dying,' he stuttered, hardly able to speak. 'I see her lying motionless on her bed, and everyone there is weeping.'

'Even the magic carpet won't help us,' sobbed Husein. But Ahmed cried, 'Yes it will, for I have an apple which will cure her. Quickly get on the carpet, both of you...'

The brothers flew through the princess's window like a tornado, and before anyone round her had a chance to realize what was happening, Nur en Nahar was already sitting up in bed, rubbing her eyes as if she had wakened from a long sleep.

'Oh, I dreamed I was dying,' she murmured, looking perplexed. 'It was no dream,' Ahmed told her. 'My magic apple saved you.'

Now that the danger of death was over, the princes started to relate all that had happened during their travels, and spoke of the rare gifts they had brought. Then they waited with some impatience for their father to choose the one who was to be Nur en Nahar's husband.

But the king scratched his bearded chin thoughtfully and said, 'There is no doubt that Ahmed's apple has saved the princess's life. But were it not for the magic tube and the flying carpet, it would have been useless. The three gifts are equally rare and wondrous, therefore it is necessary for you to compete further. The one who with his bow will shoot an arrow the furthest will be the winner!'

The very next day the princes decided to hold the shooting competition. They selected for their purpose a meadow, which stretched from the palace as far as the distant mountains.

Husein the eldest was the first to try. He aimed, and the arrow sped through the air, flying so far that all the court murmured in admiration.

Ali was the next to shoot. His arrow travelled even further, and the spectators' astonishment rewarded his effort.

The youngest prince was not downhearted by the success of his brothers. His arrow flew from his bow with such speed that no one even saw it.

Nor could anyone find it — there was not a trace of it anywhere. But the king had decided. 'Ali, my second son, is the one who deserves the princess, and he will have her as his wife. His arrow travelled further than Husein's, and it is unthinkable that Ahmed could have done better!'

The brothers accepted their father's judgement with meekness. But while the happy Ali prepared for the wedding, the sad Husein went away into the desert, there to live the life of a poor, pious dervish.

Ahmed could not get the thought of the lost arrow out of his head. He wandered towards the foothills of the mountains where the grassy meadow ended. When he reached them, exhausted and weary, he found his arrow wedged in a rocky cleft.

He took it out very carefully. He could not understand how the arrow had travelled so far — at least twice the distance of Ali's arrow.

Ahmed then noticed that the point of the arrow was missing. He searched around, till his gaze fell on a nearby dark cave. Suddenly it seemed the inner darkness was alight. Concealed iron gates were now opening and inside falling sunbeams shone upon a most beautiful maiden clothed in a grey blue robe woven from mists...

The astonished prince hardly dared to breathe. This surely must be a fairy, **69** he thought, and as if in answer the voice of this lovely creature spoke: 'I am the fairy Pari Banu, Prince Ahmed. It was I who commanded the wind to bring your arrow all the way here, and who broke off its point. Here it is.'

She opened her hand, and on her palm lay a fragment of shining metal. Then she continued, 'I have loved you for a very long time now, and I should so much like you to be my husband. That is why I led you into these mountains. Tell me whether you share my wish...'

The prince was speechless, incapable of uttering a single word. Why, Pari Banu's unearthly beauty was a thousand times greater than that of his cousin Nur en Nahar!

'How could I fail to share your wish,' he managed to stammer at last. 'But who is to give permission for our marriage? After all, I must first write out the wedding agreement with your father, as is customary!'

'Our laws are different from those of your people,' the fairy said with a smile. 'In this kingdom I am the queen, and I myself decide all matters. You are my husband from this moment.'

As soon as she had pronounced these words, the iron gates closed with a clash behind them, and Pari Banu led Ahmed into her homeland. He felt as if he had stepped straight into a fairy tale. In large, beautiful gardens filled with flowering, scented roses, hibiscus plants, oleander and tamarisk stood crystal palaces, and before them lovely damsels of breathtaking beauty sang and danced on velvety green lawns.

'The wedding celebrations will now begin,' said the fairy queen. 'It is time for us to join in them.'

Pari Banu's palace was more magnificent than any of the others. Behind glass walls, under arched gold ceilings, tables had already been prepared, lavishly laden with the most delicious dishes and bottles of the rarest wines. Haunting music trembled softly in the air like the breath of a spring breeze...

The wedding of prince Ahmed and the fairy queen lasted for one hundred days and one hundred nights, and with each passing day the prince loved his wife more dearly.

He did not give his father or brothers thought till half a year had passed — and then it flew like a small cloud across his clear brow. What were his father and his brothers doing? They surely must think that by now he had perished. He must visit them and dispel their fears.

He thought about this for several days, till Pari Banu herself spoke, 'I know you are unhappy, my prince, and I shall gladly permit you to visit your father. But you are not to reveal to anyone where you live, nor who is your wife. I fear that if you do not heed my warning our happiness will be shortlived.'

Ahmed gladly assured his wife that their life would remain their secret; he knew she was blessed with much wisdom and foresight.

Pari Banu gathered together many valuable gifts for the Indian king. She chose thirty riders to accompany Ahmed, and then bade him farewell by the iron gates of the cave.

'When you return here, have no fear. No ordinary mortal will see these gates — but to you they will open of their own accord.'

What had been happening in the meantime at the court of the Indian king?

When Ahmed had disappeared so mysteriously, his father ordered an extensive search, but it brought no results. It was then that the grand vizier recommended an artful witch as the king's advisor. With the aid of magic she discovered that his youngest son was alive. The king rewarded her handsomely, and ever since then had sought her advice.

When Ahmed appeared he wept with happiness. It had been so long since his beloved son's disappearance. He listened to his tale, how well he was faring and how happy. He himself told him that Ali was now reigning in a distant part of the Indian empire, and that Husein still chose to live in a desolate land, but that he had become the most renowned of the dervishes. He did not press Ahmed to tell him his secret, so after three days the prince was able to return without fear of hindrance to Pari Banu.

It became his habit to visit his father every month. Each time he brought valuable gifts, each time he was accompanied by his grand bodyguard of thirty riders. Ahmed's father showed no curiosity but the witch and the vizier started evil whisperings into the king's ears. 'Why doesn't Ahmed wish you to know where he now lives? He is up to no good, of that we are sure. He is only trying to blind you with his gifts. The place he comes from surely cannot be far distant, for the horses are never tired or sweaty. We warn you, do not trust him, or you will regret it. Soon he will want to oust you from your throne. Mark our words and Allah be with you!'

They talked and talked in this way about the prince, till they succeeded in poisoning the king's mind and he began to listen to their words. He insisted that Ahmed tell him his secret. But his son kept the promise he had given to his fairy wife.

One day when Ahmed left the palace as usual, the witch decided to follow him from afar. But long before she came to the cave, the prince and his retinue had disappeared. In vain she searched for a path they could have taken. All she could see were bare rocks. The iron gates remained invisible to her, thanks to Pari Banu's foresight.

72   The enraged witch strode up and down in a fury. Then she cried. 'It doesn't

matter; you may have outwitted me this time, but I'll be here waiting for you in a month's time.'

She carried out her threat. When, after a month, the prince and his riders were leaving the cave, they saw an old woman lying on the path writhing in pain.

'Oh, my good people, please help me,' she moaned. 'I am dying!'

There was no other living soul about, so Prince Ahmed turned back towards the cave, and the iron gates reopened. The sorceress pretended that she had fainted with the pain, but she was keeping an eye on all that was taking place.

Pari Banu was standing where he had left her.

'Why have you returned, my prince?'

'We found this old woman nearby,' Ahmed explained, pointing to her. 'She is dying and is in agony.'

'We will cure her,' the queen decided and straightaway she ordered two maidens to take her into the palace. Next she brought out a golden dish.

'The water from the Lion Spring is sure to make her well,' she said, and wetting her fingers in the bowl, she rubbed them gently across the old woman's brow.

The witch opened her eyes as if by a miracle.

'You have saved my life, and God is sure to reward you. Who are you, My Lady?' she asked then.

'I am Pari Banu,' the queen of the fairies replied. 'But you must ask no further questions and go home now.'

Though the old woman was besides herself with curiosity, she could do nothing but obey. The moment the iron gates closed behind her, she hurried to the palace, so that she would reach the Indian king before Prince Ahmed.

She told him what had happened and everything she had found out, adding, 'Your son is far more powerful than you, My King, and Pari Banu could easily destroy you by raising her little finger. Put them to the test. Ask for some exceptional gift — then you will know whether they are well disposed towards you.'

The king followed her advice as usual. He reproached the prince for keeping Pari Banu a secret for so long, then added slyly, 'Your wife must have great powers and I am sure she will be glad to do me a small service. I need a tent large enough to take the whole of my army. When we are on manoeuvres, we cannot take along a tent for every member of the cavalry. I want one which can be loaded onto a single horse, but which will grow on demand to such a size that it will take the whole army.'

With a heavy heart, the prince delivered his father's request to the fairy queen. But Pari Banu said, 'My beloved husband, your father's wish is easily granted. Look here.' And she showed him the palm of her hand. On it sat a tiny brightly coloured tent.

'When it is placed on the ground, it grows to a size large enough to hold the entire Indian army and their weapons. I shall gladly send it to your father.'

After a month had elapsed, Prince Ahmed visited his father as was his custom, taking with him the magic tent. But in the meantime the sorceress had been at work again, and had persuaded the king to demand another gift the following month — this time the magic water from the Lion Spring. Then, she said, they would be quite sure of his son's true feelings.

On this occasion the task was not easy even for Pari Banu. For the magic water came from the courtyard of a mountain castle, and this castle was guarded by four lions. Only the wit and wisdom of the fairy queen prevented them from tearing Ahmed apart when he rode among them. Following her advice he threw them four enormous chunks of meat, and the moment he had filled his jug from the spring, he galloped off like the wind.

'Now I know your father means to kill you,' said the fairy upon his return.

'You must take the greatest care when you are in his palace.'

By that time the witch had succeeded in making the king believe that Ahmed longed to sit on his throne and thought of nothing else. Now both the witch and the king wondered how to be rid of him for good.

'If he does not bring the water from the Lion Spring, he will die in prison,' the king declared. But the sorceress objected, 'He will assuredly bring it, just to quieten your suspicions. I have a better idea. There is a certain dwarf living in this world who kills everyone he meets with his steel cudgel. He is only three feet tall, but his beard sticks out thirty feet in front of him. I do not know of a single person who has met him and lived. Order your son to bring this dwarf here. By his hand Ahmed will die without blame being attached to yourself.' The witch laughed wickedly.

How astonished the king was when he received the water from the Lion Spring! He thanked his son and entertained him royally for the rest of his stay. But when they bade each other goodbye, the King said, 'The tasks I have set you have carried out to my satisfaction. I have only one more wish. Bring me

the dwarf with the long beard. They say he is only three feet high, and that he carries a steel cudgel on his shoulder. I am sure this desire you fulfill without difficulty and I promise I shall ask from you nothing more.'

What was the prince to do?

He hurried back to his crystal palace and told Pari Banu of his father's latest whim.

'This is what I feared,' the fairy cried. 'The dwarf does exist and is called Daibar. But the king did not tell you that he uses his steel cudgel to kill anyone who comes near. Your father knows that through Daibar he will be rid of you.'

'I refuse to satisfy my father's desire. I never wish to lay my eyes on him again,' the prince said decisively.

'Have no fear, no harm will come to you,' the fairy queen spoke softly. 'Daibar is my blood brother. Our enemies are not aware of that. So it will be enough for me to ask him to do you no harm and to go with you to your father's palace.'

They did not speak of the matter again.

A month later, however, the dwarf was waiting for Ahmed in front of the cave. He truly was a most horrific creature. The long, fiery red beard was as hard and as sharp as steel needles; his eyes were lost in his swollen cheeks and his nose drooped towards his chin. He swung his cudgel over his head with frightening speed and such dexterity that it whistled as it whirled through the air. But he welcomed the prince quite kindly.

'I am happy to know you and I shall gladly help you. But if you were not the husband of my blood sister Pari Banu, you would have not fared so well. I mean to destroy the whole human race with my cudgel,' he added threateningly.

For Ahmed the journey to the palace passed like a dream. The moment the dwarf approached the gates, the guards scattered in fright. The same thing happened in the forecourt. Whoever could took to their heels — the emirs, the soldiers, the servants. And all Daibar did was toss his cudgel round his head and smile merrily.

They entered the palace. The prince could not help laughing at the panic and commotion which then followed. Everyone disappeared as if someone had waved a magic wand — everyone but the king, his vizier and the witch. They were rooted to the spot in sheer terror.

'Why did you call me to you?' asked Daibar, approaching the throne threateningly. The terrified king did not utter a word. 'So you would make a fool of me, would you?' stormed the dwarf, and swinging his cudgel, he killed
with one swift blow the king, the sly vizier and the wicked witch.

'Now you will reign in India!' he cried, turning to the prince. And Daibar set the prince on the throne. His eyes wandered for a moment round the hall, then he slung his cudgel over his shoulder and went away, humming happily. 'Give greetings and love to my sister Pari Banu!' he shouted as he left.

As soon as the dwarf disappeared, the royal palace sprang to life again. The servants, the soldiers, the guards, the emirs and judges gathered round and all of them proclaimed glory to their king, Ahmed and their queen, Pari Banu, begging them humbly to rule wisely and justly to the end of their days.

Rapunzel

There was once a man and his wife, and for a long time they had been longing for a child, but in vain. At last, the woman was in hope that heaven would grant her wish. At the back of their house there was a little window overlooking a magnificent garden full of the most beautiful flowers and herbs. However, a high wall surrounded the garden, and no one dared to enter it, for it belonged to a witch who was very powerful and of whom the whole world stood in awe.

One day the woman was standing at this window looking down into the garden, when she noticed a bed which was planted with the finest rampion. It looked so fresh and green that it made her mouth water and she was possessed by the desire to eat some. This craving grew from day to day, but she knew she never could get any. So she began to pine away and looked pale and miserable. Her husband, in great alarm, asked her, 'What ails you, my dear?'

'Alas,' she replied, 'if I can't eat some of the rampion from the garden behind our house, I shall die.'

The husband, who loved her, thought, 'Rather than let your wife die, you shall fetch her some of the rampion, cost what it may.' So when dusk came, he climbed over the wall into the witch's garden, hurriedly cut a handful of rampion, and took it to his wife. She at once made it into a salad and ate it up with great lust. She found it so tasty, so very tasty, that her desire grew three times as strong the next day. If it was to be stilled, her husband once more had to climb over into the garden. So at dusk, he let himself down again but just as he had clambered over the wall, his heart stood still, for there was the witch confronting him.

'How dare you come into my garden like a common thief and steal my rampion?' she said eyeing him angrily. 'This shall cost you dear.'

'Alas,' he answered, 'temper justice with mercy, it was from dire necessity that I resolved to come. My wife has seen your rampion from her window and her longing is so strong that she will die if she does not get some to eat.'

Thereupon the witch's wrath abated, and she said to him, 'If it is as you say, I will let you take home as much rampion as you like. Only I make one condition. You must give me the child that your wife is going to give birth to. It will be well off and I will care for it like a mother.'

In his anguish the man agreed to everything, and the moment the wife gave birth the witch appeared, christened the child Rapunzel (rampion), and took it away with her.

Rapunzel grew up to be the most beautiful girl under the sun. When she was twelve years old, the witch shut her up in a tower in a forest. It had no stairs or doors, only a little window quite high up at the top. When the witch wanted to get in, she stood down below and called, 'Rapunzel, Rapunzel, let down your hair.'

Rapunzel had magnificent long hair, as fine as spun gold. When she heard the witch call, she loosened her tresses and wound them round a hook by the window. She let them fall down, and the witch climbed up by Rapunzel's braids.

It came to pass a few years later that the King's son, riding through the forest, came close to the tower. Suddenly, he heard someone singing. The voice was so charming that he stopped to listen. It was Rapunzel who in her loneliness amused herself by letting her sweet voice resound. The Prince wanted to climb up to join her and sought for the tower door but there was none to be found.

He rode home, but the singing had touched his heart so deeply that he went out into the forest every day and listened. Once, as he was standing behind a tree, he saw the witch come near and heard her call, 'Rapunzel, Rapunzel, let down your hair.'

Then Rapunzel let her braided hair fall down and the witch climbed up.

'If this is the ladder by which to come up,' he thought, 'I will try my luck once myself.'

The very next day, when dusk began to fall, he went up to the tower and cried, 'Rapunzel, Rapunzel, let down your hair.'

Presently the plaits came down and the King's son climbed up by them.

At first, Rapunzel was terribly frightened when a man came into her room, for she had never set eyes on a man in her life. But the Prince talked to her most kindly telling her that his heart had been so deeply moved by her singing that he knew no peace and had to come to see her. Then Rapunzel lost her fear, and when he asked her if she would take him for her husband, and she saw that he was young and handsome, she thought, 'He will love me better than old Mother Gothel,' and she said, 'Yes,' and laid her hand in his.

She said, 'I would be glad to go with you, but I do not know how to get down. Will you bring a skein of silk every time you come? I shall weave it into a ladder, and when it is ready, I will come down, and you will take me on your horse.'

They arranged that meanwhile he should always come to see her in the evening, for the old woman came by day.

Nor did the witch discover anything until Rapunzel broached it one day
80 and said to her, 'Please tell me, Dame Gothel, how is it that you are much

heavier to pull up than the young Prince who will be here before long?'

'Oh, you wicked child,' yelled the witch, 'what do I have to hear from you? I had thought I cut you off from all the world, and yet you have deceived me!'

In her rage she clutched Rapunzel's lovely hair, wound it several times round her left hand, picked up a pair of scissors with her right, and snip, snap the lovely tresses lay on the ground. She was merciless and took poor Rapunzel into a wilderness, where she was forced to live in greatest wretchedness and sorrow.

Yet on the very day she had cast Rapunzel away, the witch fastened the plaits she had cut off to the window hook. When the Prince came again he cried, 'Rapunzel, Rapunzel, let down your hair.'

Then the witch lowered the hair. The Prince climbed up, but above he found not his beloved Rapunzel but the witch, who looked at him with evil and venomous eyes.

'Oh ho,' she cried mockingly, 'you have come to fetch your dearly beloved, but the pretty bird sits no longer in her nest, and she can sing no more, for the cat has snatched her away, and it will scratch your eye out for you, too. Rapunzel is lost to you, you shall never set eyes on her again.'

The Prince was beside himself with grief and in his despair flung himself down from the tower. He escaped with his life, but had his eyes scratched out by the thorns among which he fell. He wandered about in the forest blind and feeding on nothing but roots and berries. He could do nothing but lament and weep over the loss of his most beloved Rapunzel. Thus he roamed about in utter misery for some years and, at last, found himself in the wilderness where Rapunzel had been living in dire poverty with the twins that had been born to her, a boy and a girl.

He heard a voice and it seemed to him very familiar, so he went on in its direction. When he got there, Rapunzel recognized him and fell on his neck in tears. Two of them wetted his eyes and, at once, his eyes grew quite clear and he could see as well as ever.

He took her and their twins to his kingdom, where he was joyfully received, and they lived long in happiness and contentment together.

The Fisherman and His Wife

Once upon a time, there was a fisherman and his wife who lived together in a hovel close by the sea. Every day the fisherman went out fishing and he fished and fished.

Once he sat angling and gazing into the bright water; he sat and sat.

Then his hook suddenly went to the bottom, deep down below and, when he pulled it up, he brought out a large flounder. Then the flounder said to him, 'Listen fisherman, I pray you, let me live. I am not a real flounder but an enchanted Prince. What help will it be to you that you kill me? Why, I wouldn't even taste good. So put me in the water again and let me swim away.'

'Well,' said the man, 'you do not need to talk so much. A flounder that can talk I should have let swim away anyhow.'

With this he put it back into the clear water and the flounder swam down to the seabed, leaving a long stream of blood behind him. The fisherman got up and went to his wife in the hovel.

'Husband,' said the wife, 'didn't you catch anything today?'

'No,' said the man. 'I just caught a flounder who said he was an enchanted Prince, so I let him swim away again.'

'And didn't you make a wish first?' said the wife.

'No,' said the man, 'what should I have wished for?'

'Oh,' said the wife, 'it is terrible to have to live forever in this hovel. It smells and it is disgusting. You might have wished for a little cottage for us. Go back at once and call him. Tell him we want to have a little cottage. He is sure to do it for us.'

'Ah,' said the man, 'why should I go there again?'

'Well,' said the woman, 'because you caught him and let him swim free again. He is sure to do it. Go on!'

The man didn't really feel like going, neither did he wish to act against his wife's advice. So he went to the sea once more. When he got there, the sea was quite green and yellow and not at all as clear as before. So he stood there and said,

> *'Flounder, flounder in the sea,*
> *Come, I pray you, here to me.*
> *For my wife, my Ilsebill,*
> *Wills not as I should will.'*

Then the flounder came swimming up to him and said, 'Well, what does she want?'

'Oh,' said the man, 'when I caught you, my wife says I ought to have wished something for myself. She no longer likes living in a hovel. She would like to have a cottage.'

'Just go there,' said the flounder, 'she will have it all.'

So he went home and there his wife sat no longer in the hovel; there stood a little cottage instead and his wife was sitting outside on a bench. Then she took him by the hand and said, 'Come in and see how much better it is.'

So they went in and there was a little porch in the cottage, a pretty little living room and bedroom where their bed stood. There was a kitchen and pantry, with all the finest utensils made of tin and brass, all that a kitchen should have. And behind the cottage, there was a little yard, with chickens and ducks and a trim little garden with vegetables and fruit in it. 'See that,' said the wife, 'isn't it nice?'

'Yes,' said the husband, 'and so it shall stay. Now we shall live quite content.'

'We'll see about that,' said the woman.

So all went well for about a week, then the woman said, 'Listen, husband, the cottage is far too narrow and the yard and the garden are so small. The flounder could have given us a bigger house. I should like to live in a big stone castle. Go to the flounder, tell him he should give us a castle.'

'But wife,' said the husband, 'the cottage is good enough as it is. Why do we need a castle to live in?'

'Ah, be off with you,' said the woman. 'Go to him, the flounder can do this quite easily.'

'No, wife,' said the man, 'the fish has given us the cottage. I have no mind to go to him again, the flounder might get offended.'

'Go all the same,' said the woman. 'It's well in his power and he'll be glad to do it. Just go and see him!'

The man did not feel like going, his heart was so heavy. He said to himself, 'It is not right,' but in the end he went.

When he came to the sea, the water was purple and dark-blue, grey and thick, but calm enough. Then he stood there and said,

> 'Flounder, flounder in the sea,
> Come, I pray you, here to me.
> For my wife, my Ilsebill,
> Wills not as I should will.'

'Well, what is it she wants?' said the flounder.

'Ah,' said the man rather troubled, 'she wants to live in a stone castle.'

'Just go home,' said the fish. 'She is standing before the door.'

The man went off and thought he would be going home to the cottage. But when he got there, there now stood a big stone castle. His wife was standing on the steps about to enter and she took him by the hand and said, 'Come in.'

Then he went in with her. There was a great hall with a marble floor and lots of servants everywhere who quickly opened the great doors. The walls were hung with lovely tapestries and, in the chambers, nothing but golden chairs and tables, crystal chandeliers hanging from the ceilings, and carpets covering all the floors. Food and the choicest wines were on the tables which looked as if they would break under the load.

Behind the house was a big courtyard with stables and cowsheds and the most splendid coaches. There was a magnificent garden with the loveliest of flowers and fine fruit-trees and a pleasure-grove, quite half a mile long. There were stags and roes and hares: all that a man's heart could ever desire.

'Well now,' said the woman. 'Isn't it nice?'

'Ah yes,' sighed the man, 'and so it shall stay. Now we shall live in this fine castle and be content.'

'We'll see about that and sleep on it,' said the woman. And with that they went to bed.

Next morning, the wife was the first to wake up. It was just before daybreak and from her bed she saw the glorious land lying before her. The man was still stretching himself, so she dug him with her elbow, and said, 'Man, get up and take a look out of the window. Look, we could be King and Queen over all that land. Go to the flounder, and say we would like to be King and Queen.'

'Oh, wife,' said the man. 'Why should we be King and Queen? I have no wish to be King.'

'Well, if you won't be King, I will. Just go to the flounder and say I wish to be King.'

'Oh, wife,' said the man. 'What do you want to be King for? I simply can't

84 ask him for that.'

'Why not? said the woman. 'Go there straight away. I must be King!'

The man was in utter distress that his wife wished to be King. 'It isn't right, it isn't right,' he thought. He did not feel like going there at all, but in the end he went.

When he came to the sea, the sea was all black and grey and the water was boiling up from below. It smelled quite foul. Then he stood there and said,

> 'Flounder, flounder in the sea,
> Come, I pray you, here to me.
> For my wife, my Ilsebill,
> Wills not as I should will.'

'Well, what is it she wants?' asked the flounder.

'Ah,' said the man, 'she wants to be King.'

'Go home, she is King already,' said the flounder.

The man went back and when he came to the castle, he saw the castle had become much bigger, like a palace. It had a great tower magnificently embellished, sentries stood before the gate, and there were many, many soldiers with drums and trumpets.

He went inside and everything there was pure marble and gold with velvet coverings and golden tassels. Then the doors of the great hall opened and the whole of the royal court was assembled there. His wife sat on a high throne of gold and diamonds and had a big golden crown on her head. The sceptre in her hand was of pure gold and precious stones and on either side of her stood six maidens in a row, each a head shorter than the one before.

Then he went and stood before her and said, 'Oh wife, so now you are King.'

'Yes', said the wife. 'Now I am King.'

So he stood and gazed at her and, having thus looked at her for some time he said, 'Oh wife, being King suits you so well. Let us wish for nothing more.'

'No, husband,' said the woman, growing quite restless. 'I am already feeling bored and can't stand it any longer. Go to the flounder. I am King, now I must be made Emperor as well.'

'Alas, wife, what do you want to be Emperor for?'

'Husband,' said she, 'go to the flounder. I will be Emperor.'

'Oh, wife,' said the man, 'the flounder can't make emperors. I can't even say that to him. There is but one Emperor in the realm. The flounder can't make you Emperor. He positively can't do that.'

'What!' said the woman. 'I am King and you are merely my husband. Go there at once! If he can make kings, he can make emperors. I simply must be Emperor. Go straight to him.'

So he had to go.

However, on his way there, he suddenly felt terribly miserable and, as he walked on, he thought to himself.

'This is not right and not a good thing. To ask to be Emperor is too impudent. The fish will get tired of it in the end.'

Just then, he reached the sea. The sea was black and thick and had begun to boil from below so that it made bubbles. Then a gust of wind blowing over it made it all frothy and the man got frightened. But he stood there and said,

'Flounder, flounder in the sea,
Come, I pray you, here to me.

For my wife, my Ilsebill,
Wills not as I should will.'

'Well, what does she want?' said the flounder.

'Alas, flounder, my wife wants to become Emperor.'

'Just go home,' said the flounder. 'She is Emperor already.'

The man went back and, when he came home, the whole palace became one of polished marble with alabaster figures and gold decorations. Soldiers were marching in front of the gate blowing trumpets and beating cymbals and drums. Inside, there were barons and earls and dukes walking about as mere servants. Doors of pure gold opened for him. He entered, and there was his wife sitting on a throne made of one solid piece of gold easily two miles high. She had a large golden crown on her head set with diamonds and carbuncles. In one hand she held the sceptre and in the other the imperial apple. On either side of her stood the life-guards, each shorter than the one before him, from an enormous giant two miles tall, to the smallest dwarf only as big as my little finger. And there were many princes and dukes standing before her.

The man went up and stood among them and said, 'Oh, wife, you are Emperor now.'

'Yes,' said she, 'I am Emperor.'

Then he stood and gazed at her for quite a long time and afterwards he said, 'Oh wife, isn't that nice that you are Emperor?'

'Husband,' said she. 'What are you standing about there for? I am Emperor now but I want to be Pope, too. Go and see the fish about it.'

'Alas, wife,' said the man, 'what more do you want? Pope you cannot be. There is only one Pope in all Christendom. He cannot make you that.'

'Husband,' said she, 'I will be Pope. Go straight to him, I want to be Pope today.'

'No, wife,' said the man. 'That I dare not tell him. That would not do, that's asking too much. The flounder cannot make you Pope.'

'Husband, what silly chatter!' said the wife. 'If he can make me Emperor, he can make me Pope as well. Go straight to him. I am Emperor and you are merely my husband, so go there at once!'

Then he got frightened and went, but he felt quite faint. He trembled and quaked and his knees and calves shook. A high wind swept over the land and clouds gathered, so that it was dark, like evening. The leaves were falling off the trees and the water rushed as if it were boiling, and crashed against the shore. In the distance ships were firing guns in distress and pitching and tossing on the billows. Yet there was still a patch of blue sky in the middle, but on every side it was as red as before a heavy thunderstorm. Then he went and

88 stood by the edge of the sea, anxious and despondent, and said,

'Flounder, flounder in the sea,
Come, I pray you, here to me.
For my wife, my Ilsebill,
Wills not as I should will.'

'Well, what is it she wants?' asked the flounder.

'Alas,' said the man, 'she wants to be Pope.'

'Go to her then,' said the flounder, 'she is Pope already.'

He went back and when he got there, there stood a big cathedral with nothing but palaces all around. He pushed his way through the crowd. Inside, everything was lit with thousands and thousands of lights and his wife was dressed all in gold, sitting on a throne much higher than the one before. Three golden crowns were on her head and all around was rich in ecclesiastical splendour. On either side of her stood two rows of lights, the largest so thick and so tall as the highest of towers, down to the tiniest of kitchen candles. Emperors and kings from every land were on their knees before her and kissing her slippers.

'Wife,' said the man, and looked at her wonderingly. 'You are Pope now, aren't you?'

'Yes,' said she, 'I am Pope.'

Whereupon he stood and looked straight at her, and it was as if he were looking at the bright sun. When he had thus contemplated her for a time, he said, 'Oh wife, how nice that you are Pope.'

But she looked as stiff as a post, and did not stir.

Then he said, 'Wife, be content. Now you are Pope, you cannot go any higher.'

'We will see about that,' said the wife.

Then they went to bed. But she was not contented. Greed would not let her sleep and she lay awake thinking of what she might still become.

The man slept really soundly. He had done a lot of running the day before. But his wife could not fall asleep and tossed from side to side all night long.

At last, the sun was about to rise and when the wife saw the dawn reddening on the horizon, she sat up in her bed, and gazed at it. And when, looking through the window, she saw the sun rise, it occurred to her. 'Could I not make the sun and moon rise?'

'Husband,' she said giving him a poke in the ribs, 'wake up and go to the flounder. I want to be like the good God himself.'

The man was still half asleep but he got so alarmed that he fell out of bed. He thought he had not heard aright, rubbed his eyes and said, 'Oh, wife, what did you say?'

'Husband,' said she, 'I cannot order the sun and moon to rise. I can only sit **89** and watch them. I cannot bear it and I know no peace any more, not even for an hour. I must cause them to rise myself.'

Then she regarded him with such a terrifying look that a shudder ran through him.

'Go at once to the flounder. I wish to be like God.'

'Alas, wife,' said the man and fell on his knees before her. 'That the fish cannot do. He can make emperors and popes but I beseech you, be sensible and remain Pope!'

Then she got into a rage, her hair flew wildly about her head, she tore open her bodice, gave him a kick and screamed, 'I simply cannot and will not bear this any longer. Go right away, will you?'

The man put on his trousers and ran off like a madman.

Outside a storm was raging and it was blowing so hard that he could hardly keep on his feet. Houses and trees were blown over and the hills trembled. Rocks rolled down into the sea and the skies were pitch-dark; there was thunder and lightning and the sea rolled with black waves as high as church steeples with crests of white foam. He couldn't hear his own voice when he cried,

> *'Flounder, flounder, in the sea,*
> *Come, I pray you, here to me.*
> *For my wife, my Ilsebill,*
> *Wills not as I should will.'*

'Well, what is it she wants now?' said the flounder.

'Alas,' he cried, 'she wants to be like God.'

'Go to her,' said the flounder. 'She is back in the hovel again.'

And there they are living to this very day.

Ali Baba and the Forty Thieves

In a certain town of Persia there once lived two brothers, one called Cassim, the other Ali Baba. Their father had died leaving them little inheritance, and by the time they divided it between them, neither could be said to be anything but poor. Fate, however, had different futures for them both. The elder brother, Cassim, married the daughter of a rich merchant and turned very greedy and envious, whereas Ali Baba took for a wife a woman as poor as a church mouse. He was honest and hard working, but never succeeded in making money. Soon he did not know where their next meal was coming from. All he had left was the roof over their heads, a good and handsome son, a willing donkey and determination not to give up.

The only way he could still make a dinar or two was by felling wood in the forest and selling it in town. He toiled from morning till night, his patient donkey at his side waiting to bring the logs back into the town. And in this way one day wearily followed another, and he was just able to scrape together enough to keep hunger away from the door of their miserable house.

One day when he was working in the forest, he saw a cloud of dust in the distance, followed by the sound of galloping hooves. He watched, his eyes following the cloud, till it came closer and he saw it was a band of wild looking riders, gleaming swords and daggers in their belts. The sight made Ali Baba hold his breath in terror. There must have been at least forty of them in all.

Ali Baba, his heart in his mouth, left the donkey to its fate and dived into the bushes, and when he was sure nobody was watching, he climbed into the crown of a tall oak tree. From there he could see everything unobserved.

The riders dismounted at the foot of the tree which grew by a large rock. Ali Baba guessed by the look of them that these men must be thieves — and dangerous ones at that. Each of the riders took off their saddle bags and turned to the rock which was overgrown by thistles and weeds.

And there the tallest of them — by his bearing and attire the leader — cried, 'Open, Sesame!'

To Ali Baba's astonishment the rocky wall shook and rattled and a door opened. The robbers entered, one by one, their leader last of all. Then the door closed behind them.

Ali Baba waited without daring to move for some time, before the mysterious riders reappeared. Ali Baba could not help noticing that their saddle bags were now slack and empty, and he had a better opportunity to examine their faces. They were unshaven, scarred and furrowed with cruel lines and creased brows, which made him shudder. This surely must be the notorious evil band of robbers who had terrorized the whole region for so long!

They all walked over to their horses, hung their bags over their saddles, and remounted. Soon they disappeared in a cloud of dust. Ali Baba followed them with his eyes, not daring to descend till they were well out of sight.

When all was quiet and still, he climbed down and sighed with relief. Now he was curious to see what was inside the cave. It seemed to him that the robbers must be using it as a hiding place for their booty.

'Open, Sesame,' he called, for he remembered the words of command the leader had uttered. The door opened, and he entered.

The rock closed fast behind him, but this did not worry Ali Baba, for after all, he knew well how to get out again.

92   To his surprise he did not find himself in a dark, eerie place. He was in

a bright, spacious vault, filled with piles of gold, jewels, rich stuffs from India and China, carpets and a heap of leather purses filled with money. 'If I toiled with a spade for a whole day, I couldn't move all that,' thought the dazed Ali Baba. He walked from wall to wall of that great cave, his head spinning, his eyes dimmed by the dazzling glitter. The enormous quantities of riches convinced Ali Baba that this cave had been used as a thieves' hiding place for many years.

But he did not dare waste time on dreams and thoughts. He had to get out, for he was much afraid that the robbers might return. Ignoring all else, he walked over to the bags of gold and gathered up as many as he could carry. Then he commanded the rock, 'Open, Sesame!'

Once outside he loaded the bags on the donkey's back, placing some logs on top to hide them from view, and set off for home.

The moment he arrived home, he locked the door behind him, to make sure no uninvited guest would enter and catch him unawares. Then, to his wife's astonishment, he emptied all the bags of gold one by one onto the floor. The bewildered woman was too stunned to utter a single word, but eyed him suspiciously, wondering if her husband had turned thief. Ali Baba soothed her, explaining where it had come from and told her that the gold was only a small portion of the treasure which had been stolen by a band of wicked robbers. Once reassured, she recovered and stifling her fears, was most anxious to count the gold.

'That would be an impossible task,' her husband objected. 'You would not be finished by the morning. It is not safe to have this money lying about so long. I must hide it straight away. The best idea is to dig a hole in the garden and bury it.' The wife agreed, but still insisted she must first find out how rich they now were. So she persuaded her husband to wait a little, then ran over to Cassim's house, which was nearby, to borrow his grain measure. Cassim was out, but his wife was glad to oblige.

'Certainly you may borrow the measure. Wait here, I'll fetch it.'

But all that time she was wondering what grain Ali Baba needed to weigh, when he was so poor. Curiosity made her stick some wax at the bottom of the measure, then she handed it over, apologizing for taking so long.

Whilst Ali Baba was busily digging the hole in the garden, his wife filled the measure with gold ten times over. Then happy and satisfied, she looked on as her husband poured it into the hole he had dug and covered it up with a thick layer of soil.

That same evening Cassim's wife had the measure back in her possession. As soon as she was alone, she looked inside, and to her amazement found a shining gold coin sticking to the bottom.

'Oh that artful Ali Baba!' she cried, and ran to Cassim to tell him of her discovery. 'Your brother is living and behaving as if he was a pauper,' she gasped, 'and all the time he's far wealthier than you! He has so much gold, in fact, that he doesn't count it, but weighs it!'

Cassim was a true miser who hated parting with a single dinar, and who envied anyone who had anything that could be envied. Greediness did not let him have a wink of sleep that night. And all the time his head was buzzing with one question. How had Ali Baba acquired all that money?

The next day, he quickly mumbled his morning prayer and then rushed off to his brother's house. He hammered on his door. Ali Baba greeted his older brother most cordially. But Cassim immediately flew into a rage. Loudly he abused him, calling him a two-faced brother, a liar and a cheat, accusing him of pretending to be poor. 'Look at you,' he shouted at last. 'Anyone would think you were a miserable pauper without a possession in the world. But I know the truth! You have to weigh your gold with the grain measure, because you have too many gold coins to count. See here,' he added, producing the tell-tale coin. 'Here is my proof. My wife found this piece of gold in the measure you borrowed. Now either you admit it and tell me everything, or I swear I'll march you off to the judge immediately and accuse you of being a thief.'

'I shall be only too pleased to explain everything,' said Ali Baba smoothly, swallowing his anger. He realized his secret was discovered and that he had no choice but to relate to his brother the events of the previous day. He even offered to share with Cassim the gold he had taken, as long as he kept the secret. And he described the very spot where the rock Sesame could be found.

'I do not advise you to go there, dear brother. That would be tempting Providence,' he warned him. 'It is better for us to be content with what I have brought than to risk falling into the hands of those terrible bandits.'

But the greedy, conceited Cassim only smiled haughtily. 'Why should I be such a fool as to be satisfied with so little, when there is a hundred times more wealth to be had? I'm not one to let such an opportunity slip through my fingers!'

Ali Baba reluctantly gave in and told his brother the magic formula. That was all Cassim needed. Hurriedly he left his brother's house and spent the rest of the day buying up all the mules in the town, till the townsfolk began to wonder if he planned to deprive the mule-sellers of their livelihood.

Once again Cassim could hardly wait for morning to come, and before daybreak he was already climbing with his caravan of mules up the hills and

through the forest towards the rock which Ali Baba had described.

'Open, Sesame!' he called, as he came to the secret door. And the rock wall opened. Cassim went inside and behind him the door closed.

Everything he saw was just as Ali Baba had described. There were riches here to fill all the boxes and bags he had brought, and there would be still more to return for! Dazed and excited he ran about the cave, examining the gold, the jewels, fingering the exquisite cloths, feasting his eyes on all the wealth that now was his. Then he started to carry the sacks of gold and precious stones and bales of materials to the entrance where he could load them on to the donkeys more easily. So consumed with greed was he that he thought of nothing else but riches.

When at last he remembered that he should be returning home, he found to his dismay that he had forgotten the name of the rock! He knew it was some kind of a grain — but which one? He called out 'Open, Barley!' then

'Open, Corn!', even 'Open, Oat!' and hopefully 'Open, Wheat!' till he had named every type of grain, except one — sesame.

And so the rock remained firmly closed, and the greedy Cassim, now almost out of his mind with terror, started shouting for help. Too late he realized that he should have listened to his younger brother's warning.

To add to his horror he heard the tramping of hooves — the thieves had returned! They could not fail to notice the mules waiting patiently by the cave's entrance. They would know at once that some intruder was inside.

'Open, Sesame!' the bandit captain commanded angrily, his sword ready in his hand. As the door began to open, the desperate Cassim tried to dive past. But before he could even glimpse the light of day, the thieves slew him, showing no mercy. They dragged his body back inside the cave, where they cut it into quarters and hung these up on each side of the entrance — to deter anyone else who might wish to enter.

Then the robbers drove the mules off into the forest, and put back in place all the treasures Cassim had stacked by the door. Last they added the load they had robbed from a caravan that day.

Soon only a cloud of dust told of the whereabouts of the thieves, and as they galloped away the dust too disappeared, and the whole region was as quiet and still and empty as before.

When Cassim failed to return home, his wife became anxious. When she could not bear the worry any longer she ran to Ali Baba's house and told him that Cassim had not come home. Ali Baba was almost sure his brother had gone to the cave, and now was very much afraid that the robbers might have found him in or near their cave. He did not wait to be asked to search for Cassim, but as soon as he had soothed his sister-in-law, he took three donkeys and set out for the forest.

He made straight for the fateful rock. Cautiously he looked around, and trying to avoid stepping on any twigs, he crept noiselessly closer. Soon he was satisfied there was no one about.

'Open, Sesame!' he spoke the magic words.

Oh, horror of horrors! What a sight met his eyes! There to right and to left hung his brother's remains. Now he knew with dreadful certainty that mercy would be shown to no man who crossed the path of these evil thieves.

In spite of the fact that Cassim had never been a good brother to him, and that there was danger that he too might be trapped by the thieves, Ali Baba was determined to bury him as a believer with full honours and respect. So he wrapped the remains in a rich cloth and loaded them on one of his asses. He covered the bundle with brushwood to hide it from curious eyes. The other two donkeys he loaded with bags of gold, and these too he covered with

96

brushwood. Then he ordered the door to close behind him and set off quickly for home.

It was nightfall by the time he drove the donkeys up to his house. He told his wife to unload the gold and to bury it, while he led the third donkey bearing Cassim's corpse to his sister-in-law's house.

Thoughts raced through Ali Baba's head — thoughts which chilled and horrified him. What was going to happen when the robbers discovered that the corpse had gone? They would surely find his tracks and trace him to his home.

He was still shaking with terror as he knocked on the door of Cassim's house. It was opened by Morgiana, his brother's highly trustworthy maid.

Swearing her to secrecy, Ali Baba told her the whole story. When he had finished, Morgiana remained silent for a time, deep in thought. At last her face lit up, and she said, 'I know what we must do! We shall pretend that my late master is not dead, but critically ill. I will hurry to the chemist in great distress and ask for medicine. And tomorrow we shall pretend that poor Cassim has died a natural death during the night, and we will bury him with full honours.'

'I knew I could rely on you,' Ali Baba whispered with a sigh of relief. 'But what about the body? It is in pieces...'

'That is of no consequence,' Morgiana assured him. 'I will bribe a cobbler to sew the pieces together again, and no one will be any the wiser. You'd be surprised what a gold coin in the hand will do! And to make quite sure he'll keep his mouth closed, I will blindfold him when I bring him here. And while I am attending to all this, you had better inform Cassim's wife of her loss, and ask her to marry you. You are allowed, after all, more than one wife, and in that way you can remain one family.'

Ali Baba at once carried out Morgiana's instructions. Cassim's wife, grief-stricken at first, did not wish to remain a widow for long and was only too glad to accept Ali Baba's proposal. Her late husband's body was duly sewn together by a rather frightened cobbler. His fears were, however, somewhat calmed by the feel of the gold coin in his pocket. Cassim was then placed in a coffin and buried with the usual rituals. After the funeral, Ali Baba moved to his new wife's house, took over the running of Cassim's business and settled happily into the role of a prosperous citizen.

But in the meantime the thieves were not wasting time.

When they discovered that Cassim's corpse was missing, together with several sacks of gold, they were convinced that the dead man must have had an accomplice who knew their hideout and the secret formula.

'We must track down this other man and kill him at once. Otherwise neither we, nor our treasure will ever be safe,' said the captain. 'I want the boldest and the cleverest man to disguise himself as a merchant, ride into the city and find out if anyone has died suddenly and recently.'

The chosen man did not take long to discover that the citizen Cassim had been struck by a sudden illness and had recently died, and that Ali Baba, his brother, had turned from a pauper into a very prosperous man.

The clever robber did not have to be told more.

Soon he was standing in the street, facing the late Cassim's house. All the buildings in that street looked exactly alike.

'I could easily make a mistake in the dark,' the thief thought to himself. So he marked the front door with a cross in white chalk. Then he hurriedly returned to the forest in the hills, where he told the captain how cleverly he had arranged everything.

But he did not take into account the intelligent Morgiana.

Soon after the thief had gone, Morgiana went out to the market. She noticed immediately the chalk mark on the door, and though she thought it might be the work of some mischievous children, she did not rule out the possibility that an enemy of her new master could be responsible. So to make

quite sure she took a piece of chalk and marked all the doors in the street with similar crosses.

In the forest in the meantime the robbers were making their plans. The captain was very pleased with his scout's discovery. He was now determined to lead the whole band of robbers to Ali Baba's house. And so, disguising themselves in the cloaks of respectable merchants, they waited for night to fall. In darkness they set out, their sharpened swords hidden by the folds of their cloaks. They little guessed what a surprise was waiting for them. When they discovered that all the doors in the street where Ali Baba lived were marked exactly alike, the captain grew angry, and ordered his men to retreat back to the woods.

Once by the rock they held a meeting to decide how to punish the clumsy scout whose plan had so miserably failed. 'We shall judge him according to our custom,' the captain spoke, and the others nodded their heads in agreement. The condemned man knew he could not live with his shame, and that his hour had come. He bent his head fearlessly and willingly, and it was chopped off there and then. For among thieves there is an understanding that whoever fails in his duty must perish.

Another volunteer rose now. This was Ahmad, the strongest and the most daring of them all. 'Fellow comrades,' he said, 'for such a task I am the most suitable; if I fail to lead you to the right place, let me face the same fate as that of my former comrade.'

'So be it, Ahmad,' said the captain. 'If you fulfill your promise, all the spoils in Ali Baba's house shall be yours. If you do not, then we shall have your head.'

But Ahmad fared no better. He did find the right house, and instead of marking it with white chalk, he stained it in a most inconspicuous place with a drop of his own blood. But the observant Morgiana noticed the little red mark, when she returned home from the market carrying fresh fish. She lost no time, but marked all the doors in the street with the same little red spot, using the blood of the fish she had bought for her purpose. Now she was quite certain that her suspicions were correct, and that someone was trying to kill her master.

When the gang of the thieves had gone back to town and had realized they had been fooled once again, the captain was filled with terrible fury. Ahmad was soon shorter by his head and the captain was at a loss what to do next. 'My men are excellent robbers, but have few brains,' he thought. 'If I continue like this I'll lose them all.'

So he decided on different tactics.

'I myself shall tackle the problem tomorrow morning,' he roared at his

men. 'And I shall not allow myself to be fooled. While I am gone, you will buy twenty mules, and forty large oil containers. But make sure you fill only two of them with oil. The others you must leave empty,' he added threateningly.

The captain then dismissed his men and the thieves, glad to escape from their chief's rage, crept away like dogs after a beating. There was little sleep for them that night, as they waited uneasily for morning to break.

The captain soon found out which house in the street belonged to Ali Baba. He did not mark it with any sign, but gazed at it for a long time, memorizing every detail. Then to make doubly sure, he counted the houses first from one end of the street, then from the other, till he came to the home of the man he wanted. Now he knew he could not make a mistake. Before dusk gathered, he was back in the hills with his men.

The robbers had been busy and everything was ready. There were nineteen mules with thirty-eight empty leather oil containers. The twentieth mule was carrying two of the large jars filled to the brim with oil.

'Now listen to me carefully,' whispered the captain cautiously. 'When we get near the city gates, each one of you is to hide in one of the oil containers and to stay there with your weapons till I give you a signal. Leave the rest to me.'

Soon it was night. A white moon sailed across the dark sky as the captain, disguised as a merchant, led the twenty heavily laden mules towards Ali Baba's house. In the bright moonlight it was easy to see and easy to count the houses. Before long he was hammering at the right door.

'Who is such a late visitor?' asked a voice from inside, and the captain replied, 'I am a merchant from a foreign land. Be kind enough, sir, to permit me and my mules to spend a night with you, if this is possible. All the markets and lodging houses are closed at such a late hour.'

Ali Baba opened the door and saw a stranger with his tired beasts. 'I welcome you, brother,' he said cordially. 'Please make yourself at home here.' And he led the crafty captain up the stairs while his servant attended to the mules.

What more could the captain want? The trusting Ali Baba suspected nothing. It never occurred to him to see in this polite merchant his vicious, blood-thirsty enemy, especially when his guest offered him the goods he had brought to sell in the city.

They ate, drank and made merry, and talked well into the night. Then Morgiana noticed that there was hardly any oil left in the lamp. She decided to fetch some, but it seemed there was not a drop left in the whole house. Then she remembered that the visiting merchant had offered olive oil to her master. She therefore picked up her jug and hastened to the yard. 'Surely he will not mind if I help myself to a litre or two,' she said to herself.

The oil containers were standing side by side near a high wall where Ali Baba's servant had put them.

The girl was about to open the first container, when she heard a whisper from inside. 'Has the time come, captain?'

Any other servant would most probably have fainted with terror, but not the faithful Morgiana! In a flash she put two and two together, and realized it was not oil, but a thief who lurked in that bulging container. Calmly she replied in a deep voice, 'Not yet, wait a little longer!'

She was greeted with the same question from inside the next container, and by the time she reached the end of the line, she had counted thirty-eight

thieves in all.

Not until she came to the last two jars did she find the oil. It was then that she suddenly had an idea. She ran back to the kitchen, and came back with a large copper kettle, which she filled with oil and placed on a fire. She stacked a bundle of fine, dry wood under the kettle to make it come to the boil as quickly as possible. When it was sizzling and bubbling, she took the kettle back to the yard, and into each of the containers she poured enough boiling oil to kill the bandit inside.

Having done this, she returned to the house, and filled the oil lamp as if nothing had happened. Next she put on a beautiful dance dress made of rich brocade, which was fastened with a diamond-studded belt, from which hung a small dagger. Then she sought out Abdullah the servant, and said to him, 'Take your drum, we are going into the dining hall to entertain our master and his guest.'

Ali Baba was delighted at her thoughtfulness, and turning to his guest, said, 'Look at my slave, dear sir. You will not find another to equal her charm

and her skill in dancing. Her cleverness is exceptional too. After a good dinner it is only right that we should be entertained by her dance.'

The captain nodded his head in agreement, but secretly he was seething with angry impatience. 'If only Ali Baba would stop this unnecessary nonsense and go to bed,' he thought. Then he could have his revenge. But he had no choice but to appear pleasant and bide his time.

Abdullah began to beat the drum and sing. Morgiana danced beautifully. She moved now fast, now slow, with grace and perfect rhythm, and her face was as fresh and lovely as spring blossom.

The dance came to an end. The girl took the drum from Abdullah and curtsied before Ali Baba, as if asking for payment. Her master gave her a dinar, and she turned then to his guest. The captain was about to take a coin from his purse, when, like a streak of lightning, Morgiana leapt to his side and thrust her sharp dagger into his heart. The robber gasped and fell lifeless to the ground.

'You wicked girl,' shrieked Ali Baba. 'What have you done? Do you want to ruin me? You'll pay for this deed with your life.'

'Be calm, dear Master,' the girl said quietly and fearlessly. 'I killed him to save you. For this man is no ordinary merchant from some distant land, but the leader of the band of robbers you so much fear. Come, I will show you, and explain everything.' And she led the stunned Ali Baba into the courtyard to the containers which held the bodies of the dead bandits. Then she told him everything from beginning to end, from the moment when the robbers had marked his house with the white cross.

Ali Baba knew then that Morgiana spoke the truth. Deeply moved by her loyalty towards him, he said, 'How can I show my gratitude? You have now saved my life many times. Your devotion is such that I can never hope to repay you. I will give you your freedom; but that is not enough. I shall give you also my son as a husband, to care for you till the end of your days, for I love you both most dearly.'

Morgiana and Ali Baba's handsome son were overjoyed to hear his decision, for they had always been fond of one another.

There was just one thing in this extraordinary tale which Ali Baba could not understand. He was quite sure there had been forty thieves in all, but only thirty-eight corpses had been found in the jars. What could have happened to the other two? Not knowing whether they were dead or alive, and perhaps waiting for their chance to revenge the deaths of their captain and comrades, he was loath to venture anywhere near the cave.

When a whole year had gone by without incident, he took courage and rode into the forest. There was no sign that anyone had visited the rock. All was quiet, and the entrance was thickly overgrown and almost hidden by bracken and bushes. Ali Baba knew then that no one had entered for a long time.

Thus reassured, he spoke the magic words, 'Open, Sesame!' He went into the cave. Everything was as he had last seen it. It was plain that no one had touched the treasure since his last visit.

'The two missing robbers must also be dead,' Ali Baba said to himself, gazing at the immense riches which now were his. But he was not grasping and greedy as Cassim had been. He filled only one bag with gold, and returned home, happy and contented.

From that day, until the day he died, he took from the treasure only what he needed. He was generous to the poor, was held in high respect by the rich and greatly loved by his family. And so his life passed in peace and happiness.

The secret of the cave he disclosed to no one, for he knew too well what tragedies human greed can bring.

The Nightingale

In China, as you must surely know, the Emperor is a Chinaman, and all around him are Chinese also. Many years have passed since what I am about to relate took place, but for that very reason it is important for you to hear the story at once, before it is forgotten.

The Emperor's palace was the most magnificent palace in the whole world; it was made entirely of fine porcelain, terribly expensive, but also terribly fragile and delicate, so that one had to be very careful indeed. In the garden grew the most wonderful, exquisite flowers and to the loveliest of these, little silver bells were fastened, which tinkled so that no one would go by without noticing them. Honestly, everything in the Emperor's garden was most excellently arranged! It was so long, that even the gardener did not know where it ended. If one kept on walking further, one came to a beautiful wood with high trees and deep lakes. The wood stretched right down to the sea, which was blue and deep. Large ships could sail close under the branches. And there in the branches lived a nightingale, who sang so sweetly that even the poor fisherman, who had so much else to do, would stand still and listen to her song when he came out at night to draw in his nets. 'Oh, how beautiful that is!' he would sigh; but he was obliged to get on with his work, and forget the bird. But if on the following night the nightingale sang again, and the
fisherman happened to be there again, he would sigh, 'How beautiful that is!'

Travellers from all over the world came to the Emperor's city; they admired the town, the palace and the garden, but when they heard the nightingale sing, they all said, 'This is best of all!'

After their return home, they talked about it all and scholars wrote many books about the Emperor's city, the palace and the garden; nor did they forget the nightingale, for they placed her above everything else. And those who could write poetry, wrote the loveliest poems, all about the nightingale of the wood by the deep sea.

The books went round the world, and some of them reached the Emperor. He sat in his golden armchair and he read and read, every now and then nodding his head; he was really delighted by the splendid descriptions of his city, palace and garden. 'But the best of all is the nightingale!' was written there.

'What is this?' exclaimed the Emperor. 'The nightingale? I've never heard of it! Is there really such a bird in my empire, in my own garden in fact? I have never heard anyone talk about it! I have to learn of such a thing from books!'

So he called his gentleman-in-waiting, who was so grand a person that if anyone of inferior rank dared to speak to him or ask him a question, he would only answer 'pish!', which has no meaning at all.

'I hear there is a most remarkable bird here, called the nightingale,' said the Emperor. 'They say it is the most wondrous thing in the whole of my empire! Why have I never been told about this?'

'I have never heard her mentioned!' replied the gentleman-in-waiting. 'She has never been presented at Court.'

'I wish her to come here tonight to sing for me!' the Emperor commanded. 'The whole world knows what I have here, and I do not.'

'I have never ever heard of her!' insisted the gentleman-in-waiting. 'But I will search for her, and I will find her!'

But where was she to be found? The gentleman-in-waiting ran up and down the stairs, and through halls and corridors, but none of the people he met had ever heard of the nightingale. So the gentleman-in-waiting ran back to the Emperor, saying that it surely must be some invention of the people who write books. 'Your Imperial Majesty should not believe all that is written in books! Much of it is pure invention and the so-called black magic!'

'But the book in which I have read it,' said the Emperor, 'was sent to me by the powerful Emperor of Japan, and therefore it cannot be untrue! I want to hear that nightingale! She must be here this evening! She has my highest favour. And if she does not come, I shall have the whole Court thrashed, after they have eaten their supper!'

'Tsing-pe!' said the gentleman-in-waiting, and off he ran again, up and down all the stairs, through all the halls and corridors, and half the Court ran with him, for none relished the idea of being thrashed. What a lot of questioning there was regarding the wondrous nightingale, who was known to all the world, but to nobody at Court.

At last they found a poor little girl in the kitchen, who said, 'Oh yes, the nightingale! I know her well! My word, how she sings! Every evening I am allowed to take a few scraps from the table to my poor sick mother, who lives down by the shore. On my way back when I grow tired and rest in the wood, I hear the nightingale sing. It makes the tears come into my eyes, for I always feel as if my mother were kissing me!'

'Dear little kitchen-maid,' said the gentleman-in-waiting, 'I will secure for you a permanent position in the Emperor's kitchen, even permission to watch the Emperor eat, if you will only lead us to the nightingale; for tonight I am to bring her to Court.'

So they all went together to the wood where the nightingale usually sang; half the Court was there. As they were on their way, a cow began to bellow.

'Ah,' said the Court pages, 'now we have her! What an extraordinary power for such a small animal! I am pretty sure I have heard her before!'

'Oh no, those are cows mooing!' said the little kitchen-maid. 'There is still a long way to go yet.'

The frogs in the pond began to croak.

'How lovely!' cried the Chinese chaplain. 'I hear her now! It sounds just like little church bells.'

'Oh no, those are frogs croaking!' said the little kitchen-maid.

And then the nightingale began to sing.

'There she is!' said the little kitchen-maid. 'Listen! Listen! There she sits!' and she pointed to a little grey bird up in the branches.

'Is it possible?' wondered the gentleman-in-waiting. 'I did not dream she **109** would look like this! How common she seems! I think she must have lost her colour at the sight of so many distinguished people!'

'Little nightingale!' cried the little kitchen-maid loudly, 'our gracious Emperor wishes you to sing for him!'

'With the greatest of pleasure!' replied the nightingale, and sang in a manner which would charm anyone's heart.

'It sounds like glass bells!' said the gentleman-in-waiting. 'And just look at her little throat moving! It really is strange that we have never heard her before. She will be a big success at Court!'

'Shall I sing again to the Emperor?' asked the nightingale, thinking that the Emperor was present.

'Most excellent nightingale!' said the gentleman-in-waiting, 'it is my great pleasure to invite you to a Court festival to be held this evening, when you will have the opportunity to charm his Imperial Majesty with your enchanting song.'

'But it sounds best here in the open!' said the nightingale. Nevertheless she followed willingly when she heard that this was the Emperor's wish.

Everything at the palace was sparkling clean. The walls and floors, which were all of porcelain, glittered in the light of thousands of lamps. The loveliest flowers — the ones with the merriest and loudest tinkle — were arranged along the passages; here too was much hurrying and scurrying and quite a draught, which made the flower-bells ring all the louder, so that one could not hear one's own words.

In the middle of the grand hall, where the Emperor sat, a golden perch was built for the nightingale to sit on. The whole Court was present and the little kitchen-maid was allowed to stand at the back near the door, now she had the title of a true maid of the kitchen. Everybody was dressed in his best clothes and they all gazed at the little grey bird, to whom the Emperor now signalled with a nod.

The nightingale sang so wonderfully, that tears came into the Emperor's eyes and rolled down his cheeks. And the nightingale sang all the more beautifully, and her song touched everyone's heart. The Emperor was so delighted, that he announced that the nightingale should have his golden slipper to wear round her neck. But the nightingale thanked him and said she was already well rewarded.

'I have seen tears in the Emperor's eyes, and that to me is the very greatest reward! The Emperor's tears have strange power. Heaven knows I have been sufficiently rewarded!' And then she sang again.

'This is the prettiest piece of coquetry I have ever known,' said the ladies

present. They filled their mouths with water, so they could cluck when anyone spoke to them—they imagined themselves to be nightingales too! And even the footmen and the chambermaids showed they were quite content, and that means a lot, for they are the most difficult people to satisfy. Yes, indeed, one can truly say the nightingale was a great success.

She was to remain at Court, to have her own cage and the right to fly out twice a day and once a night. She was always accompanied by twelve attendants, each holding on to her by a silk ribbon tied round her leg, and they held her tight. Such an outing was no fun at all.

All the city was talking about this wondrous bird. And when two people met, one would say only 'Night—!' and the other would add 'gale!' and they would sigh and understand each other perfectly. Eleven grocers named their children after the nightingale, but not one of them managed to give out a single melodious note.

One day the Emperor received a large parcel which was marked, 'Nightingale' on the outside.

'This will most probably be another book about our famous little bird!' thought the Emperor. But it was not a book, but a clever little toy—an artificial nightingale, intended to resemble the living one. It was covered with diamonds, rubies and sapphires. When wound up, it could sing one of the songs which the real nightingale sang, wagging its tail of glittering gold and silver at the same time. Round its neck a little band was fastened, and it read, 'The nightingale of the Emperor of Japan is poor compared with the nightingale of the Emperor of China.'

'How fantastic!' everyone cried. And the one who had brought the artificial bird was immediately given the title of Chief Imperial Nightingale Bringer.

'Now let them sing together! What a duet that will be!'

So they had to sing together, but it did not work out very well, for the real nightingale sang in her own way, and the artificial bird according to its wheels.

'It is not his fault,' said the Court music-master, 'his timing is exceptionally good, and he is of a good school!' So the artificial bird was now to sing alone. He was quite as successful as the real nightingale, but so much prettier to look at.

Thirty-three times he sang the very same tune, and yet he was not weary at all. Some would have liked to hear him right from the beginning again, but the Emperor was of the opinion that the real nightingale should now sing a little—but where was she? Nobody had noticed that she had flown through the open window towards her own green woods.

'What is the meaning of this?' said the Emperor. All the courtiers abused the nightingale, saying what an ungrateful creature she was. 'But we still have the best of the pair!' they said, and the artificial bird had to sing once more. They were hearing that same tune for the thirty-fourth time, but still they did not know it well, for it was quite a difficult one. The Court music-master was full of praise for the artificial bird, he insisted, in fact, that he was better than the real nightingale, not only in his dress of beautiful diamonds, but inside as well.

'For you see, my noble lords and ladies and Your Imperial Majesty above all, you must consider this, with the real nightingale you can never know what is coming but with the artificial bird everything is fixed beforehand. That is how it is and that is how it will be! We can take him to pieces, we can open him up and understand with our human mind, how the mechanism works, how his wheels are put together, how they move, and how one thing follows

112 another!'

'That is exactly my opinion too!' said everybody, and the Court music-master was given permission to show the bird to the Chinese people on the following Sunday. 'Let them hear him sing too,' said the Emperor.

So they heard him, and were as merry as if they had been drinking tea, for it is tea that makes the Chinese merry. And they all said 'Oh!' and held up their forefinger which they also call 'nibbler', and nodded their heads. But the poor fisherman, who had heard the real nightingale, would say, 'It sounds quite nice and it is rather like it, but something is missing!'

The real nightingale was banished from the empire.

The artificial bird was given a place on a silken cushion right by the Emperor's bed. All the presents he had received, gold and precious stones, lay round him, and in rank he was now raised to the title of High Imperial Bedside Table Singer; in fact his place was number one on the left, for the Emperor regarded the side where the heart is as the place of highest honour, and the heart is on the left side even in an Emperor. The Court music-master wrote twenty-five volumes about the artificial bird; they were terribly learned and long, and full of the most difficult Chinese words; so everyone preferred to say they had read them and understood them, for otherwise they would have been considered stupid and would have been punished.

And so a whole year went by. The Emperor, the Court, and all the Chinese knew every note of the artificial bird's song by heart, down to the last cluck, and that was exactly why they liked the song so much. They could now sing with him, and sing with him they did. The boys in the street would sing 'zezeze, cluck, cluck, cluck!' and so would the Emperor.

But one evening, when the artificial bird was singing away and the Emperor lay in bed listening, something suddenly went 'rip!' inside the bird. Something had snapped. There was a whirring sound, all the wheels went round, and the music stopped.

The Emperor jumped quickly out of bed and summoned his physician; but what use was he? So a watchmaker was called in, and he, after much talking and much examining, managed to make the bird work again, but he warned that he would have to be treated with care and used only rarely, for the pegs were almost worn out, and it was not possible to guarantee that new ones would make the bird sing. This was such a blow! Now the artificial bird was allowed to sing only once a year, and even then he managed this only with great difficulty. The Court music-master, however, made a short speech full of long words; he pronounced the bird as good as ever, and so it was as good as ever.

Five years went by. Suddenly the whole country was stricken with great grief, for in their hearts the people loved their Emperor; but now he was ill, and it was said that he would not live. A new Emperor had already been chosen, and outside the palace people stood about in the street, asking the gentleman-in-waiting how the Emperor was.

'Pish!' he would say, shaking his head.

Cold and pale the Emperor lay in his enormous, magnificent bed. The whole Court thought him already dead, and so everyone ran to greet the new Emperor. The men-servants ran out to talk about it, and the maids organized a big coffee party. Carpets and covers were laid in all the halls and passages throughout the palace, so not a single step would be heard. It was so still and so quiet everywhere.

But the Emperor was not yet dead. Stiff and pale he lay in his splendid bed with the long velvet curtains and the heavy golden tassels. The top of one window was slightly open, and the moon shone down on the Emperor and on his artificial bird.

The poor Emperor could hardly breathe; there seemed to be something pressing on his chest. He opened his eyes and saw that it was Death, who had put on the Emperor's crown, and held with one hand his gold sword and his magnificent banner with the other. And out of the folds of the big velvet curtains round the bed, the strangest heads were peering in. Some were truly

hideous, others looked kind and gentle; they were all the bad and the good deeds of the Emperor. They had come to watch him, now that Death sat on his heart.

'Do you remember?' they whispered one after another. 'Do you remember?' And they told him so much that the sweat broke out on his forehead.

'I never knew that!' moaned the Emperor. 'Music! Music! The great Chinese drum!' he cried. 'I don't want to hear what they say!'

But they kept on in their reproach, whilst Death, like a proper Chinaman, nodded his head to every word.

'Music! Music!' screamed the Emperor. 'My precious little golden bird, sing, I beg you, sing! I gave you gold and precious stones; with my own hands I hung my gold slipper round your neck—sing, I beg you, sing!'

But the bird was silent; no one was there to wind him up, and he could not sing without. And Death kept on staring at the Emperor with his great hollow eyes. It was so silent there, so dreadfully silent!

All at once the sweetest singing was heard from near the window. It was the little nightingale, who was sitting outside on a branch. She had heard of the Emperor's suffering and had come to sing to him of hope and comfort. And as she sang, the spectral forms round the bed grew fainter and fainter, the blood flowed faster and faster through the Emperor's feeble body, and even Death himself listened and urged the nightingale, 'Sing on, little nightingale, sing on!'

'Yes I will, if you give me the magnificent gold sword! And if you give me the splendid banner and the Emperor's crown!'

And Death gave up each of these treasures for a song, but even afterwards the nightingale continued to sing. She sang of the silent churchyard, where white roses bloom, where the elder-tree spreads sweet fragrance, and where the fresh grass is soaked with the tears of the bereaved. Then Death became homesick for his own garden, and he floated out of the window like a cold, white mist.

'Thank you, thank you, you heavenly little bird!' said the Emperor. 'I know you well! I drove you from my country and empire! Yet you have sung away those evil visions from my bed, and Death from my heart! How shall I reward you?'

'You have rewarded me already!' said the nightingale. 'When I sang to you the first time, you rewarded me with the tears which filled your eyes, and for that I will never forget you. They are the jewels which warm a singer's heart! But now you must sleep, so you will grow well and strong! I will sing for you!'

And she sang and the Emperor fell into a sweet sleep.

When the Emperor awoke, feeling strong and healthy, the sun was shining in to him through the windows. None of his servants had come to him, for they all thought him to be dead. But the nightingale was there still, singing away.

'You must stay with me for ever!' said the Emperor. 'You shall only sing when you wish to do so. And I will smash that artificial bird into a thousand pieces!'

'Don't do that!' said the nightingale. 'He served you well, as best as he could. Keep him as before. I cannot build my nest in the palace and live here; but let me come whenever I feel like coming. I will sit in the evening on a branch close to the window and sing to you to make you happy, but also thoughtful. I will sing to you of good, and of evil, which is kept from you. I will sing to you of those who are happy, and of those who are sad. Such a little singing-bird as I flies far and wide; to the poor fisherman, to the peasant's cottage, to all who live far away from you and your Court. I love your heart more than your crown, and yet your crown has the fragrance of something holy. I will come and sing for you again. But you must promise me one thing.'

'Everything I will promise!' cried the Emperor. He was standing now in his imperial robes which he had put on himself, and he held the heavy gold sword to his heart.

'One thing I ask of you! Let no one know that you have a little bird who tells you everything. Then everything will be all right!'

And then the nightingale flew away.

The servants came in to look at their dead Emperor. There they stood in a daze, and the Emperor said, 'Good morning!'

The Poor Miller's Boy and the Cat

In a certain mill lived an old miller who had neither wife nor children.

There were three boys who worked for him and once, when they had served him for many years, he called them and said, 'I am old now and only fit to sit behind the stove. Set out for far countries and whichever of you brings me back the best horse, to him I will give the mill. In return he shall take care of me until my death.'

The third of the lads, however, was the stable-boy, Hans, whom the others took for a simpleton. They grudged him even the chance of getting the mill, and thought anyway that he wouldn't really want it.

Then all the three set out together and, when they reached the edge of the village, the two said to simple Hans, 'You may as well stay here, you will never in your life get even a nag.'

All the same, Hans did go with them and, when it was night, they came to a cavern and there they lay down to sleep. The two clever lads waited till Hans was asleep, then they climbed out and left little Hans lying there. They thought what a fine clever thing they had done. But mind, even so, they shall not prosper!

When the sun rose, Hans woke up to find himself lying in a deep cavern. He looked around on every side and cried, 'Oh dear, where am I?' Then he got up and clambered up out of the cavern, went into the forest, and thought, 'Here I am all alone and deserted, how can I ever find a horse now?'

As he thought this, he met a small tabby cat who said in quite a friendly way, 'Hans, where are you going?'

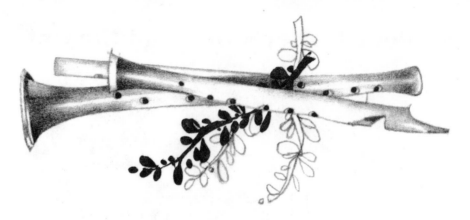

'Oh, you cannot help me,' said Hans.

'I know very well what your wish is,' said the little cat. 'You want to find a handsome horse. Come with me and be a faithful servant to me for seven years, and I will give you one, such a beauty you have never seen in your life.'

'Well, isn't this a strange cat,' thought Hans. 'But I will chance it and see if what she says is true.'

She took him with her into her enchanted little house, and there she had none but kittens serving her. They leapt nimbly up and down the stairs, and were merry and cheerful. In the evenings, when they sat down to dinner, three of them made music; one played the bass-viol, the other the fiddle and the third put a trumpet to her mouth and blew up her cheeks for all she was worth.

When they had risen from the dining table, it was carried away and the cat said, 'Now, Hans, come and dance with me.'

'No,' he replied. 'I couldn't dance with a pussy-cat. I have never done such a thing in my life.'

'So, take him to bed,' she said to the cats.

Thus one of them lighted him on his way to the bed-chamber, one took off his shoes, another his stockings and, finally, one blew out the candle.

Next morning, they came again and helped him get out of bed. One put on his stockings, one tied his garters, one fetched his shoes, one washed him and another dried his face with her tail.

'That feels very soft,' said Hans.

He, too, had to serve the cat, however, and chop wood into fine sticks every day. To do that, he was given an axe of silver, some wedges and a saw, also of silver, and a mallet of copper.

Well, he chopped the wood fine, stayed in the house, had his good meat and drink, but never saw anyone but the tortoiseshell cat and her servants.

One day she said to him, 'Go out and mow my meadow, and dry the grass.'

She gave him a scythe of silver and a whetstone of gold, but bade him return everything in good order again.

So Hans went and did as he had been bidden. This accomplished, he carried the scythe, the whetstone and the hay to the house, and asked if she was not yet ready to give him his reward.

'No,' said the cat, 'you must first do some more things for me. Here are planks of silver, a carpenter's axe, a square, and everything that is needed, all made of silver. With these you must build me a little house.'

So Hans built the little house, and said that he had done everything now, and still had no horse. Even so, the seven years were gone like six months. Then the cat asked if he would like to see her horses, and Hans said he would. Thereupon she opened the little house for him and the moment she opened the door, there were twelve horses standing there. Oh, so proud, shiny and glistening that the heart in him rejoiced to see them.

The cat gave Hans something to eat and to drink and said, 'Go home, I will not give you your horse now, but in three days' time I will come and bring it.'

So Hans got ready to depart and she showed him the way to the mill. But in all the seven years Hans had been with her, the cat had not given him any new clothes, so he had to keep on the ragged old smock which he had worn when he first came and which had become much too small for him everywhere.

When he got home, he found the other two miller's boys there. They certainly had brought with them a horse each, only the one that belonged to the first was blind, and the other's was lame.

They asked him, 'Where is your horse, Hans?'

'It will come in three days' time,' said Hans.

They laughed, saying, 'Well, Hans, where do you expect to get a horse from? That will be a beauty, for sure.'

Hans went into the dining-room, but the miller said he should not sit down to eat with them, as his smock was so worn at the elbows and in rags that they would be ashamed should anyone call.

So they gave him a little food to eat outside and, when they went to rest in the evening, the other two did not allow him to lie in a bed. So in the end, Hans had to creep into the goose-house and lie down on some hard straw.

When he awoke, the three days had passed and there came a coach with six horses. Oh, how they shone! They were a delight to behold. A servant brought the seventh horse which was for the poor miller's boy.

Then a resplendent Princess stepped out of the carriage and went into the mill. This Princess was the little tortoiseshell cat whom poor Hans had served for the seven years.

She asked the miller where his lowliest servant was.

'He's in such rags and tatters that we cannot have him in the mill,' said the miller. 'He lies in the goose-house.'

Then the King's daughter, for such she was, said that they should go at once and fetch him. So they fetched Hans out of the goose-house and he came holding his old smock together to cover himself.

Then the servant unpacked some magnificent garments, washed him and dressed him and, when he was ready, no king could have looked more handsome.

Then the Princess asked to see the horses brought by the other miller's boys and they brought the one horse which was blind and the other which was lame. Then she bade the servant bring the seventh horse, and the miller said that such a magnificent horse had never yet come into his courtyard.

'This is for the third miller's boy,' the Princess said.

'Then it is he who must have the mill,' said the miller.

But the Princess said to the miller that he was to have the horse and keep his mill as well. Then she took her faithful Hans, bade him sit in the coach, and drove off with him.

First, they drove to the little house which he had built with the silver tools but now it had become a great castle, and everything inside was of silver and gold. Then she married Hans and he was rich, so rich that he had enough money to last for as long as he lived.

No one should say that he who is foolish will never make good.

The Water of Life

Once upon a time there was a King who was so ill that no one believed he could still escape with his life. The King had three sons and they were very much grieved at their father's sickness. They went down into the palace garden and wept. There they met an old man who asked them the cause of their sorrow. They told him that their father was so ill that he would certainly die, for nothing seemed to help him. Then the old man said, 'There is yet one means I know of; that is the Water of Life. If he drinks it he will get well again. The only thing is it's difficult to find.'

Then the eldest son said, 'I will make sure to find it,' and he went to the sick King and begged him to let him go abroad to seek the Water of Life, for it alone could cure him.

'No,' said the King, 'the danger is too great, I'd rather die than expose you to it.'

However, so long did the young man entreat him that the King at last agreed.

The Prince thought, 'If I bring the water, then my father will love me best, and I shall inherit the kingdom.'

So the Prince set out and when he had ridden a certain time, a dwarf was standing in his way, who called to him, saying, 'Whither away so fast?'

'Stupid dwarf,' said the Prince, 'that's none of your business.'

But the little dwarf got angry and cast a bad spell on the young man.

Before long the Prince came to a gorge in the mountains, and as he rode on it seemed to become narrower and narrower till at last he could not go a step **123** further; it was impossible to turn the horse, or even to dismount, so he sat there stuck fast. The sick King waited for him a long time, but he never came.

Then the second son said, 'Father, let me go forth into the world and seek the Water of Life,' and he thought in his heart, 'if my brother is dead, the kingdom will fall to me.'

At first the King would not let him go either, but at last he gave in. So the Prince set out on the same road as his brother had taken, and he, too, met the dwarf who stopped him and asked where he was off to in such a hurry.

'Little busybody,' said the Prince, 'it's none of your business,' and rode on without looking back again.

However, the dwarf bewitched him, and just like his brother he found himself in a mountain gorge, and could go neither forwards nor backwards. But that is how the haughty fare.

When even the second son failed to return, the youngest begged permission to leave the country and fetch the water, and the King had to let him go in the end.

When the dwarf met him and asked where he was off to in such a hurry, he stopped and talked to him and answered saying, 'I am going in search of the Water of Life, for my father is very sick.'

'And do you know where it is to be found?'

'No, that I don't,' said the Prince.

'Well, as you have been friendly to me and not haughty like your false brothers, I will help you and tell you how to find the Water of Life. It springs from a well in the courtyard of an enchanted castle, but you shall never get in unless I give you an iron rod and two loaves of bread. With the rod strike three times on the iron castle gate, and it will spring open. Inside two hungry lions will be lying with their jaws open, but throw each a loaf, and they will be quiet. Then make haste and take some of the Water of Life before it strikes twelve, otherwise the gate will shut again and you will be imprisoned.'

The Prince thanked him, took the rod and the bread, and set out on his way again. And when he reached his destination, everything was as the dwarf had said. The gate sprang open at the third stroke of the rod, and when he had fed the lions with the bread, he entered the castle and came into a great hall.

There he found a number of enchanted princes. He took the rings off their fingers and also a sword and a loaf of bread lying there. In the next chamber he found a beautiful maiden. She was very happy to see him, kissed him and said he had broken the spell she was under, and should have the whole of her kingdom, and that if he came again in a year, their wedding would be celebrated. She also told him where the well with the Water of Life was to be found, but added he must hurry and draw the water before it struck twelve.

Then he went on, and finally came to a chamber with a fine, freshly made bed in it. As he was tired, he decided to take a little rest. So he lay down and fell asleep. When he awoke, the clock was striking a quarter to twelve. Thereupon he sprang up full of fear, ran to the well, drew some water out of it with a cup that was standing nearby, and hurried to get out in time. Just as he was going through the iron gate, the clock struck twelve, and the gate closed with such a force that it sliced off a piece of his heel.

He was happy to have the Water of Life, and set off for home. On his way he encountered the dwarf again. When the dwarf saw the sword and the loaf, he said, 'There you have won something of great value. With that sword you will be able to strike down whole armies, and the bread will never run out.'

The Prince did not want to come home to his father without his brothers, and said, 'Good dwarf, can you tell me where my two brothers are? They set out earlier than I in search of the Water of Life and didn't come back.'

'They are shut fast between two mountain-sides,' said the dwarf, 'I imprisoned them there by my spell, because they were exceedingly haughty.'

The Prince entreated him so long to free his brothers that the dwarf finally let them go, but he warned him against them saying, 'Be on your guard, they have bad hearts.'

The Prince was overjoyed to see them when they came back, and told them how he had fared.

Then they rode on together, and found themselves in a country pestered with famine and war, and the King already believed that he must perish, so dire was the need.

The Prince went to him and gave him the bread, and he fed the whole kingdom with it. The Prince also let him have his sword, with which he defeated the armies of his enemies, and henceforth could live in peace and quiet. Then the Prince took his sword and his loaf back, and the three brothers rode on. But they were to pass through two more lands where hunger and war raged, and each time the Prince gave the Kings his bread and sword, and now he had saved three countries.

And then they embarked on a ship and sailed across the sea. During the voyage the two elder brothers spoke together.

'The youngest has found the Water of Life, and we have not; for this Father will give him the kingdom, which by rights belongs to us, and thus he will deprive us of our fortune.'

This made them revengeful, and they came to an agreement that they would cheat him. They waited till he was fast asleep, then poured out the **125**

Water of Life from his cup into their own, and filled their brother's cup with salty sea-water.

When they came home, the youngest brought the sick King his cup for him to drink the water that was to make him well again. Scarcely, however, had he drunk a drop of the salty sea-water than he became even more ill than before. And while he was lamenting over this, the two elder sons came and accused the youngest of wanting to poison their father, saying it was they who brought the true Water of Life, and handed it to him. No sooner had he drunk of it than he felt his illness disappear and became hale and hearty as in his young days.

After this the two went to the youngest brother, and said, 'True, you found the Water of Life. But we had all the trouble and now we have the reward. You should have kept your eyes open, for we took it away from you while you were asleep upon the sea. And when the year is up, one of us will go and bring the fair Princess here. But take care not to betray any of this. Our father does not trust you, and if you say a single word you shall lose your life. If you keep silent, however, you will be spared.'

But the old King was angry with his youngest son, and believed he had sought to take his life. So he summoned the court to assemble and pronounce the sentence on him that he should be secretly killed.

One day when the Prince was riding to the hunt, the King's huntsman had been ordered to go with him. When they were all alone away in the forest, the huntsman looked so sad that the Prince said, 'My good man, what is the matter with you?'

The huntsman answered, 'I dare not tell you, but I must.'

Then the Prince said, 'Just speak out, I will forgive you.'

'Alas,' said the huntsman. 'I am to shoot you dead, the King has ordered it so.' This frightened the Prince who said, 'My dear man, spare my life. I will give you my royal clothes, give me yours in return.'

The huntsman said, 'With all my heart. For I could never have shot you anyway.'

Then they changed clothes, and the huntsman went home, but the Prince went away through the wood.

Some time after, three carriages full of gold and precious stones came to the old King for his youngest son. These had been sent by the Kings who had beaten their enemies with the Prince's sword and fed their countries with his bread, and now wanted to show their gratitude.

Then the old King thought, 'Is it possible that my son really was innocent?' And he said to his men, 'If only he were still alive! How it grieves me that I had

him killed!'

'He is still alive,' said the huntsman. 'I didn't have the heart to execute your command,' and told the King what had taken place.

Then the King let it be proclaimed throughout all kingdoms that his son was to be allowed to come home again where he would be graciously received.

Meanwhile, the Princess in the enchanted castle had a road built of glittering gold and told her courtiers that whoever came riding on horseback straight over it would be the right man and should be let in. But whoever came on one side of the road would not be the right one, and was not to be admitted.

Soon the time had passed, and the eldest son thought he should go to see the Princess, say that he had been her deliverer, and receive her hand in marriage and her kingdom into the bargain. So he rode forth, and when he came to the castle and saw the beautiful golden road, he thought, 'It would be a terrible pity to ride on it,' and he turned aside and rode to the right of it. However, when he came riding to the gate, the servants told him he was not the true bridegroom, and should turn back.

Soon after that the second Prince set out, and when he came to the golden road, the moment his horse set foot on it he thought it would be a shame to ride on it as it might get damaged. So he turned away and rode to the left of it. But when he came to the gate, the guards said he was not the true bridegroom either and he too should turn back.

Now that the full year had passed, the third Prince wanted to come out of the forest and go to his beloved to forget his sorrows in her dear company. So he set out thinking of her all the time and longing to be with her, and did not notice the golden road at all. So his horse rode over it right in the middle, and when he came to the gate, it was opened to him and the Princess welcomed him with great joy. The marriage was celebrated and, when it was over, she told him that his father had summoned him to his presence and had forgiven him.

So he went on horseback to him and told him how his brothers had deceived him. The old King wanted to punish them, but they had gone to sea and never came back to the end of their days.

The Ugly Duckling

It was so lovely in the country! It was summer; the wheat was yellow, the oats were green, the hay was stacked up in the grassy meadows, while the stork paraded about on his long red legs, chattering away in Egyptian, for this was the language he had learned from his mother. Thick woods spread all around the fields and meadows, and deep lakes were in the middle of the woods. It was indeed beautiful in the country! The warm sunbeams fell upon an old manor-house surrounded by a deep moat and, from its walls all the way down to the water's edge, large burdock leaves grew—they were so tall that little children could stand upright under the largest ones. This spot was as wild as any in the densest forest. And this was the place a duck had chosen to build her nest. She was doing her best to hatch little ducklings, but she was tired of sitting on the eggs, for it was taking so terribly long and she rarely had visitors. The other ducks preferred swimming along the canals to climbing up to see her for a bit of gossip under a burdock leaf.

At last the eggs started to crack, one after another, with a cry of 'peep-peep!' All the eggs were coming to life, with little heads popping out.

'Quack, quack! Quick, quick!' said the mother duck encouragingly, and the baby ducklings hurried as best as they could, peering under the green burdock leaves on all sides. Their mother allowed them to look as much as they wished, for green is so good for the eyes.

'What a big place the world is!' wondered all the ducklings, now that they had so much room to move about.

'So you think this is the whole world?' the mother instructed them. 'The world stretches a long way past our garden, all the way to the parson's fields! But I have never been there. Are you all here now?' And she got up. 'Oh no, you're not all here yet. The largest egg is still there. How much longer is this one going to take? I am really sick to death of it!' And with that she settled down again in the nest.

'How are you getting on?' asked an old duck, who came by for a visit.

'This one egg is taking simply ages!' complained the nesting duck. 'It is not even trying to crack. But just look at the others; they are the prettiest ducklings I've ever seen! They all take after their father, that scoundrel of a fellow—he doesn't even drop in to see me!'

'Let me see the egg which doesn't want to crack!' said the old duck. 'Believe me or not, it's a turkey egg! They played the same trick on me once. When

I think of the trouble and bother I had with those youngsters; imagine, they were afraid of water! I couldn't get them to go in, though I squeaked and quacked and hissed and snapped — nothing was the slightest bit of use! Show me that egg! Yes, quite definitely it's a turkey egg! Leave it alone and teach your other children to swim instead!'

'I think I'll sit on it a while longer!' the duck announced. 'I've sat on it for so long now, I'll last out a bit longer!'

'As you like!' said the old duck, and waddled away.

The big egg burst open at last. 'Peep, peep!' cried the newly born as he tumbled out. He was huge and ugly. The duck looked at him closely. 'How awfully big that duckling is!' she wondered. 'He's not a bit like the others! Could it be a young turkey-cock after all? We'll know soon enough! He'll get in the water, even if I have to push him in myself!'

The next day the weather was beautiful. The sun shone down on all the burdock leaves lining the wall. The mother duck waddled with all her family behind to the canal. Splash! and she was in the water. 'Quack, quack!' she cried, and one duckling after another jumped in. At first, the water closed over their heads, but they came straight up again and swam quite easily. They all floated merrily along, even the ugly, grey duckling.

'That's no turkey!' the mother duck said to herself. 'Just look how nicely he uses his legs, and how erect he holds himself! He's my baby! Come to think of it, he isn't at all bad-looking, when one takes a closer look! Quack, quack! Come along now with me, I'll lead you into the world and introduce you to the duck-yard. Take care to keep close to me, so nobody treads on you, and keep a look-out for the cat!'

They came into the duck-yard. The noise there was deafening, for two duck families were fighting over an eel's head— and the cat got it in the end.

'You see, such is the way of the world!' said the mother duck, licking her beak, for she too fancied the eel's head. 'And now on your feet!' she ordered. 'Show me how quick you can be and go and bow to that old duck over there! She's the most distinguished of all the ducks here. She is of Spanish blood, that's why she is so plump. As you see, she has a red rag round her leg — that is exceptionally beautiful and the greatest distinction any duck can have. It means that they would hate to lose her, and so she must be easily recognizable to everybody, animals and people! Hurry now, and don't turn your feet inwards! Well brought up ducklings always place their feet well apart, like father and mother! Like this! Bow nicely now and say "quack, quack!"'

The little ducklings did as they were told. But the other ducks eyed them up and down, quacking loudly, 'Oh no, not another bunch! As if there weren't enough of us already! And fie! How ugly that duckling is! We shan't put up with him!' And one of the ducks flew straight at him and bit him in the neck.

'Leave him alone!' cried the mother duck. 'He's doing no harm!'

'But he's far too big and far too conspicuous!' said the duck that had bitten him. 'So we'll go on nipping him!'

'You have pretty children, mother!' said the old duck with the rag round her leg. 'They are all pretty but one, and that hasn't turned out well at all! I wish you could remake it!'

'That is impossible, your ladyship!' said the mother duck. 'He may not be handsome, but he has a kind heart and he swims beautifully, like any of the others, in fact a little better than the rest. I am confident he'll grow into a beauty, or that in time he'll at least not look so big. But he was so long in that egg, it must have affected his figure!' She scratched the duckling fondly behind his neck and stroked his feathers on his back. 'Besides,' she added, 'he's a drake, so looks don't matter that much! I just hope he grows big and strong to fight through life.'

'The other ducklings are so charming!' praised the old duck. 'Make yourselves entirely at home, and if you come across an eel's head, do bring it along to me!'

And they made themselves at home.

But the poor little duckling, who had been the last to hatch and who was so ugly to look at, was nipped and pecked and teased by ducks and hens alike.

'He's such a monstrous fellow!' they all said. And the turkey-cock, who had been born with spurs on and so fancied himself as an emperor, puffed himself out like a ship in full sail, and made straight for the duckling, gabbling away till his face turned scarlet. The poor little duckling hardly knew what to do, or where to turn. He was upset because he was so ugly and the laughing-stock of the whole duck-yard.

That is how it was the first day and things grew worse and worse. Everybody was against the poor duckling, even his brothers and sisters were unkind to him, and said, 'If only the old cat would get you, you ugly creature!' And even his mother sighed, 'I wish you were far away!' The ducks bit him, the hens pecked at him, and the maid who fed the poultry kicked him.

So the little duckling fled, flying over the hedge. The little birds in the bushes were frightened and flew up in the air, and the duckling thought, 'That is because I am ugly!' He closed his eyes and ran on. And so he came to some wide marshes, where wild ducks were living. He stayed there all night, for he was tired and weary.

In the morning the wild ducks flew up and saw the newcomer. 'Who are you?' they asked. The duckling turned in all directions, greeting everyone as nicely as he knew.

'You really are uncommonly ugly!' said the ducks. 'But what does it matter, if you don't want to marry into our family!'

Poor duckling! He had not even thought of marrying! All he wanted was to be allowed to stay among the reeds and drink a little marsh water now and then. For two whole days he lay there. Then two wild geese came along, or to be more precise, two wild ganders. Not much time had passed since they pecked their way out of their egg-shell, so they were somewhat impertinent.

'Look here, friend!' they called to the ugly duckling. 'You're so ugly that we quite like you! Come with us, and be a bird of passage, like us! A stone's throw away from here, on a neighbouring marsh, there are a few adorable, beautiful wild geese, all maiden young ladies, and they are calling, "Hiss! Hiss!" You might be quite a success, in spite of your ugliness!'

Bang—bang! it echoed suddenly from above, and both the ganders fell dead into the reeds. The water turned blood-red. Bang—bang! it echoed once again and whole flocks of wild geese soared upwards from the reeds. And shots rang out again. There was a grand shoot on. The hunters had circled the marsh, some in fact were sitting in branches of trees, which stretched right over the reeds. Blue smoke drifted in little clouds between dark trees, rolling far out over the water. The hounds hurtled through the mud — splash! splash! The reeds and rushes were swaying in all directions. It was terrifying for the poor duckling. He turned his head to hide it under his wing, but just then an 133 enormous dog appeared right by his side. His tongue was hanging right out and his eyes were gleaming. He thrust his open jaw right towards the duckling, barred his sharp teeth and snap!—he was gone, gone without even touching him.

'Thank heaven!' sighed the duckling. 'I am so ugly that even the dog doesn't want me!'

And he lay there quite still, while the shots whistled through the rushes.

Not till much later in the day did silence reign again. But the poor duckling did not dare to get up even now. He waited several hours more before he looked around and then he hastened away from the marsh as fast as he could. He ran over fields and meadows but the wind was strong and only with difficulty could he fight his way forward.

Towards evening he came to a shabby little cottage. It was so wretched that it couldn't make up its mind on which side to fall, and that is the only reason it remained standing. The wind swept round the little duckling so fiercely that he had to sit tight on his tail, so as not to be blown right over. And all the time it grew worse. But then the little duckling noticed that the door of the cottage had come off one of its hinges, and was therefore hanging so crookedly that it was possible to slip through the gap inside.

In the cottage lived an old woman with a tom-cat and a hen. The tom-cat, whom she called Sonny, could arch his back and purr; he also knew how to make sparks fly, but you had to stroke him the wrong way first. The hen had tiny short little legs and was therefore called Chickatiny Shortie; she laid some beautiful eggs, and the old woman loved her as her own child.

The next morning they noticed the strange duckling at once and the tom-cat began to purr and the hen to cackle.

'What's going on?' asked the old lady, looking round. But her sight was rather poor and so she mistook the duckling for a plump duck, who had gone astray.

'What a valuable catch!' she said. 'Now I shall have duck eggs—that is if it isn't a drake! We must test it out.'

So the duckling was taken in on trial for three weeks, but no eggs appeared.

Now the tom-cat was the master of the house and the hen the mistress and they always used to say 'we and the world', for they believed they were half of the world—and the better half at that! The duckling thought it possible to have a different opinion, but the hen would not stand for this.

'Can you lay eggs?' she asked.

'No.'

'Shut your beak then!'

And the tom-cat asked, 'Can you arch your back till your fur stands on end? Can you purr and make sparks fly?'

'No.'

'In that case keep your opinion to yourself when sensible people are talking!'

So the duckling sat in a corner, feeling thoroughly sad at heart. Then he remembered the fresh air and the sunshine. He felt a strange yearning to float on water and in the end he just couldn't help himself and had to confide in the hen.

'What's the matter with you?' she asked. 'You don't have any work to do, that's why you have such fancy ideas in your head! Lay some eggs or purr, and you'll get over it!'

'But it is so wonderful to float on water!' said the duckling. 'It is so wonderful when the water closes over your head while you dive to the very bottom!'

'Sounds most delightful, I'm sure!' said the hen. 'Are you quite mad? Ask the tom-cat, he is wiser than anyone I know, if he likes to float on water, or dive under! I don't even want to speak about what I think! Ask the old woman, our mistress, in all the world there's no wiser creature than she! Do you think she longs to float and to duck her head under water?'

'You don't understand me!' complained the duckling.

'If we don't understand you, who would understand! Surely you don't think yourself wiser than the tom-cat and our old lady, without mentioning myself at all! Forget those fancies, my child, and thank the Creator for all you have been given! Haven't you arrived in a warm room, where there's company you can learn a lot from? But you're a muddler and it's not particularly entertaining having to put up with you! But you should believe me, for I mean well. I am telling you unpleasant facts, but that's how to tell true friends. Now set to work and lay some eggs and learn to purr or make sparks fly!'

'I think I will go out into the wide world,' said the duckling.

'Very well then, go!' replied the hen.

And off the duckling went. He floated on water and dived, but all the animals ignored him, because of his ugliness.

Autumn came, the leaves in the woods turned yellow and brown, and the wind caught them and sent them dancing; there was a wintry chill in the air. The clouds were heavy with hail and snow and on the fence sat a crow who croaked 'Ow, ow!' from sheer cold. Brr, the very thought of the winter was enough to give one the shivers! The poor duckling was certainly not very comfortable.

One evening, just after sunset, a whole flock of large, beautiful birds flew out of the bushes. The duckling had never seen anything so beautiful before. They were dazzling white, with long graceful necks. They were swans; they gave out the strangest of cries, spread their magnificent, long wings and flew away from the cold regions to warmer countries, across the immense, open sea. They rose high, so high, and the ugly little duckling's heart was gripped with the strangest feeling. He spun round and round on the water, straining his neck high after them and letting out a cry so loud and so strange that it frightened even him. He could not forget the beautiful, lucky birds! When they were lost from sight he dived straight to the bottom. When he came up again, he was almost beside himself. He didn't know what they were called or where they were flying to, yet he loved them as he had never loved anybody before. But he wasn't envious, not in the least—for how could he even think of wishing such beauty for himself—he would be happy just to be accepted by the other ducks—he, the poor ugly creature!

The winter was cruel, bitterly cruel. The duckling had to swim to and fro on the pond, to keep it from freezing up altogether. But every night the hole in which he swam grew smaller and smaller, and a crust of ice formed on it, too. The duckling was forced to keep his little legs going all the time to prevent the gap from closing altogether. In the end, faint with exhaustion, he lay perfectly still and froze fast in the ice.

Early the next morning a farmer was passing by. Seeing the duckling, he went down to him, broke the ice with his clog and took him home to his wife. There he revived.

The children wanted to play with him, but the duckling was afraid they wanted to hurt him, and in his terror he flew straight into the milk-pan, spilling the milk all over the room. The farmer's wife screamed and waved her hands; the duckling flew into the butter-tub and then into a barrel of flour and then up again. What a sight he looked! The farmer's wife went on screaming, chasing him with a pair of tongs, and the children were falling over one another trying to catch him shrieking and laughing. Luckily for him the door was open. The duckling flew into the bushes into the newly-fallen snow, where he lay in a daze.

It would be too sad to tell of all the misery and suffering the duckling had to endure that cruel winter. When the sun began to shine warmly again, he was lying on the marsh among the rushes, the larks were singing, the beautiful spring had returned!

Then the duckling opened his wings. They were stronger now than before and bore him forwards mightily. Before he realized it, he found himself in a huge garden, where the apple-trees were in full bloom and fragrant lilac hung on long green branches over the winding stream. Oh, how beautiful it all was, how spring-like, how fresh! And out of the thicket right in front of the duckling came three beautiful white swans; they spread their wings and swam lightly, so lightly on the water. The duckling recognized the magnificent birds and was seized with a strange sadness.

'I'll fly over to the kingly birds! They'll peck me to death for daring to go near them when I am so ugly. So what! It's better to be put to death by them than to be bitten by the ducks, pecked at by the hens, kicked by the girl who tends the poultry, and to suffer so in winter!'

And so he flew into the water and swam towards the beautiful swans. They saw him and turned towards him, their wings humming. 'Kill me then!' said the poor creature, and he bowed his head to the surface, waiting for death. But what did he see in the clear water? There, underneath him, he saw his own reflection. No longer was he the clumsy, dirty-grey bird, ugly to all—he was a swan!

It matters not if one is born in a duck-yard, if one has been hatched out of a swan's egg!

The young swan was truly happy now after all his hardships. The big swans swam round him and stroked him with their beaks.

Some little children came into the garden. They threw bread and grain into

the water, and the smallest one of them cried, 'There's a new swan!' And the others chanted, 'Yes, a new swan has come!' They clapped their hands and danced about and ran to fetch their father and mother. Bread and buns were thrown into the water and everybody said, 'The new swan is the prettiest! It is so young and so lovely!' And the old swans bowed before him.

The young swan was suddenly overcome with shyness. He tucked his head under his wing, not knowing what to do. He was so very happy, but not at all proud, for a good heart is never proud. He recalled how he had been laughed at and cruelly treated. Now everyone was saying he was the loveliest of all these lovely birds. The lilacs bent their branches right down to him and the sun shone warmly and brightly. The wings of the young happy swan were suddenly humming and with his slender neck stretched out the swan cried joyfully, with all his heart, 'I never dreamt of so much happiness, when I was the ugly duckling!'

The Evil Brothers

It so happened that during the reign of Haroun al Raschid, Abdallah Fadil, the emir of Basra, had not sent in his taxes which were due.

Haroun thought there must be a good reason for the emir's lapse, for Abdallah was one of his most honoured, reliable subjects. He decided therefore to go to Basra to see for himself.

Abdallah received him with many apologies, assuring him the payment to the caliph was ready. And as the presence of such an honourable guest demands, he organized a huge feast for Haroun and his retinue which continued into the night.

When it was time to retire, the emir ordered that a bed be prepared by his own so that they might rest side by side.

Haroun could not sleep, but pretended he was no longer awake. So it was that he heard Abdallah rise and leave the bedroom. He too left his bed and, unseen, followed at a distance, curious to see what his friend would do. They went through several long passages till the emir came to a spacious hall, thickly carpeted, in the centre of which was a large divan framed in ebony. To the caliph's surprise two black hounds were tied to the frame with gold chains.

As soon as they saw Abdallah, they barked and wagged their tails, showing how pleased they were to see him. But the emir picked up a whip and beat them both with such force, that they fell into unconsciousness. Yet afterwards he stroked them gently, soothing them with his own hand, and gave them drink and food, whilst all the time he said prayers for them. At last he took the candle and returned to his chamber.

Though such behaviour seemed most strange to Haroun, all the next day he gave no sign, nor mentioned what he had witnessed.

But when the episode was repeated the following night and on the third night too, the caliph could no longer hold back his curiosity. On the third morning, when they had breakfasted and prayed, he said, 'Emir Abdallah, I have been destined to find out about your two black hounds and about the strange way you treat them. You must tell me truthfully what it all means. Why do you beat them into unconsciousness and why afterwards do you treat them as if they were of your own blood?'

'They truly are of the human race, apostle of God,' Abdallah replied respectfully. 'But so that you may know the entire truth, I shall have to relate the whole story, and have the dogs for witnesses.'

Haroun al Raschid was only too pleased to agree to such a suggestion. So the emir fetched both the hounds and began his tale:

'I am the youngest of three sons of a wealthy merchant Fadil. My father called his first-born Mansur, and my second brother is named Nasir.

'We had a very happy childhood, but as soon as we grew up, our father fell ill and then passed away. He left us much wealth in the form of money and possessions, also a spacious house and a prosperous business.

'It was after the funeral, when all the slaves had been released, the Koran had been read and the alms had been distributed to the poor, that I asked my brothers whether they wished all the possessions to be split into three parts, or whether they wanted to remain under the same roof and live together as before.

141

'Mansur and Nasir both asked for their shares. So they were given the money and goods. To me they left the house and the business of their own free will, and went off to seek their fortunes in a distant land.

'It was in winter, exactly a year later, when I was busily working, that they suddenly returned, without a single dinar, starving and trembling with cold. I gave them my fur coats and fed them well. And they told me how they went into business in Cairo and Baghdad, making great profits, and how when they were aboard a ship sailing back to Basra, they were caught in a violent storm and were lucky to escape with their lives. It was in poverty therefore that they made the rest of their way home, begging for food to keep alive. At last they reached their old home.

'I listened to all their complaints against a merciless fate and said to them, "Dear brothers, whilst it was your destiny to suffer on your travels, God showed his generosity to me. He allowed me to enlarge my property by business dealings to the same size as it was at the time of our father's death and before we split it into three parts. Take a third each once again. I am confident you will do better."

'I acted on my decision. Mansur and Nasir worked as merchants again, but this time I insisted that they remained in Basra, so that I could keep my eye on them. But although their earlier journey had been full of bitter experiences, they were not content, but thirsted for adventures and easy riches in distant lands.

'They managed to convince me, so that I gave in to their wishes and after thorough preparations all three of us set off on our voyage.

'We hired a ship and loaded it in Basra with merchandise to be sold in other places, and in this ship we sailed along the coast from town to town.

'But though we made easy profit by buying and selling, we met not only good fortune, but also misfortune.

'One day we ran out of water on board. We anchored off a small island and went in search of a spring. I climbed a hill, and there witnessed a very unequal struggle. A black dragon was pursuing a helpless white snake. It caught up with the snake and buried its talons in the snake's body. Unable to bear such an unfair fight, I seized a large stone and struck the dragon with such force it fell down dead on the spot.

'To my amazement the white snake in that instant turned into a beautiful damsel who walked over to me and said, "It is thanks to you, Abdallah, that I am saved. I am the genie Saida. If ever you are in trouble, you too will have help from me..."

'Thereupon the earth parted and she disappeared.

'My brothers, in the meantime, had found water, so we set sail again. Some

days later the captain brought the ship to another foreign shore, so that we might replenish our supplies.

'Not far from the place where we anchored I saw a large imposing city with high walls, fortifications and iron gates. Surely here we could get everything we needed!

'But when I inquired who would accompany me to the city, they all refused, even my own brothers. Such a plan was most dangerous, they said, for only unbelievers lived in these regions, and to put ourselves in their hands could only lead to disaster.

'What else could I do but go on my own? I relied on destiny and put myself in the hands of the Almighty. I set out towards the city gates, not knowing what to expect. Reality surpassed all expectations. Every single person I came across, from the guard by the gates to the merchants, tradesmen, soldiers, ordinary men and women in the market, as well as the viziers, the sultan and the sultana in the palace — everyone in that city had been turned to stone! I could gather as much gold, silver and precious stones as I desired. But as soon as I touched anything, it turned to dust — so rotten was it with the passing of time.

'I wandered about the palace chambers, finding only deathly stillness and everywhere signs of the abrupt, unexpected end of activities. Suddenly my ears caught the melodious whisper of a girlish voice, reciting verses from the Koran, the only human voice left in the whole city!

'Curious to see the owner of the voice speaking words which sounded to me like heavenly music, I went on and came face to face with a maiden more beautiful than a fresh rosebud, her radiance equal to that of the sun.

'The maiden, who was reclining on soft cushions, rose and greeted me like an old friend, "Peace be with you, Abdallah, the delight of my eye!"

'It was with difficulty that I hid the excitement I felt at seeing such beauty. But I could not hide my curiosity and I showered her with questions, wanting to know how she came to know me and my name, and why it was that she was the only human being alive in this city turned to stone.

'In reply she told me a story which explained everything that I had so far seen:

'Her father, apparently, was a mighty ruler of a large kingdom and during his reign he amassed a huge fortune. But instead of thanking the one and only God for his good fortune, he worshipped an idol made by human hand from precious stones. And all the dignitaries, the wealthy citizens, the soldiers, the simple folk, in short all the inhabitants of the whole kingdom worshipped similar images.

144   'It so happened that one day a traveller dressed in green entered the palace,

his face lit by the holy radiance of believers. It was he who reprimanded the king for worshipping idols and urged him to become a Muslim. Not only did the king not heed the stranger's words, but tried to bring about his destruction. The king ordered that all idols be brought into the palace and placed side by side, till there was no space left.

'Then the king and all his subjects fell to their knees before their gods, praying that their wrath would pursue the stranger.

'But the traveller's faith proved too strong for them. No harm came to him, but he in turn knocked down the king's idol, and with outstretched hands asked his own God to turn the unbelievers to stone. And in that instant the whole city was turned to stone — except for the king's daughter. She escaped this terrible fate because she was predestined by Allah to turn to the true faith.

'The Muslim stranger then introduced the princess to the teachings of the Koran and it was he who also foretold that I would venture into her city, and would lead her away as my wife.

'I returned to my ship with many precious things. Radji my wife was the greatest treasure of all.

'Even my brothers could not take their eyes off her, and demanded that I gave her to them. Then I realized for the first time how greedy and selfish they were. I divided the jewels and gold fairly among us, but refused to share Radji. I guarded her closely till the spires of Basra appeared on the horizon.

'I was sure that then all would be well, that no disaster could occur, and I gave way to drowsiness. I slept.

'This was what Mansur and Nasir were waiting for. They seized me and tossed me overboard into the foaming waves. I was bidding this world goodbye, when suddenly I was helped by someone I had almost forgotten. It was the genie Saida. She had been constantly watching over me, hoping to repay the debt she felt she owed me after I had saved her from the dragon.

'Turning into a huge bird, she plucked me from the vicious waves and in a trice put me down on the deck of the ship.

'Alas, it was too late, for when Radji realized what had happened, she plunged into the sea after me. Only my own brothers were standing there, gaping in terror and astonishment to see me alive. But they soon regained their composure and embraced me heartily, as if they had not tried to end my life.

'Saida then stepped in. She wanted to punish them with death there and then for their wicked deed. It took all my efforts to persuade her to spare at least the life of my brothers.

'So she turned them into these low hounds and instructed me to beat them each night into unconsciousness, warning me that if I disobeyed, I would be whipped by her.

'This was what happened the very first night, when I did not heed the order. Even today, after twelve years, I can still feel the blows of her whip, so I no longer forget her instructions.

'So thus is my story, oh Caliph,' Abdallah ended with a sigh, and bowed his head.

'What an unusual tale,' remarked Haroun al Raschid, and asked, 'Have you forgiven your brothers?'

'Why, of course, my master! All I ask now is that they forgive me for all the beatings I have had to give them. Everything else depends on God.'

'In that case I shall instruct Saida to take away her curse,' the caliph
146   announced. He wrote a letter, sealed it and handed it over to Abdallah,

saying, 'Free your brothers from their chains and do not beat them again. When Saida comes, you must not be afraid, but give her this letter...'

Abdallah then bade Haroun goodbye, showering him with thanks. When the caliph and his attendants had disappeared from sight, he turned back. He unchained the dogs straight away, and ordered a lavish table to be prepared for him and for them.

The servants and guards thought their master must have gone out of his mind, to dine with beasts, and they refused to touch the remains from the feast. But Abdallah paid no attention to their objections, and had beds prepared for his dog-brothers alongside his own.

Suddenly the ground opened and Saida stood there.

'Why have you freed the hounds? Why are you honouring such traitors, instead of beating them? Would you like me to turn you into a dog too?' she cried, her eyes gleaming with anger.

The emir handed over the letter from Haroun al Raschid and she read it carefully.

'I am the daughter of the king of the genies,' Saida then said, 'and I cannot act without my father's permission. Wait till I have consulted him. I shall let you know his decision presently...'

Saida then disappeared, but soon she was back.

'You shall have your way,' she said, 'for the caliph of the believers has also great powers over us. But I warn you, your brothers are false and treacherous and will bring you no good.'

With that she poured some liquid into a bowl, muttered a few words of a magic formula and sprinkled the liquid on both the dogs.

Immediately Mansur and Nasir stood before them, youthful and handsome as of old. There was much joy and rejoicing, laughter and happy tears and none of them noticed that Saida disappeared. They drank together and talked and celebrated till the break of dawn, when they all set out to see the caliph.

Haroun al Raschid received both the culprits graciously and showered gifts upon them, though at the same time he reprimanded them for their past wickedness.

So it came about that after twelve years Mansur and Nasir began living again the life of human beings. Abdallah made them his assistants, bought them magnificent houses and found them beautiful wives. His kind heart forgot all past sorrows and grievances.

The brothers, however, though they behaved warmly and lovingly towards Abdallah, nursed only hate and envy in their hearts. They had not learned their lesson. They were jealous that their brother was an emir, highly honoured by the people. They were furious that no one showed them such respect and thought that if they could only get rid of their brother, the caliph might make them the joint emirs of Basra.

Their hate grew day by day, till they could bear it no longer, and they agreed to kill their brother. They invited him to Mansur's house, which stood by the river. There they prepared many highly intoxicating drinks for the occasion.

The unsuspecting Abdallah came gladly, and soon was talking with them merrily, raising the glass to his lips constantly. His brothers made sure it was always full.

It was very late when Abdallah fell into a deep sleep in his chair. But Mansur and Nasir were wide awake. They were on their feet like lightning as soon as they heard their brother's loud, regular breathing. Now was the moment to pounce on their helpless victim and strangle him.

At last they thought they had achieved their evil intention, as they dragged the lifeless body onto the terrace and threw it into the river.

The next morning both these evil plotters went to see the caliph Haroun al Raschid. Falling on their knees, their eyes full of tears, they explained that Abdallah's deeds had angered the genie Saida and that she had carried him away from this world.

But they underestimated the caliph's wisdom and character. The ruler immediately summoned the genie to justify her action.

And the daughter of the king of the genies said, 'Oh King of all believers, how true my words of warning were regarding these treacherous brothers. Why, they themselves strangled Abdallah and threw him into the river, so that the water would close over him forever and hide their guilt. Happily they

149

did not complete their evil deed. Abdallah was not dead, but unconscious. So before he sank to the river bed, I changed into a large fish and carried him to the opposite shore, where he is now recovering.'

Hearing this, the caliph became so angry that he gave an immediate order for justice to be carried out. Mansur and Nasir that very day were beheaded before Abdallah's palace.

What in the meantime was happening to their brother? On the far shore of the river, consciousness did not return to him until it was bright daylight. There was not a living soul about — all he could see was an endless, sandy plain.

An hour or so later his eyes were gladdened by the sight of an approaching caravan. They would surely have pity and help him.

And they did. He was made comfortable, fed and clad. And the leader of the caravan, who had studied how to heal the sick, attended to Abdallah himself.

So it happened that after one month of travelling Abdallah came into the land of Persia. He had still not completely recovered, so they spent that night in a lodging house. There the emir was told of a pious, learned woman who lived in a nearby hermitage, who knew how to cure all illnesses and who was therefore visited by the sick from near and far.

Sick as he was, Abdallah set out to see her. From inside, as he approached he heard a voice, a well-known, long unheard, beloved voice.

'Welcome to you, Abdallah!' it said.

Yes! It was Radji, the light of his world, the beloved of his heart, whom he had once led from the city of stone.

They had so much to tell one another! Abdallah learned that the traveller in green, who had turned her father to stone, had rescued her from the sea and had taught her how to cure all illnesses — and he also had foretold the day of their reunion.

What more is there to tell?

Abdallah immediately recovered completely, and with the help of the pious traveller they both returned to Basra. There they learned of the just punishment which had met the evil brothers. The caliph, overjoyed at seeing them, had the marriage agreement speedily prepared, and from that day on they were never again parted.

Five Peas in a Pod

There were five peas in a pod. They were green and the pod was green, so they thought the whole world must be green, and quite rightly too! The pod grew and the peas grew, arranging themselves according to their dwelling; they sat all in a row.

Outside the sun shone and warmed the pod, and the rain made it transparent. Inside it was damp and cosy, light in daytime and dark at night, just as it should be, and the peas kept on growing bigger, and as they sat there, they kept on thinking more and more, for after all, they had to do something.

'Are we going to stay here for ever?' each one of them said. 'I'd hate to harden from so much sitting about. I almost believe that outside there is something, too.'

The weeks went by. The peas were turning yellow and the pod was turning yellow.

'The whole world is turning yellow!' they said.

Suddenly they felt the pod jerk; it had been picked and then put into a coat pocket with many other full pods.

'Now they will surely open us!' said the peas, and waited.

'I'd like to know which one of us will get the farthest,' said the smallest pea. **152** 'We'll soon find out.'

'What must happen, will happen,' said the biggest.

Snap! the pod burst open and all the five peas rolled into the bright sunshine. They found themselves in a child's hand; a little boy held them and said they were exactly right for his gun. And straightaway one pea was placed in the gun and was fired.

'Now I am flying into the big world! Catch me if you can!'

And it was gone.

'And I,' said the second pea, 'I will fly straight to the sun, for that is quite a pea and will suit me fine!'

And it was gone.

'We'll sleep wherever we get to,' the others said. 'But we'll end up somewhere!'

First they rolled to the ground, before ending up in the gun, but they got there in the end.

'We'll get the farthest of all!'

'What must happen, will happen!' said the last pea, and then it was fired into the air and found itself flying towards an old board under a little garret room, straight into a crevice where there was moss and soft earth; and the moss closed round it. There it stayed hidden, but not forgotten by God.

'What must happen, will happen!' said he.

In the little garret room lived a poor woman who spent her days cleaning stoves, sawing logs and doing other heavy work, for she was very strong and diligent, but she remained poor all the same. In a tiny chamber of the house lay her half-grown, only daughter. She was very delicate and frail, for she had spent the whole year in bed and it seemed that she could not live nor die.

'She will join her sister!' the woman said. 'I had two children, but it was hard for me to look after them both, so God decided to share them and took one to Himself. I should like to keep the other one, the one I have left, but He doesn't want them to be separated, so she too will go above to her sister!'

But the sick maiden lived on. She lay patiently and quietly in her bed all day, whilst her mother went out to earn a little money.

It was spring and early one morning, just when the mother wanted to leave for her work, the sick maiden looked at the bottom window pane through the little window on to the floor.

'What is that bit of green peeping out by the window pane? It is moving in the wind!'

The mother went over to the window and opened it slightly.

'Oh,' she said, 'it is a little pea, with its green petals shooting out. How did it get into this crevice? Now you have a little garden and can watch it!'

And she pulled the bed of the poorly child nearer to the window, so the girl could see the growing pea more clearly. Then the mother went to work.

'Mother, it seems to me I am getting better!' the maiden said that evening. 'The sun has shone on me so warmly today. The pea is growing so very nicely, I too want to grow and improve and get well in the sunshine!'

'If only this could happen!' said the mother, but she never thought it could be so. Nevertheless she made a little trellis for the small green herb, which had brought happiness to her child, so it would not break in the wind. She fastened the twine to the board and to the upper window frame, so the pea shoots would have something to cling to and to twist around, as they grew. And grow they did.

'Well I never! It is in bud!' the woman cried out one morning and now she, too, was filled with hope and faith that her sick daughter would get well. Her mind recalled how much livelier the little girl's speech was of late and how only the previous morning she had sat up in bed without any help, and gazed **154** with shining eyes upon her very own little pea garden.

A week later the little patient got up for the very first time for more than an hour. Happily she sat in the warm sunshine; the window was open and outside she could see the fully developed pale pink pea flower. The little girl bent her head and gently kissed its fragile leaves. It was a very special day.

'God himself must have planted this little herb and made it grow, so it would give you hope and joy, my darling child, and me too!' the mother said happily, smiling at the bloom as at God's angel.

But now to the other peas! Yes, the one who was shot into the big world, crying 'catch me if you can!' fell in a gutter and then ended in a pigeon's craw, where it lay like Jonah in the whale's stomach. The two lazy peas fared the same and got no farther, they were gobbled up by pigeons, which made them very solidly useful indeed. And the fourth, the one that wished to fly to the sun, fell in a drain and remained for days and weeks in the foul-smelling water, swelling to quite a size.

'I am growing so wonderfully fat!' said the pea. 'I may even go pop! I don't think any other pea could get any farther, or have got any farther. I am the most remarkable of all the five peas from our pod.'

And the drain showed its agreement with this.

But under the garret window stood a young girl with shining eyes, the glow of good health on her cheeks; clasping her hands over the pea flower, she thanked God for it.

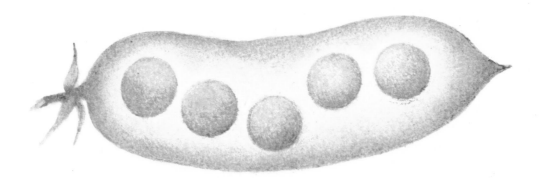

Merry Andrew

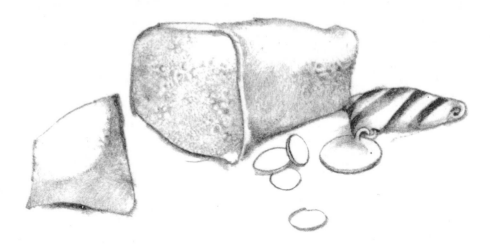

Once upon a time there was a great war, and when the war came to an end, many soldiers got their discharge. Well, Merry Andrew also got his and nothing else with it but a small loaf of army bread and four farthings in cash, and with that he went his way.

Now St. Peter had sat down by the wayside disguised as a poor beggar, and when Merry Andrew reached the spot, begged alms of him.

The soldier replied, 'Dear beggarman, what am I to give you? I've been a soldier and have got my discharge, and have nothing else but this small loaf of army bread and four farthings in cash. When that is gone I'll have to go begging just like you. Even so I'll give you something.' Then he divided the loaf into four parts, gave the apostle one of them and added a farthing.

St. Peter thanked him, went on, and once again crossed the soldier's way as a beggar but in a different guise. When the latter came along he begged him for a gift as before. Merry Andrew spoke the same as before, and again gave him a quarter of the loaf and a farthing.

St. Peter thanked him and went on, and for the third time, in another shape, he sat down as a beggar by the wayside, and addressed Merry Andrew. And even the third quarter of the loaf did Merry Andrew give him, and the third farthing.

St. Peter gave his thanks, and Merry Andrew went forth, and now he had no more than a quarter of the loaf and one farthing left. With that he went into an inn, ate the bread, and used the farthing to order some beer to go with it. When he was ready, he journeyed onwards, and again St. Peter, this time disguised as a discharged soldier, stopped him saying,

'Good day, comrade, can you give me a piece of bread and a farthing for a drink?'

'Where am I to get it?' answered Merry Andrew. 'I've got my discharge and nothing else but a loaf of army bread and four farthings in cash. I met three beggars on the road and gave each of them a quarter of my bread and one farthing. The last quarter I ate in an inn, and with the farthing I bought myself a drink. Now it's all out, and if you haven't anything left either, we could go begging together.'

'No,' said St. Peter, 'we needn't go quite as far as that. I know a little about healing and with that I should earn enough to provide for myself.'

'Well, I know nothing about that,' said Merry Andrew, 'so I must go begging all by myself.'

'Just come with me,' said St. Peter, 'and if I earn anything, you shall have half of it.'

'That's fair enough,' said Merry Andrew. And so they set out on their way together.

Then they came to a peasant's cottage where they heard heart-rending cries and lamentations. So they went in, and there a man was lying dangerously ill and almost dying. His wife was wailing and weeping loudly.

'Stop your wailing and weeping,' said St. Peter. 'I will make your husband whole again.' He took an ointment out of his pocket, and cured the sick man immediately so that he could get up and was in perfect health again. With great rejoicing the man and his wife said, 'How can we reward you? What shall we give you?'

St. Peter, however, would not take anything, and the more the peasant and his wife begged him to, the more he refused. But Merry Andrew nudged St. Peter, saying, 'Do take something, we badly need it.'

At last the peasant woman brought a lamb and told St. Peter that he really must take it but he wouldn't have it. Then Merry Andrew nudged him in the side and said, 'Do take it, you silly devil, we could really do with it.'

So finally St. Peter said, 'All right, I will take the lamb, but I am not going to carry it. You must carry it if you want it.'

'I'll carry it all right,' said Merry Andrew, and took it on his shoulder.

Then they set off and came into a forest. By then the lamb began to weigh Merry Andrew down, and being hungry he said to St. Peter, 'Look, that's a nice place. There we might cook the lamb and eat it.'

'I don't mind,' answered St. Peter, 'but I know nothing about cooking. If you want to do the cooking, there is a kettle for you. Meanwhile, I'll go and walk about a little till it is ready. But you mustn't start eating before I am back again. I'll make sure to be on time.'

'Well, go then,' said Merry Andrew, 'I can cook and I'll manage all right.'

Thereupon St. Peter went away, and Merry Andrew killed the lamb, made a fire, threw the meat into the kettle, and boiled it. The lamb was quite ready but still the apostle was not back yet. Merry Andrew took it out of the kettle, carved it, and found the heart. 'That's supposed to be the best,' said he and tasted it, but finally ate it all up.

At last St. Peter came back and said, 'You may eat the whole lamb yourself. I'll just have the heart, give me that.'

Then Merry Andrew took a knife and fork, and made as if he was anxiously looking about among the lamb's flesh, but could not find the heart all the same. Finally he said, 'There just isn't one.'

'Well, where can it be?' said the apostle.

'I don't know,' replied Merry Andrew, 'but look, what fools we both are looking for the lamb's heart and neither of us remembering that a lamb has no heart.'

'Oh,' said St. Peter, 'that's a new one on me. Every animal has a heart, why shouldn't the lamb have one?'

'No, of course not, brother,' said Merry Andrew. 'A lamb just hasn't got a heart. Give it another thought, and you'll come to realize that it really hasn't got one.'

'All right, all right,' said St. Peter, 'if there isn't any heart, then I needn't eat anything of the lamb, you can eat it all yourself.'

'Well, what I can't eat now, I'll take along in my knapsack,' said Merry Andrew, and he ate half the lamb and put the rest in his knapsack.

They went on, and then St. Peter made a stream of water flow across their path, and they had to wade through it.

St. Peter said, 'You go ahead.'

'No,' answered Merry Andrew, 'you go ahead,' thinking as he did so, 'if the water is too deep for him, I will stay back.'

Then St. Peter strode through the water, and it only reached to his knees. Then Merry Andrew started to wade across, but the water rose and reached to his neck. Then he cried out, 'Help, help, brother.'

'Then will you confess that you have eaten the lamb's heart?' said St. Peter.

'No,' answered Merry Andrew, 'I haven't eaten it.'

Then the stream swelled even higher and rose to his mouth.

'Will you now confess that you have eaten the lamb's heart?' said St. Peter.

'No, help, help, brother,' cried the soldier.

So St. Peter asked once again, 'Will you confess that you have eaten the lamb's heart?'

'No,' answered Merry Andrew, 'I haven't eaten it.'

But St. Peter did not want to let him drown, so he made the water sink, and helped him across.

Then they went on and came to a kingdom where they heard that the King's daughter lay hopelessly ill. 'Hey ho, brother,' said the soldier to St. Peter, 'this is a chance. If we cure her, we're made for life!' Suddenly, St. Peter did not walk fast enough for him. 'Now swing your feet, brother,' he said to him, 'that we may get there in good time.'

But whatever Merry Andrew tried to do to urge and drive him on, St. Peter walked slower and slower till they heard that the Princess was dead.

'That's the end,' said Merry Andrew. 'That comes of your sleepy kind of walk.'

'You be quiet,' said St. Peter. 'I can do more than just cure the sick, I can bring the dead to life.'

'Well,' said Merry Andrew, 'if that is so, then I am well pleased, but your feat should earn us at least half the kingdom.'

Then they went to the royal palace where everybody was plunged into deep sorrow. However, when St. Peter told the King he would bring his daughter back to life, he was taken to her and said, 'Bring me a kettle of water.'

When it was brought, he ordered everybody out. Merry Andrew alone was allowed to stay with him. Then he cut off all the dead girl's limbs, threw them into the water, lit a fire under the kettle, and let them boil. When all the flesh had come off the bones, he took out the fine white bones, laid them on a table, and arranged and set them together in their natural order. When that was done, he stepped towards her and said three times, 'In the name of the Most Holy Trinity, dead woman, arise!'

And at the third bidding the King's daughter arose, alive, whole and beautiful.

This made the King rejoice greatly, and he said to St. Peter, 'Demand your reward. Even if it is half of my kingdom, it shall be yours.'

But St. Peter answered, 'I desire nothing in return.'

'Oh, holy simplicity!' thought Merry Andrew to himself, nudged his comrade and said, 'don't be so stupid! You may not want anything, but I need
160 something.'

St. Peter still refused to take anything but the King saw how eager the other was to have something, and ordered his treasurer to fill Merry Andrew's knapsack with gold.

Thereupon they went on their way, and when they came to a forest, St. Peter said to Merry Andrew, 'Now we will divide the gold.'

'Yes,' he answered, 'let's do that.'

Then St. Peter divided the gold, and divided it into three heaps.

Merry Andrew thought to himself, 'What a crazy idea he's got in his head now. He makes three lots, and there are only two of us!'

'Now I have divided it quite exactly,' said St. Peter. 'One share for me, one share for you, and one for the man who ate the lamb's heart.'

'Oh, I ate that,' answered Merry Andrew and swiftly pocketed the gold. 'You can trust me when I say it.'

'How can that be true?' said St. Peter. 'Indeed, you said a lamb hasn't got a heart.'

'Oh goodness, brother, what an idea! Of course a lamb has a heart like any other animal. Why should it be the only one to have none?'

'Well, all right, all right,' said St. Peter, 'keep the gold yourself, but I will not stay with you any longer. I will go my way alone.'

'Please yourself, brother,' answered the soldier. 'Good-bye and farewell.'

Then St. Peter took a different road, and Merry Andrew thought, 'It's just as well that he is trotting off, he certainly is a droll fellow!'

Though he now had enough money he did not know how to manage it, and he squandered it, gave it away, and was penniless again after a short time.

Then Merry Andrew came to a country where he heard that the King's daughter had died.

'Oh, ho!' he thought, 'this may come in useful. I'll bring her back to life again, and see that I get paid for it handsomely.' So he went to the King, and offered to raise the dead girl to life again.

The King had heard that a discharged soldier was roaming the land bringing the dead back to life and thought that Merry Andrew was the man. Something, however, made him unsure about him, and first he consulted his councillors. They said he might as well let him try it, since his daughter was dead anyway.

Then Merry Andrew had a kettle of water brought, and bade everyone go out. He cut off all the girl's limbs, threw them into the water, and made a fire underneath, just as he had seen St. Peter do. The water began to boil, and the flesh fell off. Then he took out the bones and laid them on the table, but he did not know the order in which to lay them and placed them in all the wrong directions.

Then he stood before them and said, 'In the name of the Most Holy Trinity, dead woman, arise!' He said it three times, but the bones did not stir. Then he said it thrice more but again in vain. 'You treasure of a girl, get up,' he cried, 'get up, or it won't go well for you.'

Suddenly St. Peter appeared in the shape of a discharged soldier. He came in through the window and said, 'You godless man, what are you up to there? How can the dead maiden arise when you have thrown her bones about in such confusion?'

'Dear brother, I did it all as well as I could,' said Merry Andrew.

Then St. Peter said, 'I will help you once more out of your predicament, but let me tell you, if you try anything like this again, you will not get away with it. Nor may you either demand or accept anything from the King for having done this.'

Then St. Peter laid the bones in the right order and said three times, 'In the name of the Most Holy Trinity, dead woman, arise.' And the King's daughter arose, healthy and beautiful as before.

Then St. Peter went away again through the window.

Merry Andrew was glad to see that it all had turned out so well, but still he was much vexed that he was unable to take anything for it.

'I would just like to know what that fellow has in his head, for what he gives with one hand he takes away with the other. It makes no sense!'

Now the King offered Merry Andrew whatever he might wish for, but he did not dare openly to take anything. However, by means of hints and cunning he got the King to have his knapsack filled with gold, and with that he went on his way.

As he was going out, St. Peter was standing at the gate and said, 'Just look what kind of a man you are! Didn't I forbid you to take anything? And here you are, with your knapsack full of gold!'

'How can I help it when they put it in?' answered Merry Andrew.

'Well, let me tell you this,' said St. Peter. 'Don't you ever dare to try anything of the kind again, or it will fare ill with you!'

'Well, brother, don't worry. Now I have gold, why should I bother about washing bones?'

'Yes,' said St. Peter, 'and a long time that gold will last! But to prevent you from treading forbidden paths again, I will endow your knapsack with the power that anything you may wish to be in it shall be there. Farewell, you will never see me again.'

'Good-bye,' said Merry Andrew. 'It's just as well you're going away. I certainly shan't follow you!' And he gave no further thought to the magic

power which had been bestowed on his knapsack.

Merry Andrew travelled about with his money and squandered and threw it away like the first time. When he had no more than four farthings left, he happened to be passing by an inn, and thought, 'The money must go,' and he ordered three farthings' worth of wine and one farthing's worth of bread.

As he was sitting there drinking, the smell of a roast goose rose up to his nose. Merry Andrew looked about and peeped, and saw that the landlord had two geese roasting in the oven. Then he recalled how his comrade had told him that anything he might wish to have in his knapsack would appear there. 'Oh ho! I must try that with the geese,' thought Merry Andrew. So he went outside the door and said, 'I wish those two roast geese out of the oven and into my knapsack.' So saying, he unbuckled his knapsack, looked in, and there they were! 'It works!' he said. 'Now I am a made man.'

Then he went away to a meadow and took out the roast geese. Just as he was enjoying his meal, two journeymen came along and stared at the goose which was still untouched with hungry eyes. 'One is enough for me,' thought Merry Andrew, and called the two journeymen and said, 'take the goose, and eat it to my good health.'

They thanked him, went with it to the inn, ordered half a bottle of wine and a loaf of bread, and began to eat.

The landlady was looking on and said to her husband, 'Those two men are eating a goose. Do go and see if it's not one of ours from the oven.'

The landlord ran up and saw it. The oven was empty! 'You pack of thieves,' he cried. 'Pay for it at once, or I'll whip you with a hazel branch!'

The two travellers said, 'We are no thieves. A discharged soldier out there in the meadow made us a gift of the goose!'

'You shan't make a fool of me,' said the landlord. 'The soldier was here, but he went out by the door like an honest fellow. I kept an eye on him. You are the thieves and shall pay!'

But they could not pay, so he took a stick and thrashed them out of the door.

Merry Andrew went his way and came to a place with a magnificent palace and a poor inn not far from it. He went to the inn and asked for a night's lodging, but the landlord would not take him in saying, 'There's no more room, the house is full of noble guests.'

'How surprising,' said Merry Andrew, 'that they come to you and not to the splendid palace.'

'Indeed,' answered the landlord, 'it's quite an affair to spend a night there. Those who did try it never came out alive again.'

'If others have tried it,' said Merry Andrew, 'I'll give it a try too.'

'You leave well alone,' said the landlord. 'It may cost you your life.'

'It won't be directly a matter of life and death,' said Merry Andrew, 'just give me the keys and a lot of food and drink to take along.'

So the host gave him the key and food and wine. With that Merry Andrew went into the palace, had a good supper, and when he at last felt sleepy, he lay down on the floor, for no beds were there.

He soon fell asleep, but in the night he was awakened by a great noise. When he roused himself, he saw nine ugly devils in the room, who had formed a circle and were dancing round him.

'Well, dance as long as you like, but none must come too close,' said Merry Andrew.

But the devils pressed on ever closer, and almost stepped on his face with their dirty feet.

'Be quiet, you devil phantoms!' he said, but they behaved worse and worse. Then Merry Andrew got angry and cried, 'I will soon make you quiet!' and he got hold of a leg of a chair and struck out in the very midst of them. But nine devils against one soldier were too much in the end, and when he struck out at the one before him, the others at the back seized him by the hair and pulled at it unmercifully. 'You pack of devils!' cried Merry Andrew. 'This is too much, but just you wait! Into my knapsack, all nine of you!'

In a trice they were in it, and he buckled it up, and threw it into a corner. All at once everything was still, and Merry Andrew lay down again and slept till it was bright day.

Then came the innkeeper and the nobleman who owned the palace to see how he had got on. When they saw him safe and sound they were amazed and said, 'Didn't the ghosts harm you?'

'Certainly not,' sait Merry Andrew. 'I've got them, all the nine of them, in my knapsack! You may now live in your palace quite at ease. No one will ever haunt it again.'

The nobleman thanked him, gave him rich presents, and asked him to remain in his service, saying he would take care of him for the rest of his life.

'No,' replied Merry Andrew. 'I'm used to wandering about, I'll move on.'

So he went away, and stepped into a blacksmith's yard, laid the knapsack with the nine devils in it on the anvil and asked the blacksmith and his apprentices to give it a good pounding. Then they pounded with their big hammers for all they were worth so that the devils raised a most pitiable howl.

When he opened his knapsack again, eight devils were dead, but one, who had been sitting in a crease, was still alive, slipped out, and went back to Hell.

Then Merry Andrew travelled about the world for a long time, and there **165** would be a great deal to tell about him if only one knew. But at last he grew old and began to think about his end. So he went to a hermit who was known to be a pious man and said to him, 'I am tired of roaming about and now want to strive to get into the kingdom of Heaven.'

The hermit replied, 'There are two roads, one wide and pleasant leading to Hell, the other, narrow and rough, leading to Heaven.'

'I would be a fool,' thought Merry Andrew, 'to take the narrow, rough road.'

So he set out and went the wide and pleasant way, and finally came to a big black gate, which was the gate of Hell. Merry Andrew knocked, and the porter looked to see who was there. But when he saw Merry Andrew he was terrified, for he happened to be the very ninth devil who had been shut up in the knapsack and had got away with a black eye. He quickly pushed the bolt in again, and ran to the chief of the devils, and said, 'There is a fellow outside with a knapsack and wants to come in, but for the life of you don't let him in, or he will wish the whole of Hell into his knapsack. Once he had me pitilessly pounded in it.'

So they shouted out to Merry Andrew that he should go away again.

'If they don't want me here,' he thought, 'I will see if I can find a lodging in Heaven, after all, I've got to stay somewhere!'

So he turned about, and went on till he got to the gate of Heaven. He knocked at it and St. Peter happened to be there. Merry Andrew recognized him at once and thought, 'Here I find an old friend of mine, I should get on better.'

But St. Peter said, 'You would like to get into Heaven, wouldn't you?'

'Please let me in, brother,' pleaded Merry Andrew. 'I must get in somewhere. If they had taken me into Hell, I shouldn't have come here.'

'No,' said St. Peter, 'you shan't get in here.'

'Then, if you won't let me in, take your knapsack back, for I won't have anything at all of yours any more,' said Merry Andrew.

'Well, give it here,' said St. Peter.

Then Merry Andrew gave him the knapsack through the bars, and St. Peter took it and hung it beside his seat. Then Merry Andrew said, 'Now I wish myself inside my knapsack!' In a trice, he was inside it, and sitting in Heaven, and St. Peter had to let him stay there.

Fate and Riches

Once a long time ago in Baghdad there lived two good friends, Sad and Sadi. Though Sadi was rich and Sad was as poor as a church mouse, they loved each other dearly. Neither would dream of doing a single thing without the other and they agreed on all questions except one. This one exception they argued about forever.

Sadi, the rich man, believed that money could buy happiness.

'The more money a person has,' he said, 'the more independent of others he is, and the better and more comfortably he can live.'

But Sad, the poor man, thought differently. 'Riches are useful and important enough,' he would say, 'but happiness is a matter of Fate. If Fate is against you what good is money?'

'What nonsense!' Sadi objected. 'Hard work and cleverness will bring riches, so anyone can guide his own fate.'

Every time they met they argued about this matter. Then one day, as they were strolling together along a street in Baghdad, Sadi suddenly said:

'Let us find out which one of us is right. Hasan, the rope-maker, lives nearby. He makes ropes from morning till night. But, as he has five children, he earns scarcely enough to keep them, his wife and himself alive. If I were to give him two hundred dinars, he could buy more flax and employ an assistant too. He would grow rich in no time at all. Surely you must see that he would then be happier!'

Sad was not convinced but agreed to test his friend's idea. And so the two went together into Hasan's shabby little shop.

'How long have you been a rope-maker, Hasan?' Sadi asked.

'All my life, sir,' Hasan replied. 'And this shop was my father's and my grandfather's before me.'

'A very long time indeed,' said Sadi. 'But tell me, why is it that you can barely scrape a living?'

The rope-maker's face was full of sorrow.

'With the money I earn I can buy only very little flax for the next day. And what is left scarcely keeps hunger away from my door...'

'What if I were to give you, Hasan, two hundred dinars?' Sadi asked. 'Would you spend them, or would you use them to make your business grow?'

'Oh, dear sir, if you truly mean what you say, then in no time at all I should become the richest rope-maker in Baghdad,' Hasan answered.

Sadi smiled, and handing a purse to the rope-maker said, 'Here are two hundred dinars exactly. In six months we shall return to see what changes for the better have occurred in your life.'

Night had almost fallen, so Hasan closed the shop and hurried home. He wanted to hide the purse straight away in a safe place. But, alas, there was not a single cupboard or a single drawer in his poor little house. So he took out two dinars to buy a little food and wound the rest securely inside his turban.

He hurried off to the market to buy meat for supper. It had been so long since he, his wife or children had tasted good food. He chose a fine piece of

meat and feeling pleased and happy he started off for home. And as he walked he made all sorts of plans which would change his poor life.

But, alas! Just as he was nearing home and his head was full of wonderful ideas, a hungry vulture dived out of the darkening sky. It made straight for Hasan's supper. The rope-maker defended himself bravely against the claws of the thieving bird. But in the struggle his turban fell from his head to the ground. The vulture forgetting the meat, at once pounced on it. It screeched once and seizing the turban in its beak flew off. It was as if the evil bird knew that now it had caused far greater distress to Hasan.

The poor rope-maker almost burst into tears. All his wonderful dreams and plans had vanished in an instant. And what, he thought miserably, was he going to say the kind rich man when he returned in six months?

Allah provided and Allah took away, Hasan said to himself at last with **169** a deep sigh. And next morning he set to work again and toiled just as hard and for just as little as he had always done.

Sadi and Sad appeared in the rope-maker's shop exactly six months later. Hasan wasted no time in telling them of the misfortunes which had befallen him. As he listened Sadi kept shaking his head. He could not believe Hasan's story.

'But this man has a reputation for honesty,' Sad defended him. 'Surely you must see that I am right, that it is Fate that decides what is to be. Riches alone cannot bring happiness.'

'I cannot agree with you,' said Sadi, 'but I shall give the rope-maker a second chance. Here are another two hundred dinars.' And he tossed a second purse to Hasan. 'Now,' he said, 'surely you can keep your promise. In three months' time I shall return to see for myself.'

Sad and Sadi then went away, leaving Hasan on his knees, calling after them his words of thanks.

'This time I shall find a much safer hiding place for the money,' Hasan promised himself. And he thought about it all the way home.

But the idea only came to him after he had shut the door behind him. In a corner stood an old jug filled with bran. This, he thought, was the ideal hiding place.

There was not a soul in the house, so quickly Hasan poured some of the bran out of the jug. Then putting the purse of dinars inside, he covered it over with bran.

Satisfied, Hasan hurried back to his shop. Little did he guess what was to happen that day.

In the middle of the afternoon a pedlar stopped at his door. He was selling clay powder which the wives of poor men used to wash their hair. Hasan's wife would like to have bought the powder... but as she had not a single copper, she wondered what she could offer instead. Her glance fell upon the jug filled with bran. Such a thing was of no use to them at all. At last she persuaded the pedlar to take the jug in exchange for the powder. Who knows how far away the money was by the time the rope-maker returned home? Oh, how he groaned, how he mourned when he discovered what had happened. He blamed himself for keeping the whole affair secret from his wife. But more than anything he feared what Sadi and Sad would have to say when they returned.

The three months flew past like lightning and once again the two friends were standing before the miserable Hasan, waiting to hear his story.

'You're a good-for-nothing and a spendthrift,' the rich Sadi shouted at the end. 'I don't believe a single word of it.'

But Sad only said, 'Now you can see that riches will not win over Fate. I believe that it will take only a single copper to make this man happy. Rope-maker, please accept my gift this time, and do with it as you wish. We shall meet again in three months' time...'

The poor rope-maker was relieved that everything had gone so smoothly. He took the offered coin gratefully, and saw the two friends to the door with many bows and words of thanks.

He forgot all about the copper till late that evening, when a neighbour of his, who was a fisherman, called on him and asked, 'Please, Hasan, lend me just one copper. I need to have my nets mended before tomorrow morning...'

Why shouldn't one beggar help another? After all, whoever heard of anyone growing rich from one little coin?...

'Thank you for helping me, Hasan. Tomorrow my first catch shall be yours,' said the fisherman, as he hurried out with his nets.

What a surprise was waiting for Hasan the next day: The fisherman came to him carrying in his arms a fish as long as a table.

'Never have I caught such a large fish,' he laughed. 'But it is yours, neighbour. It was the first one in my net.'

Hasan did not want to accept such a fine gift, but the fisherman would not listen to his protests. So he thanked his neighbour and told his wife to cook the fish for supper.

Gladly his wife set to work. Suddenly she caught sight of something bright inside the fish. It shone like a fragment of coloured glass. The children saw it too and begged to be given the little glass to play with.

Their mother let them have it and off into the street they ran to show it to their friends. They played with their new toy until daylight had faded and the little glass gleamed and glittered in the darkness.

It so happened that a goldsmith was walking past and his eye was attracted by the glitter. He bent over the children to find out what they were playing with. He was amazed to see a magnificent diamond, more beautiful than any diamond he had ever seen. This time Fate was on Hasan's side. The goldsmith was an honest man, and he paid him one hundred thousand dinars for the precious stone.

The poor rope-maker was rich at last. Before the month was out, he had bought out every rope-making workshop in Baghdad. Outside the city he had a fine palace built in the centre of a beautiful park. Instead of a mean little shop, a large and grand building belonging to Hadji Hasan the Rope-Maker stood in the square.

When Sadi and Sad paid him a visit, they did not recognize the place. Only the familiar face of Hasan made them enter and listen to his tale.

Afterwards the grateful Hasan invited them both to visit his elegant palace outside the city. How they admired his splendid gardens full of flowers, trees, shrubs and birds from many lands.

But even now Sadi argued. 'I really can't believe, my friend, that you have come to all these riches thanks to one single copper coin. To find a diamond inside a fish too is just as amazing as losing the four hundred dinars before. Go on, own up that the money I gave you has helped you to this fortune!'

Hasan turned red at the injustice of this remark. The kindly Sad, seeing this, quickly began to praise Hasan's lovely garden, trying to cover up the awkward moment. Pointing to a nearby tree, he said, 'Look Hasan, not only have you the most unusual foreign plants, but also the most unusual nests.'

It was true — something white gleamed among the branches, something which no bird could have built. Hasan at once commanded his slaves to bring

him the strange nest.

One glance was enough. He could scarcely believe his eyes. But it was indeed his old turban, the one the greedy vulture had carried off.

'At last here is proof that I have spoken the truth,' he said, turning to Sadi. 'In this very turban your money is hidden.' The rich man unwound the material. The dinars were still inside, just as Hasan knew they would be. Thereupon Hasan, Sad and Sadi too rejoiced at this happy find. And the good Sad hoped that surely now his friend would be convinced of Hasan's honesty.

But it was not so. As all three were returning to Baghdad on horseback, Sadi turned to Hasan once more.

'By bread and salt, which are the mark of our brotherhood, tell me the truth. Did you not find the second purse of two hundred dinars helpful in making your fortune?'

What could Hasan reply? He was filled with bitterness at Sadi's lack of faith **173** in his word. But little did he dream that his truthfulness would soon be proved a second time.

It was dead of night when at last they reached Baghdad. The horses were worn out and hungry. Fodder must be found at once for the poor beasts.

The whole town was asleep and for a time they searched in vain. At last a slave returned to Hasan, his master. In his hands he carried an old jug.

'This is the only thing I could find, my master. And I fear the bran it holds is old but the whole town has closed down till morning.'

But Hasan stopped him. He recognized that old jug.

'Put your hand into this jug, Sadi,' he commanded. 'Surely you will recognize your own purse.'

And so for a second time the rich man was convinced. At last he had to agree with his friend Sad. 'Riches do not lead to riches. Only the will of Allah, written in the Book of Destinies, decides what is to be will be.'

The Little Match Girl

It was dreadfully cold. The snow was falling fast and it was almost dark. This was the last evening of the old year, New Year's Eve. And in this cruel cold and darkness a poor little girl was still wandering about the streets, with bare head and feet. When she had left her home she had slippers on, but they were much too large—indeed, they were last worn by her mother, that is how large they were. And whilst the little girl was running across the street, to get out of the way of two fast carriages, they had dropped off her feet. One of the slippers was lost for good; a boy ran off with the other, he thought it might come in useful one day as a cradle.

The little girl walked along the street, her bare feet quite red and blue with the cold. She carried a little bundle of matches in her hand, and a whole pile of them in her tattered old apron. No one had bought anything from her the whole day; no one had given her a single penny. She wandered through the streets starving and frozen, a pitiful little thing.

Snowflakes fell on her long, golden hair, which curled charmingly round her shoulders, but the little girl did not think about her beauty at all. Lights were glimmering behind every window and the wonderful smell of roast goose came to her from several houses; it was, after all, New Year's Eve! It was of this the little girl thought.

She found a corner made by two houses, one of which jutted out into the street slightly further than the other, and there she crouched. She drew her little feet right under her, but could not warm them—she was even colder than before. Yet she dared not go home, for she had sold no matches and had earned not a single penny. Her father would only beat her and besides, her home was almost as cold as the street, they hardly had a roof over their heads and the wind always whistled through their attic room, though they filled the worst chinks with straw and rags.

Her little hands were stiff with cold. Oh, how nice it would be to warm them over the flame of a match! If only she dared take one from the bundle, strike it against the wall, and warm her fingers... she drew one out, and with a strike—how it sparkled, how it burned! It was a bright, warm flame, like the flame of a candle, and she held her hands over it.

What a wondrous light it was! It seemed to the little girl that she was sitting by a large iron stove with brass ornaments and a brass chimney; how beautifully blazed the fire within! The little girl stretched out her feet to warm them too—but alas, at that moment the flame died. The stove vanished and the little girl sat on the cold pavement with the burnt match in her hand.

She struck a second match against the wall; it kindled and flamed, and as its glow fell on the wall, the wall became as transparent as a veil and through it the little girl could see right into the room. A table stood inside, spread with a sparkling white damask cloth and the most delicate china; the deliciously smelling roast goose stood at one end, stuffed with apples and plums! And,

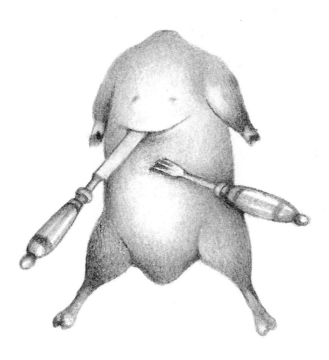

nicest of all, the goose, with knife and fork in her breast, jumped down from the dish, and waddled along the floor right up to the poor little girl. But then the match went out and all the little girl could see was the cold, grey wall.

She lit yet another match. As it flared up, she found herself before the most beautiful Christmas-tree. It was even larger and prettier than the one she had seen last Christmas through the glass door of a rich merchant's house. Hundreds of candles lit up the green branches, and gay decorations, such as she had seen in shop windows, looked down upon her from the tree. The child stretched out her little hands towards them—then the match burnt out. The Christmas candles, however, burned on, rising higher and higher and the little girl could see that they became bright stars in the sky. One of them fell, drawing a long, fiery tail through the sky.

'Someone is dying!' whispered the little girl, for her old grandmother—the only person who had been kind to her, and who was now dead—used to say, 'Whenever a star falls, an immortal spirit returns to God.'

The child struck yet another match against the wall; it flamed up, and in its glow her dear grandmother appeared, so bright and happy, and as gentle and loving as always.

'Grandmother!' cried the little girl. 'Take me with you! I know you will disappear when the match dies—you will vanish like the warm stove, like the lovely roast goose and the beautiful Christmas-tree!' and she quickly lit the rest of the matches left in the bundle, to keep her grandmother as long as she could. The matches gave out such a splendid glow, that it was brighter than daylight. Never before had grandmother looked so pretty and so tall. She took the little girl in her arms, and together they flew in joy and in glory high, so high, till they came to the place where cold, hunger and pain are never known—they were in Paradise!

But in the freezing morning-hour, a little girl crouched in the corner of the wall, her cheeks glowing, her lips smiling—but she was dead. She had frozen to death on the last night of the old year. The dawn of the New Year lit up the lifeless child, crouched there with the matches in her lap, with the one bundle burnt out.

'She wanted to warm herself,' people said. But none of them knew of the wondrous visions she had seen, or the bright glory in which she left with her grandmother into the joys of the New Year.

The Snow Queen

First story

*The Mirror
and its Fragments*

Now then, let us start. When we get to the end of the story, we shall know more than we know now. It is about a wicked magician. He was one of the wickedest of all, a real demon!

One day he made a mirror which had the magic power of making everything good and beautiful that looked into it, shrink almost to nothing; but all the things which were useless and ugly were thoroughly magnified and grew even worse. The loveliest landscapes reflected in this mirror would look like boiled spinach and the very nicest people would turn ugly or would stand on their heads without any stomachs, and their faces would be so distorted that no one could recognize them. Moreover, if one of them had a freckle, he could be sure that in the mirror it would spread all over his nose and mouth. This was most entertaining, thought the demon. If a kindly, pious thought passed through someone's head, the mirror showed such a grimace, that the demon couldn't help but roar at his magnificent invention.

All those who went to the School of Magic—for he had his own School of Magic—said to everyone that a miracle had happened. For the first time, they said, one could see what the world and the people really looked like. They ran with the mirror from place to place throughout the world, and in the end there wasn't a country, or a man left who had not been distorted in it. Then they decided to fly up to Heaven, to make fun of the angels and God himself. The higher they flew with the mirror, the more the mirror grimaced, till they could hardly hold on to it. Then all at once the mirror, grinning devilishly, started to shake so much, that it shot out of their hands and crashed to the ground, where it broke into hundreds of millions, billions, and even more little pieces. And this is why it caused even more unhappiness than before, for some of the fragments were hardly larger than a grain of sand and they flew about in the world. When they got into people's eyes, they stuck fast there, and the people saw everything the wrong way, or they had eyes only for what was bad. For each tiny fragment of the mirror had retained the same power that the whole mirror had had. Some people even got a tiny splinter of the mirror wedged in their hearts, and this was indeed dreadful. Such a heart would then be like a lump of ice. Some pieces were large enough to be used as window-panes, but it was a mistake to look through them at your friends. Other pieces found their way into the glass of spectacles, and then everything went wrong when the people put their glasses on in order to see properly and fairly.

The wicked demon laughed and laughed, till his sides ached—it was most enjoyable the way it tickled.

There are still some little splinters of the glass flying about in the air.

And now, listen to this!

Second story

A Little Boy
and a Little Girl

In a large town, where there are so many houses and people that there is not enough room for everyone to have their own little garden, and where most people therefore have to be content with flowers in pots, there in that town lived two poor children, whose garden was somewhat larger than a flower-pot. They were not brother and sister, but they loved each other just as much. Their parents were neighbours, and lived opposite in two attics; and where the roof of one house touched the other and where the gutter ran along between, there was a tiny window jutting out of each house. You only had to step across the gutter to get from one window to the other.

The parents of these children each had a large wooden box standing outside their window, in which they grew the herbs they needed, and also a little rose-tree. There was one in each box and it grew beautifully. The parents then had the idea of placing their boxes across the gutter in such a way, that they almost reached from window to window and looked exactly like two flower-beds. Pea vines hung down over the boxes, and the little rose-trees were shooting out, entwining their long shoots round the windows, bending over to each other. It looked like a festive arch of greenery and flowers. As the wooden boxes were rather high, and the children knew they must not climb on them, they were now and then allowed to step out through the window to each other and to sit on the little stools under the rose-trees. It was so pleasant for them to play there together.

The winter, of course, put an end to such pleasures. The windows were quite often frozen up and then the children would heat coins on the stove, and, pressing them against the frozen pane, would make little peepholes, clear and round. And behind each of them a bright little eye would sparkle.

The boy was called Kay and the little girl's name was Gerda. In summer they could get to each other in a single leap from the window but in winter they first had to run down so many stairs, and then climb all the way up again, while outside a snowstorm raged.

'White bees are swarming out there!' said the old grandmother.

'Have they a queen bee?' asked the little boy, for he knew that real bees have one.

'Indeed they have!' the grandmother replied. 'She flies in the thickest of the swarm. She is the biggest of them all, and never stays quietly on the ground, but flies up into the black cloud again. Many a wintry night she flies through the streets of the town and peers through the windows, and then the windows freeze in a strange, wondrous way, as if they were flowers.'

'Yes, I have seen them!' both the children cried, knowing now that this was true.

'And can the Snow Queen come in to us?' asked the little girl.

'Do let her come!' said the little boy. 'Then I'll put her on the hot stove, and she will melt.'

But the grandmother stroked his head and told them other stories.

That evening, when little Kay was back home and half undressed, he

climbed on to the stool by the window and peeped out through the little hole. A few snowflakes fell outside just then and one of these—the largest one—came to rest on the edge of one of the wooden flower-boxes. The snowflake grew and grew, and in the end it took the form of a woman dressed in the finest white veils, which seemed to be made of millions of shining starry flakes. She was extremely beautiful and grand, but she was made of ice, glittering, dazzling ice—yet she was alive. Her eyes shone like two bright stars, but there was no rest nor repose in them. She nodded towards the window and beckoned with her hand. The little boy grew frightened and jumped off the stool and, at that moment, it seemed that some big bird flew past the window.

The next day the frost bit hard, but soon afterwards it thawed, and then came spring—the sun shone, green shoots sprang from the ground, the swallows built their nests, the windows were opened and the children sat down again in their little garden in the gutter high up in the roofs.

The roses blossomed beautifully that summer. The little girl had learnt a hymn in which there was something about roses; it reminded her of her own. And she sang this hymn to the little boy and he sang with her:

> *'We'll hear little Jesus down below*
> *In the valley, where sweet roses grow!'*

And both the children held each other by the hand, kissed the roses, and gazed into God's bright sunshine, talking to it, as if little Jesus himself was there. What lovely summer days these were and how delightful it was to sit together by the rose-trees, which seemed as though they would never stop blooming!

One day Kay and Gerda were sitting outside, examining a picture-book of animals and birds, when, just as the clock in the high church tower was striking five, Kay said: 'Oh dear! What's this sharp pain in my heart! And now I've got something in my eye!'

The little girl put her arms round his neck. Kay blinked his eyes. No, there was nothing to be seen.

'I think it's gone!' he said. But gone it had not. It was one of the glass-splinters from the magic mirror; you remember, that horrid glass which made everything big and good that was reflected in it become small and nasty, while everything mean and ugly became magnified and every fault became plain to seen at once. Poor Kay! A little splinter also got right into his heart. Shortly it would turn into a lump of ice. It hurt no more now, but the glass was there.

185

'Why are you crying?' asked Kay. 'It makes you so ugly! There's nothing wrong with me! Ugh!' he cried suddenly, 'this rose is all worm-eaten! And look, that one is all lop-sided. How ugly these roses really are! They're like the boxes they're growing in!' Then he kicked the box hard and tore off both roses.

'Kay, what are you doing!' cried the little girl. When he saw how it grieved her, he pulled off another rose and ran in through his window, away from kind little Gerda.

After this, whenever Gerda came to him with the picture-book he said it was for babies, and whenever the grandmother told stories, he interrupted her with some 'but' or another. And whenever he had the chance, he would hide behind her, put on her spectacles and speak just as she did. He imitated her perfectly, and this made people laugh at him. Very soon he could mimic all the people in the street. He would imitate anything that was odd or not very nice about them, and so people said, 'That lad has a remarkable head on his shoulders!' But it was the work of the glass in his eye, and the glass that was wedged in his heart. This was why he tormented even little Gerda, who loved him with all her heart.

One winter's day, when the snowflakes were tumbling down, he came out with a large magnifying glass in his hand, and holding out his blue coat-tail, he let the snowflakes fall on to it.

'Look in the glass, Gerda!' he said. Each flake now was much larger and looked like an exquisite flower, or a ten-pointed star. It was indeed a beautiful sight.

'Isn't it extraordinary!' said Kay. 'These are far more interesting than real flowers! And there isn't a single blemish in them, they are absolutely perfect — so long as they don't melt!'

Soon after this Kay came back wearing thick mittens and carrying a sledge on his back. He shouted right into Gerda's ear, 'I've been allowed to sledge in the big square where the others are playing!' and he was gone.

The boldest boys in the square often tied their sledges to the farmer's cart, and thus rode a good way along with him. This was great fun. When they were at the height of their enjoyment, along came a big sleigh. It was painted white and the person sitting in it was wrapped in a rough white fur coat and wore a rough white fur cap. The sledge drove twice round the square, and by then Kay managed to tie his little sledge to it—and now he was being pulled along. Faster and faster they rode, making straight for the nearest street. The person who drove the large sleigh kept turning round, nodding kindly to Kay, as if they had known each other of old. Whenever Kay tried to untie his sledge, the

driver would nod again, and so Kay stayed put. They drove right out of the city gates. And then the snow started to fall so thickly and so fast, that the boy could not see his own hand, as they tore along. So he let go of the rope, trying to free himself from the large sleigh. But it was no use; his sledge held on fast, and flew like the wind. So he started to shout, shout loudly, but no one heard him and the sleigh went racing on through the snow-storm. From time to time his little sledge gave a jump, as though passing over ditches and hedges. He was really terrified, and he so wanted to say the prayer 'Our Father', but all he could remember was the multiplication table.

The snowflakes grew bigger and bigger, till in the end they looked like big white hens. All at once they flew to one side, the sleigh stopped and the driver stood up. The fur coat and cap were entirely of snow, and the person who wore them was a lady, tall and slender, and dazzlingly white—it was the Snow Queen!

'We have driven far,' she said. 'But how freezing it is! Wrap yourself in my bearskin coat!' And she sat him in the sleigh by her side, and wrapped her coat around him; he felt as if he were sinking into a snowdrift.

'Are you still cold?' she asked, and then kissed his forehead. Ugh! That kiss was colder than ice and went straight to his heart, which was already half ice. He thought he should die, but only for a moment, then he felt better for it, and no longer felt the cold.

'My sledge! Don't forget my sledge!' he remembered it first. And his sledge was tied to one of the white hens which flew behind with the sledge on her back. The Snow Queen kissed Kay once more, and he forgot little Gerda, her grandmother, and everyone at home.

'Now you will not have any more kisses!' said the Snow Queen, 'or I'll kiss you to death!'

Kay looked at her. She was so beautiful! He could not imagine a wiser and lovelier face. She no longer appeared to him to be of ice, as when she had sat outside the window, beckoning him. In his eyes she was perfect, and he felt no fear. He told her how well he could count in his head and that he could do fractions, and that he knew how many square miles each country had and how many inhabitants. And all the time she smiled. It occurred to him then that all he knew was not, after all, enough, and he gazed up into the great wide space above. And the Queen flew with him, rising high above the black cloud, while the storm raged and roared, as if it were singing some old, old songs. They flew over forests and lakes, over seas and lands. Beneath them the cold wind whistled, the wolves howled, the snow glittered and over the plain flew black, screeching crows. High above shone the moon, so big and bright and Kay watched it through the long, long winter's night. During the day he slept at the feet of the Snow Queen.

Third story

The Flower Garden of the Woman who Knew Magic

But what happened to little Gerda, when Kay did not return? Where could he be? No one knew, no one could explain. The boys could only say that they had seen him fasten his sledge to a beautiful large sleigh, which had driven off into the street and then through the city gates. No one knew where he could be and many tears were shed; little Gerda cried so much and for so long. Then they said that he must be dead, that he must have been drowned in the river which flowed past the town. Oh, what long, gloomy winter days these were!

At last came the spring with its warm sunshine.

'Kay is dead and gone!' said little Gerda.

'This I do not believe!' said the sunshine.

'He is dead and gone!' said she to the swallows.

'This we do not believe!' replied the swallows, and in the end little Gerda herself did not believe it.

'I will put on my new red shoes,' she said one morning; 'the ones which Kay has never seen. Then I'll go down to the river and ask after him.'

It was early morning. She kissed her old grandmother, who was asleep, put on the red shoes and went out alone through the gates of the town to the river.

'Is it true that you have taken my little playmate from me?' said she. 'I will give you my red shoes, if you return him to me!'

And the waves seemed to be beckoning to her strangely. So she took off her red shoes, the dearest things she had, and threw both into the river. But they fell close to the shore and the ripples brought them straight back to her on the bank. It seemed the river did not want to accept the dearest things she had, now that she no longer had little Kay. But Gerda thought she had not thrown the little shoes far enough, so she stepped into a little boat which lay among the rushes and, standing at the farthest end of it, she threw the shoes into the water. But the boat was not tied up, and her jerky movement made it float **189** away from the bank. Gerda swiftly tried to get back on shore, but before she was able to do so the boat was more than a yard out and was floating away faster and faster.

Little Gerda was terribly frightened and she started to cry, but no one heard her but the sparrows. And they could not carry her ashore, but they flew along the bank, twittering as if to comfort her: 'Here we are, here we are!' The boat raced with the current. Little Gerda sat in it perfectly still in her stockinged feet. Her little red shoes floated behind the boat, but they could not reach it, for the boat glided on faster than they did.

Beautiful were the banks of that river, with exquisite flowers, old trees, and hillsides dotted with sheep and cows; but there was not a single person to be seen.

'Perhaps the river will take me to little Kay,' thought Gerda and she became more cheerful, stood up and gazed for many a long hour at the beautiful green shores. In time she came to a big cherry orchard, in which stood a little house with curious red and blue windows and a thatched roof. Two wooden soldiers stood in front of the house, their guns pointing at anyone who happened to sail by.

Gerda called to them, thinking that they were alive, but of course they did

not answer. She came quite near to them, for the current carried the little boat to the land.

Gerda called louder still, whereupon an old woman came out of the house, leaning on a stick. On her head she wore a large sun-hat, with most beautiful flowers painted on it.

'My poor little child,' said the old woman, 'however did you get on that great, strong stream, which has carried you far into the wide, wide world?' And the old woman stepped right into the water, hooked her stick on to the boat, pulled it ashore, and lifted little Gerda out.

And Gerda was happy to be on dry land, though she was a little afraid of the strange old woman.

'Come and tell me who you are, and how you came to be here!' said she.

And Gerda told her everything. The old woman shook her head and said, 'Hm, hm!' And when Gerda had finished and asked whether she had seen little Kay, the old woman said that he had not passed by, but that he would surely come; and Gerda should stop being so unhappy, and should taste her cherries and look at her flowers, which were more beautiful than in any picture-book — and each could tell her a story. Then she took little Gerda by the hand and they went together into the little house, the old woman locking the door behind them.

The windows were very high and their panes were red, blue and yellow. In them daylight shone in all colours—it was something truly beautiful. And on the table some lovely cherries were placed, and Gerda could eat as many as she liked. And while she was eating, the old woman combed her hair with a golden comb, and the hair curled and shone so beautifully golden round her gentle little face, which was so round and as fresh as a rose.

'I have longed for a lovely little girl like you!' said the old woman. 'Now you will see how well we two are going to get on!' And as she combed Gerda's hair, Gerda thought less and less of her playmate Kay, for the old lady was well versed in magic, though she was not a wicked sorceress; she practised magic only for her own amusement and now she wished very much to keep little Gerda. She therefore went into the garden, pointed her stick at all the rose-trees and all the roses; no matter how beautifully they were blooming, they all instantly sank down into the black earth and no one would have guessed that they had ever grown there. The old lady was afraid that if Gerda looked at roses, she would remember her own, and little Kay, and would run away.

Then she led Gerda into the flower garden. Oh, how fragrantly it smelt, how beautiful it was! Every imaginable flower from all the four seasons grew there with the most exquisite blooms. No picture-book could have been more **191** colourful or beautiful. Gerda skipped for joy and played among the flowers, till the sun set behind the tall cherry-trees. And then she was given a lovely little bed with crimson silk eiderdowns, stuffed with blue violets. Gerda fell asleep and had such beautiful dreams as a queen might have on her wedding day.

The next day she was again allowed to play with the flowers in the warm sunshine and so many a day passed. Gerda knew every little flower in the garden, but no matter how many there were, she felt there was one missing—though she could not tell which one. Then one day she was sitting, looking against the sun at the old woman's wide hat with the flowers painted on it, and the most beautiful among them was a rose! The old woman had forgotten to take off the rose from her hat, when she made all the others disappear into the ground. This often happens when things are done in haste.

'How is it,' said Gerda, 'that there are no roses here?' And she ran among the beds and searched and searched, but she did not find a single rose. And she sat down and cried. Her hot tears happened to fall on the very spot where a rose tree had disappeared into the ground. As the tears moistened the soil, the tree suddenly sprang up, as fresh and blooming as before. Gerda threw her arms around it, kissing the roses, and thought of the lovely blooms at home, and with them of little Kay.

'Oh, how could I have forgotten for so long!' cried the little girl. 'I set out to find Kay! Don't you know where he is?' she asked the roses. 'Do you think he is dead and that he will never return to me?'

'He is not dead!' said the roses. 'We have been in the ground, and that is where all the dead are, but Kay is not among them!'

'Thank you!' said little Gerda. Then she went over to the other flowers, looked deep into their cups and asked, 'Don't you know where little Kay is?'

But every flower was sunning itself, dreaming its own story or fairytale. Little Gerda could hear as many of these as she wished, but not one of them knew anything about Kay.

What did the tiger-lily say?

'Can you hear the drum? Bum-bum! It has only two notes, always: bum, bum! Listen to the women's lament! Listen to the chorus of the priests! The Hindu woman stands in her long scarlet robe on the funeral fire, the flames leaping around her and around her dead husband. But the Hindu woman thinks only of the living person who stands there in the crowd, the man whose eyes burn more fiercely than the flames, the man whose eyes set her heart on fire more than the flames which shortly will turn her body to ashes. Can the
192   flame of the heart die in the flames of the funeral fire?'

'I do not understand that at all!' said little Gerda.

'That is my fairy-tale!' said the tiger-lily.

'What says the convolvulus?'

'High above a narrow mountain path towers an ancient castle. Thick evergreens cover its old red walls, twining leaf by leaf all the way to the balcony; and there stands a lovely maiden. She leans over the balustrades, her eyes fixed on the path. No rose hangs more freshly on its spray than she, no apple-blossom carried far from the tree by the wind trembles more than she. How her magnificent silky robe rustles! 'Will my dearest one never come?' says she.

'Is it Kay you mean?' asked little Gerda.

'I speak only of my fairy-story, of my dream,' replied the convolvulus.

'What says the little snowdrop?'

'Between two trees on strong ropes hangs a long board, a swing. Two pretty little girls are swinging on it, their dresses as white as snow and with long green silk ribbons fluttering from their hats. Their brother, who is bigger than they, is standing on the swing, his arm round the rope to keep himself steady, for in one hand he has a little cup and in the other a straw — he is blowing soap bubbles. The swing swings and the bubbles fly away. The last still hangs to

the edge of the straw, bending in the wind. The swing swings on. A little black dog, as light as the bubbles, stands up on its hind legs, and wants to get on to the swing, too. Away flies the swing, the dog flops down and barks angrily. The bubbles burst; a swinging board, a fleeting picture of a bubble — that is my song!'

'Maybe that what you tell is beautiful, but you tell it so sadly and you don't mention Kay at all. What say the hyacinths?'

'There were three lovely sisters, transparent and delicate they were. One had a red dress, the second blue, and the third pure white. Hand in hand they danced by the silent lake in the clear moonlight. They were not fairies, but daughters of men. There was such a sweet fragrance there, and the girls disappeared into the wood; the fragrance grew stronger still. Three coffins, with the three lovely maidens inside, glided from the wood's thicket on to the lake. Fireflies flew around like little glittering, hovering lamps. Sleep the dancing maidens, or are they dead? The scent of the flowers says that they are dead. The evening bells peal out for them!'

'You're making me quite sad!' said little Gerda. 'You have such a strong smell! I have to keep thinking of the dead maidens. Can little Kay really be dead? The roses have been under the earth, and they say "No!".'

'Ding, dong!' rang out the hyacinth bells. 'We are not ringing for little Kay, we don't know him! We are only singing our song, the only song we know!'

And Gerda went over to the buttercup, which shone brightly from among its glistening green leaves.

'You are like a little bright sun!' said Gerda. 'Tell me, if you can, where to find my little playmate.'

And the buttercup glittered so beautifully and looked at Gerda again. What song would the buttercup sing? But that too had nothing to do with Kay.

'On the first day of spring, God's sun shone warmly upon a little courtyard. The beams were sliding down the white walls of a neighbour's house; growing close to it were the first yellow blossoms, glittering like gold in the warm sunshine. And old grandmother sat outside in her rocking chair, her granddaughter, a pretty but poor servant girl, had just come home from a short visit. She kissed her grandmother; there was gold, heart's gold in that loving kiss, gold on the lips, gold in the heart, gold in the bright first morning light! These three golds make me strong and bold! There, that is my little story!' said the buttercup.

'My poor old grandmother!' sighed Gerda. 'Yes, she must be missing me and wishing for me, just as she wished for and missed little Kay. But I shall soon return home, and bring Kay with me. It is no use asking the flowers, they **194** only know their own little songs, they can't give me a proper answer!' And so she tucked up her little skirt so as to be able to run faster. But as she jumped over a narcissus, it caught her leg. So she stopped, looked at the tall yellow flower and said, 'Have you, perhaps, anything to tell me?' and she stooped down to the narcissus. And what did it say?

'I can see myself, I can see myself! Oh, oh, how sweetly I smell! Upstairs, in a tiny attic room, stands a little dancing-girl, half dressed. First she stands on one leg, then on both, kicking out at the whole world. She herself is nothing but an illusion. She pours water from the teapot on to a piece of material she is holding in her hand—it is her bodice. Cleanliness is a worthwhile thing! Her white dress hangs on a hook, it too has been washed and dried on the roof. The girl puts the dress on and ties a saffron-yellow scarf round her neck; this makes the whiteness of the dress stand out even more. Leg up! See how she stands on one stalk! I can see myself! I can see myself!'

'I don't really care if you do!' said Gerda. 'Such talk is not for me!' And with that she ran to the edge of the garden.

The gate was shut, but Gerda worked at the rusty lock till it loosened and the gate sprang open and then little Gerda ran out barefoot into the wide world. Three times she looked round, but there was no one following her. In the end she could run no more, and she sat down on a large stone. And when she glanced round, she found that the summer was gone and it was already late autumn. This was not apparent in the lovely garden, where there was always sunshine and where flowers bloomed all the year round.

'Oh dear, how I've been delayed!' said little Gerda. 'Why, it's autumn already! Now I mustn't rest!' And she rose and went on her way.

Oh, how sore and tired her little feet were, how cold and raw were her surroundings! The long willow-leaves had already turned yellow, and the dew ran down them in large drops; the leaves were falling off the trees, one by one; only the sloe still bore fruit, but the berries were so sharp it set one's teeth on edge.

Oh, how grey and gloomy was the big wide world to her that day!

Fourth story

The Prince and the Princess

Gerda was forced to rest again. Suddenly a large raven hopped along the snow to where she sat. For a long time he just gazed at her intently, wagging his head. Then he said, 'Caw! Caw! ello! ello!' He couldn't say it better, but he meant the little girl well and asked where she was going to all alone in the big wide world. How well Gerda understood the word 'alone', how well she knew its sad meaning! She told the raven her whole story and asked if he had seen Kay.

And the raven nodded his head and said, 'Perhaps yes, perhaps yes!'

'What are you saying?' cried the little girl, nearly squeezing the raven to death, so hard did she kiss him.

'Now be sensible, sensible!' said the raven. 'I think it could be little Kay! But I certainly believe he has forgotten you for the Princess!'

'Does Kay live with a Princess?' asked Gerda.

'Why, yes!' said the raven. 'But it is so hard for me to talk in your language. Do you understand raven speech? If so, I can talk much better!'

'No, that I have never learnt,' said Gerda. 'But my grandmother knew it. She also knew the secret language. How I wish I'd learnt!'

'It doesn't matter!' said the raven, 'I will talk as best as I can, though it's bound to be frightful!' And he told her all he knew.

'In the kingdom where we are now lives a Princess, who is truly clever; but then she reads all the newspapers in the world, and then forgets them again, that is how clever she is. The other day she was sitting on the throne — and they say it is not much fun at all — and she began to hum a song, which goes like this: "Why shouldn't I get married! There's some sense in that!" said she, and so she decided she would get married. But she wanted a husband who would know how to answer when spoken to; one who wouldn't just stand, looking high and mighty, for that sort of thing is such a bore. So she asked the drummers to bring all the court ladies together, and when they heard what the Princess wanted, they were really delighted. "I really like that," and "I was thinking the same only the other day," they said. Believe me, that every word I say now is true!' said the raven. 'I have a tame sweetheart, who walks about the palace freely and she told me all this!'

His sweetheart, of course, was another raven, for birds of a feather flock together, and so it had to be a raven for a raven.

'The newspapers, came out at once, edged with a border of hearts and with the Princess's monogram. They said that any young man who was good-looking was free to go to the palace and talk to the Princess. The one who would show himself most at home in the palace, and who could speak the best with her, would be chosen by the Princess for her husband.'

'Oh yes!' said the raven, 'It is as true as I am standing here.'

'People poured to the palace, there was so much pushing and shoving, but nobody had any luck the first nor the second day. They all could speak well enough outside in the streets, but the moment they went through the palace gates and saw the royal guard all in silver and then the lackeys on the staircase in gold, and the huge brightly lit halls, they were dumbfounded. And when they stood before the throne where the Princess sat, they couldn't even mutter a single word, except to repeat the last word she had uttered. The Princess, of course, wasn't in the least interested to hear it again. It was as though the men had snuff stuffed into their tummies, and were in a trance. But once they were back in the street again, they talked then alright! There was a long queue stretching from the city gates to the palace. I went myself to have a look! They were hungry and thirsty, but nobody from the palace gave them as much as a glass of water. A few, the cleverest ones, did bring some bread and butter, but they didn't share it with their neighbours, but thought to themselves, "Let him look hungry, then the Princess won't want him!"'

'But Kay, what about little Kay?' asked Gerda. 'When did he come? Was he in the crowd?'

'Patience, patience! We are just coming to him! It was on the third day that a little man arrived without a horse or carriage, and he marched bravely straight to the palace. His eyes shone like yours and he had lovely long hair, but otherwise he was poorly dressed.'

'That was Kay!' cried the delighted Gerda. 'Oh, so I have found him at last!' And she clapped her hands with happiness.

'He carried a bundle on his back,' said the raven.

'No, that would be his sledge,' said Gerda. 'You see he left home with a sledge!'

'It is possible it was a sledge!' said the raven. 'I didn't look too thoroughly. But I do know from my tame, beloved raven, that when he walked through the

palace gates and saw the royal guards in silver, and on the staircase the lackeys in gold, he wasn't in the least put off, but nodded to them in a friendly manner and said, "It must be boring to stand on the stairs. I'm going inside!" The halls were flooded with lights. Cabinet councillors and their excellencies were walking about barefooted, carrying golden trays. It was just the place to make anyone feel solemn. The boy's shoes creaked horribly, yet he wasn't frightened, not in the least!'

'That most certainly was Kay!' said Gerda. 'I know he had new shoes, I have heard them creaking in my grandmother's parlour!'

'Yes, they creaked alright!' said the raven. 'And the boy went up cheerfully to the Princess, who was sitting upon a pearl as large as a spinning-wheel. All the court ladies with their maids and the maids' maids, and all the gentlemen with their servants and the servants' servants, who also had their pages, were standing all around. The nearer they were to the door, the more self-conscious they looked. One would hardly dare look at a servants' servants' page, who always walks about in slippers, so proudly he stands in the door!'

'That must be frightful!' said little Gerda. 'And did Kay win the Princess?'

'If I hadn't been a raven, I should have won her myself, though I am engaged. They say he talked as well as I talk when I converse in raven speech. This I know from my beloved. He was plucky and bright. He had not come to woo the Princess, only to hear how clever she was; and he found she truly was clever, while the Princess in turn found him clever too!'

'To be sure, that was Kay!' said Gerda. 'He was so clever, he could do mental arithmetic, even fractions! Oh, please be kind and take me to the palace!'

'That's easily said!' said the raven, 'but not so easily done. I'll speak about it with my beloved, perhaps she will advise us. For I may as well tell you that a little girl such as you must never show herself there officially!'

'But I want to go there!' said Gerda. 'When Kay hears that I am here, he will come out straightaway and take me inside!'

'Wait for me by those steps!' said the raven, and he flew off, wagging his head.

The raven did not return till the evening, when it was dark. 'Caw, caw!' he cried. 'My beloved sends you her love! And here is a piece of bread for you, she took it from the kitchen; they have plenty of bread, and you must be hungry! There is no chance of you getting into the palace. You have bare feet. The guards in silver and the lackeys in gold wouldn't allow it. But don't cry; you will get there. My sweetheart knows a little back staircase which leads to the bedroom, and she also knows where to get the key!'

And together they went into the garden, down the grand avenue where leaf after leaf fell off the trees. And when the palace lights went out, one by one, the raven led little Gerda to a back door, which was ajar.

Oh, how Gerda's heart hammered with fear and longing! It was as though she was about to do something wrong and yet all she wanted was to be sure whether little Kay was really there. Surely it would be him! She remembered so clearly his wise eyes, his long hair. She could see him smile as he used to when they sat together at home under the roses. He would surely be happy to see her and to hear what a long journey she had undertaken for his sake, and to learn how broken-hearted everyone was at home when he failed to return. Oh, this was fear and joy all in one.

They came to the staircase. A little lamp burnt on a cupboard. In the middle of the floor stood the tame raven, turning her head in all directions and looking at Gerda.

'My fiancé has told me so much about you, my little lady,' said the tame raven. 'Your life's adventures, as one can say, are so touching! Do please take the lamp, and I'll lead the way. We'll go the straight way, there we shan't meet anyone!'

'It seems as if someone were following us!' said Gerda, as something swished near. It was like shadows along the wall, horses with flowing manes and slender legs, huntsmen, ladies and gentlemen on horseback.

'Those are only dreams!' said the tame raven. 'They come to fetch the noble people's thoughts. That is a good thing, for then you will be able to observe them better in bed. I do hope that when you find such honour and favour, you will show a thankful heart!'

'There's no need to talk like that,' said the raven from the wood.

Now they entered the first hall. The walls were covered in rose-coloured satin, embroidered with beautiful flowers. Here the dreams rushed past them so swiftly that Gerda did not catch even a glimpse of the noble people. Each hall was more magnificent than the last and filled Gerda with awe. At last they reached the bedchamber. The ceiling looked like a big palm tree with leaves of precious glass; in the centre of the room were two beds on a pillar of gold, and these were in the form of lilies. One was white, and in this lay the Princess. The other was red, and in this Gerda hoped to find little Kay. She pushed aside one of the red leaves, and saw a brown neck. Oh, it was Kay! Aloud she called out his name, holding the lamp close to his head and all at once the dreams swept back into the room on their horses. He awoke, turned his head... but it was not little Kay.

The Prince resembled him only about the neck, though he was young and handsome. And from the white lily-bed the Princess looked out and asked what was the matter. Then little Gerda wept and told her the whole story and all the two ravens had done for her.

'You poor child!' said the Prince and the Princess. They praised the ravens, saying that they were not in the least cross with them, as long as they did not make a habit of doing that sort of thing. But this time they must be rewarded.

'Would you like your freedom?' asked the Princess. 'Or would you like to become the Court ravens, and live on the abundance of the kitchen scraps?'

And both the ravens curtsied and chose to stay at Court. They were thinking of their old age, and said it would be nice to be comfortable in 'the twilight of their lives', as they put it.

Then the Prince got out of his bed and made Gerda sleep in it. Gerda clasped her little hands together and thought, 'How kind men and animals are to me!' Then she closed her eyes and slept happily. All the dreams came flying back, and now they looked like angels of God, pulling a sledge with Kay on it, nodding to her. But it was only a dream and the moment she awoke, it vanished.

The next day she was dressed from head to toe in silk and velvet. She was invited to stay at the palace, where she would surely enjoy herself. But Gerda only begged for a little carriage with a horse, and a pair of little boots, so she could drive off again into the wide world in her search for her dearest Kay.

She was given both boots and a muff. When she was ready to leave, a new carriage of pure gold drove up to the door with the coat of arms of the Prince and Princess glittering upon it like a star. The coachman, footmen, and postilions—for postilions were there too—all wore gold crowns. The Prince and Princess helped her into the carriage and wished her good luck. The raven from the wood, who was now married to his beloved, accompanied her for the first three miles. He sat next to her, for he couldn't bear to travel with his back to the horses. The other raven stood at the gate flapping her wings; she did not go with them, for her head hurt from living so well and eating so well! In the coach was a pile of sugar biscuits and under the seat were fruit and ginger-nuts.

'Farewell! Farewell!' cried the Prince and the Princess, and little Gerda cried, and the raven cried too. So they passed the first few miles. Then the raven, too, bade her goodbye, and this was the hardest parting of all. The raven flew up into a tree and flapped his black wings for as long as the coach, which gleamed like the bright sun, was still in sight.

Fifth story

The Little
Robber-Girl

They drove through the dark forest, and the carriage shone like a flame. Its brilliance attracted the notice of some robbers and the fierce glow burnt into the robbers' eyes, so that they could not bear it.

'That is gold! Gold!' they cried, and rushing forward from the forest, they stopped the horses, killed the postilions, the coachman and the footmen, and then pulled little Gerda out of the carriage.

'She's beautifully plump, she's been fattened on nut kernels!' said the old robber-woman, who had a long bristly beard and eyebrows hanging down over her eyes. 'She'll be as delicious as a little fat lamb! What a feast she'll make!' And she drew out her polished knife and the knife glittered most menacingly.

'Ooh!' the old hag suddenly cried out. She had been bitten in the ear by her own little daughter, who was clinging to her back and who was as wild and naughty as anything. 'You horrid child!' shouted the mother, missing the chance of cutting Gerda's throat. 'Let her play with me!' said the little robber-girl. 'Let her give me her muff and her nice dress, let her sleep in my bed with me!' And she bit hard again, making the old robber-woman leap into the air and twist round and round. All the robbers laughed and cried, 'Look how she dances with her youngster!'

'I want to go in the coach!' said the robber-girl, stamping her feet. And she got her own way, for she was terribly spoilt and stubborn. She climbed in with Gerda, and off they drove over bramble and stubble deeper into the forest. The little robber-girl was about as tall as Gerda, but stronger, broader, and with a darker skin. Her eyes were quite black, and almost sad. She put her arm round little Gerda's waist and said, 'They won't kill you as long as I don't get angry with you! I expect you're a Princess?'

'No, I am not,' Gerda replied, and she told her about everything that had happened and how very much she loved little Kay.

The robber-girl looked quite seriously at her, lightly nodding her head, and said, 'They mustn't kill you! And if I get angry with you, I'll do it myself!' Then she dried Gerda's eyes and put both her hands into the pretty muff that was so soft and warm.

At last the carriage came to a halt. They were in the courtyard of the robbers' castle. Much of it was in ruins. Crows and ravens were flying out of the holes in it and enormous bulldogs, each looking as if he could eat a man, were leaping into the air, though they did not bark, for that was forbidden.

In a large, smoky hall a huge fire was blazing on the stone floor. Soup was boiling in a big copper pot, and hares and rabbits were turning on the spit.

'Tonight you shall sleep with me and all my little pets!' said the little robber-girl. They had food and drink, and then went to a corner, where there

were blankets and straw. Above this bed nearly a hundred pigeons were sitting on sticks and perches. They seemed to be asleep, but they moved slightly when the little girls arrived.

'They are all mine,' boasted the robber-girl, seizing one of the nearest and holding it by the legs and shaking it, till it flapped its wings. 'Give him a kiss!' she cried, slapping Gerda with the bird's wing. 'The wood rabble sits over there!' she continued, pointing to a number of laths nailed across a high hole in the wall. 'Those two are real rascals! If you don't lock them in properly, they fly off at once. And this is my dear old favourite!' And she tugged at the horns of a reindeer, who had a bright copper ring round his neck and was tied to a large stone. 'He's another one we have to keep on a tight rope, or he'd be off. Every evening I tickle him under his neck with a sharp knife. He's scared to death of that!' And the little girl drew a long knife out of a crack in the wall, running it over the reindeer's neck. The animal struggled and kicked with his legs and the robber-girl laughed and pulled Gerda into bed with her.

'Are you taking the knife to bed with you?' asked Gerda, eyeing the knife with fear.

'I always sleep with my knife!' said the little robber-girl. 'One never knows what may happen. But now tell me again what you told me earlier about Kay, and why you came into the big wide world.'

So Gerda began all over again, and up above the wood-pigeons cooed in their cage, while the other pigeons slept. The little robber-girl put her arm round Gerda's neck, and holding the knife in the other, she snored loudly in her sleep. But Gerda could not close her eyes throughout that night, not knowing whether she was going to live or die. The robbers sat by the fire, singing and drinking, and the old robber-woman turned somersaults. Oh, what an awful sight it all was for the little girl.

Then all at once the wood-pigeons said, 'Coo, coo! We have seen little Kay. A white hen was carrying his sledge, he was sitting in the Snow Queen's carriage, which sped silently through the wood, while we lay in our nest. The Snow Queen breathed upon us young ones, and all but the two of us died. Coo, coo!'

'What are you saying up there?' Gerda cried. 'Where was the Snow Queen going? Do you know anything about it?'

'She was most likely going to Lapland, where there is always snow and ice! Ask the reindeer who is tied over there.'

'That's the place for ice and snow, a grand place to know!' said the reindeer. 'There you can run about freely in the wide, glistening valleys! There the Snow Queen has her summer tent, but her real home is a castle up near the North Pole, on the island called Spitzbergen.'

'Oh, Kay, my little Kay!' sighed Gerda.

'Lie still,' said the robber-girl sharply, 'or my knife will end up in your tummy!'

In the morning Gerda told her everything the wood-pigeons had said and the little robber-girl looked very serious, nodded her head and said, 'Very well, very well! Do you know where Lapland is?' she asked the reindeer.

'Who should know better than I?' said the reindeer, his eyes sparkling. 'That is where I was born and bred, that is where I have romped in the snowy plains!'

'Now listen,' said the robber-girl to Gerda. 'As you see, all our menfolk are away, but mother is still here and here she'll remain. But, during the morning, she will drink from that big bottle and after that she usually naps. Then I will do something for you!' With that she jumped out of bed, flung her arms round her mother's neck, tugged at her beard and said, 'My dearest nanny-goat, good morning!' And her mother pinched her nose, till it turned purple and blue, but it was all in fun.

When later her mother had drunk from the bottle and was having a nap, the robber-girl went up to the reindeer and said, 'I'd love to tickle you many more times with this sharp knife of mine, for you are always so very funny, but never mind. I am going to untie you and let you out, so you can run to Lapland. But you've got to go like the wind and take this little girl for me to the Snow Queen's castle, where her playmate is. You must have heard what she said, for she spoke loud enough and you have big ears!'

The reindeer leapt for joy. The robber-girl lifted little Gerda up, and was careful enough to tie her on firmly. She even gave her a little cushion to sit on. 'And here,' she said, 'are your fur boots, for it is going to be cold, but I am going to keep the muff, it is too pretty to part with. But I won't let you freeze. Here are my mother's mittens, they are enormously large, they'll reach right up to your elbows. Now hands in! Your hands now look as ugly as my mother's!'

And Gerda wept for joy.

'Stop snivelling!' said the robber-girl. 'Now you should look happy! Here are two loaves and a ham, so you won't go hungry.' She tied both on to the reindeer's back. Then she opened the door, called all the big dogs inside and, cutting the rope with her knife, said to the reindeer, 'Now run! But take great care of this little girl!'

And Gerda stretched out her hands in the enormous mittens to the robber-girl, and bade her goodbye. And the reindeer flew off as fast as he could, over bushes and briars, through the big forest, over swamps and deserts. The wolves howled and the ravens shrieked 'Ish, ish!' from the sky. One might have fancied the sky was sneezing red.

'Those are my dear Northern Lights!' cried the reindeer. 'See how beautifully they shine!' And he ran on, faster and faster still, night and day he ran. The loaves were eaten and so was the ham, when at last they came to Lapland.

Sixth story

The Lapland Woman and the Finnish Woman

They stopped at a little house. A miserable little house it was. The roof was almost touching the ground, and the door was so low, that whoever wished to go in or out had to crawl on their stomachs. Nobody lived there except an old Lapland woman, who was cooking fish over an oil-lamp. And the reindeer told her Gerda's whole story but first he told her his own, which he thought far more important. Gerda was so freezing cold, she could not speak.

'Oh, you poor things!' cried the Lapland woman. 'You have still a long way to go! You have a hundred miles journey into Finland, where the snow Queen dwells in the summer and burns blue lights every night. I will write a few words for you on a piece of dried cod, for I have no paper, but you can take it with you to a Finnish woman, who will advise you better than I can.'

So when Gerda was warm and had eaten, the Lapland woman wrote a few words on a piece of dried cod, asked Gerda to look after it well and tied her to the reindeer again. Onwards they sped. 'Ish, ish!' sounded from the sky, and the wondrous Northern Lights shone right through the night. And so they rode into Finland, and knocked at the Finnish woman's chimney, for she did not even have a door.

It was so very hot within, that the Finnish woman walked about almost naked. She was little, and very grubby. She immediately took off Gerda's clothes and her mittens and boots, for otherwise she would have been much too hot. Then she laid a slab of ice on the reindeer's head, and read the message written on the dried cod. She read it three times, and by then she knew it off by heart, so she threw the fish into the pan. After all, the cod was quite good to eat, and the Finnish woman was not one to waste anything.

Then the reindeer told her his own story and next little Gerda's tale. The Finnish woman blinked her wise eyes, but said nothing.

'You are so wise,' said the reindeer. 'I know you can tie with a single thread all the winds of the world together. When a sailor loosens one knot, he gets a favourable wind; if he undoes the second, it blows sharp, and if he unties the third and the fourth, so great a storm will rage that whole forests will be flattened. Could you not mix this little girl a drink which would give her the strength of twelve men, and so enable her to overpower the Snow Queen?'

'The strength of twelve men,' mumbled the Finnish woman, 'yes, that should do it!' She walked over to a drawer, took out a large roll of skin and opened it out. Strange letters were inscribed on it, and the Finnish woman read till the sweat ran down her forehead.

But the reindeer pleaded so earnestly for little Gerda, and Gerda looked so entreatingly at the Finnish woman with eyes full of tears, that the Finnish woman began blinking her eyes again and drew the reindeer into a corner, where she whispered to him, placing at the same time fresh ice on his head.

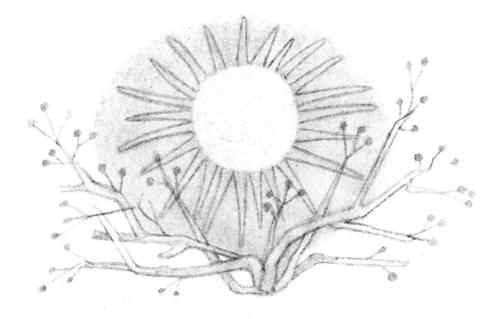

'Little Kay is indeed with the Snow Queen, where he may have anything he desires or thinks of. He is therefore quite convinced that it must be the best place in the world. But that is because he has a glass-splinter in his heart, and a glass-splinter in his eye. These splinters must come out, or he will never feel like a human again, and the Snow Queen will go on holding him in her power!'

'But can't you give little Gerda something to give her power over things?'

'I cannot give her greater power than that she has already! Can't you see how great is that power? Can't you see how human beings and animals must serve her, how without mishap she has got far in the world, in her bare feet? She must not think she needs such power from us; it is in her heart and comes from the heart of a lovely, innocent child. If she cannot find her own way to the Snow Queen, if she cannot herself take out the splinters from Kay's heart and eye, then we cannot help her. The Snow Queen's gardens begin two miles from here. You can carry the little girl there. Put her down by the big bush which bears red berries in the snow. Do not dawdle there, but hurry back here!' Then the Finnish woman lifted little Gerda onto the reindeer's back, and he ran off as fast as he could.

'Oh, I have forgotten my boots, I have left my mittens!' cried little Gerda, remembering quickly in the bitter cold. But the reindeer did not dare to stop and he ran on and on, till he came to the big bush with the red berries. There he put Gerda down, kissed her on the lips, the tears rolling down his cheeks, and ran quickly back again. And there stood poor Gerda, without shoes, without mittens, in the middle of that dreadful, ice-cold Finland.

She ran on as fast as she could, only to be met with a whole regiment of snowflakes. But they were not falling from the sky, the sky was perfectly clear and brightly lit by the Northern Lights. The snowflakes were running along the ground, and the nearer they came, the bigger they grew. Gerda well remembered how big and mysterious they had looked that time she saw them through the magnifying glass. But here they were big and terrifying in quite a different way—they were alive—they were the Snow Queen's front guards. They had the strangest of shapes. Some looked like great ugly hedgehogs, others like a whole mass of writhing snakes with their heads sticking out, and others like little fat bears with bristling hair, dazzlingly white—all living snowflakes.

Little Gerda now prayed 'Our Father'. And the cold was so fierce that she could see her own breath rising from her mouth like smoke. The smoke became denser and denser, turning into little transparent angels, that grew bigger and bigger the moment they touched the ground. Each one of them wore a helmet and carried a spear and a shield in his hand. More and more of them appeared, and by the time Gerda had finished her prayer, there was a whole legion round her. They stabbed the hideous snowflakes with their spears, till they broke into hundreds of pieces, and little Gerda walked quite safely and happily on. The little angels stroked her feet and her hands, so Gerda did not feel the cold as much, but walked swiftly on towards the Snow Queen's palace.

But first, let's take a look at how Kay is getting on. He of course was not thinking of little Gerda, least of all that she now stood at the palace gate.

Seventh story

*What Happened in the Snow Queen's Palace,
and Afterwards*

The palace walls were made of drifting snow, the windows and doors of sharp winds. There were more than a hundred halls, depending on how the snow drifted. The biggest hall stretched into the distance for many a mile. They were all illuminated by the strong Northern Lights and were incredibly large, fearfully empty, icy cold and dazzlingly white. Cheerfulness here never entered. Never was a party held here, with games like blind-man's buff and tap-a-paw. Never was there a small coffee-morning for select white young lady-foxes. Vast, empty and cold were the halls of the Snow Queen; the Northern Lights flashed so regularly, that one could work out when it would be at its highest point and when at its lowest. In the centre of the empty, endless hall was a frozen lake. The ice on it was broken into thousands of pieces, but each piece was so exactly like the next, that it was a true work of art. And in the middle of the lake sat the Snow Queen; she would say then that she was sitting on the mirror of reason, and that hers was the best, in fact the only such mirror in the world.

Little Kay was quite blue with cold, indeed almost black. But he did not feel it, for he had been kissed by the Snow Queen, which sent away the shivers and turned his heart into a lump of ice. He was playing about with some sharp, flat pieces of ice, pulling them and building them on top of each other in different ways, trying to form a pattern, just as people do with Chinese puzzles. Kay could make pictures too, the most curious of patterns—in his eyes these patterns were something quite exceptional and of the greatest importance. That was because of the glass-splinter in his eye! He made patterns which formed whole words, but he never managed to find the right patterns to make the one word he really wanted: eternity.

The Snow Queen said to him: 'If you can put that word together, you shall be your own master and I will give you the whole world and a pair of new skates.' But Kay could not do it.

'Now I am off to the warm countries!' said the Snow Queen. 'I want to peep into the black pots! By that she meant the mountains which spit fire, Etna and Vesuvius, as we call them. 'I'll whiten them up a little! They need it. It will be good for the lemons and grapes!' With that the Snow Queen flew away and Kay was left all alone in the empty hall of ice many miles long.

He gazed at the pieces of ice and thought and thought till his head ached and throbbed. So still and so stiff he sat, that one would have believed he had frozen to death.

It was then that little Gerda walked into the palace through the big gates of sharp winds. But she had said an evening prayer, and the winds immediately died down, as though they had gone to sleep, and Gerda entered the empty, vast, cold halls – and saw Kay. She knew him at once, her arms flew round his neck, she held him tight and cried happily, 'Kay, my dear little Kay! At last I have found you!'

But Kay remained perfectly still, stiff and cold. Little Gerda shed hot tears and they fell upon his chest and penetrated his heart, where they melted the piece of ice and swallowed up the glass-splinter. Kay looked at Gerda, and Gerda sang the hymn:

> *'We'll hear little Jesus down below*
> *In the valley, where sweet roses grow!'*

Then Kay burst into tears. He wept till the glass-splinter fell out of his eye, and then he recognized Gerda and joyfully cried, 'Gerda! Dear little Gerda! Where have you been all this time? And where was I?' And he looked all around him. 'How cold it is here, how bare, how oppressive is this vast empty space!' And he held Gerda tight and she laughed and cried for joy.

It was so wonderful to see that even the bits of ice started dancing round them, and when they got tired and laid down to rest, they formed the very letters of the word the Snow Queen had said if Kay ever put them together, he would become his own master, and she would give him the whole world and a new pair of skates besides.

Then Gerda kissed his cheeks, and they became rosy and glowing. She kissed his eyes, and they started to sparkle like hers. She kissed his hands and feet and he was once again completely healthy. Let the Snow Queen come home whenever she likes! Kay's charter of release was written there in letters of sparkling ice!

Holding each other by the hand, they walked out of the big palace. They talked about grandmother and about the roses high on the roof. And wherever they walked, the winds dropped and the sun shone through. And when they came to the bush with the red berries, they found the reindeer waiting for them. With him was another, young reindeer, whose udder was full. She gave the children her warm milk and kissed them both on the lips. Then they carried Kay and Gerda first to the Finnish woman, where they warmed themselves in the hot room and were told how to get back home, and then to the Lapland woman, who made them new clothes, and mended Kay's sledge.

And the old reindeer and the young hind ran alongside, accompanying them all the way to the border of that country. And there, where the first sign of green was showing from the soil, Kay and Gerda bade the pair of reindeer and the Lapland woman goodbye.

The first little birds began to twitter, the wood was in green bud and suddenly a horse came galloping out of it. Gerda recognized it for it had been

harnessed to the gold coach. A young girl sat astride the magnificent horse, a bright scarlet cap on her head, and pistols in front of her. It was the little robber-girl, who had grown tired of staying at home, and had decided to travel first north and then to other parts of the world if she did not like it. She recognized Gerda straightaway, and Gerda recognized her. How happy was their meeting!

'A fine roamer you are!' she said to little Kay. 'I wonder if you deserve to have people running after you to the ends of the earth!'

But Gerda stroked her cheeks and asked after the Prince and the Princess.

'They've gone away to foreign lands!' replied the robber-girl.

'And the raven?' asked little Gerda.

'The raven? Why, the raven is dead!' she replied. 'The tame sweetheart is a widow now, and wears a piece of black wool round her leg. She moans awfully though it is all put on, I say. And now tell me all that has happened and how you found him!'

And Gerda and Kay both told her.

'And so rang the bell, there's no more to tell!' said the robber-girl and taking them both by the hands, she promised to come and see them if she ever passed through their town. With that she rode away into the big wide world.

Kay and Gerda walked on hand in hand, and wherever they walked it was spring, beautiful spring, with bright flowers and lots of green leaves.

By and by they came to a town where church bells were ringing. They recognized the tall towers and the big town; it was the one where they lived. So they walked into it and went to grandmother's door and then up along the stairs into the room where everything was exactly as it had been before. The clock said 'Tick, tick!' and the hands moved round. But as they went in through the door, they found that they had become grown-up people. The roses in the gutter were blooming by the open windows and over there stood the tiny stools. And Kay and Gerda sat down, each on their own, holding each other by the hand. Like a bad dream, they forgot the cold, hollow splendour of the Snow Queen's palace. The grandmother was sitting in God's bright sunshine, reading aloud from the Bible: 'Unless ye become as little children, ye shall not enter into the Kingdom of Heaven!'

And Kay and Gerda gazed into each other's eyes, understanding now the words of the old hymn:

'We'll hear little Jesus down below
In the valley, where sweet roses grow!'

So there they both sat, grown up and yet children, children at heart.

The Magic Tree

One day at the end of the last century, a small white boy was walking across a plain in the middle of Africa. His parents had recently arrived in the continent to try to farm the barren land. The boy was very tired so he sat down in the shade of the only tree that he could see for hundreds of yards around. As he sat in the shade a soft breeze began to blow and stirred the twigs of the old tree.

'So someone has come again. I have no more magic. Go away.'

The boy was frightened. 'Who said that?' he cried in terror.

'I did,' said the breeze in the tree.

'But I.. I... don't understand.'

'You want nothing from me?' asked the breeze in the tree.

'Only the shade of your branches,' said the boy. 'Why do you ask?'

'Child. I have been here for many hundreds of years. I was planted by the god of the Creation to serve the tribes that once lived here.

'When I grew to maturity there were many peoples living all around. They were poor but hardworking. They tilled the soil and planted their crops and they were happy. There were four main tribes and two or three minor ones and they all worked together in harmony. One day the elders came to me and said, "Give us some relief from our poverty. We work in the hot sun from morning until night and we barely scrape a living."

'So I gave them the gift of a wonderful animal. It could survive on only a little grazing and it could breed quickly. The people were very happy, and with the animal they became rich and prosperous. It gave them much milk. Their carcasses were full of fine meat. Clothes could be made from their skins, and their bones could be used to make beautiful ornaments.

'The tribes became so rich that they stopped tilling the land and brought in servants from far away to do the work for them.

'At first, they treated the servants well, but as they became richer, they became greedier and began to be cruel and harsh.

'One night the servants' witch doctor came to me. He had painted his body in bright colours and he wore horns on his head. There were ornaments around his neck and over his shoulders.

217

'"Oh tree," he said to me. "We have heard that you have magic power. When we came here at first we did not mind working for our masters. They treated us with kindness and consideration. But now they are cruel and treat us badly. They whip us and starve us, no matter how hard we work for them. Give us our freedom."

'I did as they asked. I told the witch doctor that at the next full moon I would make the breeze blow through my branches and call all the villagers to me. I would keep them there until the slaves had made good their escape.

'And when the full moon came, I called the tribes to me. I used my magic to root all the tribesmen to the spot while their servants escaped. I held them there for two days to give them time to get far away, and when I knew they would be safe, I released their masters from my magic.

'But the servants were not only content with their freedom. They took all the herds and left nothing for their old masters.

'I did not think that the tribes would know that it was I who was responsible for the freedom of their servants, but they soon realized what had happened.

'They came back later and said, "Tree. We realize that you gave our servants their freedom and we know, too, why you did so. We treated them so badly. But now we have nothing. Help us."

'And so I gave them a seed that would grow into a rich grass that would feed them and any animals that they had. And they planted it and they grew rich again. But they had learned their lesson. They cultivated their own fields and cared for their own animals. And they were happy.

'But then the white man came. And he was envious of the lush fields and fat livestock. So he took them for himself and made slaves of the tribes. They returned to me and asked yet again for help. I gave them a germ that would cause fever in the white man. "But you must not touch anyone who catches the fever, otherwise you too will die," I said.

'They took the germ and soon many of the white men caught the fever. At first there was no danger to themselves. But one stupid girl had fallen in love with her white master and as he lay in his fever she kissed him, and so she became ill. And then her family. Soon the fever had touched all the people, black and white, and it spread to the animals.

'Within weeks everyone was either dead or had left the area and I was left alone with my magic. So I called to the god of the Creation. "My magic has brought nothing but pain and tyranny and suffering. Take it from me."

'And the god of the Creation replied, "I'll do as you ask, but I leave you one gift."

218   '"What is it?" I asked him.

"'I will not tell you. But from now on you will have one gift to bestow on anyone who comes to you.'"

'To this day I do not know what it was. But no one comes here any longer, so it does not matter.'

By this time the little white boy was feeling refreshed, so he stood up and left the shade of the tree.

He told no one what he thought had happened.

His parents decided to build their house quite close to the tree. At first it was a simple structure, but they worked hard and they prospered. Soon they could afford to extend it. They built terraces and verandahs and the house became the most important in the area.

One day some builders came and erected a fine seat around the trunk of the tree.

The following day the boy and his mother and sister came to sit on it and enjoy the shade that the tree's branches afforded.

'How wonderful it is to sit in the cool shade on such a hot day as this,' said the boy's mother. 'We are so lucky to have this tree so close to the house.'

'It's almost like a gift from the gods,' laughed the daughter.

And the little boy looked up into the tree's branches and smiled.

The Pied Piper of Hamelin

The town of Hamelin was in an uproar: there were mice and rats everywhere!
Rats in the houses, rats in the barns, rats in the streets, rats in the palace and
the Mayor's office. Mice ran about all over the place. They hid in the pantries
and kitchens, eating everything they could find. They hid in the wardrobes
and made nests among the clothes, they scampered about in the Council
Chamber and their squeaking made it difficult for the Mayor to be heard.

'Something has got to be done!' announced the Mayor, brushing a cheeky
mouse from his hat where it was eating the feather. 'This state of affairs simply
cannot be allowed. I haven't had a wink of sleep for three weeks and my wife
tells me that as soon as she bakes any bread the mice and rats queue up
outside the kitchen and when her back is turned, they rush in and devour it
all.'

'That's right, that's right,' said Adolphus the Corn Merchant. 'I have put
padlocks on all my storeroom doors but it's no use, the rats chew their way
through the walls and raid the corn and barley. If this goes on we shall starve
in a few weeks.'

'Look at my cloak,' said Bartholomew the Tailor, 'the mice have nibbled
away all the fur from the edge and last night began to eat the silk lining. We
shall have nothing to wear if no one rids us of these pests.'

'Worst of all,' said the Town Clerk solemnly, 'several rats have eaten three
books of the laws passed by the Council and unless we stop them no-one will
know what to do or how to behave.'

'We will offer a reward to whoever can rid us of these creatures,' said the
Mayor. 'How much do you think would be suitable?'

'Not too much,' said the Town Clerk.

'One hundred crowns and not a penny more!' said the Mayor.

A large notice was nailed to the Town Hall door and the people of Hamelin
waited to see who would come and save them. Not a single person arrived and
in desperation the Mayor and the Council raised the reward to five hundred
golden crowns, and sent the Town Crier of Hamelin out into the countryside
to tell everyone about it.

And then, in May, a strange man arrived at the Town Hall.

'Well,' said the Mayor, looking scornfully at the man's tattered clothes.
'What do you want?'

'I am the Pied Piper,' responded the tattered man. 'I can rid you of the   **221**

plague of rats and mice. Is it true there is a reward of five hundred golden crowns?'

'It is,' said the Mayor, 'but I don't believe that you can do it.'

'Oh, but I can,' said the tattered man, 'but you must promise that I shall receive the reward if I succeed.'

'Of course, of course,' said the Mayor, but already his crafty mind was working out how to cheat the Pied Piper.

The Pied Piper strode out of the Town Hall and took a thin reed pipe from his pocket. Putting it to his lips he began to play a strange tune. The sound of the flute curled round the houses like wisps of smoke. To the amazement of the citizens of Hamelin, the rats and mice began to pour out into the streets. As the Pied Piper walked along, still playing his pipe, the horde of rats and mice followed him, out of the town, across the countryside and away from Hamelin.

The next day the Pied Piper came back to Hamelin, but not a single rat or mouse followed him. He marched up to the Town Hall and demanded his reward.

'The reward was offered to the person who would rid Hamelin of all the rats and mice,' said the Mayor. 'It will not be given if one single rat or mouse remains.'

'That is so,' said the Pied Piper. 'The reward is mine.'

'Then what is this?' asked the Mayor, taking from his pocket a tiny, terrified mouse (a mouse that he had caught the day before and hidden away so that he could cheat the Pied Piper).

'No reward for you,' said the Mayor. 'This little mouse proves that you have not done what you claimed.'

The Pied Piper looked steadily at the Mayor. 'I will give you one month to reconsider,' he told him, 'and if, when I return, you do not deal with me fairly, then I shall take my own reward, and it will be something that you cannot afford to lose,' and he turned on his heel and left.

'Ha!' said the Mayor, 'what can a ragamuffin like that do?'

The month passed and the Pied Piper returned.

'Will you give me my reward?' he asked.

'No,' replied the Mayor.

'Very well then,' said the Pied Piper.

Once again he took out his pipe and began to play the haunting tune. This time it was not the rats or mice who followed him, but all the children of Hamelin. They followed the Pied Piper away from Hamelin and not one of them ever returned. So the town of Hamelin paid a far greater price than they expected, and all because of the greed of the Mayor.

Little Ida's Flowers

'My poor flowers are quite dead!' sobbed little Ida. 'Only last night they were so pretty and now all the petals are drooping. Why?' she asked the student who was sitting on the sofa. She happened to be terribly fond of this student, for he could tell stories and could cut out the loveliest pictures: hearts with little dancing ladies in them, flowers and huge palaces with doors that you could really open. He was such a jolly student! 'Why do the flowers look so poorly today?' little Ida asked once again, pointing to the whole withered bunch.

'Do you know what's wrong with them?' said the student. 'These flowers went to a ball last night, and that's why their little heads are drooping!'

'But flowers surely can't dance!' little Ida protested.

'Oh yes they can,' said the student. 'When it grows dark and the rest of us are asleep, they dance about to their heart's content. They have a ball almost every night!'

'Are children allowed to go to those balls?'

'They are,' said the student. 'Tiny daisies and lilies of the valley.'

'Where do the prettiest flowers dance?' asked little Ida.

'Have you not often been beyond the gate of that great palace where the King lives in summer—where there's such a beautiful garden filled with flowers? You must have seen the swans—they always swim near when you throw them crumbs. I bet you anything that's where they hold the ball!'

'I went to that garden only yesterday with my mother,' said Ida. 'But all the leaves had dropped from the trees and there wasn't a flower to be seen. Where are they all? In the summer I saw so very many!'

'They are in the palace!' said the student. 'You see, after summer as soon as the King with his courtiers moves back to town, the flowers rush out of the garden into the palace and have a merry time. If you could see them! The two most beautiful roses sit on the throne and are King and Queen. The scarlet cockscombs line up at their side and stand and bow. They are the royal pages. Then all the prettiest flowers arrive and the ball begins. Blue violets play the part of little naval cadets, and they dance with hyacinths and crocuses, and call them young ladies! Tulips and the large yellow lilies are old ladies; they keep their eye on things, making sure that everyone behaves and everything goes off nicely.'

'Doesn't anybody punish the flowers for dancing in the King's palace?' asked little Ida.

'No one really knows anything about it!' answered the student. 'It is true that sometimes at night the old caretaker who looks after the palace comes along with his enormous bunch of keys. But the minute the flowers hear the keys jingling, they stand as still as statues and hide behind the long curtains, with only their little heads peeping out. "There are some flowers here," the old caretaker will mutter. But he can't see them.'

'How lovely!' cried little Ida. 'Could I see the flowers?'

'Of course you can,' the student announced. 'Next time you go to the palace, just remember to look in at the window, and you'll see them for sure. I did so today and just imagine, there was a tall yellow daffodil stretched out on the sofa. It was a lady-in-waiting.'

'Can the flowers from the Botanic Gardens go there too? Can they make such a long journey?'

'They certainly can,' said the student. 'For they can fly when they want to. Surely you've noticed those pretty butterflies—the red, yellow and white ones—that look like flowers? That is exactly what they have been. They jump off their stalks high into the air, flap their little leaves as if they were wings, and off they fly! And because they are very well behaved, they are allowed to

fly in daytime too, and don't have to go back home and sit still on their stalks. So in the end, those leaves turn into real wings. You've seen it for yourself! It is quite possible, of course, that the flowers from the Botanic Gardens have never been in the King's palace and that they don't even know that it is such a merry place at night. But I'll tell you something, it will be quite a surprise for the professor of botany, who lives right next door to the Botanic Gardens – I think you know him! Next time you go into his garden, tell one of the flowers that a grand ball is taking place at the palace. It will pass the word to the others and they'll fly off. When the professor goes into the garden, there won't be a single flower left, and he will be quite baffled as to where they have gone!'

'But how can the flower tell the others? After all, flowers can't talk!'

'That they can't,' replied the student. 'But they make themselves understood by signs. Surely you've noticed, whenever a breeze blows, how they bow and move all their little green leaves? To them it is just as plain as talking!'

'Does the professor understand their language?' Ida asked.

'Why, of course! One morning he went into his garden and saw a big

stinging-nettle moving its leaves and paying court to a beautiful scarlet carnation. It was saying, "You are so pretty and I like you so very much!" But the professor won't put up with things like that. He smacked the stinging-nettle's leaves, for they are really its fingers, but he stung himself and from that day he doesn't dare touch a single nettle.'

'How funny!' laughed little Ida.

'Do you think it is right to stuff the child's head with such nonsense?' said the disapproving, surly councillor, who was paying a visit and was sitting on the sofa. He didn't like the student, and always grumbled when he saw him cutting out those funny or fascinating pictures. Sometimes it was a man hanging on the gallows, clutching a heart in his hand, for he was the stealer of hearts. Sometimes an old witch, flying on a broomstick, carrying her husband on her nose. The councillor didn't like this at all and he would say, as he was saying now, 'Is it right to stuff the child's head with such nonsense? What silly imagination!'

But all the same, little Ida found everything the student told her most amusing and most entertaining and she kept on thinking about it. The flowers were drooping because they were tired after dancing right through the night—they must surely be ill. Ida took them to her other toys which were standing on a pretty little table. The table drawer, too, was full with lovely

things. Ida's doll Sophie was asleep in a doll's bed, but little Ida said to her, 'You must get up now, Sophie, and make do with the drawer for a bed tonight. These poor little flowers are ill and so must lie in your bed, then perhaps they'll get better!' She lifted the doll from her bed, but the doll looked grumpy and said not a word, for she was very cross at being turned out of her bed.

Then little Ida placed the flowers in the doll's bed, covered them with a blanket and told them to lie nice and quiet, that she would make them some tea, so they could get well and be up again in the morning. She drew the curtains by the bed, so the sun would not shine in their eyes.

All that evening she thought of nothing else, but what the student had told her. And when it was time for her, too, to go to bed, she peeped behind the curtains hanging in front of the windows where her mother's lovely flowers stood, hyacinths and tulips. She whispered to them so very softly, 'I know you're going to the ball tonight!' The flowers pretended not to understand and never moved a petal but they didn't fool little Ida.

When she was tucked up in bed, she thought for a long while how lovely it would be to see the pretty flowers dancing in the King's palace. 'I wonder if my flowers have really been there?' she thought, and fell asleep. During the night she woke up again. She had been dreaming about flowers and the student, and of the miserable councillor who was cross with the student for stuffing her head with nonsense. There was complete silence in the bedroom where little Ida lay. A night-light was burning on the table and her father and mother were asleep.

'I wonder if my flowers are still in Sophie's bed?' little Ida said to herself. 'I would so like to know!' She sat up in bed and gazed at the half-opened door, and could just see all her toys and the flowers. She listened hard, and it seemed to her that a piano was being played, but softer and more beautifully than she had ever heard before.

'I'm sure all the flowers are dancing in there now!' she said to herself. 'How I'd love to see them!' But she didn't dare get up, for fear of waking her father and mother. 'If only they would come in here,' she thought. But the flowers did not come and the music sounded so wonderful. At last little Ida could bear it no longer, it was all too beautiful. She slid out of her little bed, crept to the door and peeped into the next room. Oh, what a pretty sight she saw there!

No night-light was burning in that room, yet it was brightly lit; the moon was shining through the window right into the centre of the room. All the tulips and hyacinths were standing in two long rows on the floor; not a single one remained in the window, all that was left were their empty pots. The flowers were dancing on the floor so gracefully round one another, turning and holding one another by their long green leaves. Sitting at the piano was a large yellow lily, which little Ida was sure she had seen that summer, for she remembered that the student had said to her, 'Good gracious, doesn't it look like Miss Lina!'—one of little Ida's friends. Everyone had laughed at him then, but now little Ida also saw that the lily was very like her friend and that whilst playing the piano, it behaved like her too—turning its long yellow face first to one side, then to the other and nodding in time to the lovely music.

Now she saw a large blue crocus jump right on to the centre of the table, where all the toys were, walk right up to the doll's bed and pull aside the curtains. There lay Ida's poorly flowers but they got up straightaway, and nodded to the others as if to say they wanted to dance, too. An old chimney-sweep doll, whose bottom lip was broken off, stood up and bowed to the pretty flowers. They didn't look sick at all now, but jumped about with the others and were very merry.

Suddenly it sounded as if something had fallen off the table. Little Ida looked to see. It was her carnival rod jumping down among the flowers for it seemed to think it was one of them. It was actually very pretty, and on its top sat a little wax doll with a wide-brimmed hat exactly like the one worn by the councillor. The carnival rod hopped to the flowers on its three red legs and stamped about heavily, for it was dancing the mazurka. The other flowers couldn't stamp.

All at once the little wax doll on the carnival rod started to grow big and tall, twisting round above the paper ribbons, shouting loudly, 'Is it right to stuff the child's head with such nonsense? It's all that silly imagination!' Just then he looked the very image of the councillor in his wide-brimmed hat for he was just as yellow and just as grumpy. But the paper ribbons on the rod whipped his skinny legs, so he cowered and shrank back, turning into a tiny wax doll again. What fun it all was! Little Ida couldn't stop herself laughing. The carnival rod went on dancing and the councillor had to dance with it. It made no difference whether he grew big and tall, or whether he shrank back into a yellow wax doll with the wide-brimmed hat. At last, some of the flowers pleaded for him, especially the ones who had lain in the doll's bed, and so the carnival rod stopped dancing. Just then, a loud knocking was heard from inside the drawer, where Ida's doll Sophie lay together with lots of other toys. The chimney-sweep ran to the edge of the table and lying on his tummy, he stretched and managed to pull the drawer slightly open.

Sophie stood up and gazed round her wonderingly. 'You're having a ball!' she cried. 'Why wasn't I told?'

'Will you dance with me?' asked the chimney-sweep.

'As if I would dance with a fellow like you!' she said and turned her
230 back on him.

Then she sat on the drawer, hoping that at any moment one of the flowers would come and ask her to dance. But nobody came. So she coughed, 'A'hem, a'hem, a'hem!' But still nobody came. The chimney-sweep danced by himself and made a good job of it, too!

As none of the flowers seemed to notice Sophie, she tumbled from the drawer on to the floor, with quite a bang. Now all the flowers crowded round her, asking if she had hurt herself, and they were all so very kind to her, especially the ones which had lain in her bed. But Sophie hadn't hurt herself one little bit. All Ida's flowers were thanking her for the lovely bed, and were making such a fuss of her. They led her to the centre of the room, where the moon was shining, and danced with her, with the other flowers forming a circle round them. Sophie now was truly happy! She announced they could keep her bed, that she didn't mind sleeping in the drawer one little bit.

But the flowers said, 'We thank you most sincerely, but we cannot live much longer. Tomorrow we shall be quite dead. But tell little Ida, that we would like to be buried in the garden where the canary already lies. Then in the summer we'll grow again and will be prettier than ever!'

'Oh, you mustn't die!' Sophie said, kissing the flowers.

At that moment the door opened and a crowd of flowers came dancing inside. Little Ida couldn't make out where they had come from—and told herself they must surely be the flowers from the King's palace! Right in front were two lovely roses with little gold crowns on their heads. They were the King and the Queen. Next came beautiful violets and carnations, greeting everyone around. They brought music with them. Big poppies and peonies had pea-pods for instruments and they blew them till their cheeks were red. Bluebells and little white snowdrops tinkled like real bells. It really was lovely music. Many other flowers followed, and they all danced together, the blue violets with the red daisies, ragged robins with lilies of the valley—and they all kissed each other. It was such a delightful sight!

Then at last the flowers bade each other good night and little Ida, too, crept back into bed, where she dreamed of all she had just seen.

When she got up in the morning, she rushed to her little table to see if the poorly flowers were still there. She drew aside the curtains by the doll's bed. All the flowers were still there, but they were quite withered; much more so than the previous day. Sophie lay in the drawer where she had been put, looking very sleepy.

'Do you remember what you're supposed to tell me?' asked little Ida. But Sophie just looked stupid and didn't utter a word.

'You are not nice at all,' said Ida, 'and yet everyone danced with you!'

232 Then she picked up a little cardboard box, on which pretty little birds were

drawn, and opening it, she placed the dead flowers inside. 'This will be your beautiful coffin,' she said to them. 'And when my cousins arrive, they will help me to bury you in the garden, so that you will be able to grow again next summer, prettier than ever!'

Ida's cousins were two bright boys called James and Adolphus. Their father had given them each a new bow and arrow and they had brought them to show to Ida. She told them about the poor flowers and how they had died, and asked the boys to bury them. The two boys walked in front, their bows over their shoulders, and little Ida followed with the dead flowers in the pretty box. They dug a small grave in the garden. Ida kissed the flowers, then laid them, with the box, in the ground. And Adolphus and James fired their arrows over the grave, for they did not have a shotgun, or a cannon.

The Little Prince of the Sun

The islands of Tonga lie in the South Seas, and many hundreds of years ago they were ruled by a very powerful king. He had one daughter who was said to be the most beautiful girl in the world, and he was very proud of her. But the king was so jealous of her beauty that he refused to let anyone, other than her handmaiden, see her.

The handmaiden felt sorry for her beautiful mistress and one day she said to her, 'It is so sad that you are always shut up within the palace walls. Why, you cannot even swim.'

'I have heard of swimming, but although I know I would like it, my father would never allow me to go to the seashore,' said the princess.

'It is your birthday tomorrow,' said the maid. 'Why do you not ask your father if you can go out as a special treat?'

So, the princess went to the king and asked if, just this once, she could leave the palace and go swimming.

The king thought for a minute and said, 'I hate to see you sad, so I will arrange something as a surprise.'

The next morning, the king escorted his daughter down to the seashore. All his subjects had been commanded to stay indoors so that they could not see her. During the night, the king had had a shaded causeway built out to the nearest island.

'There, my daughter,' he said. 'You may walk out to the island and there you may spend the day swimming, out of sight of any of my people.'

So the princess went out to the island and happily splashed about in the warm, deep green water. After an hour or two she lay down on the sand to rest. While she lay there, the god of the Sun passed over the island and shone down on the princess. As his rays warmed her she smiled up at him and her smile was so beautiful that he immediately fell in love with her.

The next day the princess asked her father if she could return to the island and she looked so beautiful, kissed by the sun, that her father willingly gave his permission.

And so, every day from then on the princess swam in the warm seas around the island and would then lie down and allow the sun to kiss her, for she grew to love the sun as much as he loved her. The two lovers were blissfully happy

and eventually the princess gave birth to a handsome baby boy whom she called 'Little Prince of the Sun'.

As the child grew, he became the most handsome boy in the islands. He could run faster than anyone else, throw the javelin further and swim long after the others had tired. He was also very proud and would boast to his friends, 'The king is my grandfather, and my mother is the most beautiful woman in the world. I am the best among you all.' And because he was so strong and proud, the others always agreed with him.

One day he went too far. He picked a quarrel with the smallest boy in the village and forced him to the ground. As he sat astride him, the little prince forced him to say, 'You are the best in all the islands, because your grandfather is king, and your mother is a beautiful princess.'

One of the other boys watching suddenly shouted, 'Your grandfather may be king and your mother a beautiful princess, but who is your father? At least we all have fathers and you do not.'

And all the other boys began to taunt him, calling, 'Who's got no father? Who's got no father?'

The little prince was enraged and began to chase the others away, but their taunts rang in his ears. 'Who's got no father? Who's got no father?' And he began to cry. Huge salt tears rolled down his cheeks as he ran back to his house. 'Mother,' he called and threw himself into her arms. 'The boys in the village said I do not have a father. Tell me, who is my father?' And he cried so hard that his whole body became racked with pain.

The princess felt so sorry for her son that she said to him, 'My child, do not cry. Your father is a great king. No one in the whole world has a father as powerful as yours.'

'But who is he?' demanded the child.

'Other children have ordinary mortals as their fathers. But you, my son, are the child of the god of the Sun. He is your father!'

The boy stopped crying immediately. 'If my grandfather is king, and you, my mother, are his daughter, and my father is the sun, then I am much too grand to live on this island. How can I talk to the other boys if the sun is my father?'

The princess was horrified at these words, but before she could ask anything the boy continued, 'I must leave here and go and visit my father.' He stood up and kissed his mother tenderly. 'I will come back when I have spoken to him.'

And with these words he left the house despite his mother's pleadings. She ran towards the door to call after him, but the boy had disappeared into the **236** forest and she never saw him again.

The Little Prince of the Sun crossed the forest and went to the cove where his boat was anchored. He hoisted the sail and when the tide was high enough he pushed his boat into the water. The wind blew him towards the east and at mid-day the sun was right overhead. The Little Prince cried out to him, 'Father! Father! Stop, it is me, your son.' But the sun did not hear him and continued his journey to the west. The Little Prince tried to follow him, but the wind blew him in the wrong direction. He watched sadly as his father raced across the skies and slipped out of sight over the western horizon.

That night the Little Prince was all alone in the dark, dark ocean. When it was at its darkest, the Little Prince remembered that the sun rose in the east, so he raised his sail and sailed to the point where his father would rise from the sea in the morning.

When the first rays of light spread over the ocean the next morning, the Little Prince called out, 'Father! Wait for me.'

'Who calls me?' asked the sun.

'Me. Your son,' said the Little Prince. 'You must know me. I am the son of the Princess of the Islands of Tonga and of you, god of the Sun.'

'You are my son?' asked the sun.

'Yes, I am. Oh please stop and talk to me.'

'My son, I cannot. What would the people say if I did not shine in the sky? I must go or I shall be late.'

'Please stay. Hide behind a cloud and come down and talk to me,' pleaded the Little Prince. 'If you are behind a cloud, the people will not know that you have come down to talk to me.'

The sun admired the boy's intelligence and wit, so he called on a cloud and under its cover he slid down to the surface of the water. There the father and son talked. 'Tell me of your life on the islands,' said the sun.

So the boy told his father of his mother and of his grandfather; about his friends and how he was the best swimmer and the fastest runner in all the islands. And the sun told the Little Prince many of the secrets of the sky. Eventually the sun told the child that he must continue his journey across the sky or else men and women would begin to get alarmed. 'Stay here till night comes and my sister, the moon, appears. When she leaves the water to begin her journey across the sky, call to her and tell her that you are her nephew, my son. She will offer you a choice of two gifts.'

'And which one should I take?' asked the boy.

'One is called Melaia and the other Monuia. Ask her for Melaia and you will have eternal happiness. If you disobey and take Monuia, then great misfortune will come your way. Goodbye, my son.'

And the sun went back behind the cloud and began to race across the sky. **237**

The people looked up and said, 'Look. The sun is late and is now rushing across the sky much faster than usual.'

The Little Prince took down his sail and stayed where he was until nightfall. When the night came he raised his sail and skimmed across the ocean to where the moon would rise. The moon saw the boat and the handsome young boy sailing in it.

'Boy,' she called out. 'Why do you sail like the wind across the seas to look into my face?'

The Little Prince stopped his boat right in front of the moon and said, 'I am the child of your brother, the sun, and the princess of the Islands of Tonga. My name is the Little Prince of the Sun and you, Moon, are my aunt.'

The moon was astonished and said, 'How wonderful to have a human nephew. But move your boat, for I must begin my journey. Look, the stars are already in the sky.'

'If I do, Aunt, you must give me the gift that my father said you would offer me.'

'I have two gifts in in my possession,' laughed the moon knowingly, 'which one did the sun tell you to ask for?'

Now the Little Prince was a devious child. When he was told to do one thing he always did the other. Always! So he said to the moon 'My father told me to ask for Monuia. So may I have it, please?'

The moon was horrified. 'He said Monuia! Are you sure that he did not say Melaia?'

'No, Aunt. He said that you were to keep Melaia and that you were to give me Monuia.'

'I cannot give him Monuia,' said the moon to herself. 'Surely my brother would not want to harm his son.'

So she took Melaia from her purse and handed it to the boy. 'Here,' she said, 'here it is. But you must not open it until you are safe on your own island.'

Unbeknown to both the moon and the boy, the sun had been watching all this from the opposite horizon. He had delayed his setting until the moon had talked to her nephew. When he saw what had happened, he was furious, and with the last ray of light he stretched out across the sky unseen by either his son or the moon. He removed Melaia from the boat and put Monuia in its place. He returned Melaia to his sister's pocket.

As the boy sailed away, the moon began to rise in the sky and to hurry across it to make up for lost time.

The people below looked up and said, 'How strange. The moon was late

and now she is running through the stars.'

The boy sailed on and across the ocean until he was in sight of his own island. 'I cannot wait to open my present until I am home, surely it will not matter if I open it before.'

So he picked up Monuia from where it lay and took it out of its covering. His eyes lit up with joy when he saw the most beautiful oyster shining in the dying light of the moon.

'Such an oyster must contain a magnificent pearl,' and he took his knife and opened the oyster. Inside there was such a pearl as no man had ever seen before. The Little Prince was about to take it from the shell when, as if by command, a storm began to blow. The little boat was tossed around on the waves, but the boy was oblivious to the danger. He could not keep his eyes away from the pearl. Suddenly from out of the stormy seas every type of fish began to rise to the surface and to swim towards the little boat. There were dolphins, sharks, tuna fish, eels, and even whales. But still the Little Prince was unaware of anything but the pearl.

The storm continued and more and more fish were swimming towards the boat. Just before they came close to the boat, they submerged and swam under it. As if by magic they all surfaced at once, tossing the boat high out of the water.

Poor child. He was tossed out of the boat and he landed deep in the ocean. He stood no chance of saving himself. He was dead before he knew what was happening. As he splashed through the surface, the oyster snapped tightly shut and nipped the top of his little finger off.

The Little Prince's body was never found. It lies deep down in the South Seas. The oyster, however, was washed ashore on his island a few days later. Inside it there was the most magnificent black pearl shaped like the top of a finger. No other pearl like it has ever been found before or after.

You see, Monuia was the goddess of the tide, which the moon controls and which can bring danger to those who disregard her.

Daedalus and Icarus

The ancient city of Athens has always been the mightiest city in Greece. Even today its temples and palaces, squares and meeting places are still impressive. Imagine how Athens must have looked when it was young, when the great Acropolis was first built.

This huge temple to Pallas Athene, the patron goddess of the Athenians, stands on the hill of the Acropolis, overlooking the paved streets and smaller temples of the city. Inside the Acropolis once stood a proud and awesome statue of the goddess. This statue was said to be so lifelike that when the people of Athens prayed to her she bowed her head to receive their prayers. Who built such a statue? Who could have made such a strange and wonderful thing?

This is the story of the man who was believed to have built not only his statue but many of the beautiful temples and palaces of Ancient Greece; the man who built the fabulous maze which surrounded the dreaded Minotaur of Crete. The man whose name meant 'cunningly wrought'. This is the story of Daedalus and his son Icarus.

Even when Daedalus was a young man he began to make wonderful sculptures. Most statues at that time were stiff and straight, their eyes were blank and they looked blindly out at the people who came to see them. The statues that Daedalus made looked as if they might step down and walk among the men and women of Greece. Some of these statues showed men throwing the discus — a popular sport in Greece; some of them showed the athletes and sportsmen who took part in the great Olympic Games that were held every four years. The statues that Daedalus made of the statesmen and leaders of that time showed them as if they were real men, not stiff and unnatural stone models. Their eyes seemed real, their robes looked as if they might move in the cooling breezes that blew through Athens.

Even more than this, the temples, palaces and houses that Daedalus designed were more comfortable than the houses built by any other architect. Their mosaic floors, pillared halls and painted walls proclaimed the genius of Daedalus. Whenever a new temple was built or a great palace was created for the rulers of Athens it was Daedalus who was asked to design it.

No wonder then that Daedalus became the greatest artist in all Greece. Students came from all parts of the ancient world to learn from him, songs were written praising him and his name was known all over Greece.

Daedalus became proud and haughty, and when one of his students, the son of his sister, began to show great promise as an artist, Daedalus began to watch him carefully.

Daedalus' nephew Talus learned fast, and soon there was very little that Daedalus could teach him. Talus knew how to carve the fine marble from the mountains round Athens, how to take a rough block of this milky stone and turn it into a fine likeness of a man. He carved little sculptures of animals; cats and dogs which seemed so real that they might jump down and scamper away. Then he turned his hand to making pottery. He invented a wheel on which beautiful vases could be made: vases which were smooth and shapely, unlike the crude pottery that had been made before. He even made small models of shrines to the gods. Talus became well thought of and some of the rich merchants of Athens began to ask him to design their marble villas.

Daedalus watched this and grew more and more jealous. He did not feel pleased that Talus had learned his skills only from him. He didn't listen when people told him how proud he must be of his nephew and how well he had taught him. Daedalus began to forget that he himself could still make fine sculptures, that he was still the greatest artist in Greece. He only looked at what Talus had made. He would not allow Talus to build any of the great temples of Athens and never asked for his help.

He tried to ignore Talus, but wherever he went people spoke so well of his

nephew that Daedalus could never forget him. At last he became determined to destroy him.

One evening Daedalus sent a message to Talus asking him to come to a high cliff beside the sea near Athens. He pretended that he wished to ask for Talus' advice about a temple that was to be built there. Talus received the message, and, glad that his uncle, who had seemed so strange and silent recently, wanted to see him, hurried off to the meeting place.

Daedalus was waiting for him, pacing around the cleared space which was littered with blocks of marble ready to be carved into statues of the gods. Below him he could hear the thunder of the waves on the sharp rocks at the base of the cliffs. He looked around. This was a desolate place, a mile or so from the city and far away from curious eyes.

'Yes,' thought Daedalus. 'This place is ideal for my plan. No one can see me and the sea is deep and full of deadly currents.'

He looked down at the crashing waves and for a moment almost changed his mind. 'Talus is so young... my sister's only son... just a few years older than my own son Icarus...' he thought to himself, but then he hardened his heart again.

'There must be only one great sculptor and architect in Greece, and it must be me,' he said to himself. 'The gods will surely forgive me for what I do, I have built many temples to them, surely they will forgive me...'

The voice of his nephew broke into his thoughts.

'Uncle, this is indeed a wild and magnificent place for a temple, see how the mountains surround us and the sea stretches before us.'

Talus walked towards Daedalus and stood by him. Daedalus put his arm round the young man's shoulders and turned towards the cliff edge.

'See how far the sea stretches into the distance,' he said, urging Talus towards the crumbling stone that marked the edge of sheer and fatal drop into the sea.

It was done swiftly; a scuffling of feet, a muffled cry and Talus fell into the darkness towards the hissing waves.

Daedalus turned away from the cliff, sickened at what he had done. Fearfully he looked up into the darkening sky, afraid that the gods had seen him. Pulling his robe round his face he crept back to Athens.

The gods had indeed seen what Daedalus had done and Pallas Athene was determined that Talus should not die. As he plunged downwards she turned him into a bird before he could reach the sea. She had saved him from death and for evermore Talus would swoop and cry round her temple on the Acropolis – one of the white seabirds that forever give thanks to the wisest of

goddesses.

Daedalus hardly dared to go out among the men and women of Athens. He was sure that his face must show the dreadful thing that he had done. The days passed and at first Talus was not missed, but then people began to wonder.

'Where is Talus, the nephew of Daedalus?' they asked.

'Why does Daedalus look so pale and frightened?' they murmured in the streets.

'Daedalus was jealous of his nephew, anyone could see that,' they whispered in the alleyways.

'Perhaps Daedalus has...' they muttered in the squares of Athens.

Still the body of Talus was not found. Weeks passed and Daedalus began to feel bolder. He began to go out and about again, but wherever he went people stared after him.

'There goes Daedalus,' they hissed. 'His nephew Talus is missing, such a strange thing...'

'See how pale Daedalus looks, as if he had a guilty secret,' they said, and their voices followed Daedalus around.

Even the white birds that circled the temple of Pallas Athene seemed to be crying out — Talus... Talus... Talus...

Daedalus was frightened. No one dared to openly accuse him, for the body of Talus was still missing. But now, instead of being the proudest artist in Greece, Daedalus was the man who everybody thought was a murderer, and he knew that they were right. He had to get away, away from the whispering voices and the accusing stares.

He packed his belongings and persuaded one of the Athenian fishermen to take him and his son Icarus far, far away from Athens. And so they sailed far across the stormy waters of the Mediterranean Sea until they came to the island of Crete.

Minos, the King of Crete, was a strange man. He had heard of Daedalus, of the marvellous palaces and temples that Daedalus had built, and he had also heard that Daedalus was thought to have killed Talus. Minos did not care, for he had need of this man. Only Daedalus could help to hide the dreadful secret that this King kept in his heart.

Parsifae, the Queen of Crete, had a son, but this was no ordinary child. He was born with the body of a human but the head and shoulders of a bull. As the child of Minos and Parsifae became stronger he grew into a monster whose terrible rages could not be controlled. Minos knew that Daedalus was the only man who could build a palace large enough and strong enough to hide his monster son, a palace so complicated and strange that no one could enter it. Even if they did, they would never be able to find their way out.

'If you build a palace for the Minotaur, you may stay here and I will protect you from the Athenians,' Minos told Daedalus. 'You and your son will have the finest house and everything you could ever want. I will pay you handsomely and you will be safe.'

Daedalus agreed. He wanted Icarus, his son, to grow up without being taunted and bullied for having a murderer for a father.

For five years Daedalus worked at building the most fantastic palace the world had ever seen. Made from the pinkish stone of the island it had hundreds of rooms, countless courtyards and galleries and thousands of pillars. Some of the walls were painted with bright pictures. Carvings surrounded the doorways and windows, the floors were paved with mosaics and patterned slabs of marble, but strangest of all were the passageways. These twisted and turned like a nest of serpents, doubling back on themselves. Some of them led nowhere, some made a complete circle and returned to the outside of the palace.

One of these passageways, so secret that only Daedalus and Minos knew where it was, led to a room at the centre of the palace. Here, far away from the outer walls, the Minotaur, the terrible son of Minos and Parsifae, was to live. The half-human, half-bull monster whose roars and screams would never be heard by the outside world.

When the palace was finished and the Minotaur safely hidden inside, Daedalus was tired. The island of Crete, although beautiful, was not as lovely as Greece. Daedalus was homesick. His son was nearly a grown man and Daedalus wanted to return to Athens.

'Surely the Athenians will have forgotten about Talus by now,' he thought.

He went to Minos and told the King that he wished to leave and take Icarus with him. Minos persuaded Daedalus to stay a little longer; he had no intention of letting this brilliant artist go.

'It is the feast day of my wife, Parsifae,' he told Daedalus. 'Make me a present for her, something that will astonish and amaze her.'

Daedalus set to work again. He made the most magnificent wooden model of a cow, so lifelike that no one believed it was carved.

When it was finished he went to Minos again.

'Now may I leave?' he asked.

But Minos still would not let him go, and Daedalus realized that he must devise a way to escape from Crete, a way that would take both himself and his son far across the Mediterranean to his beloved Greece. Daedalus knew that Minos had hundreds of fast and well armed ships.

'The sea is too dangerous,' he thought. 'The only way to escape is through the air: I must make wings for Icarus and myself and like birds we will fly to freedom.'

Daedalus secretly began to collect birds' feathers. From the wings of the tiniest thrush to the great pinions of the eagle, Daedalus hoarded the feathers until at last he had enough. He built a light framework of the hollow stems of reeds and attached the feathers to this with wax. When one pair of wings was finished he made another pair for his son Icarus.

At dead of night he and Icarus crept to the top of the highest cliff in Crete. They strapped the wings to their arms and launched themselves into the darkness.

The wings worked well and they flew on and on over the sea towards Athens. As dawn broke, Daedalus and his son could see the cliffs and islands of the Greek coast ahead of them in the distance. They looked down and saw the sea below them, wrinkled and blue. They looked up and saw the clouds and the sun above them and curious birds circling around them, wondering what these two strange winged creatures were.

Icarus loved flying.

'Look at me,' he called to his father. 'I can fly higher than you.'

'Come down, come down!' called Daedalus. 'The feathers are only glued to your wings with wax and the sun is too hot. Fly lower where the sea breeze can cool you. If the wax melts you will fall.'

But Icarus would not listen and flew up and up towards the sun, and the wax began to melt. Soon the feathers began to fall and spiral down towards the sea. At last so many feathers had fallen that the wings could no longer hold Icarus up and he fell, like a thunderbolt, down and down towards the blue Mediterranean.

Daedalus looked down at the sea. There was no sign of his son and he saw ahead of him the very cliff where he had murdered Talus.

He realized then that the gods had punished him for the death of Talus by taking the life of Icarus. He had no heart now to return to Greece. Instead he flew on towards Sicily. There he spent the rest of his life. Although he made many statues there he was never happy again. None of the statues he carved ever smiled, and their eyes always looked towards the cliffs of Athens and the sea which claimed the life of his son Icarus.

The Six Swans

Once upon a time a King was out hunting in a large forest, and pursued a deer with such zeal that none of his men could keep up with him. When evening came, he made a halt, looked around him, and saw that he had lost his way.

He sought for a way out of the forest, but could find none. Then he saw an old woman with a wobbly head coming towards him who turned out to be a witch. 'Dear lady,' he addressed her, 'can you show me the way through the woods?'

'Oh yes, Your Royal Highness,' she answered, 'of course I can, but there is one condition. Unless that one is fulfilled, you shall never get out of the forest, and shall starve to death in it.'

'What sort of a condition?' asked the King.

'I have a daughter,' said the old woman, 'she is as beautiful as any girl you can find in the world and well deserves to become your wife. If you will make her your Queen, I will show you the way out of the forest.'

Afraid of dying a miserable death, the King agreed, and the old woman led him to her cottage where her daughter was sitting by the fire. She received the King as though she had been expecting him, and then he saw that she was indeed very beautiful. Yet there was something he did not like about her, and he could not look at her without secret dread. He lifted the maiden on to his horse, the old woman showed him the way, and he arrived at his royal palace again, where the marriage was celebrated.

The King had already been married once before, and had seven children by his first wife who had died. He had six boys and one girl, whom he loved beyond anything in the world. Now he was afraid that their stepmother might not treat them well and even do them some harm. So he took them to a lonely castle which stood in the middle of a forest. It lay so hidden, and the way was so difficult to find that he would never have found it himself had not a wise woman given him a ball of yarn of such wonderful property that when he threw it in front of him it unwound by itself and showed him the way.

However, the King went so often to visit his dear children that the Queen found his absence strange. She was curious to know what he was doing all alone out in the forest. She bribed his servants with a large sum of money, and they disclosed the secret to her, and even told her of the ball of yarn which alone could show the way. Now she knew no peace till she had found out where the King kept the ball of yarn. Then she made tiny little shirts of white silk, and as she had learnt witchcraft from her mother, she sewed a charm in each of them. One day, when the King had ridden out hunting she took the little shirts and went into the forest, and the ball showed her the way.

The children seeing someone coming from the distance thought it was their dear father coming to see them, and full of joy ran out to meet him. Then she threw one of the little shirts over each of them, and the moment the shirts touched their bodies, they turned into swans, and flew away.

The Queen went home pleased with her work, and believed herself rid of her stepchildren, but the maiden had not run out with her brothers to meet her father, so the Queen knew nothing about her. Next day the King came to see his children, but found only the little girl. 'Where are your brothers?' asked the King.

'Alas, dear father,' she answered, 'they are all gone and have left me here quite alone,' and she told him how from her little window she had seen all her brothers changed into swans flying away over the woods, and showed him the feathers which they had dropped in the courtyard.

The King was sad, but did not know that it was the Queen who had done the evil deed and, as he feared that the maiden might also be stolen from him, he wanted to take her away with him. But she was terrified of her stepmother, and begged him to let her stay at least one night in the forest castle.

The poor girl thought, 'It's not right for me to stay here any longer. I will go and look for my brothers.' And when night came she ran away and went straight into the forest. She went on and on throughout the night, and the next day as well without stopping till she was so weary that she could not walk any further.

Then she saw a woodman's hut, went up and found a room with six little beds in it. However, she did not dare to lie down in any of them, but crept under one, and lay down on the hard floor in order to spend the night there. When the sun was about to set, she heard some rustling and saw six swans flying in through the window. They alighted on the floor, and blew at one another's feathers till they blew them all off, and their swan skins pealed off like a shirt. The maiden looked on and recognized her brothers, and full of joy

she crept from under the bed. The brothers were no less pleased to see their little sister but their joy was not for long.

'You simply cannot stay here,' they said to her, 'this is a robbers' hide-out. When they come home and find you here, they will kill you.'

'But can't you protect me at all?' asked their little sister.

'No,' they replied, 'we may take off our swan skins for a mere quarter of an hour every evening, and during that time we have our human form, but afterwards we turn into swans again.'

The sister cried and said, 'Can't you be disenchanted?'

'Alas, no,' they answered, 'the conditions are too hard. Anyone who wants to break the spell must not speak or laugh for six years, and during that time must sew six shirts for us out of starwort. If a single word leaves your lips, then all the labour is lost.' And by the time the brothers had finished speaking, the quarter of an hour had passed, and they flew out of the window again changed back into swans.

However, the maiden firmly resolved to save her brothers even if it should cost her life. She left the hut, went into the middle of the forest, settled herself in a tree, and spent the night there. Next morning she went out, and gathered starwort, and began to sew. She did not talk to anyone, and she was in no mood for laughter. She merely sat at her labours.

When she had been there for some time, it chanced that the King of that country was hunting in the forest, and his huntsmen came to the tree on which the maiden was sitting. They called out to her saying, 'Who are you?' But she made no reply. 'Come down to us,' they said, 'we will do you no harm.'

She only shook her head. When they kept harassing her with questions, she threw her gold necklace down to them hoping to satisfy them by doing so. But they wouldn't stop, so she threw down her girdle, and when this did not help, her garters, and gradually everything she had on that she could dispense with. Eventually she was left with nothing but her shift. However, the huntsmen would not let themselves be put off by this, but climbed the tree, brought the maiden down, and led her before the King.

The King asked, 'Who are you? What were you doing up there in the tree?'

She did not answer, however. He asked in all the languages he knew, but she remained as mute as a maggot. However, as she was so beautiful, the King's heart was touched and he fell passionately in love with her. He wrapped her in his cloak, took her on his horse, and brought her to his palace. There he had her clad in rich robes, and she shone in her beauty like the brightness of the day, but no one could make her utter a single word. He made
her sit by his side at the table, and her demure behaviour and her modesty

pleased him so much that he said, 'This is the girl I desire to marry and I shall have no other in the world.' And a few days later he married her.

But the King had a wicked mother who was dissatisfied with the marriage and said evil things about the young Queen. 'Who knows where the wench who cannot speak comes from,' she said. 'She is not worthy of a king.'

A year later, when the Queen gave birth to her first child, the King's mother took it away from her while she was asleep and smeared her mouth with blood. Then she went to the King and accused her daughter-in-law of being a cannibal. The King did not believe it and would not allow anyone to do her any harm. She sat all the time silently sewing shirts and took no notice of what went on around her.

The next time, when she again gave birth to a pretty boy, the wicked grandmother repeated her cruel plot, but the King did not believe anything against his wife.

He said, 'She is too pious and good to do such a thing. If she weren't dumb and could defend herself, her innocence would be proved.'

However, when for the third time the old woman robbed the mother of her new-born babe and accused the Queen, who uttered not a word in her defence, the King had no other choice but to hand her over to the court, and she was sentenced to be burnt at the stake.

The day arrived when the sentence was to be carried out. It happened to be the last day of the six years during which she had not been allowed to speak or

laugh, and by keeping her silence she had delivered her dear brothers from the power of the spell. The six shirts were ready, only the left sleeve was still missing on the last one. As she was being led to the stake, she laid the shirts over her arm, and when she was standing up there and the fire was just about to be kindled, she looked round, and there came six swans flying through the air. Then she saw that their deliverance was at hand, and her heart was moved with joy. The swans came fluttering towards her and dropped down so that she could throw the shirts over them; and the moment the shirts touched them, the swan skins fell off them, and her brothers stood before her in their human form and were fine and handsome—but for the youngest who had his left arm missing and instead had a swan's wing on his back. They embraced and kissed each other, and the young Queen went up to the King who was completely bewildered, began to speak and said, 'Dearest husband, now I may speak and reveal to you that I am innocent and wrongly accused,' and she told him about his mother's deception who had taken the three children away and hidden them. Then to the King's great joy they were fetched, and by way of punishment the wicked mother-in-law was bound to the stake and burned to ashes.

But the King and Queen and her six brothers lived for many years in happiness and peace.

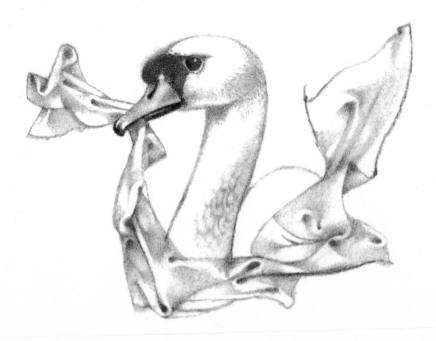

The Snowman

'I am all a-crackle, it's so beautifully cold!' said the snowman. 'And that biting wind, when it nips, most certainly blows life into one! But how that glare up there glares at me!' By that he meant the sun, which was just about to set. 'I shan't give her the pleasure of even batting an eyelid, and will stand firm on my ground.'

His eyes were two triangular pieces of tile, his mouth a part of a broken old rake, which gave him teeth too.

He had been born to the cheering of boys and to the greeting of ringing sleigh-bells and the cracks of whips.

The sun went down and the full moon rose, round and large, shining brightly in the blue air.

'There she is again, but this time she is turned the other way round!' cried the snowman, for he thought the sun had reappeared. 'But I've stopped her from glaring! Let her hang and shine up there, so I can see myself clearly. If only I knew what one should do to be able to move! How I wish I could move! Then I would slide on the ice, the way I've seen the boys doing. But I don't know how to run.'

'Go away! Go away!' barked the old watch-dog. He was a bit croaky, and had been right from the day he had stopped being a house-dog, lolling about under the stove. 'That sun will teach you how to run! I saw it happen last year to your predecessor, and before that to his predecessor. Go away! Go away! Away they all go!'

'I don't understand you, my friend,' said the snowman. 'Do you mean to say that the creature up there will teach me to run? When I looked her straight in the eye the first time, she ran well, sure enough. But now she's sneaked back again from the other side.'

'You don't know anything!' said the watch-dog. 'But then you've only just been thrown together today! What you see up there now is the moon; what went down was the sun. She will be back again tomorrow, and will be sure to teach you how to run to the ditch. We're in for a change of weather. I can feel it in my left hind leg. The weather is on the change, to be sure.'

'I don't understand him,' said the snowman. 'But I have a feeling that it is something unpleasant. That glare which glared at me, and then went down, the one he calls the sun, is no friend of mine.'

'Go away! Go away!' barked the watch-dog again. He turned round his tail three times, then crawled into his kennel to sleep.

There was, indeed a change in the weather. In the morning thick, damp fog settled over the whole district. An icy wind was blowing, and a sharp frost was in the air. What a wonderful sight it was when the sun rose! Trees and bushes were covered with hoarfrost and looked like a forest of white coral, with the branches studded with glittering, silvery blossom. Countless twigs and sprigs, which in summer one cannot see for the leaves, now stood out clearly, each and every one. It was like delicate lace, so dazzling white it was, as though a brilliant light streamed from every spray. The silver birch stirred in the wind and seemed to be as full of life as trees are in summer-time. How

indescribable was all the splendour! When the sun came out, oh, how everything sparkled, as if sprinkled with diamond dust. And on the snow-covered plain, large diamonds sparkled, you would think they were countless, tiny candles burning, whiter than the white snow itself.

'How very beautiful!' exclaimed the young woman, who came into the garden with a young man. They stopped right by the snowman and gazed at the glistening trees. 'It is never so beautiful in the summer!' said she.

'And we never see such a grand fellow as this in the summer,' added the young man, pointing to the snowman.

The young woman laughed, gave a friendly nod to the snowman and danced away with her friend across the snow, which crunched under their feet as if it were starched.

'Who were those two?' said the snowman to the watch-dog. 'You've been in this garden longer than I have. Do you know them?'

'Of course I do,' said the watch-dog. 'She strokes me and he gives me bones with bits of meat. I never bite them.'

'But who are they?' asked the snowman.

'Sweethearts!' said the watch-dog. 'They are going to move into the same kennel and gnaw on the same bone. Go away! Go away!'

'Are those two as important as you and I?' asked the snowman.

'Why, of course, they belong to our owners!' said the watch-dog. 'It's pathetically little a fellow knows who was born only yesterday. I can see this with you! I, on the other hand, am old and experienced, and I know everybody in this place. And there was a time when I didn't stand here chained up in the freezing cold. Go away! Go away!'

'The frost is lovely!' argued the snowman. 'Tell me more, tell more! Only stop rattling that chain, it makes my inside all a-crackle.'

'Go away! Go away!' barked the watch-dog. 'In those days I was still only a puppy, a tiny, pretty puppy, so they say. I used to lie on a soft velvet stool, sometimes even in the lap of my noble master or mistress. And I was kissed on my nose and my paws were wiped on an embroidered handkerchief. They called me "Poppet" and "Cuddles". But then I grew too big for them, so they gave me to the housekeeper. What a comedown that was, right into the basement! You can see into the room from where you stand. But in that room I was the master. Yes, at the housekeeper's I was the master. It may have been a poorer place than the one above, but it was far more comfortable. There were no children to squeeze me and drag me around as they did upstairs. My food was just as good, and there was much more of it! I had my very own cushion and then there was the stove. Such a stove; at this time of the year it is the most wonderful thing in this world! I always crawled right under it, out of everyone's sight. Oh, I dream of that stove even now! Go away! Go away!'

'Is a stove really so beautiful?' asked the snowman. 'Does it look like me?'

'It is the exact opposite of you. It is as black as soot! And it has a long neck with a brass ring. It devours wood, till flames shoot out of its mouth. You have to stay right near it, then you'd see how very cosy it is! If you look through the window from where you stand, you must be able to see it!'

And the snowman looked in and saw a truly black, polished object with a brass ring. The fire shone from underneath it. The snowman felt most peculiar, he felt something he could not even explain to himself. He was overcome by something he did not recognize.

'And why did you leave her?' asked the snowman, thinking that the stove must be a she. 'How could you leave such a place?'

'I was forced to, of course,' said the watch-dog. 'They threw me out and tied me to this chain. I bit the young master in the leg, for he kicked away the bone I was gnawing. I said to myself, a bone for a bone! But they didn't understand that at all, and so I've been chained ever since and I've lost my clear voice;

just listen how hoarse I am. Go away! Go away! And that was the end of my wonderful life!'

The snowman was no longer listening. He was still staring into the housekeeper's basement flat, into her room where the stove was standing on its four iron legs, looking as big as the snowman himself.

'I've got such a funny, crunching feeling inside,' said he. 'Will I never get inside? It is such a modest wish, and surely our modest wishes must come true. It is my greatest wish, my only wish; it would be rather unjust if it didn't come true. I must get in there, I must cuddle up to her, even if it means breaking the window.'

'You will never get in there!' said the watch-dog. 'And if you did get to the stove, you would be gone straightaway!'

'I am as good as gone now,' said the snowman. 'It seems to me I am falling to bits.'

All day long the snowman stared through the window. At dusk the room was even more inviting. A pleasant glow came from the stove, such as the moon and the sun cannot give, a glow such as only a stove can give when it is well fed. Whenever its door was opened, the flames shot out as was their custom, making the snowman's white face glow bright red and flooding his chest with scarlet light.

'I can't bear it,' he said. 'She's so beautiful when she puts her tongue out at me!'

The night was very long, but not for the snowman. He stood engrossed with his beautiful thoughts, which straightaway froze solid.

In the morning the basement windows were frozen up; they were covered in the most lovely frosty flowers any snowman could wish to see, but they hid the stove. The flowers did not want to melt, and so the snowman could not see her. Everything crunched and crackled; it was the sort of frosty weather to make any snowman truly happy, but our snowman was not happy at all. He could have been happy and he should have been happy, but he was unhappy, for he was suffering with stove-sickness.

'That is a dangerous illness for a snowman,' said the watch-dog. 'I suffered with it too, but I got over it. Go away! Go away! We're in for a change in the weather!'

And the weather did change. It started to thaw.

As the thaw increased, the snowman decreased. He said nothing, he complained not, and that is a good sign.

One morning he collapsed. Where he had stood, something that looked like a broomstick was left sticking in the air. He had been built by the boys round that broomstick.

'Now I understand why he was paining,' said the watch-dog. 'The snowman had a poker in his body, and the poker moved him. But now it's all over. Go away! Go away! Gone!'

And soon the winter was gone too.

'Go away! Go away!' barked the watch-dog. But in the yard little girls sang:

> *'Flower, sweet primrose, show us your face;*
> *Now willow, 'tis time to bud, make haste!*
> *You, cuckoo and lark, come and sing,*
> *February's end brings us spring!*
> *I shall sing too, tweet-tweet! Cuckoo!*
> *Beautiful sun, shine for us, do!'*

Then, no one gave a thought to the snowman.

Hasan the Goldsmith

Nobody remembers now when it happened; it was so long ago. But one thing is certain: in those ancient times a young goldsmith named Hasan lived in Basra, and though he was not exactly prosperous, he was very popular on account of his pleasant and handsome appearance, and his kind, likeable

nature.

Now while the goldsmith sat in his shop one day after the afternoon prayers, a stranger entered. By his attire he was a Persian and on his head he wore a large scarlet turban. Though he had never met Hasan, he showered him with compliments, praising his work and his handsome looks in a voice as sweet as honey.

'I do not have a son, Hasan,' he confided with a sigh, 'and I should like to look upon you as if you were my own boy, for in this short time I have grown most fond of you. To prove I am sincere and serious, I am going to chase poverty from your door forever, by teaching you the secret art of making pure gold out of ordinary copper.'

Young Hasan dared not believe his own ears, but the stranger continued, 'I shall convince you. Light the charcoal and melt some copper. Then you will see for yourself!'

Hasan obeyed. He cut an old copper plate into small pieces and threw them into the crucible and blew upon it with the bellows till the pieces turned to liquid. Then the Persian took a small paper bag from his turban and sprinkled some of the yellow powder it contained into the melted copper. Red smoke rose from the crucible and the stranger said, 'When the smoke evaporates, you will be convinced of the truth of my words.'

And truly — there was a lump of gold gleaming in the crucible! When Hasan saw this, he was so astounded he could barely stammer out words of thanks. But the Persian interrupted. 'Now you can see I mean what I say. But to become wealthy it needs more than one lump of gold. We have to find much more of the magic ingredient to add to the copper. I know how to prepare it — it is made from herbs which grow at the very top of Cloud Mountain. If you agree, we will go there.'

Of course Hasan wanted to go! He could hardly wait. Visions of wealth had clouded his senses and reason, so he replied without hesitation, 'I am ready now. I have no idea where this Cloud Mountain lies, but I am confident you will lead me to it.'

'The Cloud Mountain lies on a distant island in the middle of the sea,' whispered the Persian, as if he feared that he might be overheard. 'My boat is anchored in the harbour; we can sail forth today. The magic herbs are in full bloom just now.'

That was all the young goldsmith needed to hear. Hurriedly he locked up the shop, and long before the stars brightened the night sky, they were sailing across the wide sea.

The next day came and went, and the second, and the third … The sun rose and set many more times before the morning came when the ship quickened her speed and the sky darkened with strange black clouds.

'We are nearing our destination,' the Persian said to Hasan. And truly it was so. A black speck appeared in the sea, and the nearer they came, the larger it grew, and soon they could make out the outline of a mountain rising from the sea. It was well named Cloud Mountain, for its summit was lost in the clouds.

They anchored by the shore.

'How can we reach the summit?' Hasan asked, gazing at the sheer impassable mountain walls.

'I have thought of that,' said the Persian, and out of his bag he took a golden drum and a pair of golden drumsticks. He proceeded to beat the drum, whereupon three camels appeared, attracted by the sound. The Persian slaughtered them all and stripped one of its skin. He then sewed the skin up again, leaving a small opening underneath.

'Now listen well, Hasan,' he said. 'You are to crawl into this skin and wait for the vultures to come and carry you off to the summit. As soon as they fly out of sight again, cut yourself free, climb out and gather the herbs you will see around you.'

'How am I to get back?' asked Hasan anxiously.

'Don't worry, I will help you down, but now you must hurry and hide in the skin. And remember, you must only pick the plants which are in flower!'

Hasan thereupon entered the skin — and he was just in time too. Piercing cries were already echoing from the clouds as three enormous vultures dived down. In the twinkling of an eye each one seized a dead camel and rose into the clouds. Smiling with satisfaction under his scarlet turban, the Persian watched their flight until they disappeared from view.

Some time later Hasan felt himself being put down. He was on firm ground again. He peered out from inside the skin, and seeing nothing of the vultures, he widened the opening and crawled out.

He was on the peak of Cloud Mountain. All around him grew herbs with golden flowers and many old human bones lay among them. Hasan did not let that worry him. He picked the magic herbs till there was not a single plant left. Then he walked over to the edge of the step cliff and shouted down. 'I have them all ready. What do you want me to do now?'

'Tie them into a bundle, and throw them down to me,' the Persian's voice called from a great distance.

Hasan did as he was told, tied the herbs in a big bundle and threw them over the top.

'What now, sir? How do I get down?' he cried.

'You will never come down again, you fool, unless you want to throw
yourself down to a certain death! I am leaving you up there for the vultures to

tear you apart, and for the sun to bleach your bones as it bleached the bones of all those who came before you!' cried the Persian, laughing wickedly.

'What about our friendship? You said that you think of me as your own son... You cannot forsake me! You cannot leave me here alone!' Hasan protested, almost in tears.

'What would I want with your friendship? I am Bahran, the follower of Fire and the greatest enemy of all Muslims,' cried the voice from below. 'Surely you do not think I would have told you the secret formula if I could have obtained the herbs myself! I curse you and all your generation in the name of Fire!' the Persian added, his voice full of hate. Then he picked up the bundle of herbs and walked off calmly towards his ship.

Hasan was speechless with fright. So that was it then. His reward for helping Bahran was to be left at the mercy of the wild, merciless vultures...

I would rather perish by leaping into the sea than wait to be torn apart by them, he thought. Sadly he recited a passage from the Koran, begging God for his deliverance — for only the will of the Almighty determines our destiny — and then he plunged from the summit of Cloud Mountain into the foaming, turbulent sea.

He lost consciousness as he fell, but it must have been the will of Allah that he did not die. He woke to find himself being carried by the waves to safety on a great rock. Carved out of this rock a staircase wound upwards. Hasan climbed to the top and found to his amazement a palace built entirely of gold!

Hasan had to protect his eyes, so fierce was the dazzling glare of the whole building. Nevertheless he took courage and walked through the gates. He came upon two damsels sitting on the terrace playing chess. They were as beautiful as the face of the moon — more beautiful than anything and anyone Hasan had ever seen. He stopped hesitatingly before them, bowing his head in greeting. The youngest one called, 'You must be Hasan the blacksmith, whom Bahran brought here this year! Come and tell us how you escaped from his clutches!'

They know me, thought the bewildered Hasan, and he told the maidens everything that had happened to him from first to last.

'Oh, that wicked scoundrel!' cried the older girl, when he had finished.

'We have been living on this side of Cloud Mountain for as long as we can remember, and we do not have much idea what happens on the farther side. You see, our father is the king of the genies, and he gave this palace to me and to my sisters, for he considers this to be the safest place in the world. We have heard that Bahran comes here once a year, always in the company of a different youth, but we never dreamed what an evil fate he prepares for

them. Now that we know, and with your help, we will repay him in full!'

'Until then you must stay and be our companion,' added the younger girl merrily, and Hasan gladly agreed.

He discovered there were altogether six beautiful daughters of the king of the genies living in the palace, and that each day they took their turn to hunt and to cook. For Hasan they chose a private chamber whose richness and elegance matched their own, and they treated him as a true brother. It was therefore not surprising that he did not miss the outside world.

Time sped by as fast as the running tide, and before he realized it, a whole year had passed. The very morning Bahran was once again due to sail, to Cloud Mountain, the eldest princess said to Hasan, 'The time for revenge is here, and your weapons are ready!'

She signalled with her hand, and the servants brought Hasan a saddled horse of the finest breed, dressed him in an officer's attire and armed him with a sharp sword. Then they all rode out through the gates.

The ship lay already anchored by the shore. As they drew near, Bahran was in the act of forcing a frightened young Muslim to crawl into the camel skin. **265**

'Stop!' Hasan cried, riding like the wind to their side. 'Or you will be struck down by an awful fate.'

At seeing him alive, Bahran's knees started to shake, so terrified was he. By then the young goldsmith was looming over him.

'I can see that you have not given up your evil practices, so I have come to settle the score!' Hasan stormed, and before the wretched Bahran had a chance to defend himself, he was shorter by his head.

Hasan took the drum and the drumsticks from him and turned to the young Muslim, who was eyeing him with awe. 'Board the ship and sail for home, for nothing but destruction awaited you here.'

The ship was soon lost from sight, and Hasan returned with the princesses to the golden palace, where they all continued to enjoy life to the full.

But it was written in the book of destiny that a day would come which would

completely alter the course of Hasan's life. It happened that the princesses were invited by their father, the king of the genies, to attend the wedding of one of their royal relatives. Because of Hasan, the damsels would have preferred to remain in their golden palace, but they had to respect their father's wish.

'Be of good cheer,' they said to comfort him. 'Our house is your house. You are our brother now. You can make merry, you can hunt and feast and read whilst we are gone, and the time will pass quickly till our return.'

They were to be absent for more than two months. When they bade him farewell, the eldest princess handed him the keys to all their rooms and said, pointing to one particular key, 'This key opens the door of a chamber which you must not enter. Pay attention to this warning, if you want peace to remain in your heart...'

Hasan asked no questions. He was too saddened by the thought that he was

to be separated from his dear sisters. Heavy-hearted, he watched them ride away from the palace.

Now that he was alone, Hasan passed the time hunting and eating and reading. As the days went slowly by, boredom and loneliness made him dispirited and gloomy, and he took to wandering about the empty palace passages and luxurious chambers, examining and admiring their elegance. But he became obsessed with the thought of opening the forbidden door. Though he hesitated for some days, in the end curiosity overcame him. He turned the key and pushed open the door.

There was no luxurious chamber here — just a bare room with a flight of stairs at the far end. These stairs, however, were thickly carpeted and the walls above them were studded with jewels. Hasan hesitated only a moment, gathered his courage and then he climbed the stairs. They led him into a maze of passages and chambers, which eventually opened out on the roof of the palace. There beneath him lay green fields and beautiful gardens full of wild beasts and birds, and beyond was the roaring, foaming sea. Hasan walked in till he came upon a sparkling green pool bordered by magnificent, scented flowers, shrubs and trellises adorned with bars of gleaming gold and emeralds and pearls, each the size of a pigeon's egg.

'Not even the most powerful of all rulers possesses such wealth,' Hasan marvelled in amazement at what he saw. And he sat down under a hedge to enjoy all the perfection round him.

He was out of sight just in time, for at that very moment there was a sudden rustle of wings and a large and beautiful white bird flew from the skies onto the soft green lawn. It looked around carefully, but did not see the young intruder who was hidden by the branches.

To Hasan's surprise the bird began to peck the feathers on its chest and to tear them apart with its talons. The skin suddenly split open and a damsel stepped out, whose loveliness almost took Hasan's breath away. Her mouth had the beauty of Solaiman's with lips like coral, her cheeks were like anemones, her eyes like the eyes of a gazelle; her hair was blacker than the darkest night, and when her face broke into a smile, her teeth were as dazzling as pearls strung on a necklace of gold.

Hasan could not tear his eyes away from this vision of loveliness and he felt waves of joy and love flooding his heart. Too late he knew now why the princesses had not wished him to pass through the forbidden door, for he felt quite overcome with love for this beauty.

At long last he forced his gaze away and in a trance retraced his steps to the palace. He must try not to give his secret away! He must not let anyone know

where he had been!

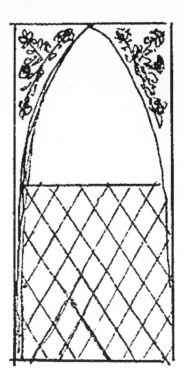

But he could not sleep, or eat, or drink, or rest. He could only weep and pine and long for the beautiful damsel, who had set his heart on fire with love.

And then the two months had passed and a cloud of dust in the distance announced the princesses' return. There was hustle and bustle by the palace gates and soon Hasan could hear the six familiar voices calling his name.

They were shocked to see his changed appearance — so thin, so pale, so weak. But he pretended nothing was amiss, and listened with a forced smile to their chatter about the journey and their stay.

He made himself join in the conversation, but his heart was not with them, and his usual happy nature was gone. As days passed he grew so frail from desire to see again the unknown damsel that he became too ill to leave his bed.

Perhaps he would have died of sorrow, if it had not been for the youngest princess — the one he loved best. She spent endless hours at his bedside, caring for him, fearing for him, pleading to know what was wrong, till in a moment of weakness he confided in her.

'You poor unfortunate man!' she cried, when she heard his secret. 'Why, that was our beautiful sister Manarassanah, who must never be seen by a human eye! Not even we — her sisters — can ever speak to her. It is the will of our father, the king of the genies. You must forget her, for your love can lead only to sorrow...'

'Alas, dear sister, it is too late, I cannot forget her. I am so consumed with love that if I cannot win Manarassanah for my wife, I shall die,' Hasan replied, despair in his voice, tears in his eyes.

What could the princess do? In vain she tried to comfort and cheer him. The youth she had chosen as a brother was growing weaker with each hour, wasting and withering like a fine fresh sprig dries out and withers in the merciless heat of the desert. In the end the youngest sister told the others and persuaded them to agree that in spite of the danger, they would help their brother.

One morning they came to his bedside and the youngest princess said, 'We cannot permit our own brother to perish, though we shall not escape punishment and shall probably never see you again. But you must remember my words, Hasan. When you come to the pool and Manarassanah throws her feathered dress aside, take her hand and do not allow her to touch even lightly the plumage. Otherwise she will be back in the powers of the king of the genies and you will never meet her again.'

On hearing these encouraging words, Hasan came to life again. He rose from his bed and hastened through the forbidden door...

Everything went well and a little later he returned with the smiling Manarassanah. Her face told of her own love for the kind and handsome youth.

The princesses made preparations for their wedding, and by the following day the golden palace was buzzing with activity, merriment, singing and dancing in honour of Hasan and his bride.

Hasan joined in as in a dream, for such magnificent celebrations were unheard of even at the sultan's court!

When after forty days and forty nights the festivities ended, Hasan knew the time had come for him to leave Cloud Mountain with his bride. He was homesick and it was not safe to prolong their stay, for the king of the genies was expected to arrive any day.

The princesses gave them many fine gifts of gold and jewels which were put into large chests. When all was ready for their departure, Hasan beat the golden drum and three camels appeared. He sat on one, Manarassanah on the second, and the third was laden with the chests. As they were about to leave, the youngest sister, unobserved by anyone else, handed a sealed package to Hasan, and whispered, 'This bag contains Manarassanah's dress of bird feathers. You must not destroy them, but as long as you hold them in your possession, she will be yours. Hide them well, for she must never find them, or you will lose her to our father again...'

270   The princesses were loath to see Hasan go — they had grown to love him even more as their own true brother. So they all wept as Hasan left with his bride — the youngest of them most of all.

Once home, Hasan reopened his business. But it was no longer a poor little shop, but a large, imposing place with many workrooms and sales rooms which soon became renowned far and wide. All the rich gentry, wealthy merchants and the viziers were his important and frequent customers, and more than once he was honoured by an order from the sultan himself.

Hasan lived happily with Manarassanah and it seemed that nothing could mar their joy. But, alas, when the thought of harm or evil could not have been further from their minds, disaster struck.

The young goldsmith had to go away for several days on business, and Manarassanah remained at home alone. Out of boredom and curiosity she began to go through all the rooms and halls of their house, till at last she entered the chamber where her husband had hidden the sealed bag containing her feathered dress. Eventually she came upon the package and broke the seal. As soon as her eyes rested on the feathers, she was filled with an unexplainable, irresistible urge to turn into a bird once more. She hesitated

for a moment — for it seemed as if an inner voice was warning her against it. Then she shrugged her shoulders and thought: 'I'll only try it on again, and then put it back in its place, and no one shall be the wiser.'

She put on the feathered dress and turned into the white bird. Then a strange, invisible force seemed to draw her towards the open window. The wings opened of their own accord, and Manarassanah found herself flying high above her house. Alas, too late, she realized that she was back in the power of the king of the genies. Now she knew it was his will which was compelling her to fly far, far away to his residence, to the distant Island of Wak.

Hasan, now on his way home, heard the plaintive cries of his wife far above him. Baffled, he gazed up into the skies, where the sound seemed to come from. He saw the beautiful white bird, he heard Manarassanah's final despairing words, 'You will find me on the Island of Wak! The Island of Wak...'

Nothing but a small white speck remained in the sky now... and soon that too was gone...

Hasan realized immediately what must have happened during his absence. He groaned with the pain which pierced his heart, and covering his face with his hands, wept bitter tears. What hope was there that he would ever see his beloved Manarassanah again?

But as the day passed by in mourning and weeping for his lost wife, it occurred to him that there was one place where he might find help. He must go immediately to seek his sisters on Cloud Mountain. The thought comforted him, and he decided to leave at once. He closed his shop, beat the golden drum, and in a trice the three camels were flying across the desert like shadows chasing sunbeams.

They did not stop till they came to the golden palace. The moment the princesses saw Hasan, they rushed through the gates to greet him.

'What brings you here, dear brother?' asked the youngest one. 'You must know that when you led Manarassanah from here, the king of genies turned into your enemy — so this territory is dangerous for you!'

'Your father has my beloved wife back in his possession as he always wanted,' Hasan whispered, and sighed. And he told them all that had happened. 'I am here to beg for your help,' he added. 'Where is the Island of Wak and how can I reach it?'

The princesses looked embarrassed and remained silent. At last the eldest one spoke. 'The journey to the Island of Wak lasts seven human lives; not even your fastest camels can shorten it!'

'That is because your journey will be strewn with seven times seven mortal

dangers, which an ordinary human being cannot avoid,' explained another sister.

'It is said that only the person who has the magic cap and magic rod can survive the trip,' interrupted the youngest princess. 'These two things have more power than the all powerful king of the genies! But all we know is that they belong to a wicked magician, and that he has hidden them in a cave...'

'I shall find the magic cap and rod, and I shall set Manarassanah free. Where can I find the magician?' Hasan cried out impatiently.

The answer did not please him.

'We do not know, dearest brother, his whereabouts, for whoever puts the cap on his head, becomes invisible, and with the aid of the rod he can go anywhere he desires...'

'If it is necessary and that is my destiny, I shall search for the magician till the end of my days,' Hasan announced.

In this he stood firm. He left soon afterwards, and as the golden palace disappeared before him, he was carried by the three camels across the parched desert, over mountains and valleys and seas. Hasan did not know how many nights passed before he came to a small island in the middle of a vast ocean. There was not a living soul in sight, and at first it seemed the island was uninhabited. He noticed at the foot of a rocky slope an opening into a cave, and went to investigate. As he approached, he heard the quarrelsome voices of two boys. 'Mine is the cap and yours is the rod!'

'No, I want the cap. Come outside and let's settle this once and for all!'

Before Hasan realized what was happening, the lads appeared, the long searched for cap and rod in their hands. 'You decide, stranger,' said the bigger boy. 'Our father was a mighty magician and when he died, he left us this cap and this rod. But we are not sure which one belongs to whom.'

'I will be the judge,' Hasan agreed at once. 'Go and find a pair of stones of identical size; whoever throws his stone the furthest will get the cap. While you are looking, I shall hold on to both cap and rod.'

'That seems very fair,' said the boys enthusiastically and ran off to the beach to find the stones.

The moment they were gone, Hasan put the cap on his head and said to the rod, 'Take me to the Island of Wak!'

The earth rumbled and trembled, and four spirits as black as coal swished through the air to his side. They seized the young goldsmith by his hands and feet and flew off as swiftly as an arrow to the island of the king of the genies, while on the ground below the two sons of the magician gaped after them in astonishment.

Hasan was so afraid the spirits might let him drop that he kept his eyes tightly shut all the way. Not until the flight was over and he felt firm ground under his feet did he dare open his eyes and examine his surroundings.

He was on the Island of Wak. All around him there were genies, marids and other spirits running to and fro, but not one of them paid him any attention. 'This must be because I have the cap on my head and I am invisible,' Hasan thought. So unseen and confident, he began his search for Manarassanah.

He traversed the whole island, he searched every corner of every house, the markets, the gardens, even the barracks of the guards. There was not an inch left unsearched, except for the royal palace. But in the palace too there was no sign of his beloved wife. He was just about to give up in despair when fortune smiled on him at last. He was standing by the heavy iron gates which led into the underground prison when he overheard the conversation of two guards. One was telling his companion that the king kept his daughter, Manarassanah, in the deepest dungeon, so that he, Hasan, would never find her.

Hasan's first impulse was to rush into the dungeon. But he decided that it would be wiser to wait till nightfall when everyone was asleep and no one would discover till morning that he had carried off the princess.

He curbed his impatience and waited. At last night came and Hasan, the cap on his head, slipped silently through the maze of dark, winding passages and low damp stairways till he came to the dungeons. The dampness and the gloom depressed him. Would he ever find his beloved wife? He seemed to have been searching and groping in the blackness for so long without success. But then at last he came to a door. Behind it lay the sleeping princess!

How his heart raced, how it pulsed with joy! Taking the cap off his head, he lightly stroked the girl's pale cheek.

'Hasan!' she cried, and fainted with sheer happiness at seeing her beloved.

276 Hasan wasted no time. He had heard a sound on the stairway behind them.

Quickly he said to the rod, 'Take us to the golden palace on Cloud Mountain!'

And once again the rod did not fail him. A swarm of little spirits dived to their side and in a trice they were both being lifted out of the dungeon, out of the prison, and carried swiftly through the paling night.

When Hasan dared at last to glance over his shoulder, he was dismayed at what he saw. The king of the genies was in close pursuit, riding like the wind in a gold coach drawn by a team of marids. He was so near, in fact, that Hasan could see his face — and his angry, threatening expression terrified him.

'Bring fog and mist down upon our pursuer!' Hasan commanded the rod, and immediately all behind them was enveloped in a thick white blanket.

Below land and sea came into view alternately. Manarassanah opened her eyes and huddled close to Hasan for protection. As she opened her lips to speak, an angry voice roared from behind, 'You will not escape me! You belong to me.'

The king of the genies was again close behind.

'Let the rain pour down behind us!' Hasan cried, and a torrent of water slowed down the gold carriage for the second time.

Now they could see before them the familiar outline of Cloud Mountain, and on it a speck which shone like the glittering sun — the golden palace!

But the king of the genies was approaching closer yet again... 'I have you!' he cried, rising in his carriage, his sword ready to strike.

But Hasan once more shouted to the rod, 'Bring thunder and lightning!'

A fiery arrow sliced the sky in half, and with a tremendous crash it shattered the gold coach into a thousand pieces.

Hasan and Manarassanah were now standing in the palace forecourt, and the six sister princesses were running towards them. But before they could embrace, their father, the king of the genies stood before them. His turban was as high as the tallest turret and his thick white beard flowed to the ground.

'Are you not aware that you cannot escape the king of the genies and that I shall punish you, no matter who you are?' he stormed at Hasan.

'I do not fear you, for you accuse me unjustly,' Hasan bravely replied. 'I too have magic to help me. With this cap and the rod I can escape from you always. But that is not so important. The only thing that matters to me is the love of your daughter Manarassanah, who is mine according to our proper marriage contract. Oh king of kings,' Hasan humbly continued, 'I shall gladly give you the rod and the cap to win your favour and heart.'

The old king's wrath was dying.

'If it is as you say, I shall accept your offer. Give me the rod and cap...'

Hasan passed him both the cap and rod without hesitation. But the king of the genies unsheathed his sword, and brandishing it above his head, he cried menacingly, 'Now you are defenceless, I am going to cut off your head!'

'Then slay me too, father!' begged Manarassanah as, weeping, she fell to her knees by Hasan's side.

To the astonishment of everyone present the old king's hand which held the sword fell to his side, and a contented smile lit his face.

When he spoke, his voice was gentle. 'I was testing your love. The Almighty is compassionate and he must have ordained that your love is so strong that nothing will part you. Be happy in life and in love, my children. It is the will of Allah.'

Ondin and the Salt

In Austria, many hundreds of years ago, there lived an old fisherman called Friedl. He lived in a large house on the banks of a large lake, with his daughter, Gunde. Friedl was very old and could not handle his fishing tack very well, so it was left to Gunde to do most of the fishing. Every morning, she would row out into the middle of the lake and spend the hours hard at work. When she returned home, her father would inspect the morning's catch and no matter how many fish she had caught, he was never satisfied.

Friedl was much too mean to pay for a servant, so poor Gunde spent the rest of the day cleaning and cooking, but she did not really mind because she loved her father dearly.

As well as being hard working, Gunde was also extremely beautiful, and many men from far and near had asked Friedl for her hand in marriage. But each time Friedl refused. Who else would do his fishing, clean his house and cook his meals? If Friedl allowed Gunde to marry he would have to pay three servants to do her work.

Gunde was not upset. Although she had liked all the men who had asked her to marry them, she had not yet been in love.

One day, however, a handsome young hunter came to live in the forest. His name was Antoine and as soon as Gunde saw him she fell head over heels in love with him. And as soon as he set eyes on Gunde, he fell hopelessly in love with her. The happy couple spent hour after hour walking through the forest and along the shores of the lake, talking about the future and how happy they would be when they were married.

Gunde and Antoine decided on a day when Antoine should come to the cottage and ask Friedl for Gunde's hand. On the appointed day, Antoine duly turned up, his heart beating wildly.

Now, Antoine was as brave as any man and better-looking than most, but he was poor — as poor as poor could be. So when Friedl asked him if he would be willing to pay for the servants that he would need to replace Gunde, Antoine could only shake his head. 'Then go,' said Friedl. 'Come back when you are rich enough and then you may marry Gunde, but until then I forbid you to see her.'

Gunde was an obedient child and did mean to stop seeing Antoine, but her love for him was so strong that occasionally she would slip out of the house to meet her lover. 'One day you will be rich,' she would say comfortingly to him, 'and Papa will have to let us marry, then.'

But Antoine knew that no matter how hard he worked in the forest, he would never be able to afford to pay for three servants. And he grew sadder and sadder.

One night after one of their meetings when the two lovers had talked and talked about what life would be like when they were married, Antoine was unable to sleep, so he decided to go fishing. The day had been very cold and the moon shone down from the cloudless sky. Stars twinkled and glittered from the velvet blackness and as Antoine walked to the lakeside he could not help but be filled with wonder by the beauty of the night. When he arrived at the water's edge, he cast his line and sat under an old oak tree and began to think of his dear Gunde.

After a few minutes, the line tightened and the rod was almost snatched from his hands. Antoine stood up and began to pull in the line. But the fish was not going to give in easily. 'It must be enormous,' thought Antoine as he struggled to land the monster. It took a long time and every ounce of his strength, but at last he managed it. He gave a huge tug and suddenly the monstrous fish came from the water.

Only it was not a fish. It was unlike anything Antoine had ever seen before. It was like a little green man with long hair. It had arms and legs, but where its hands and feet should have been, there was webbing, just like a frog.

'Who are you?' asked Antoine, more afraid than he showed.

The little creature muttered something incomprehensible, and as he spoke two great tears rolled down his cheeks. 'I meant you no harm,' said Antoine. 'Are you hungry?'

The little fellow nodded.

'Then come with me back to my house and I will give you something to eat.'

Antoine held out his hand and the little thing took it in his webbed hand and the two made their way through the forest to Antoine's cottage. They ate a little fish and drank a little wine and soon the little man was smiling and happy. Antoine was now feeling sleepy and he said to the little fellow, 'Go, sit by the fire and sleep.' But the little man was afraid of the flames. Antoine had to coax him into a chair. When he held out his hands to the heat, the little man did the same, and the look of fear vanished and a smile spread across his strange little face. Within a few minutes he was sleeping peacefully and Antoine left him and went to bed.

The next morning, Antoine expected the little man to be gone. But no, there he was sitting by the embers of the fire. 'Do you have a name?' asked Antoine for the umpteenth time. The little green creature nodded.

'Then do tell me what it is. If you are going to stay here, I must know what to call you.'

The little man croaked something that Antoine could not make out. It sounded like 'Ondin'.

'Ondin?' he enquired and the little man nodded.

From then on, Ondin followed Antoine like a dog. When they went hunting, he would run hither and thither through the undergrowth and fetch the game that Antoine had caught. He was a very inquisitive little creature and loved to look at everything in sight. When the two went near the lake, the little man jumped up and down with great joy. Water was obviously his element, but when Antoine asked him if he wanted to return to his beloved water, Ondin shook his head and jumped up into Antoine's arms.

One day, about a week later, as the two were crossing the forest a herd of deer passed by. Ondin became very agitated and ran into the undergrowth to hide from them.

'Poor thing,' thought Antoine, 'he is obviously afraid of the fine stag,' and followed him to try to comfort him. He found Ondin sitting by a small stream, shivering with fear.

'It's all right,' said Antoine. 'No one is going to harm you,' and he stooped down to pick Ondin up. But as he did so he lost his footing and slipped on a patch of smooth rock. In his panic to right himself he dropped Ondin into the water. A few seconds later, the little green creature came to the surface with such an expression of distaste on his face, and with such a spluttering and spitting that Antoine thought he was having some kind of fit.

Ondin managed to clamber back onto the bank, still spitting and shaking.

'What on earth is the matter?' asked Antoine.

The little man pointed at the water and spat again.

Antoine knelt down with a puzzled expression on his face and scooped up some of the water from the stream into his cupped hands. When he sipped the water an even more puzzled expression came over his face. For the water was salty and they were many miles from the sea.

In those days, salt was one of the most valuable things that there was, and people who were lucky enough to own salt mines were very rich indeed. Antoine ran home as fast as he could and picked up a spade. He returned to where Ondin was still sitting, and began to dig as quickly as his muscles would allow him. He had only gone down a few inches when the spade hit **281**

something hard. He threw it to one side and began to clear the loose earth away with his hands. Within a few instants he was looking at a beautiful white vein of pure salt. As he dug wider he could see that the salt vein stretched for a great distance and went as deep as he could imagine.

He hugged Ondin and said, 'Now I will be rich and Friedl will have to let me marry Gunde.'

The man and the strange creature made their way back to the hut where Antoine washed and put on his best clothes. He cleaned Ondin, too, and together they went into town to register their claim on the salt vein.

Word of Antoine's good fortune soon spread around the town, and wherever he went, people crowded round him to congratulate him.

'It is all his doing,' Antoine would say pointing at Ondin. 'If he had not fallen into the stream, I would still be a poor hunter.'

Antoine bought himself a suit of fine cloth and a pair of beautiful leather boots. The next morning he was up bright and early and put on his new clothes. With Ondin at his side, he rowed across the lake to Friedl's house. Gunde saw him from her window and rushed to meet him.

'I have come to ask for your hand in marriage again,' said Antoine as the two embraced.

'But you know what Father said. You must pay for three servants to do my work, if he is to allow me to marry you.'

'That is no problem now,' said Antoine. 'Thanks to this little fellow here, I am now a rich man and could afford thirty servants.'

'What is it?' asked Gunde, nervously recoiling from the little green man.

'My dearest friend, my faithful companion,' said Antoine and explained how he had caught Ondin when he had been fishing after their last moonlight meeting.

'Then I hope that you will be my friend, too,' said Gunde and bent down to kiss the little creature. 'For if Father allows us to marry, I shall owe all my happiness to you.'

Ondin had never been kissed before and he drew back from Gunde's lips.

Antoine laughed and coaxed him to allow Gunde to kiss him.

The happy lovers went inside the cottage and, of course, Friedl had no alternative but to give his permission for the wedding.

Two weeks later the forest echoed to the sounds of laughter and merrymaking. The churchbells pealed joyfully across the lake and everyone agreed that the bride was the most beautiful they had ever seen. Antoine looked so handsome in his fine new clothes that all the women were envious of Gunde. And even Ondin looked smart. Gunde had made him a beautiful suit of green silk which he wore, with tremendous pride. And this time when

Gunde bent down to kiss him after the wedding, he did not recoil. He decided that he quite liked being kissed by such a pretty lady, and every night from then on when Antoine and Ondin returned from their salt mine, Gunde would kiss, first, her handsome husband, and then, her favourite little green man.

And the three of them lived happily ever after.

And today, in the Austrian mountains salt is still mined. But it could have lain there undiscovered, if not for an unhappy lover who went fishing one night when he was unable to sleep.

The Tinder-Box

A soldier came marching along the high road—left, right, left right! He had
a knapsack on his back and a sword by his side, for he was returning home
from the wars. And on the road he met an old witch; she was awfully ugly,
with a bottom lip hanging right down to her chest. 'Good evening, soldier!'
she said. 'What a nice sword you have, and what a large knapsack! You're
a real soldier to be sure! Now you'll get as much money as you want!'

'Thank you very much, old witch,' said the soldier.

'Do you see that big tree?' asked the witch, pointing to a tree standing close
by. 'It's quite hollow inside. Climb up to its top and you'll see a hole, through
which you can slip right down deep into the tree. I'll tie a rope round your
waist, so I can pull you up again when you give me a shout!'

'And what am I to do inside that tree?' asked the soldier.

'Why, fetch money from there!' said the witch. 'To be sure, when you get
right down to the bottom, you'll find yourself in a big passage, which will be
brightly lit, for there are over a hundred lamps burning there. Then you will

see three doors, which you'll be able to open, for in each lock there is a key. When you enter the first room, you'll see a large chest in the middle of the floor, with a dog sitting on top of it. His eyes are as big as tea-cups, but don't mind that! I'll give you my blue-checked apron, just spread it on the floor. Then go over to the dog, take him and put him down on this apron, open the chest and help yourself to all the money you want. It contains only copper. If you prefer silver, go into the next room. Only there you will find a dog with eyes as big as mill-wheels but don't mind that. Just sit him down on my apron and help yourself to the money! But if perhaps you prefer gold, you can have as much as you can carry, if you go into the third room. The dog who sits on that money-chest has such eyes, each one as big as a tower. Imagine, what a dog! But don't mind that! Sit him down on my apron, then he won't harm you.'

'That doesn't sound too bad,' said the soldier. 'But what am I to give to you, old witch. You'll want something from me, to be sure!'

'Not at all,' said the witch. 'I don't want a single coin. Just bring me the old tinder-box my grandmother forgot there when she was last down.'

'Very well then,' agreed the soldier. 'Tie the rope round my waist!'

'Here it is,' said the witch, 'and here is my blue-checked apron.'

With that the soldier climbed up the tree, dropped down the hole and found himself, exactly as the witch had said, in the large passage where hundreds of lights were burning.

He opened the first door. Brrr! There sat the dog with eyes as big as tea-cups, glaring at him!

'What a fine fellow you are!' said the soldier, putting him down on the witch's apron and helping himself to as many copper coins as his pockets would hold. Then he closed the chest, put the dog back on it and went into the next room. And there, to be sure, sat the dog with eyes the size of mill-wheels.

'Don't stare at me like that,' said the soldier, 'you could strain your eyes.' And he sat the dog on the apron. But when he saw the heap of silver coins in the chest, he threw away all the coppers and filled his pockets and his knapsack with the silver. Then he went into the third room. Oh, what a horrid sight it was! The dog in there really did have eyes as big as towers.

'Good evening!' said the soldier, lifting his cap in salute, for he'd certainly never seen such a dog. He examined him for a while, but then thought, enough is enough, and sat him on the apron and opened the chest. Gracious me! What a lot of gold. For that he could buy the whole town and all the sugar pigs in the cake shop and all the tin soldiers, and whips and rocking-horses in the world!

286 This certainly was money! The soldier threw away all the silver, which filled his pockets and knapsack, and stuffed them with the gold instead. In fact his pockets, his knapsack, his cap and boots were all so full, he could scarcely walk! Now he had money! He sat the dog back on the chest, slammed the door and shouted.

'Pull me up again, old witch!'

'Have you got the tinder-box?' asked the witch.

'Why, to be sure, I clean forgot about that,' said the soldier, and went back to get it. The witch pulled him up, and there he was, back on the road, with his pockets, boots, knapsack and cap full of money.

'What are you going to do with that tinder-box?' asked the soldier.

'That's none of your business!' snapped the witch. 'You've got your money! Now give me my tinder-box!'

'Stuff and nonsense!' said the soldier. 'You tell me right now what you want it for, or I'll draw my sword and cut off your head!'

'I shan't!' cried the witch.

So the soldier cut off her head. And, as she lay there, the soldier tied all the money in her apron, slung the bundle over his shoulder, put the tinder-box in his pocket, and set off for the town.

It was a grand town and the soldier went into the very best inn, where he ordered the very best room and his favourite food—for he was a rich man now, with all that money.

The servant who cleaned his boots thought, of course, what ridiculously shabby old boots they were for such a rich gentleman, but then he hadn't bought any new ones yet. The next day he had new boots and also smart new clothes! Now the soldier had become a grand gentleman and people were telling him of all the wonderful sights in the town, about the King and what a pretty Princess his daughter was.

'How can I see her?' asked the soldier.

'She isn't to be seen,' was everyone's reply. 'She lives in a big copper castle, which is surrounded by lots of walls and towers! Nobody but the King is allowed in, because it has been foretold that she will marry a common soldier, and our King wouldn't like that.'

'I'd most certainly like to see her,' thought the soldier, but see her he could not, for it wasn't allowed.

From now on he lived a merry life, going to the theatre, driving through the royal park, and giving away lots of money to the poor, which was nice! But then he well remembered from days of old how hard it was to be without a penny. Now he was rich, and well-dressed, and had lots of friends, who all said what a fine fellow and a true gentleman was he. The soldier loved hearing that! But, as he was spending money each day in this manner and never

getting any back, in the end he was left with nothing but two coins. He had to move from the magnificent rooms into a tiny little attic right under the roof; he had to clean his own boots and mend them with a darning-needle and none of his friends bothered to visit him, for so many steps led to that room of his!

Once, when it was a really dark evening and the soldier couldn't even buy himself a candle, he suddenly remembered that there was still a bit of a candle left in the tinder-box which he had taken from the hollow tree, with the help of the witch. He took out the tinder-box and candle-end, but the moment he struck a light and the sparks flew from the flint, the door burst open and, before the soldier stood the dog with eyes as big as two tea-cups whom he had seen in the tree, and he said:

'What are my master's commands?'

'Well I never!' wondered the soldier. 'What a funny tinder-box this is, when I can get whatever I like with it! Find me some money!' he ordered the dog, and in a flash the dog was gone! And in a flash he was back again, a big bagful of coppers in his mouth.

Now the soldier knew what a magnificent tinder-box it was! If he struck once, in ran the dog who sat on the chest of coppers; if he struck twice, in ran the one who had the silver money, and if he struck three times, in ran the one who had the gold.

And so, the soldier moved back into his splendid rooms, dressed himself in fine clothes and soon all his friends began to know him again and to love him once more.

One day the soldier thought, 'It really is rather ridiculous, that nobody is allowed to see the Princess! Everyone says how beautiful she is! But what good does it do her, when all the time she has to sit in that big copper palace with all those towers! Am I never to see her? Now where is my tinder-box!' He struck it once and there stood the dog with eyes like tea-cups.

'I know it's the middle of the night,' said the soldier, 'but I so dearly want to see the Princess, if only for a moment!'

The dog was out of the door and, before the soldier knew what was what, there he was again, carrying the Princess. There she sat, fast asleep on the dog's back and she was so beautiful that it was plain to see at once she was a Princess. The soldier couldn't help himself, he had to kiss her hand. Then the dog ran back again with the Princess.

In the morning, when the King and Queen were drinking tea, the Princess said she had such a strange dream that night, all about a dog and a soldier. She was riding on the dog's back, and the soldier had kissed her.

'That's a fine carry-on,' exclaimed the Queen. And she ordered one of the elderly ladies-in-waiting to sit by the Princess's bedside the next night to see whether it really was a dream, or what was the meaning of it.

The soldier longed terribly to see the beautiful Princess again, and so the dog appeared in the palace, took the Princess and ran off with her for all he was worth. But the elderly lady-in-waiting put on a strong pair of boots and ran after him just as fast. And, when she saw the dog and the Princess disappear into a big house, she said to herself, 'Now I know where it is!' and with a piece of chalk, she drew a big cross on the gate. Then she returned home and went to bed, and the dog with the Princess returned, too. But when the dog saw the cross chalked on the gate of the house where the soldier was living, he took a piece of chalk and drew a cross on every gate in town. This indeed was a clever idea, for now the lady-in-waiting would never find the right gate.

Early the next morning the King and Queen came to see where it was the Princess had been that night, and the lady-in-waiting and all the court officials went with them.

'Here it is!' exclaimed the King, when he saw the first door with a cross on it.

'Oh no, dear man, it's over there,' said the Queen, seeing another door with a cross on it.

'But here's the cross, and here's another!' they all cried, for no matter where

they looked, there were crosses on the gates. Now they realized that all the looking in the world wouldn't help them.

The Queen, however, was a very clever woman, who could do more than ride about in a coach. She took a big pair of golden scissors, cut up a large piece of silk and made a nice little bag from it. This bag she filled with fine buckwheat seed and fastened it to the Princess's waist. When this was done, she snipped a little hole in the bag, so the seed would trickle out, leaving a trail wherever the Princess went.

That night the dog reappeared, put the Princess on his back and ran off with her again to the soldier, who loved her terribly and wanted so very much to be a Prince, so he could marry her.

The dog did not notice the grain trickling out of the bag all the way from the palace to the soldier's window, which he reached by running up the wall with the Princess on his back. So, in the morning, the King and the Queen saw quite plainly where their daughter had been, and they took the soldier and put him in jail.

There he now sat. Brr, how dark and boring it was, and to top it all, they said, 'Tomorrow you'll hang.' These were not glad tidings and what's more, the soldier had left the tinder-box at his lodgings in the inn. In the morning he could see through the iron bars of the little window, how all the people rushed out of town to see him hanged. He heard drums and saw soldiers marching. Everybody was running, even the cobbler's apprentice in his leather apron and slippers. He was running so fast that one of the slippers flew off, landing right by the wall where the soldier sat behind the iron bars, looking out.

'Hey, cobbler boy, not so fast,' said the soldier. 'It won't start before I appear! But wouldn't you rather turn round and run to my old lodgings and bring me my tinder-box? I'll give you four coins. But you'd better run like the wind!' The cobbler's boy was always glad of a copper or two, so he dashed away for the tinder-box, gave it to the soldier and, well now, let's wait and see!

Outside the town a big gallows had been erected and round it stood soldiers and hundreds of thousands of people. The King and the Queen sat on magnificent thrones facing the judges and the whole Council.

The soldier was already standing on the ladder, but as they were about to put the rope round his neck, he said that it was always the custom of the court to grant the offender one simple, harmless wish, before carrying out the punishment. He would so love to smoke his pipe once more, for, after all, it would be his very last smoke here on earth.

The King didn't want to refuse such a wish, and so the soldier took out his

tinder-box and struck it once, twice, three times—and straightaway all the three dogs were there, the one with eyes as big as tea-cups, and the one with eyes like mill-wheels, and the one with eyes like towers.

'Help me now from being hanged!' said the soldier, and with that the dogs flew at the judges and all the councillors, seizing some by the leg, others by the nose, tossing them high up into the air, so that when they hit the ground again, they were smashed to pieces.

'Not me!' objected the King, but the biggest dog seized him and the Queen and threw them up after the others. The soldiers grew frightened and the people all shouted. 'Good soldier, you shall be our King and you shall marry our beautiful Princess!'

Then they put the soldier into the King's carriage, and all the three dogs danced in front shouting 'hurrah' and the boys whistled through their fingers and soldiers saluted in his honour. The Princess left the copper palace and was made Queen, which was much to her liking! The wedding lasted eight days and the dogs sat at the table with the rest, eyeing it all with wonder.

The Emperor's New Clothes

Many years ago there lived an Emperor so very fond of fine new clothes, that he spent all his money on dressing himself up. He didn't care for his soldiers, he didn't care for the theatre or for rides to the forest, he cared only, but only for showing himself off in new clothes. He had a robe for every hour of the day and, just as it is said about a King, that he is 'in council', it was said of him, 'The Emperor is in the dressing-room'.

The big city, where the Emperor lived, was a very busy one, and every day many strangers came to it. One day, two swindlers arrived. They pretended to be weavers, saying they could weave the most magnificent cloth imaginable. Not only were the colours and patterns exceptionally beautiful, but any clothes made from this material had the magic power of being invisible to anyone unfit for his job, or terribly stupid.

'These would be fantastic clothes,' thought the Emperor. 'If I wore them, I would find out who in my kingdom is unfit for his post; I could tell the clever ones from the dim-witted! Oh yes, that cloth must be woven for me at once!'

And he paid the two impostors a lot of money in advance, so they could commence their work.

The swindlers set up two looms and pretended to work, but the loom was quite, quite bare. They brazenly asked for the finest silk and the richest gold thread. This they pushed into their own sack.

'I would really like to know how far they've got with that material!' thought the Emperor, but a queer feeling gripped his heart at the thought that anyone stupid or unfit for his post wouldn't be able to see the material. Though he was quite convinced that he didn't need to worry about himself the slightest bit, he thought it best to send someone else first to see how it looked. All the people of the town knew of the strange power of the material, and they were all eager to see how unfit or stupid their neighbour was.

'I'll send my old honest minister to the weavers,' the Emperor decided.

'He's the best one to judge that cloth, for he has plenty of sense and no one carries out his job better than he!'

So the old honest minister went off to the hall where the two swindlers sat, working away at the empty looms.

'Gracious me,' thought the old minister, his eyes rolling, 'I can't see a thing!' But aloud he said nothing.

Both the swindlers asked him to step nearer, and enquired how he liked the lovely pattern and the beautiful colours. Then they pointed to the empty loom and the poor old minister opened his eyes wider than ever, but he still couldn't see a thing, for of course there was nothing there.

'Goodness me!' thought he. 'Am I that stupid? I never thought I was, and nobody must find out! Am I unfit for my post? No, it would never do for me to admit I can't see the cloth!'

'Well, why don't you say something?' said one of the weavers.

'Oh, it's a wonderful cloth! Truly magnificent!' said the old minister, peering through his spectacles. 'Such pattern and such colours! Yes, I'll certainly tell the Emperor how exceptionally nice it is!'

'We're happy to hear that!' said the two weavers and they named the colours and the special pattern. The old minister listened most carefully, so he could repeat it all to the Emperor upon his return. And this he did.

The swindlers now asked for more money, more silk and gold thread, saying they needed it for weaving. They put the lot into their own pockets, not a single thread reached the loom and they went on weaving, as before.

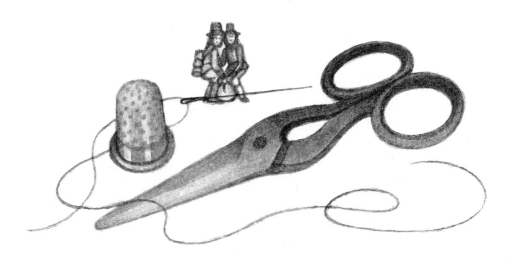

A little later, the Emperor sent another worthy official to see how the weaving was progressing and if the cloth would soon be ready. He fared the same as the minister. He looked and looked, but as there was nothing there but the empty looms, he saw nothing.

'Well, don't you think this is a beautiful piece of cloth?' asked both the swindlers, pointing at and explaining the magnificent pattern which of course wasn't there at all.

'I'm not stupid!' thought the official, 'could it be then that I'm unfit for my office? That would be most strange! I mustn't let anyone see!' And so he praised the cloth, which he couldn't see at all, assuring them of his pleasure from seeing the lovely colours and the magnificent pattern. 'Yes, it is truly exquisite!' he told the Emperor.

The whole town was talking about the magnificent material.

Now the Emperor wished to see it, while it was still on the loom. He left with a whole group of selected men, the two elderly, experienced officials among them, to visit the two crafty weavers who were weaving away for all they were worth without a single thread on the loom.

'Isn't this material truly magnificent?' asked the two worthy officials. 'Just look at that pattern, Your Highness, and those colours!' and they pointed at the empty loom, for they assumed that the others could see the cloth.

'What's this?' thought the Emperor. 'I can't see anything! Oh, this is terrible. Am I stupid? Am I, perhaps, unfit to be an Emperor? That would be the very worst fate which could befall me! — Why, this material is truly beautiful!' he said aloud, 'I give it my official approval!' and he nodded his head with satisfaction, while he looked at the empty loom. He didn't want to admit he couldn't see a thing.

All his followers looked and looked, with no more result than the rest. All the same, they said, like their Emperor, 'Oh, it's truly beautiful!' and advised him to wear clothes made from the magnificent material for the first time in the grand procession which was soon to take place. 'It is fantastic, exquisite, magnificent!' were the words that passed from mouth to mouth and one and all were most delighted with it. The Emperor gave each of the swindlers a knight's cross for his button-hole and the title of Court High Weaver.

Before the morning of the procession the swindlers sat up all night by their looms, with more than sixteen lights burning. People could see for themselves how busy they were to finish the Emperor's new clothes. They pretended to take the cloth off the loom, they snipped the air with their big scissors, they sewed with a needle without thread and, in the end they said, 'There, now at last the clothes are ready!'

The Emperor came there in person with his noble gallants, and both the swindlers raised one hand as if holding something, and said, 'These are your trousers! Here's the coat! Here's the cloak!' and so on. 'They are as light as gossamer! You would almost think you haven't a stitch on, but that's the very beauty of them!'

'How very true!' nodded all the gallants, but they saw nothing, for there was nothing to see.

'Your Imperial Highness, be gracious enough to take off your clothes now!' said the swindlers. 'We shall dress you in the new ones, over there, please, in front of that large mirror!'

The Emperor took off all his clothes and the weavers pretended to dress him in all the individual garments they were supposed to have made, and they held his waist as if fastening something round it. That was supposed to be the train. And the Emperor turned and twisted before the mirror.

'Oh, how they suit you! What a perfect fit!' everybody cried. 'What a pattern! What colours! What exquisite robes!'

'The canopy which is to be carried over Your Highness in the procession is waiting outside,' the master of ceremonies announced.

'Very well, I am ready,' said the Emperor. 'They fit me well, don't you think?' And he turned round in front of the mirror just once more, for he wanted everyone to think he was looking at the magnificent robes.

The chamberlains who were to carry the train fumbled about on the floor, pretending to pick up the train. They walked along, their empty hands in the air, not daring to show that they couldn't see a thing.

And thus the Emperor marched in the procession under the beautiful canopy, and all the people in the street and at the windows said, 'Oh, how wonderful are the Emperor's new clothes! What a magnificent train he has to his robe! How splendidly they fit!' Nobody wanted to admit that he couldn't see anything, for then he would have been unfit for his post or would have been awfully stupid. Never had the Emperor's clothes been such a success.

'But the Emperor hasn't got anything on!' cried a little child.

'Dear God, listen to the voice of the little innocent!' said the father, and it was whispered from man to man what the child had said.

'He hasn't anything on, that's what a little child says, that he hasn't anything on!'

'Why, he hasn't a thing on!' all the people shouted at last. And the Emperor went all goose-pimply, for he knew they were right, but he thought, 'I have to last out till the procession is over.' And so he marched on even more proudly, while the chamberlains walked behind him, bearing the train that wasn't there at all.

Orion

If you look up into the sky on a clear, dark night, you may be able to see a group of stars called Pegasus. There are hundreds of stars in Pegasus, and one of them is called Pelai.

Pelai lived in a magnificent palace with his lovely wife and their beautiful daughter. One day the daughter looked down to the Earth and saw a young hunter called Orion. Orion was as tall and handsome as any of the gods in the sky and the girl fell in love with him immediately.

Orion was out hunting one day shortly after the girl had first seen him, and as he turned into a clearing in the forest, he came upon the most beautiful girl he had ever seen. It was the daughter of Pelai, who, as soon as light had come to the sky, had slipped out of her night palace and come down to earth. Orion fell in love with her as deeply as she had fallen in love with him. The happy couple spent the day hunting and laughing and walking hand-in-hand through the forest, as lovers do. When night approached, the girl said: 'I must leave now. I must return to my father's palace in the night sky. We can never meet again. For I am allowed but one trip to your world. If I try to come back, my heavenly light will be put out forever.'

Orion was heartbroken. 'Then I must come to you,' he whispered.

'Your love will have to be the strongest of all if you are to ascend to the sky and live with me,' the girl said gently, and disappeared.

Poor Orion. His love was the strongest of all. But how could he find a way to the heavens?

Day after day, Orion would climb to the highest cliffs, scale the tallest trees, and even, in utter despair, reach out as far as he could. But it was of little use. The night sky was as far away as ever. Orion sat down and wept. As he shed his tears, an old woman walked by. 'My son,' she said as she passed, 'why do you cry? You are young. You are handsome. What has made you so sad?'

'Oh woman,' wailed Orion. 'Love has made me weep so,' and he explained his plight to the old woman.

She listened silently and when he had finished she said, 'There is only one way for you to ascend to the heavens. You must gather your most precious possession and offer it to the night gods tomorrow when the moon is high. If they are pleased with your offering, they will take you to live amongst them.'

Orion was overjoyed and rushed home to find his most treasured possession. As a hunter, his bow and arrow were of great value to him, so he gathered them up. He was about to leave his humble hut and return to the clearing when he remembered the belt that his parents had given him when he had reached manhood. It was studded with precious stones and his parents had sacrificed much to afford it.

With his bow and arrow and his belt he ran back to the clearing and waited until the sun was at its highest. There was a thin veil of clouds covering the stars, but exactly when the moon should be at its highest, the sky cleared and Orion could see the shining stars.

Suddenly, a soft voice whispered in the breeze, 'Orion, what is your most precious possession that you can offer?'

'My bow and arrow, by which I make my living,' said Orion.

The breeze wrenched the bow and arrow from his hands and Orion watched it disappear upwards and upwards.

A few seconds later the breeze whispered, 'It is indeed a precious gift, but we want your *most* precious possession.'

So Orion took the belt from around his waist and held it up to the stars. Again the breeze wrenched it from his hands and Orion watched as it disappeared heavenward.

'It is indeed a precious gift, but there is something else that you have that is even more precious,' whispered the breeze.

'I have nothing else of value,' cried Orion.

'There is one thing so precious that if you offer it to the gods they will grant you your wish.'

'Nothing. There is nothing more,' sobbed Orion.

'Then I leave,' breathed the wind.

'No. Wait!' cried Orion. 'My most treasured possession I cannot give away, for it is not mine to give. It was entrusted to me and in return I gave a similar gift.'

'What is it?' demanded the breeze.

'It is the love that my sweetheart gave to me. That is my most treasured possession.'

As soon as he had said the words, the breeze became stronger and wrapped itself around Orion pulling him upwards and upwards and upwards, until at last he was in the sky looking down at the world.

'My love,' a voice behind him whispered. Orion turned round and there was his beloved. 'You had to know that my love was your most treasured possession before you could come here. I am so happy that you knew it.'

The happy couple embraced and have been together in the sky ever since.

The Voyages of Sinbad the Sailor

There was once a rich merchant who had a son called Sinbad. When the merchant died, he left Sinbad a vast amount of money and precious jewels. Sinbad was lazy and spent all his day with undesirable friends, squandering his wealth. Within a few years he had spent most of his inheritance.

One day he happened to pick up an old book and his eyes fell upon these words:

'Three things are more important than any other: the day of death is more important than the day of birth, the living dog is more important than the dead lion, and poverty is less important than the grave.'

He thought about these words for some time and realized how silly he had been. So he sold what was left of his possessions and decided to invest the money he raised in a journey overseas to buy precious things which he could resell at a profit when he returned. He would spend what he had raised on hiring a ship and crew and with anything left over, he would buy goods to sell overseas to pay for his purchases.

So that is what he did. He went to the bazaar and spent some money on goods for trading. Then he hired a few porters and ship and crew, and then they set sail. They crossed the Persian Gulf and sailed into the Sea of Levant.

One day, the ship approached a beautiful island and the captain cast anchor. The merchants were enchanted by the loveliness of the place and were eager to set their feet upon land. So they went directly ashore. There some lit cooking fires, others washed in the island's clear streams and still others, Sinbad amongst them, walked about enjoying the sight of the trees and greenery.

They had spent many hours in these pleasant pursuits when all at once the ship's look-out called to them from the gunwale:

'Run for your lives. Return to the ship. That is not a real island, but a great sea monster stranded in the sea on whom the sand has settled and trees have sprung up so that he looks like an island. When you started your fires it felt the heat and moved. In a moment it will sink with you into the sea and you will all be drowned. Run! Run!'

All who left, left their gear and goods and swam in terror back to the ship. But Sinbad had walked too far to get away in time. Suddenly the island shuddered and sank into the depths of the sea; the waters surged over Sinbad and the waves crashed down upon him. He had nearly drowned when a wooden tub in which the crew had been bathing floated his way. He jumped into it and began to paddle with his arms towards the ship. The captain, however, was in such a fright that he set sail immediately with those who had reached the ship, heeding not the cries of the drowning.

Darkness closed in around Sinbad and he lay in the tub, certain that death was at hand. But after drifting for an entire night and a day, the tides brought him to the harbour of a lofty island. He caught hold of one of the branches and managed to clamber up onto the beach. Alas, he could walk no farther, for his legs were cramped and numb, and his feet swollen. So he crawled on his knees until he came upon a grove of fruit-laden trees amidst springs of sweet water. Sinbad ate and drank and his body and spirit began to revive.

After several days, Sinbad set out to explore the island. As he walked along the shore he caught sight of a noble mare tethered on the beach. He went up to her and she let out a great cry. Sinbad trembled in fear and turned to leave.

Before he had gone very far, a man came out of a cave, followed him and asked, 'Who are you?'

'Sinbad,' the surprised merchant replied.

'Where have you come from?' asked the man.

'I am a stranger who was left to drown in the sea, but good fortune led me to this island.'

When the man heard Sinbad's tale, he took his hand and led him to the entrance to the cave. They entered, descended a flight of steps and he found himself in a huge underground chamber as spacious as a ballroom.

Sinbad looked around and said, 'Now that I have told you of my accident, pray tell me who you are, why you live under the earth and why that mare is tethered on the beach?'

And so the man began his story:

'I am one of many who are stationed in different parts of the island. We are grooms of King Mirjan who guard and protect all of his horses. The mare you saw was one of a magical breed that eats not hay, but is nourished by the light of the moon.

'Every month when the moon is at its fullest, we bring the mares to the beach and then hide ourselves in these caves. In the morning when the moon has worked its spell, we return with the mares to our master. And now I shall take you, too, to the king.'

The rest of the grooms soon arrived, each leading a mare and the grooms set out, journeying to the capital of King Mirjan. The groom introduced the king to Sinbad, wherupon Mirjan gave him a cordial welcome and asked to hear his tale. So Sinbad related all that had happened. When he had finished the king said, 'Your rescue is indeed miraculous. You must be a blessed man destined for great things.' And the king promptly made Sinbad his harbour master, showered him with gifts and all manner of costly presents.

Sinbad lived in this way for a long while. And whenever he went to the port, he questioned the merchants and travellers for news of his home, Baghdad, for he was weary of living among strangers and hoped to find some way to return home. But he met no one who knew of his beloved city, so he despaired.

One day a large ship came sailing into the harbour. When it had docked, the crew began to unload the cargo while Sinbad stood by and recorded the contents. 'Is there anything left in your ship?' Sinbad asked when the crew seemed to have finished.

'There remains in the hold only assorted bales of merchandise whose owner was drowned near one of the islands on our course. We are going to sell the goods and deliver the proceeds to his people in Baghdad.' When Sinbad asked for the drowned merchant's name, the captain replied, 'Sinbad the Sailor.'

On hearing this, Sinbad let out a great cry.

'O captain, I am that Sinbad who travelled with you. I was saved by a wooden tub that carried me to this island where the servants of King Mirjan found me and brought me here. These bales are mine and I pray you to release them to me.'

But the captain did not believe Sinbad.

'O captain,' Sinbad exclaimed, 'listen to my words. I will tell you more about my voyage than you have told me, then you will believe me.'

So Sinbad began to relate to the captain the whole history of the journey, up to the tragedy of the island. The captain then realized the truth of Sinbad's story and rejoiced at his deliverance saying, 'We were sure that you had drowned. Praise be to the power that gave you new life.'

The captain gave the bales to Sinbad, who opened them up and made **305** a parcel of the finest and costliest of the contents as a present to King Mirjan.

Having done so and been honoured with even costlier presents from King Mirjan, Sinbad returned to Baghdad with the crew of the ship.

With all the presents that the King had given him, Sinbad was rich and settled down again in Baghdad.

Sinbad was leading a most pleasurable life until one day he took it into his head to travel around the world. So he brought a large supply of merchandise, went down to the harbour and booked a passage on a brand new ship. At last, fate brought him to an island, fair and green filled with fruit-bearing trees, fragrant flowers and singing birds. Sinbad landed and walked about, enjoying the shade of the trees and the song of the birds. So sweet was the wind and so fragrant were the flowers that he soon fell into a deep sleep. When he awoke he was horrified to find that the ship had left without him.

Giving himself up for lost he lamented, 'Last time I was saved by fate, but fate cannot be so kind twice. I am alone and there is no hope for me.'

He was so upset that he could not sit in one place for long. He climbed a tall tree and, looking in all directions, saw nothing but sky and sea and trees and birds and sand. But after a while his eager glance fell upon some great thing in the middle of the island. So he climbed down from the tree and walked to it. Behold, it was a huge white dome rising high into the air.

Sinbad circled around it but could find no door. As he stood wondering how to enter the dome, the skies darkened. Sinbad thought that a cloud had hidden the sun, but when he looked up he saw an enormous bird of such gigantic breadth that it veiled the sun.

Then Sinbad recalled a story he had heard long ago from some travellers. It told of a certain island where lived a huge bird called the roc, which fed its young on elephants. As Sinbad marvelled at the strange ways of nature, the roc alighted on the dome, covered it with its wings, and stretched its legs out on the ground. In this strange posture the roc fell asleep. When Sinbad saw this he arose, unwound his turban and twisted it into a rope with which he tied himself to the roc's legs.

'Perhaps,' he thought, 'this bird will carry me to inhabited lands. That will be better than living on this deserted island.'

In the morning the roc rose off its egg, for that is what the dome was, and spreading its wings with a great cry, soared into the air dragging Sinbad along, but never noticing him. When the roc finally alighted on the top of a high hill, Sinbad, quaking in his fear, wasted no time in untying himself and running off. Presently he saw the roc catch something in its huge claws and rise aloft with it. Looking as closely as he dared Sinbad realized it was

a serpent as gigantic as had ever roamed the earth; yet it seemed puny compared to the roc.

Looking further around, Sinbad found that he was on a hill overlooking a deep valley, which was surrounded by mountains so high that their summits disappeared into the clouds. At the sight of the wild and impassable country Sinbad moaned, 'Woe is me: I was better off on the island. There I had fruit to eat and water to drink, but here there are neither trees nor fruits nor streams and I will surely starve.'

Then Sinbad took courage and went down into the valley. Imagine how amazed he was to find that the soil was made of diamonds and it swarmed with snakes and vipers as big as palm trees. Sinbad ran for his life. Again he lamented at his misfortune.

As Sinbad walked along the valley, a roc flew overhead and dropped a slaughtered beast at his feet. Looking at the beast he had an idea. He took his knife from his belt and cut the meat into large, sticky pieces. When he had done this he threw the chunks into the valley. Suddenly the air was filled with huge eagles who swooped down into the diamond-filled valley and picked up the meat. Because the meat was so sticky, the precious stones stuck to it. Sinbad ran after them and shooed them away, picking up the diamonds as he did so.

When he had gathered all the diamonds, he unwound his turban and laid all the meat on it. He tied it around himself and lay on his back and waited. A few minutes later, one of the huge eagles flew overhead and seeing the juicy meat, swooped down. He picked the meat up in his mighty talons, the turban and Sinbad with it. They flew for many miles, until Sinbad saw that they were passing over a huge, blue lake. He let out a loud cry and the startled bird dropped him, diamonds and all.

Sinbad landed in the lake with a large plop. Fortunately he was a good swimmer and swam as fast as he could for the shore. He walked along the sandy beach until he came to a small village. He asked one of the men there, how he could get to the nearest port. The man scratched his head and said, 'The nearest port is many miles from here, much too far to walk. We only have one horse in the village, so we could not sell it to you, no matter how much you offered.'

Sinbad showed the man his diamonds. 'Sir,' he said, 'if your horse is strong enough to carry two, I will give you ten diamonds for a lift. You and I can both ride on its back, and with the money you get for the diamonds you can buy ten hundred horses.'

So the man agreed to do this and the two set off. It was a long and tiring journey, but eventually they reached the port. There Sinbad sold some of the diamonds and bought beautiful silks and golden ornaments with the money he had received. He hired a boat to take him back to Baghdad, and when he arrived he sold all his goods for a huge profit and settled down in the town again, living a most pleasurable life.

But as time passed he once again grew weary of his idle life of ease and comfort. So once more he laid in a considerable supply of merchandise to trade, and set sail in a fine ship with a company of merchants. For weeks they travelled on calm seas, stopping at many ports and gaining great profits through their trade. But one day, when they were far out at sea a mighty storm arose. The waves lashed the ship and the gales drove them they knew not where. The next morning when the storm had calmed, the captain climbed up to the gunwale and scanned the ocean in all directions. Suddenly he let out a great cry and tore his garments in despair.

'O my fellow travellers,' he cried, 'the wind has driven us far off course and we have run aground at the Mountain of the Hairy Apes. No man has ever left this place alive. We are doomed.'

Hardly had he finished speaking when thousands of apes were upon them, surrounding the ship on all sides, swarming about like locusts. They were the most fearsome creatures, only two feet tall, but covered with black hair, evil-smelling, black-faced and yellow-eyed. They gnawed at the ship's ropes and cables, tearing them in two, so that the sails fell into the sea and the powerless ship was stranded on the mountainous coast. Then the apes chased all the men off the ship, stole the cargo and disappeared.

Sinbad and his companions were left on the mountain island where they fortunately found fruit and water. They ate and drank and then decided to explore the island.

They had walked for a mile or two when they came across what looked like an uninhabited house. As they came close to it they could see that it was a tall castle and the gate was open. They went in and found themselves in a large courtyard which was completely empty. They lay down and fell asleep, hoping that the castle's owner would return before nightfall.

All at once the earth trembled under them and the air rumbled with a terrible noise. The owner had returned and he was a gigantic creature shaped like a man but as tall as a tree, with eyes like fiery coals and teeth like elephant's tusks. His mouth was like a well, his lips hung loose onto his chest and his nails were as long and sharp as lion's claws.

The merchants almost fainted with terror at the sight of him. Then the giant seized Sinbad, who was but a tiny plaything in his hands, and began to run his mighty hands all over him, prodding him here and there. But Sinbad was too thin for the giant's huge appetite, so he put him down and picked up **309** another. Finding him too thin as well, the giant tried another and another until he came to the captain of the ship, who was a fat, broad-shouldered man. The giant found him tempting enough to eat and promptly did so. That done he lay down and fell asleep. In the morning he got up and left the castle.

The next night the giant returned and again the earth trembled, and again he went through all the men until he found one tasty enough for his supper.

When the giant departed the next morning the terrified men decided that they could not sit by and watch the giant eat them all.

'Let us try to slay him,' they said. 'We will build a raft of firewood and planks and keep it ready at the shore.' As soon as the giant came home, he grabbed one of the men and ate him for his dinner. He lay down and fell asleep shortly afterwards.

When the men were quite sure that the giant was sound asleep, they took two iron spits and heated the ends in a fire, until they were as red-hot as the coals themselves. They crept up to the sleeping giant and thrust the glowing spits into his eyes.

His scream rent the air and he jumped up fumbling for the men. But he was quite blind and he could not prevent the men rushing to the raft.

But even when they had passed beyond the giant's reach, they could find no respite from danger, for the sea was stormy and the waves swollen. One by one the men died until there were only three men and Sinbad left. Finally the winds cast them upon an island where they found fruit to eat and water to drink. Exhausted by their hazardous voyage, they lay down on the beach and went to sleep.

They had barely closed their eyes when they were aroused by a hissing sound and saw that a monstrous dragon with a huge belly was spread in a circle around them. Suddenly it reared its head, seized one of Sinbad's companions, and swallowed him whole. Then the beast left and Sinbad said, 'Woe to us. Each kind of death that threatens us is more terrible than the last. We rejoiced at our deliverance from the sea and apes and the giant, but we are now at the mercy of something even more evil.'

The frightened men climbed into a high tree and went to sleep there. Sinbad rested on the top branch. When night fell, the dragon returned. He looked to right and left and finally discovered the men in the tree. He stood up on his hind legs and swallowed Sinbad's companions. Again, the dragon left satisfied with his dinner. Then Sinbad climbed down and resolved to find some way to save his life. So he took pieces of wood, broad and long, and made a cage with them. He crept into the cage and when the dragon returned he saw Sinbad sitting in the cage. He immediately tried to eat him, but he could not get his jaws round the cage.

All through the night, the dragon circled around Sinbad's cage, hissing in
anger. But when the dawn came and the sun began to shine, the dragon left in
fury and disappointment.

Sinbad ran to the beach where he spied a ship on the horizon. He broke
a branch off a tree, unwound his turban from his head and tied it to the
branch. He began to wave it like a flag and at last, one of the sailors spotted
him and the ship turned to shore. They cast anchor and took the grateful
Sinbad aboard, and carried him back to Baghdad.

One day, several months later, Sinbad was visited at home by a company of
merchants who talked to him about foreign travel and trade, until the old
wanderlust came back to Sinbad, and he yearned to enjoy the sight of foreign
lands once more. So Sinbad resolved to join them on their voyage and they
purchased a great store of precious goods, more than ever before. They set out
and sailed from island to island.

After several months of travelling and trading they sailed into a furious
storm which tore the sails to tatters. Then the ship foundered, casting all on
board into the sea.

Sinbad swam for half a day, certain that his fate was sealed, when one of the
planks of the ship floated up to him and he climbed on it, along with some of
the other merchants.

They took turns paddling and soon the current drove them to an island. Sinbad and his companions threw themselves onto the beach, ate some of the fruit that they found there and then each man fell into a troubled sleep. The next morning they began to explore the island. Coming across a house, they were about to knock at the door when a host of half-naked savages ran out, surrounded them and forced them inside where the king waited. The king extended a most cordial welcome and invited them to dinner. Gratefully they sat down and were immediately served such food as they had never tasted in their lives.

Sinbad, however, was not hungry and he refused all the food that was offered to him. He was soon glad that he had done so, for as the men tasted the food they lost all their senses and began to devour it like madmen possessed of an evil spirit. Then the savages gave them coconut oil to drink, whereupon their eyes turned around in their heads and they continued to eat even more ravenously than before.

Seeing all this, Sinbad grew anxious for his safety. He watched carefully and it was not long before he realized that he was amidst a certain tribe of savages of whom he had once heard a traveller tell. Every man who came to the savages' country was given food and oil which made their stomachs expand and at the same time to lose their reason and turn into idiots. In this way, the unfortunate victims never stopped eating. Every day they were led out to pasture like cattle and grew fatter and fatter. When they were judged fat enough, the savages slaughtered them and sent them off to market.

So Sinbad understood the evil folk that he had fallen among and watched sadly as his friends ate and drank. The savages paid no attention to Sinbad, for as the days passed he grew thinner.

One day he slipped away and walked to a distant beach. There he saw the old man who was the herdsman, charged with guarding his friends. As soon as the herdsman saw Sinbad, so gaunt and bony, he realized that this was not one of the madmen and wanted to help him escape.

'If you take the road to the right,' the herdsman said, 'it will lead you away from the house of the savages.'

Sinbad followed the kind old man's advice and did not cease travelling for seven days and seven nights. He stopped only to eat and drink, for the path was strewn with roots and herbs and water was plentiful. On the eighth day he caught sight of a group of men gathering peppercorns.

'I am a poor stranger,' he said to them. 'May I have a peppercorn?'

One of the men threw him a handful and Sinbad told them the story of the hardships and dangers that he had suffered.

312   The men marvelled at Sinbad's tale and brought him to their king, to whom he repeated his tale. The king instantly liked Sinbad and invited him to stay in his sumptuous palace.

One day the king invited Sinbad out to ride with the hunt. Now Sinbad had noticed that neither the king nor his citizens had saddles on their beautiful steeds.

'Why, O Lord, do you not have saddles? Riding is much easier with them.'

'What is a saddle?' the king asked, for he had never heard of such a thing before.

Sinbad offered to make one for him, so that he could ride in greater comfort. In a few days, Sinbad had fashioned a magnificent saddle of polished leather with silk fringes and presented it to the king. The king tried it and was delighted. The next week his Vizier asked Sinbad to make a saddle for him as well. In a short time, everyone wanted a saddle, so Sinbad went into business and became a prosperous saddle maker.

Then one day the king said, 'Sinbad, I have such affection for you that I cannot permit you ever to leave. I must therefore insist that you marry one of our women so that you will remain here for the rest of your days.'

So Sinbad married a beautiful and rich lady of noble ancestry and lived with her in peace and contentment.

One sad day, however, Sinbad's wife took ill and died within a week. The mournful Sinbad was about to make arrangements for a funeral in accordance with the customs of his own country when a messenger arrived from the king.

'My lord offers you deep condolences and asks that the funeral be conducted according to the customs of our land,' the messenger said. Sinbad agreed, for he wished only to honour his wife.

Now it happened that the customs of the country were very strange. When a woman died she was buried in a deep cave and her husband, still alive, was buried with her so that she might have companionship in the afterlife.

On the day of the funeral, the whole town arrived in front of Sinbad's house and they walked in procession to the burial cave — a vast underground cavern that ran beneath a mountain. The body of Sinbad's wife was lowered down. Then the townsfolk lowered him down on a rope ladder.

Sinbad found himself in a cave filled with rotting bodies and skeletons, for it had served as a burial site since time immemorial. It was a horrible, foul-smelling place and Sinbad again lamented that the greed that had made him leave Baghdad had ended in such a way. There was no escape from the cave of death.

The day after the funeral, Sinbad noticed a mountain goat at the far end of **313**

the cave. Seeing that the beast was fat and healthy, Sinbad realized that there must be another opening in the cave, one unknown to the townspeople. So he followed the beast and after a while saw a shaft of light. Indeed, it was another opening. Sinbad joyfully climbed out and found himself high over the sea on a steep cliff which only an animal so agile as the goat could climb. Although he felt sure that he was to die there, he was thankful that he would not die in the cavern of death.

When Sinbad was near to death, a ship passed by and spotted him. The ship cast anchor and with the help of strong ropes, the sailors scaled the cliff and rescued Sinbad.

When he arrived back in Baghdad, Sinbad promised his friends and relations that he would never leave them again. This time he kept that promise.

The Two Brothers

Once upon a time there were two brothers, one rich and the other poor. The rich brother was a goldsmith, an evil-hearted man; the poor brother earned his living by making brooms, and was good and honest. The poor brother had two children, twin-brothers, who were as alike as two peas. Now and then the two boys would go to their rich uncle's house and, once in a while, they got something to eat from the leftovers.

One day, as the poor man went into the forest to fetch brushwood, he happened to see a bird that was of solid gold and more beautiful than any he had ever set eyes upon. He picked up a pebble, threw it at the bird, and was lucky enough to hit it. But only one golden feather fell, and the bird flew away.

The man picked up the feather and brought it to his brother, who looked at it and said, 'This is pure gold,' and gave him a lot of money for it.

On another day, the poor brother climbed a birch-tree to cut off a few branches. Then the same bird flew out of it and, having searched further, the man found a nest with an egg in it that was made of gold. He took the egg home with him and brought it to his brother, who said again, 'It's pure gold,' and gave him what it was worth.

At last the goldsmith said, 'I should like to have the bird itself.'

The man went to the forest for the third time, and again he saw the golden bird sitting in the tree. So he picked up a stone and threw it at the bird and brought it down and took it to his brother, who gave him a huge pile of money for it. 'Now I have something to go on with,' he thought and went home well content.

The goldsmith was crafty and cunning, and knew only too well what kind of a bird it was. He called his wife and said to her, 'Roast me the bird, and take care that none of it gets lost. I wish to eat it all myself.' It was no ordinary bird, but so wonderful that whoever ate its heart and liver would find a gold piece under his pillow every morning. The wife got the bird ready, stuck it on a spit, and roasted it.

However, it so happened that just as the wife had to leave the kitchen to do some other work, the children of the poor broom-maker came running in, saw the spit and turned it round a few times. When two small pieces fell off the bird into the pan, the one said, 'We can eat those few bits, no one will notice.' Then, as they were eating, the goldsmith's wife appeared and seeing they were eating something she said, 'What is it you are eating?'

'A few bits that have dropped off the bird,' they answered.

'That was the heart and the liver,' said the woman terrified. So that her husband should not miss anything and get angry, she quickly killed a cockerel, took out the heart and liver, and put them into the golden bird.

When it was ready, she served it to the goldsmith who ate it all himself and left nothing. The next morning, however, when he looked under his pillow hoping to find the gold piece, there was no more there than at any other time.

The two boys didn't know what good fortune had been theirs. The next morning, when they got up, something dropped with a tinkling noise on to the floor, and when they picked it up, there were two gold pieces. These they brought to their father, who was astonished and wondered how it could have come about. But when next morning they found another two, and so on every day, he went to his brother and told him the strange story.

The goldsmith knew at once what had happened. The boys had eaten the golden bird's heart and liver. In order to have his revenge, the envious and wicked man said to his brother, 'Your children are in league with the Evil One. Don't accept the gold, and don't tolerate them any more in your house, for he has them in his power and will bring ruin to you.'

The boys' father was afraid of the Evil One and, hard as he found it, he led the twins out into the forest and with a sad heart left them there.

The two children ran about the forest trying to find their way home, but they couldn't, and in the end got completely lost. At last, they came upon a huntsman who asked, 'Whose children are you?'

'We are the poor broom-maker's boys,' they answered, and told him that their father didn't want to keep them in his house because there was a gold coin lying under their pillow every morning.

'Well,' said the huntsman, 'that in itself is nothing bad as long as you stay honest and do not start idling about and become lazy-bones.'

The good man liked the children and, as he had none of his own, he took them into his house and said, 'I will take the place of your father and bring you up.' He taught them the craft of the huntsman, and the gold coins which each of them found every morning, he kept for them for the future.

When they grew up, their foster-father took them into the forest one day and said, 'You shall do your shooting test today and, if you are successful, you will become hunters.'

They went with him to lie in wait and stayed a long time but no game appeared. The huntsman looked up above him and seeing a flock of snowgeese flying in a triangle said to one of the boys, 'Now bring down one from each corner.' He did so and thus passed his test.

Soon afterwards yet another formation of geese came flying past in the form **317** of a figure two. Now the foster-father bade the other boy bring down one from each corner, and his trial-shot was also successful. The foster-father said, 'I now release you from your apprenticeship. You are accomplished huntsmen.'

Afterwards, the two brothers went further into the forest together, took counsel and came to an agreement. In the evening as they sat down to supper they said to their foster-father, 'We will not touch the wine, nor take a single morsel of food until you have granted us a favour.'

'What is your request then?' he asked.

They answered, 'We have now learnt our craft, and must try our luck in the world. Give us leave to go on our way.'

Then the huntsman said with pleasure, 'You talk like honest huntsman. That which you yearn for has also been my wish. Go on your way, you will prosper.' Then they ate and drank merrily together.

When the day came for the boys to leave, the foster-father presented both of

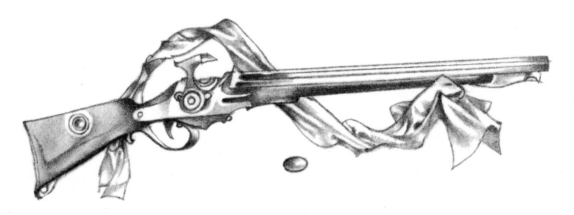

them with a good rifle and a dog, and let them take as many saved gold coins as they wanted. Then he accompanied them part of the way and, during the leave-taking, gave them a bright and shiny knife and said, 'If you ever part, thrust this knife into a tree at the crossroads. The one that comes back will see by this knife how his absent brother has prospered, for the blade will go rusty if he dies, but as long as he is alive, it will stay bright.'

The two brothers went further and further away, and came into a forest which was so large that they found it impossible to come out of it in one day. So they stayed there overnight and ate what they had in their hunting pouches. But on the second day they didn't reach the end of the forest either. As they had nothing to eat one of them said, 'We'll have to shoot something, or go hungry.' He loaded his gun and looked around. As an old hare came

running past he raised the gun, but the hare cried:

'Dear huntsman, let me live,
Two of my young to you I'll give.'

And indeed, it at once sprang into the underwood and brought out two young hares. But the little animals played so merrily and were so well-behaved that the huntsmen didn't have the heart to kill them. So they kept them, and the little hares followed close on their heels wherever they went.

Soon afterwards a fox came sneaking by, which they wanted to shoot, but the fox cried:

'Dear huntsmen, let me live,
Two of my young to you I'll give.'

And indeed, he did bring two fox cubs, but the huntsmen could not kill these either. They put them with the hares for company, and they all followed on one behind the other.

Before long a wolf came out of the brushwood, the huntsmen levelled their guns at him, but the wolf cried:

'Dear huntsmen, let me live,
Two of my young to you I'll give.'

The huntsmen added the two young wolves to the other animals, and they went along with them, too.

Then came a bear, who wanted to trot about alive a little longer, and cried:

'Dear huntsmen, let me live,
Two of my young to you I'll give.'

The two young bears were added to the others, and now there were eight animals in the company.

Then, who should come but a lion, shaking his mane. The huntsmen weren't scared and aimed at him, but the lion also said:

> 'Dear huntsmen, let me live,
> Two of my young to you I'll give.'

He, too, brought two of his cubs along, and so the huntsmen had two lions, two bears, two wolves, two foxes and two hares which followed them.

However, this was not the way to ease their hunger, and they said to the foxes, 'Listen, you prowlers, get us something to eat, for you are crafty and cunning.'

They answered, 'Not far from here is a village from which we have stolen many a chicken. We will show you the way there.'

They went into the village, bought themselves something to eat and also fed the animals. Then they went on. The foxes knew their way about the district very well, particularly where the chicken yards were, and so were able to show the huntsmen exactly where to go.

They wandered about awhile, but could find no place where they could stay together whereupon the huntsmen said, 'There's no other way. We must separate.' So they divided the animals between them and each got one lion, one bear, one wolf, one fox, and one hare. Then they took leave of each other, pledged each other brotherly love unto death and stuck the knife which their foster-father had given them into a tree. Then one went east and the other west.

The brother who had walked to the west with his animals came to a city where everything was covered in black crape. He went to an inn, and asked the innkeeper if he could give shelter to his animals. The innkeeper gave him a stable with a hole in the wall. The hare crept out and brought himself a cabbage; the fox brought himself a chicken and, when he had eaten it, a cock also. But the wolf, the bear and the lion being too big could not get out. The innkeeper led them to a place where a dead cow was lying on the grass so that they could eat their fill. And not until the huntsman had taken care of his animals did he ask the innkeeper why the city was draped with mourning crape.

'Because tomorrow our King's only daughter is going to die,' he said.

'Is she dangerously ill?' asked the huntsman.

'No,' answered the innkeeper, 'she is hale and hearty but even so she's got to die.'

'But why?' asked the huntsman.

'There is a high mountain outside the city, where a dragon lives, and it must have a pure maiden every year, or it would lay waste the whole country. Now all the pure young maidens have been given up to it except one, and she is the King's daughter. However, there is no escape, she must be given up to it, and tomorrow is the day of the sacrifice.'

321

The huntsman said, 'Why don't they go and kill the dragon?'

'Alas,' said the landlord, 'so many knights have tried it but all have lost their lives. The King has promised his daughter in marriage to the man who conquers the dragon, and after his death the victor shall inherit the kingdom.'

The huntsman said no more, but the following morning, he took his animals and climbed up Dragon's Hill with them. At the top was a small church, and inside on the altar stood three filled cups. An inscription lay beside them: 'Whoever drinks from these cups shall become the strongest man on earth, and shall wield the sword that lies buried before the threshold.'

The huntsman did not drink, instead he went out and sought the sword buried in the earth, but found it impossible to move it from its place. So he went in and drained the cups, and then he was strong enough to lift up the sword, and his hand was able to wield it with ease.

When the hour approached that the King's daughter was to be sacrificed to the dragon, she came accompanied by the King, the marshal, and the courtiers. She saw from afar the huntsman high above on Dragon's Hill and thought it was the dragon waiting for her. She hung back at first but since she knew the whole city would be destroyed if she didn't go on, she forced herself to continue her awesome journey. The King and the courtiers returned home full of grief, but the King's marshal waited behind to watch everything from a distance.

When the Princess got to the top of the mountain it was not the dragon but the young huntsman standing there. He tried to comfort her, and assured her he was going to save her. Then he led her into the church, and locked her in.

Before long the seven-headed dragon came with a loud roar. When it saw the huntsman, it was astonished and said, 'What business brings you up here on the mountain?'

The huntsman said, 'I have come to fight you.'

The dragon replied, 'So many knights have lost their lives here, and I shall soon be rid of you, too.' And the dragon breathed fire from its seven mouths. The fire should have set fire to the dry grass and the huntsman was expected to suffocate in the vapour, but the animals came at a run and trampled the fire out. Then the dragon rushed upon the huntsman, but he swung his sword so that it sang in the air and sliced off three of its heads. Then the dragon became really furious, reared itself up in the air, spat out flames of fire at the huntsman, and intended to rush at him, but the

322 huntsman once more drew his sword and cut off three more of its heads.

Then the monster lost most of its strength, and sank down intending to hurl itself at the huntsman yet again, but the huntsman, with the last of his strength, cut off its tail. Then unable to fight any more, he called up his animals who tore the dragon to pieces.

Now that the fight was over, the huntsman unlocked the church door, went in and found the Princess lying on the floor unconscious. During the struggle she had been overcome by fear and terror. He carried her out and showed her the dragon torn to pieces.

She was overjoyed and said, 'Now you shall become my dearest husband, for my father has promised me to the man who would slay the dragon.' Then she took off her coral necklace and divided it among the animals as a reward, and the lion got the little golden clasp. Then she gave her handkerchief with her name on it to the huntsman, who went and cut the tongues out of the seven dragon's heads, and wrapped them in the handkerchief to keep them safe.

After this, as he felt so weak and tired from the fight and the fire, he said to the Princess, 'We are both so faint and weary, we ought to sleep a little now.' She agreed, and they lay down on the ground.

The huntsman said to the lion, 'You shall keep watch, that no one attacks us in our sleep.'

The lion lay by their side, but he, too, was tired from the fight, so he called to the bear and said, 'Lie down beside me, I must sleep a little, but if anyone comes, wake me.'

Then the bear lay down beside him, and he called to the wolf and said, 'Lie down beside me, I must sleep a little, but wake me if anyone comes.'

Then the wolf lay down beside him but he, too, was tired, so he called the fox and said, 'Lie down beside me, I must have a little sleep, but wake me if anyone comes.'

Then the fox lay down beside him but he, too, was tired, and so he called

the hare and said, 'Lie down beside me, I must have a little sleep, but wake me if anyone comes.'

So the hare sat down beside him, but the poor hare was also tired, and fell asleep. Now the King's daughter, the huntsman, the lion, the bear, the wolf, the fox, and the hare, were all fast asleep.

However, the marshal, whose duty it had been to watch, waited until all was quiet on the mountain. Then he plucked up courage, and climbed to the top and found the dragon dead on the ground, torn to pieces. Not far from it he found the King's daughter, the huntsman and all his animals in a deep sleep. And, because he was a bad and a wicked man, he took his sword and cut off the huntsman's head and seized the Princess in his arms and carried her down the hill.

When she woke up, she was frightened to find herself being carried by the marshal. The marshal said, 'You are in my hands and you shall say it was I who killed the dragon.'

'That I cannot do,' she answered, 'for it was the huntsman with his animals who did it.'

He drew his sword and threatened to kill her, if she didn't obey him. So she was forced to promise she would say anything he wanted her to. Then the marshal brought her before the King, who was beside himself with joy.

The marshal said to him, 'I have slain the dragon and delivered the Princess. The entire kingdom therefore I demand, and her hand in marriage, as was promised.'

The King asked his daughter if what the marshal said was true.

'Yes,' she answered, 'it is true. But I shall make it a condition that the wedding shall not take place before a year and a day is out.' For she hoped to hear from her beloved huntsman during that time.

On Dragon's Hill, the animals were still lying asleep by the side of their dead master. A big bumble-bee came and sat on the hare's nose, but the hare knocked it off with his paw, and slept on. The bumble-bee came a second time, but again the hare knocked it off and went on sleeping. Then it came for the third time and stung him on the nose, and that woke him up! As soon as the hare was awake, he woke the fox, the fox woke the wolf, the wolf woke the bear, and the bear woke the lion. And when the lion awoke and saw that the Princess was gone and his master dead, he started roaring terribly and cried, 'Bear, why didn't you wake me?' The bear asked the wolf, 'Why didn't you wake me?' and the wolf asked the fox, 'Why didn't you wake me?' and the fox asked the hare, 'Why didn't you wake me?' The poor hare all alone did not know what to say in reply, and the blame remained
with him.

They were about to set upon him, but he begged them saying, 'Don't kill me. I will bring our master back to life again. I know of a mountain on which a root grows, and whoever has it placed in his mouth will be cured of any illness and healed of any wound. But the mountain is two hundred hours distant.'

'You must run there and back in twenty-four hours,' said the lion, 'and bring the root back with you.'

The hare galloped away, and in twenty-four hours he was back again bringing the root with him. The lion put the huntsman's head on again and put the root in his mouth. Immediately the heart started beating and life was restored. The huntsman was horror-struck when he did not see the maiden beside him, and thought, 'She must have gone away while I was sleeping in order to get away from me.'

The huntsman was sad and wandered about the world and let the animals dance before people. It so happened that after exactly one year had passed, he came back again to the very same city where he had saved the King's daughter from the dragon, and this time he found the city draped in crimson cloth. He asked the innkeeper, 'What does this mean? A year ago, the city was draped in black crape. What does the crimson cloth signify?'

The innkeeper answered, 'A year ago, our King's daughter should have been sacrificed to the dragon, but the marshal fought it and killed it and tomorrow their wedding is to be celebrated. That's why the city is draped in crimson for rejoicing.'

The next day when the wedding was to have taken place the huntsman said to the innkeeper, 'Would you believe it if I told you that I shall eat bread from the King's table today?' 'Nay, I wouldn't,' said the innkeeper. 'I would rather bet you a hundred gold pieces that you won't.'

The huntsman accepted the wager, and laid down a pouch with a hundred gold pieces in it. Then he called the hare and said, 'Go to the palace and fetch me some of the bread that the King is eating.'

Now the hare was the smallest and could not pass the order on to anyone else, but had to go himself. 'Alas,' he thought, 'when I leap along the streets all alone, the butcher's dogs will chase me.' As he had guessed, so it happened. The dogs chased him and wanted to tear his fur for him. But he sprang away and found shelter in a sentry-box without the soldier noticing. Then the dogs came and wanted to chase him out, but the soldier struck them with his rifle-butt so that they ran off barking and howling.

When the hare saw that the coast was clear, he sprang towards the royal palace, and straight to the King's daughter, sat down under her chair, and scratched her foot. Then she said, 'Off with you!' thinking it was her dog. **325**

The hare scratched her foot for the second time, and she said again, 'Off with you!' thinking it was her own dog. But the hare would not be put off, and scratched for the third time. Then she looked down and recognized the hare by his collar. She took him on her lap, carried him into her chamber, and said, 'Dear hare, what do you want?'

He answered, 'My master, who killed the dragon, is here and has sent me to ask for bread from the King's table.'

Then the Princess was full of joy, and she had the baker come and ordered him to bring the bread from the King's table.

The little hare said, 'But the baker must also carry it there for me, so that the butcher's dogs may do me no harm.'

So the baker carried it for the hare as far as the door of the inn, then the hare got up on his hind legs, took the bread into his forepaws and brought the loaves to his master.

Then the huntsman said to the innkeeper, 'See, the hundred gold pieces are mine.' The innkeeper was astonished but the huntsman went on, 'The King's bread I have, but I will also eat from the King's roast.'

The innkeeper said, 'Indeed, I would like to see that.' But he was no longer keen on betting. The huntsman called the fox and said, 'My little fox, go to the palace and fetch me the roast such as the King eats.'

The red fox knew how to slink along the sides of the streets and round corners without being seen by a single dog. Soon he had sat down under the Princess's chair and was scratching her foot. She looked down and recognized the fox by his collar, took him into her chamber with her, and said, 'Dear fox, what do you want?'

The fox answered, 'My master, who killed the dragon, is here and sent me to ask for a roast such as the King eats.' Then she bade the cook come, and he had to prepare the joint the way the King ate it, and carry it for the fox as far as the door of the inn. Then the fox took the roast, and brought it to his master.

'You see,' said the huntsman to the innkeeper, 'bread and meat are here, but I will also have vegetables such as the King eats.'

Then he called the wolf and said, 'Dear wolf, go to the palace and fetch me vegetables such as the King eats.'

Then the wolf went directly to the palace, because he was afraid of no one, and when he got to the Princess's chair he pulled at her dress from behind so that she had to look round. She recognized him by his collar and took him with her into her room, and said, 'Dear wolf, what do you want?'

He answered, 'My master, who killed the dragon, is here, and I am to ask for some vegetables such as the King eats.'

She bade the cook come again and had him prepare some vegetables just as the King ate them, and he had to carry them for the wolf as far as the door. There the wolf took the dish from him and brought it to his master.

'You see,' said the huntsman, 'now I have bread, meat and vegetables, but I will have a pudding as well, one that the King likes to eat.'

Then he summoned the bear and said, 'Dear bear, you are fond of licking something sweet. Go to the palace and fetch me a pudding that the King likes to eat.'

The bear ambled to the palace, and everyone got out of his way. But when he came to the sentries, they held their rifles at the ready, and would not let him pass into the royal palace. So the bear raised himself up on his hind legs, slapped the sentries with his paws with such a force that the whole guard ran away. Then he went straight to the King's daughter, placed himself behind her and growled a little. When she looked round she recognized the bear, bade him follow her into her chamber and asked, 'Dear bear, what do you want?'

He answered, 'My master, who killed the dragon, is here, and I am to ask for a sweet pudding such as the King eats.'

Then she had the pastry cook come, told him to bake a sweet pudding that the King liked and to carry it for the bear as far as the door of the inn. There the bear first licked up the sugar plums which had fallen off, then took the bowl and brought it to his master.

'Behold,' said the huntsman to the innkeeper, 'now I have bread, meat, vegetables, and a pudding, but I will also drink wine, the same wine as the King.'

He called the lion and said, 'Dear lion, you also like a good drop of wine. Go and fetch me wine such as the King drinks.'

So the lion tramped through the streets and the people ran away from him, and when he came to the sentries they wanted to bar his way, but he roared once, and everyone sprang aside. The lion went to the royal chamber, and knocked on the door with his tail. Then the King's daughter came out and got a fright when she first saw the lion, but she recognized him by the golden clasp from her necklace and bade him come with her into her chamber. She said, 'Dear lion, what do you want?'

He answered, 'My master, who killed the dragon, is here, and I am to ask for wine such as the King drinks.'

Then she bade the cupbearer to give the lion the same wine that the King drank.

The lion said, 'I will go along and see that I get the right wine.' He went down with the cupbearer, and when they came to the cellar, the cupbearer drew him the rough wine that the King's servants drank.

But the lion said, 'Wait! I want to taste the wine first.' He drew himself half a measure and swallowed it down. 'No,' he said, 'that's not the right kind.'

The cupbearer looked at him, and was about to give him wine from another cask, which was for the King's marshal when the lion said, 'Wait! I will try the wine first.' So he drew himself half a measure and drank it. 'This is better, but still not right.'

Then the cupbearer got angry and said, 'What does such a stupid beast understand about wine?' But the lion gave him a blow behind the ears that felled him roughly to the ground and when the cupbearer had picked himself up again, he led the lion in silence to a special, small cellar where the King's wine lay and from which no ordinary man had yet drunk.

The lion drew himself half a measure, and tasted it. Then he said, 'This is very likely the right kind,' and bade the cupbearer fill six bottles. Then they went upstairs but when the lion got out of the cellar into the open, he staggered from one side to the other, and was a little bit drunk. The cupbearer had to carry the wine for him as far as the door of the inn. There the lion took the basket in his mouth and brought the wine to his master.

The huntsman said, 'Now I have bread, meat, vegetables, a pudding and wine such as the King has. Now I will have a banquet with my animals.' And he sat down, ate and drank, and gave the hare, the fox, the wolf, the bear and the lion something to eat and drink from it and they all made merry, for he saw that the King's daughter still loved him. And when the feast was over, he said to the innkeeper, 'I have eaten and drunk as the King eats and drinks, and now I will go to the King's court and marry the King's daughter.'

The innkeeper asked, 'How can you do that, when she already has a bridegroom, and the marriage is being celebrated today?'

Then the huntsman pulled out the handkerchief which the King's daughter had given him on Dragon's Hill, and in which the monster's seven tongues were tied, and said, 'What I hold in my hand will help me to accomplish that.'

Then the innkeeper inspected the contents of the handkerchief, and said, 'I may believe anything, but I won't believe this. I am willing to wager my house and home on it.'

Then the huntsman took a pouch with a thousand gold pieces in it, placed it on the table, and said, 'This I wager against you.'

The King at the royal table asked his daughter, 'What did all the wild animals want which came to see you, and went in and out of my palace?'

She answered, 'I may not tell you, but send a messenger down and let him fetch the master of those animals. You will be doing what is right.'

So the King sent a servant to the inn to invite the stranger to the palace, and the servant came just as the huntsman had made the bet with the innkeeper. 'See,' said he, 'the King has sent a servant and has given me an invitation to go to the palace. But I am not going just yet,' and to the servant he said, 'I beg His Majesty to send me royal clothes, a carriage and six, and servants to wait on me.'

When the King received this reply, he said to his daughter, 'What should I do?'

She said, 'Let him come in the way he asks, and you'll be doing what is right.'

So the King sent the huntsman royal clothes, a carriage and six, and servants to wait on him. When the huntsman saw the carriage and horses and servants coming, he said to the innkeeper, 'See, now I am being fetched in the way I asked.' And he put on the royal garments, took the handkerchief with the dragon's tongues in it with him, and drove to the King's palace.

When the King saw him coming, he said to his daughter, 'How am I to receive him?'

She answered, 'Go and meet him, and you will be doing what is right.'

So the King went to meet him and led him upstairs, and the huntsman's animals followed him. The King seated him near himself and his daughter. The marshal, as bridegroom, sat on the other side, but he no longer recognized the huntsman.

Just then, the seven dragon's heads were brought in for display, and the **329**

King said, 'The dragon's seven heads were cut off by the marshal, therefore I am giving him my daughter in marriage today.'

Then the huntsman stood up, opened the seven mouths, and said, 'Where are the dragon's seven tongues?'

The marshal was panic-stricken, turned pale and did not know what answer he should make. Finally, in his confusion he said, 'Dragons have no tongues.'

'Liars should have none either,' said the huntsman, 'but the dragon's tongues shall be the victor's tokens.' He unfolded the handkerchief and there they lay, all the seven of them. And then he put each tongue back in the mouth to which it belonged, and it fitted exactly. Then he took the handkerchief on which the name of the Princess was embroidered, showed it to the maiden, and asked her to whom she had given it.

'To him who killed the dragon,' she replied.

And then he called his animals, took the collar off each and the golden clasp from the lion, showed them to the Princess and asked to whom they belonged.

She answered, 'The necklace and the golden clasp were mine. I divided them among the animals who helped overcome the dragon.'

Then the huntsman said, 'When I, exhausted from the fight, was resting and sleeping, the marshal came and cut off my head. Then he carried off the King's daughter and pretended that it was he who killed the dragon. That he is a liar I have proved with the tongues, the handkerchief, and the necklace.'

Then he recounted how the animals had healed him by means of a magic root, and that he had wandered about with them for a year, and at last had come back here and had learnt about the marshal's treachery from the innkeeper.

The King then asked his daughter, 'Is it true that this man killed the dragon?' And she replied, 'Yes, it is true; now I can reveal the marshal's infamous deed, since the truth has come to light through someone else, for under threat of force I had to promise to keep silence. This was the reason why I made the condition that the marriage should not be celebrated till after a year and a day.'

Then the King summoned twelve councillors to pronounce judgement on the marshal, and their verdict was that he should be torn to pieces by four oxen. So the marshal was executed, and the King gave his daughter to the huntsman and appointed him his viceroy.

The wedding was celebrated with much joy, and the young King sent for his father and his foster-father, and bestowed a great many treasures on them.

Nor did he forget the innkeeper. He sent for him and said, 'See, I have married the King's daughter, and your hearth and home are mine.'

'Yes,' said the innkeeper, 'so it is only fair.'

But the young King said, 'I am merciful. You shall keep your hearth and home, and as to the thousand gold pieces, I'll make a present of them to you as well.' Now the young King and Queen were of very good cheer and lived happily together. He often went out hunting, since it was his favourite pastime, and his faithful animals always went with him. Yet there was a forest nearby that was supposed to be haunted. Once in it, it was no easy matter to get out again. The young King felt a great desire to hunt there, and begged the old King for his permission to go there.

He rode out with a large hunting party and, when he came to the forest, he saw a snow-white deer and said to his men, 'Wait here till I return. I wish to give chase to that beautiful creature.' And he rode into the forest after it, followed only by his animals.

The attendants waited till evening, but the young King did not come back. So they rode home and related to the young Queen what had happened.

The young King had ridden on and on after the beautiful animal, but was never able to overtake it. When he thought it was near enough to be shot at, it bounded away, and finally vanished altogether.

Suddenly he realized that he had ridden deep into a forest. So he took his horn and blew it but received no answer, for his men could not hear it. Moreover, night was falling, and he saw that he couldn't get home that night. So he got off his horse, made a fire near a tree and resolved to spend the night there.

As he was sitting by the fire with his animals, he thought he heard a human voice. He looked round but could see nothing. Soon afterwards he heard a groan as if from above and, looking up, he saw an old woman sitting in the tree who kept wailing, 'Oh, oh, oh, how cold I am!'

He said, 'Come down and warm yourself if you are cold.'

But she answered, 'No, your animals would bite me.'

'They will do you no harm,' said the young King. 'Just come down.'

But the old woman was a witch, and she said to him, 'I will throw down a wand from the tree. If you strike them on the back with it, they won't harm me.' Then she threw down a small wand, and he struck them with it.

At once they lay still and were turned into stone. When the witch was safe from the animals, she touched the young King with a wand, too, and turned him to stone. Then she laughed, and dragged him and the animals into a ditch, where a number of similar stones already lay.

When the young King did not come back, the Queen's anguish and sorrow grew from day to day.

And then it so happened that the other brother, who had gone east when the two separated, came to the kingdom. He had been looking for work and had found none, so he had wandered around from place to place and had taught his animals to dance. Then, one day, it occurred to him that he should go and look for the knife which they had thrust into the tree trunk when they parted, that he might learn how his brother was faring.

When he got there, his brother's side was half rusty and half bright. He was alarmed and thought, 'My brother must have met with some great misfortune, but perhaps I can still save him, for half the knife is still shiny.'

Then he and his animals travelled westward, and when he came to the city, the sentries came to meet him, and asked if they were to announce him to his consort. They told him that the young Queen had been in great anxiety about his staying away so long, and was afraid he had perished in the haunted forest. To be sure, the sentries were convinced that he was the young King himself, so much did he look like him with his wild animals running after him.

Then he realized that they were talking about his brother and thought, 'I had better pretend to be him, then I can rescue him more easily.' So he let himself be escorted by the sentry into the palace and was received with great joy. The young Queen thought no other but that he was her husband, and asked him why he had stayed away so long.

'I lost my way in the forest,' he answered, 'and couldn't find my way out any sooner.'

That night he was taken to the royal bed, but he laid a double-edged sword between himself and the young Queen. She didn't know what it was supposed to mean, but did not dare to ask.

He stayed at the palace for a few days, and learnt everything concerning the haunted forest. At last he said, 'I must hunt there once more.'

The old King and the young Queen tried to dissuade him, but he insisted on going, and set out with a large hunting party. When he reached the forest, he fared just as his brother had done before him. He saw a white deer and said to his men, 'Stay here, till I come back. I wish to chase that fine creature.'

Then he rode into the forest, and his animals ran after him. He could not overtake the deer either and got so deep into the forest that he was forced to spend the night there. When he had made a fire, he heard somebody wailing overhead. 'Oh, ho, ho, ho! I am so cold!' He looked up, and there was the same witch sitting in the tree.

'If you're cold,' he said, 'then come down, granny, and warm yourself.'

'No,' she answered, 'your animals will bite me.'

But he said, 'No, they won't hurt you.'

Then she cried out, 'I am going to throw down a wand. Just hit them with it, and they won't harm me.'

Hearing this, the huntsman no longer trusted the old woman, and said, 'I won't hit my animals, you come down, or I'll come up and fetch you.'

Then she cried, 'What exactly are you going to do? You can do me no harm.'

But he replied, 'If you don't come, I'll shoot you down.'

'Shoot away,' she said, 'I am not afraid of your bullets.'

So the huntsman took aim and fired at her, but the witch was proof against lead bullets and gave a shrill laugh, and cried, 'You shall not hit me yet!'

The huntsman knew how to trick her and he tore three silver buttons off his coat and loaded his gun with them. The witch was powerless against them and, the moment he pulled the trigger, she came hurtling down with a shriek. Then he placed his foot upon her and said, 'Old witch, if you don't tell me this instant where my brother is, I'll seize you with both my hands, and throw you into the fire!'

Then the witch was really frightened, and begged for mercy, saying, 'He's in a ditch with his animals turned to stone.'

Then he forced her to go there and threatened her saying, 'Old monkey, now you shall bring my brother and all his creatures lying there back to life again, or you end in the fire.'

So she took a wand and touched the stones. Then his brother and his animals came to life again, and many others with them, merchants, woodcutters and shepherds. They got up, thanked him for their deliverance, and set out for home.

When the twin brothers saw each other again, they kissed each other, and rejoiced heartily. Then they seized the witch and put her in the fire, and when she was dead the forest opened up and became light and clear, so that the royal palace could be seen about three hours away.

The two brothers then went home together, and on the way told each other about their adventures. And when the one said that he was the King's viceroy over the whole country, the other said, 'I know that, of course, for when I came to the city I was taken for you. I was shown all royal honours and the young Queen took me for her husband. I had to eat by her side and sleep in your bed.'

When the other heard that, he got so jealous and angry that he drew his sword and struck off his brother's head. But when he saw him lying there dead with his red blood flowing, he was overwhelmed with regret. 'My brother delivered me,' he cried, 'and in return I have killed him!' and loud were his lamentations.

Then his hare came and offered to fetch some of the special root that had once saved him, raced off and brought some back. The dead brother was brought back to life, and didn't even notice his wound.

Then they went on, and the young King said, 'You look like me, wearing royal garments like myself, with the same animals following you. Let's go into the palace through opposite gates and thus appear before the old King from two sides at the same time.'

So they separated, and the sentries came to the old King at the same time from both gates announcing that the young King with his animals had returned from the hunt.

'It is not possible,' said the King, 'the gates are an hour's distance apart.'

Meanwhile, however, the two brothers entered the courtyard from both sides and mounted the steps. Then the King said to his daughter, 'Well, can you say which is your husband? The two look exactly alike. I can't tell which is which.'

Then she was in great distress and couldn't tell. At last she remembered the necklace she had given the animals, looked and found her little golden clasp on one of the lions. Then, in her joy, she cried, 'The man who is followed by this lion is my true husband!'

The young King laughed and said, 'Yes, that's the right one,' and they sat down together, ate and drank and were merry.

That night when the young King went to bed he found the two-edged sword his brother had placed there. Then he realized how true to him his brother had been.

Clever Grethel

Once upon a time there was a cook whose name was Grethel. She wore shoes with red heels, and when she went out in them she would sway and turn, and think to herself, 'You really are a pretty girl!' And when she came home, she would drink some wine for sheer joy. Then since wine awakens the appetite, she would taste the best food that she had cooked until she had eaten her fill. She said to herself, 'The cook must know what the food tastes like.'

One day, her master said to her, 'Grethel, I have a guest coming tonight. Get two fine chickens ready.'

'Very good, sir,' answered Grethel.

She killed the chickens, plucked them, scalded them in boiling water and stuck them on the spit. Then as evening approached, she put them on the fire to broil. The chickens began to sizzle and turn brown, but still the guest hadn't arrived.

Grethel called out to her master, 'If the guest doesn't come soon I must take the chickens off the fire. It will be a frightful shame if they are not eaten when they are at their juiciest.'

So the master said, 'I will go myself and fetch my guest.'

As soon as the master had turned his back, Grethel went to the spit and moved the chickens to one side and thought, 'Standing so long near the fire makes one hot and thirsty. Who knows when those two will come! Meanwhile

I'll run along to the cellar and have a drink of wine.' She ran downstairs, held a jug to the tap of a cask and pulled herself a drink. 'One good drop of wine asks for another,' said Grethel and took another drink.

Then she went upstairs and put the chickens on to the fire again, spread some butter on them, and turned the spit around. The roasted chickens smelled so good, that Grethel thought to herself, 'I should just make sure these chickens are quite all right. I think they should be tasted.' She passed her finger over the fowls, licked her finger, and said, 'Oh, my! The chickens are so good! Indeed, a wicked shame for them not to be eaten at once!'

She ran to the window to see if her master and his guest were coming yet, but saw nobody. She went to the chickens again, and thought, 'One wing is going to get burnt, so it's better I cut it off and eat it.' So she cut it off and found it very tasty.

When she had eaten it she thought, 'The other wing must come off as well, or the master will notice there's something missing.' When the two wings had been consumed, she went again to look for her master, but could not see him. 'Who knows,' she thought, 'they may not come at all. Perhaps they have found somewhere else to eat.' Then she said to herself, 'Grethel, cheer up! Once a thing is started, it should be seen through to the end. Go and have another drink and eat up the chicken. When it's all gone you'll be at peace. A gift from God must not be wasted.'

So she ran once more down to the cellar for some wine and ate up one chicken quite merrily.

When one chicken was inside her and her master still had not come, Grethel looked at the other one and said, 'Where the one is, there should be the other. The two go together. What is right for one is right for the other.' So she took the second chicken and it went the way of the first.

But as she was in the middle of her feasting, her master came back and called, 'Hurry up, Grethel. My guest will be here directly.'

'Very good, sir,' answered Grethel, 'I'll get it ready.'

Meanwhile, the master looked to see if the table was properly laid, took the big knife with which he was going to carve the fowls, to sharpen it on a stone outside.

The guest in the meantime had come, and knocked politely and courteously at the door. Grethel ran to see who was there and, when she saw the guest, put her finger to her lips and said, 'Keep quiet and make haste to get out of here. If my master catches you, you will be the worse for it. It's true he has invited you for supper, but only to cut off both your ears. Just listen, he is sharpening the knife now.'

336   The guest heard the noise of a knife being sharpened and ran out of the

house as fast as he could. Grethel was not idle either but ran screaming to her master, 'Indeed, it's a fine guest you have invited!'

'Why, Grethel? What do you mean?'

'He has just taken both the chickens. I was about to serve them from the platter when he snatched them away and ran off with them.'

'That's just like him,' said the master feeling sorry about the loss of his fine fowls.

'If only he had left me one, at least there would be something for me to eat!'

He shouted after the guest to stop but the latter pretended not to hear. Then he ran after him with the carving knife still in his hand, crying, 'Only one, only one!' meaning that the guest should leave him one chicken and not take both.

However, the guest thought he meant he should give up only one of his ears, and rushed headlong through the streets as if the devil were after him, intending to get both his ears safely home.

Aladdin

In far-off China there once lived a magician who was as ugly as he was wicked. His magic was tremendously powerful, but he was not satisfied with it. He wanted to be the most powerful and the richest magician in the whole of the world, for he knew that there were others who could equal him.

One day as he was walking in the market place his eyes fell upon a ring that was brighter than any ring that he possessed. It glittered in the bright sunshine and threw off dazzling patterns of red and blue on the canopy of the jewel-seller's stall. The magician had to have it and after long bargaining with the jewel-seller, a price was agreed which satisfied both men.

The magician rushed home with his new treasure and as soon as he was inside, he hurriedly pulled off all the rings that he was wearing and slipped the new one on. He moved his hand hither and thither, and marvelled at the glorious colours that the ring cast off. With greed and lust in his eyes, the magician watched the beautiful patterns until he could bear it no longer and he lovingly stroked the ring. Suddenly, the room darkened and was filled with smoke. The magician was terrified and began to shake with fear. He shook even more when a voice boomed out, 'Who calls the Genie of the Ring?'

'The what?' asked the magician, his voice trembling as much as his knees.

'Who calls the Genie of the Ring?' the voice repeated.

'I did, I suppose,' said the magician.

'And what do you want, o Master?' the Genie of the Ring asked.

'What can you give me?' asked the magician.

'Money, jewellery, precious metals, rich cloth, enough to satisfy most men.'

'I am not most men,' said the magician. 'I want power. I want to be the richest and most powerful man in the world.'

'For that you need the Genie of the Lamp, not the Genie of the Ring.'

'Where can I find this Genie of the Lamp?'

'Come, I will show you,' said the Genie and with a rush of wind and a blaze of sparks the two were suddenly transported to an oasis far from anywhere. In the centre of the oasis there was a trapdoor.

'There you will find the Genie of the Lamp. Under the trapdoor,' said the Genie of the Ring.

The magician rushed forward and pulled at the trapdoor. But it refused to move, even by as much as an inch.

'Foolish man,' scoffed the Genie of the Ring. 'I offered you enough to satisfy most men and you wanted more. Only one person in the whole world can open the door.'

'Who?' demanded the magician. 'Who can open the trapdoor?'

'Aladdin. Aladdin, the washerwoman's son. Anyone else who enters the garden will die instantly,' laughed the Genie and with a rush of wind and a blaze of sparks he was gone.

The magician rubbed his eyes in disbelief and suddenly found himself back in his own home.

He immediately summoned all his servants and commanded them to find out where Aladdin, the washerwoman's son, lived. One by one his servants went out and searched, and one by one they returned with no information. The magician angrily sent them out again and eventually one of the servants came back with the news that Aladdin lived in the poorest district of the town, some distance from the magician's palace.

The very next morning the magician set out to see Aladdin, and even his own servants did not recognize him. His long, dirty fingernails had been cleaned and cut. His straggly hair and greasy beard had been washed and trimmed and he was dressed in fresh, newly-laundered clothes. He quickly made his way to where Aladdin lived and when he saw the boy he rushed up to him and put his arms around him.

'Aladdin. My dear nephew. We have never met, but I am your poor father's brother. I have been travelling for many years, visiting holy places.'

'My father's brother,' said Aladdin. 'No one has ever mentioned that my father had a brother.'

'No matter, child. It is the truth. Take me to your mother. My poor brother's wife.'

The boy did as he was told and the two went into the steamy laundry where Aladdin and his mother lived.

'Sister-in-law,' cried the magician as soon as he saw Aladdin's mother.

'Sister-in-law? My poor husband had no brother,' said the woman.

'He did. Indeed he did. But we quarrelled many years ago and I have been on pilgrimage ever since.'

The woman did not believe him at first, but when the magician took ten gold coins and gave them to her, saying, 'Take this. Buy some clothes for the child,' she was happy to believe him.

For several days the magician stayed with Aladdin and his mother, insisting on paying for everything.

One day, about a week after his arrival the magician asked the woman if he could take Aladdin on a journey for a few days. By this time the widow was convinced that the magician was her brother-in-law and gave her consent.

The man and boy travelled together for several days until they came to an oasis. 'Aladdin,' said the magician. 'Raise the trapdoor, child, and bring me the lamp that you will find down there.'

Aladdin did as he was told and lifted the trapdoor. There was a flight of stairs and the magician then told Aladdin to go down them and bring him the lamp. Aladdin went down the steps and found himself in the most beautiful garden that he could ever have imagined. The trees were laden with precious jewels that dazzled Aladdin's eyes with their magnificent colours — there were pearls, diamonds, rubies and many, many more. At the end of a golden path, Aladdin could see the lamp. He made his way towards it and tried to lift it, but it would not budge. 'Uncle,' the boy cried. 'I cannot lift it on my own. Come and help me.' But the magician was afraid and called back, 'Try harder, nephew, for I cannot come into the enchanted garden.'

The boy tried and tried, but it was no good. He kept calling for his uncle and still his uncle refused to come down. After many hours the poor child was exhausted and made his way back to the steps. But the magician was furious. 'Ungrateful wretch!' he screamed. 'You shall stay there for ever. If I cannot have the lamp, then no one will.' And with that he slammed the trapdoor down, leaving Aladdin in the enchanted garden.

Poor Aladdin. He ran back through the garden looking for a way out, but there was none. Eventually he made his way back to where the lamp was and unthinkingly tried to lift it. He was amazed when he did so quite easily. He ran back to the trapdoor and shouted, 'Uncle, I have it. I have it.' But the magician was miles away and no one heard Aladdin's cries. Aladdin sat down and wept. As he did so his hands rubbed the lamp, and suddenly there was an enormous puff of smoke and with a blaze of sparks, the most enormous Genie appeared before Aladdin.

'You called me, Master. What is your command?'

'M... M... M... Master! C... C... Command,' stuttered Aladdin.

'Yes, Master! I am the Genie of the Lamp. Anything you wish shall be granted.'

'Then take me home,' cried the astonished boy and in an instant Aladdin was outside his own home. 'Mother,' he cried and rushed inside to tell her everything that had happened to him.

'We need never be poor again,' he said and rubbed the lamp. When the Genie appeared Aladdin asked him to bring gold and silver and fine clothes; and in an instant the Genie did as Aladdin had commanded. For many days, whenever Aladdin or his mother wanted anything they summoned the Genie, who did as he was asked.

One day, Aladdin was in the market when soldiers of the Sultan's army appeared and began to push the crowds roughly to one side. 'Stand back,' they cried. 'The Sultan's daughter is coming and she must not be seen. Turn around.' Everyone did as they were commanded and the Princess passed **341** through the market place. Now Aladdin had obeyed the soldiers, but found himself looking into a large mirror. As the Princess passed by, Aladdin saw her reflection in the glass and instantly fell in love with her. He ran home as fast as he could and burst into the house. 'Mother,' he gasped. 'I have seen the Sultan's daughter.'

His mother was horrified. 'But it is instant death for anyone who casts eyes on the Princess. It is the law.'

'I saw her in a looking glass,' said Aladdin. 'Mother. I must marry her!'

'Marry her!' exclaimed his mother. 'Aladdin, child, we are poor people. You cannot marry the Princess.'

'But the lamp,' said Aladdin. 'With the Genie we can become as rich as the Sultan.'

And so, despite his mother's doubts, Aladdin summoned the Genie. He commanded him to build a vast palace and to fill it with jewels and precious things.

Before the mother and son could blink, they found themselves in a sumptuous room furnished with gold and silver. Their clothes were made of the finest silks and jewels sparkled from their fingers.

The next morning the Sultan awoke as usual and went to his window to look out over his capital. He blinked once, then twice, then three times. For where there had been a vast park the night before, there now stood the most beautiful palace that the Sultan had ever seen.

The astonished Sultan immediately summoned his Vizier and demanded an explanation. The Vizier hurried from the palace and into Aladdin's splendid new home.

When Aladdin saw the Vizier approach, he went to meet him. 'Tell your master that the palace and all the precious things are for the Princess if he will give me permission to marry her.'

The Vizier ran back to the Sultan and told him what Aladdin wanted. The Sultan ordered that his daughter be brought to him, dressed in her most beautiful clothes. 'Go and bring this Aladdin to me,' he called to the harassed Vizier.

As soon as the Princess saw Aladdin she fell as deeply in love with him as he had with her.

'How did you come to build such a magnificent palace overnight? How is it that you are obviously so rich, yet I have never heard of you?' demanded the bewildered Sultan.

'Sire, my fortune I made in a far-off land. By trade,' said Aladdin, who did not want anyone else to know of the Genie of the Lamp. 'I had one million servants toil silently through the night to build the palace.'

'And why do you want to marry my daughter?'

'Because, sire, I had heard of her beauty, and now that I see her for myself I see that I was told wrongly, for no words can describe such beauty. Sire, allow me to marry her. I will make her happy. She will want for nothing.'

The Sultan thought for a few seconds. He loved his daughter very much and did not really want to lose her. But he loved riches, too. 'Very well, I consent,' he said, 'but only on condition that you take her to the palace across from mine, and that you both live there for ever.'

Aladdin was overjoyed and promised to bring the Princess back.

The wedding was the grandest that had ever been seen, and the couple were as happy as happy could be to live in their splendid palace. Everyone who saw them was astonished at how completely happy they were together and expected them to live there for ever and ever. And that is exactly what the lovers planned to do; but they had made these plans without considering the wicked magician.

Thousands of miles away, the magician was wondering what had happened to Aladdin. One day, about three weeks after Aladdin and the Princess had been married, he went into a great book-lined room and from the back of a secret drawer he took out his crystal ball. Murmuring some strange incantations, he rubbed his hands over the ball. Imagine his horror when he saw Aladdin and the Princess in their splendid palace. His voice got louder and louder and soon he was screaming a strange spell at the top of his voice. He turned three times and vanished into thin air.

He reappeared at nightfall outside Aladdin's palace. He walked around the walls and saw that it was heavily guarded. He wanted the lamp more than ever and as the night passed, he made his plans to get revenge.

The next morning, he watched as Aladdin set out on a fine horse, obviously going hunting. He then made his way to the market where he bought several beautiful new lamps.

Soon he was back outside Aladdin's palace, shouting, 'New lamps for old! New lamps for old!' From deep inside the palace, the Princess heard the strange call, and suddenly remembered the old lamp that her husband kept in a cupboard. 'How well pleased he will be to have a fine new lamp,' she thought to herself and ran to fetch it.

'Lampseller,' she called from a window. 'Wait. Here is an old lamp for a new one.'

The magician's greedy hands grabbed the lamp and his eyes lit up with joy. He had the lamp. 'Thank you, Lady,' he called up to the Princess. 'Here is your new lamp,' and with that he was off.

344   He rounded a corner out of sight of anyone and rubbed the lamp.

Instantly the Genie appeared. 'What do you require, o Master?'

'Take Aladdin's palace and the Princess to my home in Africa.'

No sooner had he spoken than there was a loud gust of wind. The palace was being hammered by a violent dust storm, and when the dust cleared, the palace had vanished.

When the Sultan awoke from his afternoon nap, he went to his window as he now always did to admire his son-in-law's magnificent palace. Imagine his horror when all that he saw was the park that had been there before. He immediately summoned his Vizier and demanded that Aladdin be brought before him. It took a few hours to find the young man, but eventually he was brought before the furious Sultan.

'What have you done with my daughter? Where is the palace?' the Sultan demanded.

Aladdin could only shake his head in astonishment as he had no idea what had happened.

'Take him away,' roared the Sultan. 'Throw him into the deepest dungeon and let him remain there until my daughter is returned to me.'

Poor Aladdin was dragged away and cast into the deepest, darkest dungeon in the palace.

Meanwhile, thousands of miles away in the depths of darkest Africa the poor Princess was weeping and begging the magician to take her back.

'Keep the palace, but let me return,' she begged.

'Never,' replied the magician. 'Now you are here, here you will stay. Not as a princess, but as my wife. Prepare yourself, my dear, for tomorrow we will be wed. Tonight we will feast.' With that, the magician departed and left the poor girl to her thoughts. She thought long and deep, and after many hours she came up with a plan.

That evening, she dressed herself in her most beautiful robes, rubbed the most expensive perfumes on her soft skin and waited for the magician. She ordered her servants to bring her the most succulent meats and the sweetest fruits. To drink, she ordered the most potent of all the wines in the cellar. When the magician appeared later, she greeted him with a deep curtsey.

'At last you have come, my master,' she said.

'Ah,' sighed the magician. 'I can see that you have thought over my proposal and are going to be sensible.'

'Come, drink with me,' the Princess said softly.

She poured two glasses of wine and watched as the magician drank deeply. She quickly filled his glass and beckoned him to the table. All through the meal she laughed and smiled and kept the magician's glass full, while she hardly drank at all.

'You are without doubt the most powerful man in the world. That weakling Aladdin is nothing compared to you,' she said after they had eaten. 'Where does your power come from?' Before he could answer, she filled his glass yet again. 'Let us drink a toast to your power,' she said and watched with great satisfaction as the magician emptied his glass.

'My power,' the magician said, 'comes from this old lamp.' As he spoke, he took the lamp from under his cloak. 'I only need to rub it gently...' He never finished his sentence. The Princess had filled him so full of wine, that he slipped to the floor, completely drunk.

The Princess picked up the lamp and rubbed it gently. Immediately the Genie appeared. 'What do you command, o Mistress?'

'Take this man and set him in a place from which he can never escape.'

The Genie stooped down and picked up the sleeping magician as easily as if he had been a piece of fluff. He disappeared for the flick of an eye, and was back. 'What else, o Mistress, do you command?'

'Take me and my palace back to where we belong,' said the Princess.

There was a sudden rush of wind and in an instant the palace was back in its proper place.

The next morning, the Sultan awoke from his troubled sleep and went to the window to look sadly at the park where the palace had once stood. He blinked once, and then twice, and then three times.

'Vizier!' he shouted. 'Come quickly. Look!'

Within a few minutes, Aladdin had been released from his deep dungeon and was reunited with his beloved wife.

'You are indeed a powerful magician, Aladdin, who can make palaces appear and disappear. But do not do it again. Next time I will not be so merciful!'

Aladdin was quick to agree, and he and his Princess lived happily together for many, many years.

And the lamp? It was locked away in the deepest dungeon in Aladdin's palace, and it is probably still there to this day.

The Darning-Needle

There was once a darning-needle so fine that she thought of herself as a sewing-needle. 'Now take good care of what you're holding,' she said to the fingers that picked her up. 'Don't drop me, please! If I fall on the floor, you may never find me again, I am so fine!'

'You're not all that fine,' said the fingers, gripping her tightly.

'Look, I come with my train!' said the darning-needle, pulling after her a long thread, but without a knot in it.

The fingers guided the needle straight to the cook's slippers, the uppers of which had split and had to be sewn together.

'This is vulgar work,' said the darning-needle. 'I'll never get through that leather, I'll break, I'll break!' And break she did. 'Didn't I tell you,' she went on. 'I'm much too fine!'

The fingers now thought the needle to be useless, but they had to hold her tight while the cook dropped some sealing-wax on her and pinned her to her scarf.

'See, I have now turned into a brooch,' said the darning-needle. 'I knew my worth would be recognized in the end; if you really are somebody, you're sure to become something!' And then she laughed, but only to herself, of course, for a darning-needle never shows outwardly that she is laughing. And there she sat in the scarf as proud as a peacock, as if she was sitting in a coach, looking round in all directions during the ride.

'May I take the liberty of asking you whether you are of gold?' she asked the pin who was her neighbour. 'You look so splendid, and you have your own head, though it is somewhat small! You should get it to grow, for it is not everybody who can be stuck up with sealing-wax!' With that the darning-needle drew herself up so proudly that she fell out of the scarf straight into the sink, just as the cook was emptying it.

'Now I am off on my travels,' said the darning-needle. 'I only hope I shan't get stuck!' But that is what she did.

'I am too fine for this world!' she said, as she lay in the gutter. 'However, I have my self-respect and that's something to cheer up any man!' And the darning-needle held herself erect and did not lose her good humour.

All sorts of things swam over her — sticks, straws, scraps of newspaper. 'Just look how they sail along,' said the darning-needle. 'They have no idea what is stuck underneath them! It is I, and I am sticking where I am! Take a look at that splinter swimming on, I bet he hasn't a single thought in his head which isn't about splinters such as he! And there goes a straw, see how it turns and twirls! Stop thinking so much about yourself! Or you'll go bump against the pavement! And those newspapers! Everyone has long forgotten

what is in them, yet they are throwing themselves about! I sit here quietly and patiently! I know what I am, and I'll stay what I am!'

One day something appeared near the needle which was so shiny that she took it for a diamond. But it was only a glass-splinter from a bottle, and as it glittered so brightly, the darning-needle spoke to it, introducing herself as a brooch. 'Surely you're a diamond!' 'Yes, something of that sort!' And so each believed the other to be very precious indeed, and they started talking about the haughtiness of the world.

'Well, I used to live in a box belonging to a young lady,' said the darning-needle, 'and that lady was a cook. On each of her hands she had five fingers and I've never seen anything so conceited as those five fingers! Yet she only had them to hold me, to pick me from the box and put me back again.'

'Did they shine at all?' asked the glass-splinter.

'Shine!' said the darning-needle, 'oh no, with them it was pure pride, pride! They were five brothers in all, all from the same family, they held themselves very erect side by side, though they were of different length. The one on the outside, Thumb was the name, was short and fat; he usually wasn't in line with the other fingers and had only one bend in his spine, so he could only bend once. But I heard it said that if he were chopped off a man, that man would no longer be fit for military service. The second finger, Sweet-tooth, poked in sweet and sour things, pointed at the sun and the moon, and it was he who pressed the pen when they were writing. Longfellow was head and shoulders taller than the rest. Ringman had a gold ring round his tummy, and the smallest one, Peer Musician, did nothing at all and was proud of that. Proud they were and proud they'll stay, and so I took to the sink.'

'And now we sit together here and sparkle,' said the glass-splinter. But then more water poured into the gutter and it overflowed its banks and carried the splinter away.

'So now he's got further, he's been promoted,' said the darning-needle. 'And I go on sitting here, for I am too fine, but I am proud of that and my pride deserves respect!' So she sat on, erect, full of her own thoughts.

'I could almost believe I was born of a sunbeam, I am so fine! And it seems to me the sun is always looking for me under the water. Why, I am so fine that my own mother couldn't find me. If I still had my old eye which broke off, I think I'd burst into tears — though I wouldn't! It is not ladylike to weep!'

One day some boys were raking about in the gutter, looking for old nails,
small coins and such like. They poked about in the dirt, having fun.

'Ouch!' cried the one who pricked himself on the needle. 'That's a fine fellow!'

'I am a fine lady,' said the darning-needle, only nobody heard her. The sealing-wax had dropped off and she was black all over, but then black is a very slimming colour and so the needle fancied herself finer than ever. 'There floats an egg-shell,' cried the boys and they stuck the darning-needle into the shell.

'White walls and I all in black,' said the needle, 'that is very becoming! Now I shall be noticed! I only hope I shan't be sea-sick, for then I would break!' But she was not sea-sick and she did not break.

'For sea-sickness a good remedy is to have a stomach of steel and always to remember that the likes of us are more than human. I've cured myself! The finer one is, the more one can stand.'

'Crunch!' said the egg-shell, as a waggon rolled over it. 'Oh, how it presses!' sighed the darning-needle. 'Now I'll be sea-sick after all! I'll break, I'll break!' But she did not break, though the waggon had passed over her. She stayed where she was — and we shall leave her there!

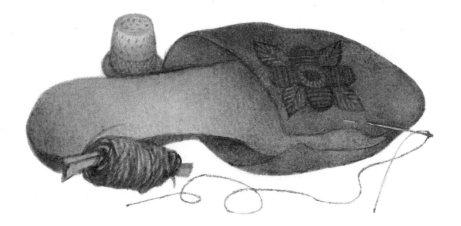